FORGOTTEN REALMS

R.A. SALVATORE
CHARON'S CLAW

THE NEVERWINTER™ SAGA
BOOK
III

COVER ART
TODD LOCKWOOD

The Neverwinter Saga, Book III
CHARON'S CLAW

Published by Wizards of the Coast LLC.

FORGOTTEN REALMS, NEVERWINTER, DUNGEONS & DRAGONS, D&D, WIZARDS OF THE COAST, and their respective logos are trademarks of Wizards of the Coast LLC in the U.S.A. and other countries. Hasbro SA, Represented by Hasbro Europe, Stockley Park, UB11 1AZ. UK. All Wizards of the Coast characters and their distinctive likenesses are property of Wizards of the Coast LLC.

PRINTED IN THE U.S.A.

Cover art by Todd Lockwood
First Printing: October 2011

9 8 7 6 5 4 3 2 1

ISBN: 978-0-7869-6223-5
620-98402000-001-EN

Library of Congress Cataloging-in-Publication Data
Salvatore, R. A., 1959-
Charon's claw / R.A. Salvatore.
    p. cm. — (Neverwinter saga ; bk. 3)
"Forgotten Realms."
ISBN 978-0-7869-6223-5
1. Drizzt Do'Urden (Fictitious character)--Fiction. I. Title.
PS3569.A462345C56 2012
813'.54--dc23

2012017358

U.S., Canada, Asia, Pacific, & Latin America, Wizards of the Coast LLC, P.O. Box 707, Renton, WA 98057-0707, +1-800-324-6496, www.wizards.com/customerservice

Europe, U.K., Eire & South Africa, Wizards of the Coast LLC, c/o Hasbro UK Ltd., P.O. Box 43, Newport, NP19 4YD, UK, Tel: +800 22 427276, Email: wizards@hasbro.co.uk

Visit our web site at **www.wizards.com**

Welcome to Faerûn, a land of magic and intrigue, brutal violence and divine compassion, where gods have ascended and died, and mighty heroes have risen to fight terrifying monsters. Here, millennia of warfare and conquest have shaped dozens of unique cultures, raised and leveled shining kingdoms and tyrannical empires alike, and left long forgotten, horror-infested ruins in their wake.

A LAND OF MAGIC

When the goddess of magic was murdered, a magical plague of blue fire—the Spellplague—swept across the face of Faerûn, killing some, mutilating many, and imbuing a rare few with amazing supernatural abilities. The Spellplague forever changed the nature of magic itself, and seeded the land with hidden wonders and bloodcurdling monstrosities.

A LAND OF DARKNESS

The threats Faerûn faces are legion. Armies of undead mass in Thay under the brilliant but mad lich king Szass Tam. Treacherous dark elves plot in the Underdark in the service of their cruel and fickle goddess, Lolth. The Abolethic Sovereignty, a terrifying hive of inhuman slave masters, floats above the Sea of Fallen Stars, spreading chaos and destruction. And the Empire of Netheril, armed with magic of unimaginable power, prowls Faerûn in flying fortresses, sowing discord to their own incalculable ends.

A LAND OF HEROES

But Faerûn is not without hope. Heroes have emerged to fight the growing tide of darkness. Battle-scarred rangers bring their notched blades to bear against marauding hordes of orcs. Lowly street rats match wits with demons for the fate of cities. Inscrutable tiefling warlocks unite with fierce elf warriors to rain fire and steel upon monstrous enemies. And valiant servants of merciful gods forever struggle against the darkness.

A LAND OF
UNTOLD ADVENTURE

PROLOGUE

The Year of the Reborn Hero
(1463 DR)

RAVEL XORLARRIN STRODE CONFIDENTLY INTO HIS MOTHER'S AUDIENCE HALL, his purple robes dancing around his loudly and rudely clacking high boots. Everyone in the room of course knew that he could walk in perfect silence; his boots, like those of most drow nobles, were imbued with that rather common magical trait. He had thrown back the black cowl of his garment so his long white hair flowed behind him, further drawing attention to himself. This was his shining moment, after all.

To the left side of the room, Ravel's older brother and sire, Elderboy Brack'thal, flashed him a simmering stare—not unexpectedly since the much younger Ravel had taken the mantle as the most powerful of the Xorlarrin children. Brack'thal had once been the object of such high honor, a mighty wizard greatly favored by Matron Mother Zeerith. But that had been before the Spellplague, during which Brack'thal had suffered terribly and his powers had greatly diminished.

In that same time, the patron of the House, the unfortunately-named Horoodissomoth, had been driven completely insane and had consumed himself in a delayed blast fireball, one he had inadvertently placed into his own vest pocket.

And so Zeerith had turned to the semi-comatose Brack'thal for seed and had produced of his loins Ravel, his brother and his son.

Every time Ravel greeted Brack'thal with "my brother, my father," the older wizard winced in anger, and the younger wizard grinned. For Brack'thal could not move against him. In personal combat, Ravel would annihilate Brack'thal, they both knew, and though he was barely out of Sorcere, the drow academy for wizards, Ravel had already built a stronger spy network and support team than Brack'thal had ever known. Like the younger magic-users of House Xorlarrin, Ravel did not even call himself a wizard, nor did Matron Mother Zeerith and the others. Powerful weavers of arcane powers like Ravel were now considered "spellspinners" in House Xorlarrin, and indeed they had tailored the material and semantic components of their spells to make their casting

1

seem more akin to the dance of a spider than the typical finger-waggling of pre-Spellplague wizards.

When he glanced to the right side of the room, Ravel took note of the House weapons master, Jearth, a poignant reminder of his vast and growing network of influence. Jearth was Ravel's closest ally, and though House Xorlarrin was widely and uniquely known for its many male magic-users, Jearth Xorlarrin was rightfully considered one of the most powerful of the current weapons masters of Menzoberranzan.

From the day of his birth, it seemed, everything had broken Ravel's way.

And so it was now. It was Ravel who had discovered Gromph Baenre's work on the magical skull gem. Ravel had dared to sneak behind the back of the mighty Archmage of Menzoberranzan—no small risk, considering that Gromph's family reigned supreme in the drow city—and also explore the inner magic of that gem. In it, Ravel had encountered the disembodied spirit, a lich, and from that creature the spellspinner had discerned some startling information indeed.

Apparently, Matron Mother Zeerith had thought the tales interesting, as well.

"Well met, Matron Mother," Ravel greeted, barely diverting his eyes from hers. Had Zeerith been angry with him, such a bold break with etiquette would have surely gotten him snake-whipped. "You requested my presence?"

"I demanded it," Matron Mother Zeerith curtly corrected. "We have determined that the cataclysm that struck the surface was the work of a primordial. The vomit of a fire beast perpetrated the catastrophe."

His head down, Ravel grinned from ear to ear. He had told her as much, for the lich in the skull gem had told him the same.

"We have determined that this primordial resides within the ancient Delzoun homeland of Gauntlgrym," Zeerith went on.

"Have you found it?" Ravel asked before he could stop the words from bursting out of his mouth. He sucked in his breath immediately and lowered his head, but not before noting the gasps from his many vile sisters, or noticing that one put her hand to her snake-headed whip. His ally Jearth, too, had winced and sucked in his breath, clearly expecting a swift and brutal punishment to rain down on Ravel.

But stunningly, Matron Mother Zeerith let the breach go unpunished, unmentioned even.

"Look at me," she commanded, and Ravel complied.

"Your pardon, Matron Moth—"

She waved him to silence.

"We do not know the way to this place, Gauntlgrym," she admitted. "But we know its region. We are grateful to you for your resourcefulness and cunning. It is no small thing to extract such information out from under the nose of that miserable Gromph and his wretched family, who deign themselves so superior to all others in Menzoberranzan."

Ravel, despite his bravado, could hardly believe the sweet words and could hardly breathe.

"We must find it," Zeerith said. "We must determine if this place, with this source of power, is suited to our designs. Too long has House Xorlarrin toiled under the smothering cloak of House Baenre and the others. Too long have we been held from our rightful position of leadership, the ultimate favor of Lady Lolth. We were the first to emerge from the Spellplague, the first to learn the new ways to weave magical energies for the glory of the Spider Queen."

Ravel nodded with every word, for Matron Zeerith's bold declarations were no secret among the nobles of House Xorlarrin. Long had they searched for a way out of Menzoberranzan. Long had they pondered the thought of founding an independent drow city. How daunting it seemed, however, for they all knew that such an act would bring the vengeance of mighty House Baenre and other allied Houses, like Barrison Del'Armgo.

But if House Xorlarrin found such a fortress as this Gauntlgrym, and a source of power as great as a primordial, perhaps they would realize their dreams.

"You will lead the expedition," Zeerith said. "You will find all the resources of House Xorlarrin at your disposal."

At the side of the room, Brack'thal's audible sigh had many heads turning his way.

"Is there a problem, Elderboy?" Zeerith asked him.

"Elderboy. . . ." he dared echo, as if the fact that he and not Ravel held that title should be an obvious enough problem for all to see.

Zeerith glanced at her daughters and nodded, and as one, the five Xorlarrin sisters took up their magical whips, multi-headed, devious magical implements whose strands writhed with living, biting serpents.

Elderboy Brack'thal growled in response. "Matron, do not! If you would allow Ravel his miscues, then so you must—"

He fell silent and took a step back, or tried to, but those drow around him grabbed him and held him fast, and as the sisters approached, their commoner male servants marching defensively before them, Brack'thal was thrown to their grasp.

The commoners dragged him out of the chamber, into a side room that many males of the House knew all too well.

"All the resources," Zeerith said again to Ravel, and she didn't lift her voice, flinch, or avert her eyes at all as the beating in the anteroom commenced and Brack'thal began to shriek in agony.

"Even the weapons master?" Ravel dared to ask, and he, too, feigned that his brother's screaming was nothing unusual or disruptive.

"Of course. Wasn't Jearth complicit in your deception of Gromph Baenre?"

It was the answer he wanted to hear, of course, but Ravel hardly smiled. He glanced over at the weapons master, who seemed to shrink back just a bit and flashed him a cold stare in response. Jearth had indeed helped him, but covertly . . . only covertly! Jearth had warned him from the beginning that he would not have his name associated with any deception involving Gromph Baenre, and now Matron Mother Zeerith had expressed it openly in the House Noble Court.

House Xorlarrin was the most magical, from an arcane and not divine standpoint, of any House in Menzoberranzan. Xorlarrin put more students into Sorcere than any other House, even Baenre, and many times the number of any House other than Baenre. And the Master of Sorcere was the Archmage of Menzoberranzan, Gromph Baenre.

No one, not Ravel, not Jearth, not even Matron Mother Zeerith, doubted that Gromph Baenre had spies within House Xorlarrin. To Ravel, this was no great issue. He had been a favored student of Gromph and the archmage would not likely move against him for such a transgression as a bit of spying.

But Jearth was a warrior and no wizard, and merciless Gromph would likely show no such deference to any swordsman.

"You will take Brack'thal, as well," Zeerith instructed.

"Subservient to me?" Ravel asked, and Zeerith grinned wickedly.

"And of your sisters, only Saribel and Berellip are available for the journey," Zeerith explained.

Ravel tightened at that, but quickly hid it, for Saribel was the youngest, the weakest, and, as far as he could tell, by far the stupidest, of the House priestesses, and Berellip, though older and more powerful, often looked upon him with open scorn and had made no secret of her dismay that House Xorlarrin allowed males so prestigious a status among the nobles. Fanatical in her devotion to Lolth, Berellip showed indifference, at best, to the arcane spellspinners, and had, on occasion, issued open threats to the upstart Ravel.

"You will argue?" Zeerith asked, and coincidentally, at that moment, Brack'thal let loose the most agonized scream of all.

Ravel swallowed hard. "Harnessing a primordial . . ." he said, shaking his head and letting his voice trail off ominously. "Has it ever been accomplished?"

"Redirect its powers, perhaps?" Zeerith asked. "You understand what we need."

Ravel bit back his next argument and considered the words carefully. What did House Xorlarrin truly need?

Room to breathe, most of all, he understood. If they could establish a fledgling city in this ancient dwarven land and have time to get their considerable magical wards in place, would the other Houses of Menzoberranzan think it worth the cost to assault them?

If this new drow city could open avenues to expanded trade, or serve as a warning post against any potential Underdark excursions by the wretched surface dwellers, would that not be a boon to Menzoberranzan?

"Ched Nasad has never been replaced," Ravel dared to remark, referring to Menzoberranzan's former sister city, a beauty of web bridges and sweeping arches, which had been destroyed in the War of the Spider Queen a century before.

"Berellip will inform you of your budget for mercenaries," Zeerith said with a dismissive wave. "Assemble your team and be away."

Ravel bowed quickly and spun around, just in time to see Brack'thal staggering back into the audience chamber, his shirt tattered and bloody, his jaw clenched and eyes bulging from the painful poison of snake-headed whips. Despite that obvious inner struggle, the Elderboy managed to control his facial muscles just long enough to toss Ravel a hateful glare.

For an instant, Ravel thought of appealing Zeerith's decision that he take his brother along, but he let it go. Brack'thal could not defeat him in single combat, after all, and they both knew it. Brack'thal wouldn't make a move against him personally. And since Ravel had been given the power to determine the composition of the expeditionary force, he'd make sure that none of Brack'thal's associates would go along.

Not that the fallen wizard had many associates, in any case.

"They are not rogues—" Ravel started to say, but Jearth stopped him short with an upraised hand.

Quietly! the weapons master insisted, flashing the word with his fingers through use of the intricate drow sign language. As he did that, Jearth brought his cloak up with his other hand to shield the signing hand from view, which the secretive drow often referred to as his "visual cone of silence."

Ravel glanced around, then brought one hand in close so that it was shielded by his own voluminous robes. *They are not Houseless rogues,* his fingers signed.

Many are.

Not all. I recognize a soldier of House Baenre. Their weapons master's assistant, no less!

Many are commoners of lower Houses.

But with a Baenre, Ravel insisted.

At least three, at my last count, Jearth signalled.

Ravel recoiled, a look of horror on his handsome black-skinned features.

Did you believe that we could assemble a force of nearly a hundred skilled drow and march out of Menzoberranzan without attracting the attention of Baenre? Of any of the great Houses? Jearth countered, his hand moving as a blur, so fast that Ravel could barely keep up.

Matron Mother Zeerith will not be pleased.

She will understand, Jearth signed. *She knows well the ever-present eyes of Baenre and Barrison Del'Armgo. She knows that I invited Tiago Baenre, who serves as first assistant to Andzrel Baenre, weapons master of the First House.*

Ravel looked at him doubtfully.

Tiago is a friend, Jearth explained.

Disloyal to Baenre?

Hardly, Jearth admitted. *Our entire plan depends upon our success of securing the powers of Gauntlgrym quickly, that the other Houses will see our fledgling city as a boon and not a rival, or at least, that they will think it not worth the cost of coming after us. In that regard, Tiago will be loyal to his House and useful to our cause if we succeed.*

You will do well to embrace Tiago when we are away, Jearth added. *Allow him a position of leadership among our expedition. Doing so will afford us a longer time period before exhausting the patience of House Baenre.*

Keep our enemies close, Ravel's fingers signaled.

"Potential enemies," Jearth replied aloud. "And only if that potential is not realized will House Xorlarrin succeed."

You doubt the power of Matron Mother Zeerith and House Xorlarrin? Ravel flashed indignantly.

I know the power of Baenre.

Ravel started to argue the point, but he didn't get far, his fingers barely forming a letter. He had tutored under Gromph Baenre. He had often accompanied Gromph to the archmage's private chambers within the compound of the First House of Menzoberranzan. Ravel was a proud Xorlarrin noble, but even the blindness wrought of loyalty had its limits.

He realized that he could not argue Jearth's point; if it came to blows, House Baenre would obliterate them.

"Would you like an introduction to Tiago Baenre?" Jearth asked aloud.

Ravel smiled at him, a clear sign of surrender, and nodded.

Young, handsome, and supremely confident, Tiago Baenre guided his lizard along the wall of an Underdark corridor. Even with his saddle perpendicular to the floor, the agile Tiago sat easy, his core muscles locked tightly, keeping him straight and settled. He wasn't leading the march of a hundred drow, double that number of goblin shock troops, and a score of driders—nay, Ravel had sent two-score goblins up ahead to make sure the way was clear of monsters—but as the leagues wore on, it became apparent to all that Tiago was guiding the pace.

His sticky-footed subterranean lizard, Byok, was a champion, bred for speed and stamina, and with, so it was rumored, a bit of magical enhancement.

He thinks us his lessers, Ravel flashed to Jearth at one juncture.

He is Baenre, Jearth replied with a shrug, as if that explained everything, because indeed it did.

The clacking of exoskeleton scrabbling across the floor drew their attention, and Ravel pulled up his own mount and turned sidelong to greet the newcomer.

"A goblin stabbed at my consort, Flavvar," said the creature. Half gigantic spider, half drow, the speaker's voice came through with a timbre that was as much insect as it was the melodic sound of a drow voice. Once this creature had been a drow, but he had run afoul of the priestesses of Lolth. Far afoul, obviously, for they had transformed him into this abomination.

"Out of fear, no doubt," said Jearth. "Did she creep up on him?"

The drider, Yerrininae, scowled at the weapons master, but Jearth just grinned and looked away.

"Did the goblin damage her?" Ravel asked.

"It startled her and startled me. I responded."

"Responded?" Ravel asked suspiciously.

"He threw his trident into the goblin," Jearth reasoned, and when Ravel looked at Yerrininae, he noted that the drider puffed out its chest proudly and made no effort to argue the point.

"We intend to dine on the fool," the drider explained, turning back to Ravel. "I request that we slow our march, as we would like to consume it before too much of its liquids have drained."

"You killed the goblin?"

"Not yet. We prefer to dine on living creatures."

Ravel did well to hide his disgust. He hated driders—how could he not?—thoroughly disgusting beasts, one and all. But he understood their value. If the two hundred goblins sought revenge and turned their entire force on the driders in a coordinated assault, the twenty driders would slaughter all two hundred in short order.

"Would you be so tactful as to do it out of sight of the goblin's companions?" the spellspinner asked.

"A better message might be delivered if—"

"Out of sight," Ravel insisted.

Yerrininae stared at him for a few moments, as if measuring him up—and Ravel knew that he and his drow companions would be constantly scrutinized by this band of dangerous allies—but then nodded and skittered away noisily.

Why did you bring them along? Jearth's hands signaled as soon as Yerrininae had started off.

It is a long and dangerous road, and ending at a complex no doubt defended, Ravel countered, twisting his hands and fingers with emphatic movement. *We are but two days out of Menzoberranzan and already we move more slowly in anticipation of a fight around every corner. Do you doubt the fighting prowess of Yerrininae and his band?*

I don't doubt the prowess of a band of devils, Jearth's fingers signed. *And they would be easier to control, and less likely to murder us.*

Ravel smiled and shook his head, confident that it would not come to that. His relationship with Yerrininae went far back, to his earliest days in Sorcere. The drider, under orders from Gromph—and no one, drider or drow, dared disobey Gromph—had worked with Ravel on some of his earliest expeditions, guarding the young spellspinner as he had ventured into the Underdark beyond Menzoberranzan in search of some herb or enchanted crystal.

Yerrininae and Ravel had a long-standing arrangement. The drider would not go against him. Besides, Matron Mother Zeerith had sweetened the prize for Yerrininae, hinting that if this expedition proved successful, if House Xorlarrin was able to establish a city in the dwarf homeland of Gauntlgrym, she would afford the driders a House of their own, with full benefits afforded drow, and with Flavvar, Yerrininae's consort, as Matron. From that position they could, perhaps, regain their standing with Lady Lolth.

"And who can guess what might happen with the goddess of chaos from there?" Zeerith had teased, not so subtly hinting that perhaps the drider curse could be reversed. Perhaps Yerrininae and his band might walk as dark elves once more.

No, Ravel did not fear that the driders would turn against him. Not with that possible reward dangling before them.

The old drow mage put down his quill and tilted his head so he could regard the door to his private room. He had been back in House Baenre for only a matter of hours, seeking a quiet respite wherein he might work some theories around a particularly effective dweomer he had witnessed in Sorcere. He had explicitly asked Matron Mother Quenthel for some privacy, and she, of course, had agreed.

Gromph might be a mere male, the Elderboy of the House, but none, not even Quenthel, would move against him. Gromph had been one of the pillars of strength of House Baenre beyond the memory of any living Baenre, noble or commoner. The eldest son of the greatest Matron Mother Baenre, Yvonnel the Eternal, Gromph had served as the city's archmage for centuries. He had weathered the Spellplague and had grown even stronger in the decades since that terrifying event, and though Gromph was quite likely the oldest living drow in Menzoberranzan, his level of involvement in city politics and power struggles, and in the spell research at Sorcere, had only increased, dramatically so, in the last years.

A thin, knowing grin creased the old drow's withered lips as he imagined the doubting expression on the face of his soon-to-be visitor. He envisioned the male's hand lifting to knock, then dropping once more in fear.

Gromph paused a bit longer, then waggled his fingers at the entrance, and the door swung in—just ahead of the knocking fist of Andzrel Baenre.

"Do come in," Gromph bade the weapons master, and he took up his quill and turned his attention back to the spread parchment.

Andzrel's boots clapped hard against the stone floor as he strode into the room—stepped forcefully, Gromph noted from the sound. It would seem that Gromph's action had embarrassed the weapons master.

"House Xorlarrin moves brashly," Andzrel stated.

"Well met to you, too, Andzrel." Gromph looked up and offered the much younger male a withering stare.

Andzrel let a bit of obvious bluster out with his next exaggerated exhale following the mighty wizard's clear reminder of station and consequence.

"A sizable force moving west," Andzrel reported.

"Led by the ambitious Ravel, no doubt."

"We believe that your student is at their head, yes."

"Former student," Gromph corrected, pointedly so.

Andzrel nodded, and lowered his gaze when Gromph did not blink. "Matron Quenthel is concerned," he said quietly.

"Though hardly surprised," Gromph replied. He braced himself on his desk and pushed up from his chair, then smoothed his spidery robes, glistening black and emblazoned with webs and crawling arachnid designs in silver thread. He walked around the side of his desk to a small shelf on the chamber's side wall.

Not looking at Andzrel, but rather at a large, skull-shaped crystal gem set on the shelf, the archmage muttered, "The eating habits of fish."

"Fish?" Andzrel finally asked after a long pause, Gromph purposely making no indication that he would clarify the curious statement, or even that he intended to turn back around, without prompting.

"Have you ever hunted fish with a line and hook?" Gromph asked.

"I prefer the spear," the warrior replied.

"Of course." There was little indication of admiration in Gromph's voice at that point. He did turn around, then, and studying the weapons master's face, Gromph knew that Andzrel suspected that he had just been insulted. Suspected, but did not know, for that one, for all his cleverness—and he was conniving—could not appreciate the sublime calculations and patience, the simple absence of cadence that was line fishing.

"A typical pond might have ten different types of fish wriggling through its blackness," Gromph said.

"And I would have speared them all."

Gromph snorted at him and turned back to regard the skull gem. "You would cast your spear at whatever swam near enough to skewer. Line fishing is not so indiscriminate." He stood up straighter and turned back to regard the weapons master, acting as if he was just realizing the curiousness of his own statement. "Even though you will see the fish you seek to impale, you will not be, in the true measure, as particular in your choice of meal as the line fisherman."

"How can you claim such?" Andzrel asked. "Because the line fisherman will throw back any fish he deems unworthy, while I would already have slain my quarry before bringing it from the pond?"

"Because the line fisherman has already chosen the type of fish," Gromph corrected, "in his selection of bait and placement, point and depth, of the line. Fish have preferences, and knowing those allows a wise angler to properly lay his trap."

He turned back to the skull gem.

"Is it possible that Archmage Gromph grows more cryptic with the passing years?"

"One would hope!" Gromph replied with a glance over his shoulder, and again he saw that the nuance of his words was somewhat lost on the poor Andzrel. "Living among the folk of Menzoberranzan is often akin to line fishing, don't you agree? Knowing the proper lures to attract and catch adversaries and allies alike."

When he turned back to Andzrel this time, he held the skull gem in one hand, aloft before his eyes. The skull-shaped crystalline gem danced with reflections of the many candles burning in the room, and those sparkles, in turn, set Gromph's eyes glowing.

Still the weapons master seemed as if he was in the dark regarding the archmage's analogy, and that confirmed to Gromph that Tiago had not betrayed him.

For Andzrel did not know that Ravel Xorlarrin had looked into this very skull gem, in which the young spellspinner had gained the knowledge of the prize that he and House Xorlarrin now pursued. And Andzrel did not have any hint that Tiago had facilitated the spellspinner's intrusion into Gromph's private chambers at Sorcere, as a favor to the House Xorlarrin weapons master Jearth, who was one of Andzrel's greatest rivals in the city's warrior hierarchy.

"House Xorlarrin moves exactly as House Baenre would wish, and to a destination worth exploring," Gromph explained clearly.

That seemed to rock Andzrel back on his heels a bit.

"Tiago is with them, by request of Matron Mother Quenthel," Gromph continued, and Andzrel's eyes popped open wide.

"Tiago! Why Tiago? He is my second, at my command!"

Gromph laughed at that. He had only mentioned Tiago in order to make Andzrel tremble with outrage, a sight Gromph very much enjoyed.

"If you instructed Tiago one way, and Matron Quenthel commanded him another, to whom should he offer his obedience?"

Andzrel's face grew tight.

Of course it did, Gromph knew. Young Tiago was indeed Andzrel's second, but that was an arrangement which few expected to hold for much longer. For

Tiago had something Andzrel did not: a direct bloodline to Dantrag Baenre, the greatest weapons master in the memory of House Baenre. Tiago was Dantrag's grandson, and thus the grandson of Yvonnel and the nephew of Gromph, Quenthel, and the rest of the noble clan. Andzrel, meanwhile, was the son of a cousin, noble still, but further removed.

To make matters worse, not a drow who had watched these two in battle thought that Andzrel could defeat Tiago in single combat—young Tiago, who was only growing stronger with the passing years.

The archmage spent a moment considering Andzrel, then recognized that he had planted the doubt and concern deeply enough—that Tiago was out with House Xorlarrin on this matter of apparent great importance would keep this one pacing his room for days.

Gromph, therefore, thought it the perfect time to change the subject.

"How well are you acquainted with Jarlaxle?"

"Of Bregan D'aerthe?" Andzrel stuttered. "I have heard of . . . not well." He seemed at a loss with his own admission, so he quickly added, "I have met him on several occasions."

"Jarlaxle always seems to set interesting events in motion," said Gromph. "Perhaps this will be no different."

"What are you saying?" the weapons master asked. "House Baenre facilitated this move by Xorlarrin?"

"Nothing of the sort. Matron Zeerith moves of her own accord."

"But we played a role in guiding that accord?"

Gromph shrugged noncommittally.

"What do you know, Archmage?" Andzrel demanded.

Gromph replaced the skull gem on the shelf and moved back to sit down at his desk, all at a leisurely pace. When he had settled once more, he turned his attention back to his parchment and took up his quill.

"I am no commoner," Andzrel shouted, and he stomped a heavy boot like the sharp crack of an exclamation point. "Do not treat me as such!"

Gromph looked up at him and nodded. "Indeed," he agreed as he reached for a corked, smoke-filled flask. He brought it before him, directly between him and Andzrel, and pulled off the cork. A line of smoke wafted up.

"You are no commoner," Gromph agreed. "But you are dismissed." With that, Gromph blew at the smoke, sending it toward Andzrel. In so doing, he released a sequence of spells in rapid order.

Andzrel looked at him curiously, startled and very much concerned, even afraid. He felt his very being, his corporeal form, thinning, becoming less substantial.

He tried to speak out, but it was too late. He was like the wind, flowing away and without control. Gromph watched him recede from the room, then waved his hand to throw forth a second burst of wind, a stronger one that not only sped Andzrel's departure, but slammed the room's door closed behind him.

Gromph knew that Andzrel wouldn't regain his corporeal form until he was far away from this wing of House Baenre.

The archmage didn't expect the annoying weapons master to return anytime soon. That brought a frown to Gromph's face, though, as he considered the expression he could elicit on Andzrel's face with the other little secrets he kept. For among Tiago's entourage on the expedition was one of Gromph's oldest associates, an old wizard-turned-warrior-turned-blacksmith drow named Gol'fanin, who carried with him a djinni in a bottle, a phase spider in another, and an ancient sword design, one which had eluded Gol'fanin for centuries because of his inability to properly meld the diamonds and metal alloys.

If the destination of the Xorlarrin expedition was as Gromph and Matron Zeerith and Matron Quenthel all expected, and if the cataclysm had been wrought of the rage of a primordial fire beast, then Andzrel's current state of outrage would seem utterly calm by comparison when Tiago returned home.

That thought pleased the old drow archmage greatly.

PART I

OLD GRUDGE

I am past the sunset of my second century of life and yet I feel as if the ground below me is as the shifting sands. In so many ways, I find that I am no more sure of myself than I was those many decades ago when I first walked free of Menzoberranzan—less sure, in truth, for in that time, my emotions were grounded in a clear sense of right and wrong, in a definitive understanding of truth against deception.

Perhaps my surety then was based almost solely on a negative; when I came to recognize the truth of the city of Menzoberranzan about me, I knew what I could not accept, knew what did not ring true in my heart and soul, and demanded the notion of a better life, a better way. It was not so much that I knew what I wanted, for any such concepts of the possibilities outside the cocoon of Menzoberranzan were surely far beyond my experience.

But I knew what I did not want and what I could not accept.

Guided by that inner moral compass, I made my way, and my beliefs seemed only reinforced by those friends I came to know, not kin, but surely kind.

And so I have lived my life, a goodly life, I think, with the power of righteousness guiding my blades. There have been times of doubt, of course, and so many errors along the way. There stood my friends, to guide me back to the correct path, to walk beside me and support me and reinforce my belief that there is a community greater than myself, a purpose higher and more noble than the simple hedonism so common in the land of my birth.

Now I am older.

Now, again, I do not know.

For I find myself enmeshed in conflicts I do not understand, where both sides seem equally wrong.

This is not Mithral Hall defending her gates against marauding orcs. This is not the garrison of Ten-Towns holding back a barbarian horde or battling the monstrous minions of Akar Kessell. In all Faerûn now, there is conflict and shadow and confusion, and a sense that there is no clear path to victory. The world has grown dark, and in a dark place, so dark rulers can arise.

I long for the simplicity of Icewind Dale.

For down here in the more populous lands, there is Luskan, full of treachery and deceit and unbridled greed. There are a hundred "Luskans" across the continent, I fear. In the tumult of the Spellplague and the deeper and more enduring darkness of the Shadowfell, the return of the shades and the Empire of Netheril, those structures of community and society could not remain unscathed. Some see chaos as an enemy to be defeated and tamed; others, I know from my earliest days, see chaos as opportunity for personal gain.

For down here, there are the hundreds of communities and clusters of farms depending on the protection of the city garrisons, who will not come.

Indeed, under the rule of despot kings or lords or high captains alike, those communities so oft become the prey of the powerful cities.

For down here, there is Many Arrows, the orc kingdom forced upon the Silver Marches by the hordes of King Obould in that long-ago war—though even now, nearly a century hence, it remains a trial, a test, whose outcome cannot be predicted. Did King Bruenor, with his courage in signing the Treaty of Garumn's Gorge, end the war, or merely delay a larger one?

It is always confusion, I fear, always those shifting sands.

Until I draw my blades, and that is the dark truth of who I have become. For when my scimitars are in hand, the battle becomes immediate, the goal survival. The greater politic that once guided my hand is a fleeting vision, the waving lines of rising heat showing rivers of sparkling water where there is only, in truth, dry sand. I live in a land of many Akar Kessells, but so few, it seems, places worth defending!

Perhaps among the settlers of Neverwinter there exists such a noble defense as that I helped wage in Ten-Towns, but there live, too, in the triad of interests, the Thayans and their undead hordes and the Netherese, many persons no less ruthless and no less self-interested. Indeed, no less wrong.

How might I engage my heart in such a conflict as the morass that is Neverwinter? How might I strike with conviction, secure in the knowledge that I fight for the good of the land, or for the benefit of goodly folk?

I cannot. Not now. Not with competing interests equally dark.

But no more am I surrounded by friends of similar weal, it seems. Were it my choice alone, I would flee this land, perhaps to the Silver Marches and (hopefully) some sense of goodliness and hope. To Mithral Hall and Silverymoon, who cling still to the heartsong of King Bruenor Battlehammer and Lady Alustriel, or perhaps to Waterdeep, shining still, where the lords hold court for the benefit of their city and citizens.

But Dahlia will not be so persuaded to leave. There is something here, some old grudge that is far beyond my comprehension. I followed her to Sylora Salm willingly, settling my own score as she settled hers. And now I follow her again, or I abandon her, for she will not turn aside. When Artemis Entreri mentioned that name, Herzgo Alegni, such an anger came over Dahlia, and such a sadness, I think, that she will hear of no other goal.

Nor will she hear of any delay, for winter is soon to be thick about us. No storm will slow her, I fear; no snow will gather deep enough that stubborn Dahlia will not drive through it, to Neverwinter, to wherever she must go to find this Netherese lord, this Herzgo Alegni.

I had thought her hatred of Sylora Salm profound, but nay, I know now, it cannot measure against the depths of Dahlia's loathing of this tiefling Netherese warlord. She will kill him, so she says, and when I threatened to leave her to her own course, she did not blink and did not hesitate, and did not care enough to offer me a fond farewell.

So again I am drawn into a conflict I do not understand. Is there a righteous course to be found here? Is there a measure of right and wrong between Dahlia and the Shadovar? By the words of Entreri, it would seem that this tiefling is a foul beast deserving of a violent end, and surely the reputation of Netheril supports that notion.

But am I now so lost in my choice of path that I take the word of Artemis Entreri as guidance? Am I now so removed from any sense of correctness, from any communities so designed, that it falls to this?

The sands shift beneath my feet. I draw my blades, and in the desperation of battle, I will wield them as I always have. My enemies will not know the tumult in my heart, the confusion that I have no clear moral path before me. They will know only the bite of Icingdeath, the flash of Twinkle.

But I will know the truth.

Does my reluctance to pursue Alegni reflect a distrust of Dahlia, I wonder? She is certain in her course—more certain than I have ever seen her, or seen anybody, for that matter. Even Bruenor, in his long ago quest to regain Mithral Hall, did not stride so determinedly. She will kill this tiefling or she will die trying. A sorry friend, a sorrier lover, am I indeed if I do not accompany her.

But I do not understand. I do not see the path clearly. I do not know what greater good I serve. I do not fight in the hopes of betterment of my corner of the world.

I just fight.

On the side of Dahlia, who intrigues me.

On the side of Artemis Entreri, so it would seem.

Perhaps in another century, I will return to Menzoberranzan, not as an enemy, not as a conqueror, not to tear down the structures of that society I once held as most vile.

Perhaps I will return because I will belong.

This is my fear, of a life wasted, of a cause misbegotten, of a belief that is, in the end, an empty and unattainable ideal, the foolish designs of an innocent child who believed there could be more.

—Drizzt Do'Urden

CHAPTER 1

THE WAR WOAD

DRIZZT WASN'T ALARMED WHEN HE AWOKE AT DAWN TO FIND THAT DAHLIA was not lying beside him in their small camp. He knew where she would be. He paused just long enough to strap on his scimitar belt and scoop Taulmaril over his shoulder, then trotted down the narrow forest paths and up the steep incline, grabbing tree to tree and pulling himself along. Near the top of that small hill, he spotted her, calmly staring in the distance with her back to him.

Despite the cold—and this morning was the coldest of the season by far, Dahlia wore only her blanket, loosely wrapped around her, drooping from one naked shoulder. Drizzt hardly noted her dress, or undress, remarkable as it was, for his gaze was caught by Dahlia's hair. The previous night, she had worn it in her stylish and soft shoulder cut, but now she had returned to the single thick black and red braid, rising up and curling deliciously around her delicate neck. It seemed as if Dahlia could become a different person with the pass of a magical comb.

He started toward her slowly, a dry branch cracking under his step, the slight sound turning Dahlia's head just a bit to regard him.

Drizzt stopped short, staring at the patterns of blue spots, the warrior elf's woad pattern. That, too, had been absent from her appearance the previous night, as if she had softened herself for Drizzt's bed, as if Dahlia was using the hair and woad as a reflection of her mood, or. . . .

Drizzt narrowed his gaze. Not as a reflection of her mood, he realized, but as an enticement to, a manipulation of, her drow lover.

They had argued the previous evening, and fiery Dahlia, braid and woad intact, had staked out her position, her intention to go after Alegni, forcefully.

But then she had come to Drizzt more gently in reconciliation, her hair softer, her pretty face clear of the warrior pattern. They had not discussed Alegni then, but neither had they gone to sleep angry at each other.

19

Drizzt walked over to join Dahlia, taking in the sight from the western edge of the hillock. He looked down across the miles to Neverwinter, shrouded in a low ground fog as the colder air drew forth the wet warmth from the great river.

"The mist hides much of the scarring," Drizzt said, his arms going around the woman, who didn't react to his touch. "It was once a beautiful city, and will be again if the Thayans are truly defeated."

"With the Shadovar haunting the streets and alleyways?" Dahlia replied, her tone harsh.

Drizzt didn't quite know how to reply, so he just hugged her a bit closer.

"They are in the city, among the settlers, so said Barrabus—the man you call Artemis Entreri," Dahlia replied.

"A foothold likely gained only because of the greater threat of Sylora Salm. If that threat is diminished, I expect that the Shadovar—"

"When their leader is dead, the threat of the Shadovar will diminish," Dahlia interrupted bluntly and coldly. "And their leader will soon be dead."

Drizzt tried to hug her closer, but she pulled away from him. She took a couple of steps closer to the edge of the bluff and rearranged her blanket around her.

"Time is not his ally, it is ours," Drizzt said.

Dahlia turned on him sharply, her gaze stern—and intensified by the threatening patterns of her war woad.

"He will know the truth," Drizzt insisted. "He will learn from Entreri of what transpired with Sylora Salm, and will know that we will come for him—Entreri admitted as much to us when he told us that he was enslaved and that he could not join us in your vendetta."

"Then the foul Netherese warlord should be very afraid right now," Dahlia replied.

"And so he will be very alert right now, with his forces pulled in tightly. Now is not the time—"

Again, Dahlia cut him short. "It is not your choice."

"As the Thayan threat diminishes, so too will our opponent's guard, and so too will his standing within the city," Drizzt pressed on against her anger. "I have met these settlers and they are goodly folk—they'll not suffer the Netherese for long. This is not the time to go after him."

Dahlia's blue eyes flashed with anger, and for a moment, Drizzt thought she might lash out at him. Even knowing her designs and determination to get Alegni, the drow ranger could hardly believe the level of intensity in that rage! He could not imagine her angrier if he had admitted to her some heinous crime he had committed against her family. He was glad that she did not have her weapon available to her at that moment.

Drizzt let a long silence pass between them before daring to continue. "You will kill Alegni."

"Do not speak his name!" Dahlia insisted, and she spat upon the ground, as if even hearing the name had brought bile into her mouth.

Drizzt patted his hands in the air, trying to calm her.

Gradually, the angry fires in her eyes were replaced with a profound sadness.

"What is it?" he whispered, daring to move closer.

Dahlia turned around but did not refuse him as he put his arms around her once more. Together, they looked down at Neverwinter.

"I'm going to kill him," she whispered, and it seemed to Drizzt as if she was speaking to herself more than to him. "No delay. No wait. I will kill him."

"As you killed Sylora Salm?"

"Had I known she named him as her enemy, I would have helped her. Had I known the identity of the Shadovar leader, I never would have left Neverwinter for Luskan or Gauntlgrym. I never would have departed the region until he was dead *by my hand.*"

She said those last three words with such clarity, such intensity, such venom, that Drizzt knew he would get nowhere in reasoning with Dahlia at this time.

So he just held her.

In the skeleton of a dead tree, peering through a crack in the rotting wood, Effron the Twisted watched the couple with great interest. The misshapen warlock heard every word of their conversation and wasn't surprised by any of it. He knew of Dahlia, knew more of her than anyone else alive, likely, and he understood the demons that guided her.

Of course she would try to kill Herzgo Alegni. She would be happier if she died trying to kill him than if they both remained alive.

Effron understood her.

The warlock couldn't deny his own emotions in looking at this elf warrior woman. Part of him wanted to leap out from the tree and destroy the couple then and there. Good sense overruled that impulse, though, for he had heard enough of the reputation of this Drizzt Do'Urden creature to realize that he ought to play this game cautiously.

Besides, he wasn't sure he wanted Dahlia killed—not immediately, at least. There were some things he wanted to know, needed to know, and only she could provide the answers.

The Shadovar warlock shade-shifted away from the spot, but did not immediately return to Herzgo Alegni's side to report his findings. Effron was nobody's slave, after all, and was not without his own resources.

He went instead to a forest region of dells and rocky ridges outside of Neverwinter. The sky was still very dark, with low clouds, and a light snow had begun to fall, but Effron knew this area well and moved unerringly to an encampment set in a shallow cave.

Sitting nearby were a handful of Shadovar—Netherese soldiers who had come through from the Shadowfell soon after Effron, at Effron's secret bidding, but who had not yet pledged their allegiance to Alegni.

When the twisted warlock shambled into their midst, they all stood up, not quite at attention but still with some modicum of respect.

"You have the globes?" the warlock asked one shade, a tall human male named Ratsis.

In response, Ratsis flashed a crooked-toothed smile and reached under the open collar of his shirt to produce a silver chain necklace set with two shadow-filled translucent globes, each the size of a child's fist. In the swirling shadowmists within each globe crawled a spider, small and furry, like a tiny tarantula. Ratsis grinned.

"For the elf woman," Effron reminded him.

"And what of her companion?" Ratsis asked.

"Kill him," Effron replied without hesitation. "He is too dangerous to capture, or to allow to escape. Kill him."

"We are seven," insisted Jermander, another of the group, a fierce tiefling warrior who wore both his pride and his unrelenting anger openly. "They are but two!"

"Eight," Ratsis the spider-keeper quietly corrected. He paused for just a moment, smiling as he rolled the globes of his necklace around, eyes glowing as he viewed his pets, and reconsidered. "Ten."

Jermander's expression showed that he did not appreciate those particular allies, which only drew a laugh from Ratsis.

"Do not underestimate these two enemies, my fighting friend," Ratsis warned.

"Do not underestimate us," Jermander retorted. "We are not fodder, pulled from the Shadowfell for the pleasure of Effron the Twisted, or even Lord Alegni."

Effron matched the warrior's stare, but he did not disagree. These particular shades were not Netherese nobles, perhaps, but neither could they be considered commoners. They were mercenaries of great reputation, the famed Bounty Hirelings of Cavus Dun, and they came at a high price indeed.

"My apologies, Jermander," Effron said with an awkward, twisted bow.

"Capture the elf woman," Ratsis said with great emphasis. "Sheathe your blades." He rolled the spider globes around his fingers again and smiled victoriously. "Be lethal with the drow, gentle with the elf."

The exchange of looks between Jermander and Ratsis revealed more than a little competition between the two, and no shortage of animosity either. Neither of those truths was lost on Effron.

"Do not fail me in killing the drow," the warlock, who also carried the weight of a Netherese noble, warned. "Fail me in capturing Dahlia alive, and you will beg for your death for eternity."

"A threat?" Jermander asked, seeming amused.

"Draygo Quick," Effron reminded him. The warrior lost his bluster at the mention of that truly powerful Shadovar. "A promise."

Effron ended with a hard stare, shifting his gaze from one mercenary to the other, then slowly walked away.

"Get the Shifter," Ratsis said as soon as Effron was gone. The Shifter had been the reason he had corrected Jermander's count when he had insisted that they were eight and not seven.

Jermander stared at him doubtfully.

"The drow's blades will pose challenges and dangers to our capture of Dahlia," Ratsis said. "I don't wish to explain Dahlia's untimely death to the likes of Draygo Quick!"

"I can move him," insisted another shade, a wiry and muscular tiefling wearing few clothes and carrying a short spear.

"As can I," declared another, one of human heritage and Shadovar skin, who was similarly armed and armored only in a fine cloth suit. He stepped up beside the tiefling and both puffed out their slender, but quite muscular, chests, seemingly in practiced unison. On this human, more than on the tiefling, such a pose seemed a jester's parody. With a mop of curly blond hair and cherubic cheeks, he appeared almost childlike, despite his honed muscles.

Ratsis wanted to laugh at these two Brothers of the Gray Mists, an order of monks that had gained some notoriety of late among the Netherese. He wanted to laugh, but he knew better than to do so. For Brothers Parbid and Afafrenfere were particularly zealous and undeniably reckless.

"I had expected that you two would be primary in killing the drow," Ratsis said to appease them, and indeed, the monks both showed the edges of a smile at his compliment. "With your quick movements and deadly fists, I would expect even one of Drizzt Do'Urden's reputation to be overwhelmed."

"We are disciples of the Pointed Step," Parbid, the tiefling, replied, and stamped his spear. "We will do both: move him and then kill him."

Ratsis glanced at Jermander, who was obviously equally amused. Jermander's look showed that their little spat had been left behind, suppressed by the almost-comical puffery of Parbid and Afafrenfere.

"I am the catcher. You are the killer," Ratsis said to Jermander. "What is your choice?"

"An eighth would suit us well," Jermander replied, to the disappointment—and apparent deflation—of the two monks. "I would take no risks here. Not at this time."

"The Shifter will demand three shares!" said Ambergris, another of the band, a dwarf convert to the Shadowfell, part shade but not quite wholly one as of yet. Her real name was Amber Gristle O'Maul, but Ambergris seemed a better fit, for she surely looked and smelled the part, with long black hair, parts braided, parts not, and a thick and crooked nose. She didn't quite look the part of a Shadovar yet, appearing more like the offspring of a duergar and a Delzoun. She'd only been in the Shadowfell for a little more than a year. But her prowess with her exceptional mace and her divine spellcasting had not gone unnoticed. Despite her lack of credentials among the Shadovar, the Bounty Hunters of Cavus Dun had taken her in and had promised to sponsor her for full admission into the empire—extraordinarily rare for a nonhuman—if she proved herself.

She seemed to understand that as she sat among this group, eagerly rolling her weapon, which she had lovingly named Skullbreaker, in her strong hands. The mace reached nearly four feet in length, its core polished hardwood, handle wrapped in black leather, its weighted end intermittently wrapped with thick rings of black metal. She could deftly wield it with one hand, or could take it up in both and bat the skull from a skeleton out of sight. She carried a small buckler, easily maneuverable so it wouldn't hinder her frequent shifts from one hand to two on the weapon.

"Perhaps you would do well to remain silent," Ratsis answered sternly. Ambergris took it with a shrug; had she supported his position here, no doubt Jermander would have turned on her with equal discipline.

"True enough," the tiefling monk Parbid remarked. "Ambergris thinks herself special because she's one of a thousand among us due to her heritage, and one of ten thousand when you add in her gender. One would think that by now she would have come to understand that her specialness is a matter of curiosity and nothing more."

"Unfair, brother," said the other monk, Afafrenfere. "She fights well and her healing prowess has helped us greatly."

"Won't be helpin' yer devil-blooded partner anytime soon," Ambergris muttered under her breath, but loud enough for all to hear.

"Perhaps she will be of use in interrogating any of her filthy kin we catch along our trails," Parbid answered Afafrenfere.

"The dwarf's point is well taken," Jermander interjected to get things back to the point. "The Shifter will demand three full shares, though her work will be no more grueling, and surely less dangerous, given her ability to escape anyone's grasp, than our own."

"We'll offer her two shares, then," Ratsis calmly replied, and Jermander nodded. "Are we all agreed?" Ratsis asked.

Ambergris stamped her foot, crossed her arms over her chest, and stubbornly shook her head, though of course, she did not have a full vote as she was not fully of the Shadovar. When Ratsis's skeptical expression conveyed exactly that, the dwarf retreated a bit and began fiddling with the string of black pearls she wore around her neck, cursing under her breath.

The two monks stood resolutely and shook their heads with a unified "nay," countering Ratsis and Jermander, who both voted "aye."

All eyes turned to the back of the camp, where a broad-shouldered woman and a fat tiefling male sat on stones. The woman sharpened her sword. The tiefling man wrapped new strands of red leather around the handle of his great flail. With every twist of leather, the weapon jerked and the heavy spiked ball, the size of a large man's head, bobbed at the end of its four-foot chain.

"Ye do what ye need doin'," the tiefling, who was called simply Bol, replied.

"Two and a half to two, then," Ambergris said with grin.

But the sword-woman quite unexpectedly chimed in with "Get the Shifter," as soon as the dwarf had made the claim. All eyes fell on her. It was the first time any of them had heard her speak, and she had been with this hunting band for tendays. They didn't even know her name, and to a one had referred to her as Horrible, or "Whore-o-Bol" as Ambergris had tagged it, a nickname that hadn't seemed to bother her, and one that had merely amused the slobbering Bol.

Or maybe it had bothered her, Ratsis mused as he looked from the woman to the dwarf, to recognize some true animosity between them. And that animosity had likely elicited the response.

"Three to two and a half, then," Jermander said, pulling Ratsis back into the conversation.

"Call it four, then!" Bol added. "If me Horrible's wanting it, then so be it."

"So what was to be a seventh-split will be a ninth," Parbid grumbled.

"Shouldn't you and your brother be out scouting for Dahlia and the drow, as we agreed?" Ratsis replied. "And if you happen upon them, do feel free to take them, and in that event, you two may split Effron's gold evenly between you."

Parbid and Afafrenfere exchanged looks, their expressions both doubtful and intrigued, as if they might just call Ratsis on his bluff.

Jermander, meanwhile, cast a less-than-enthusiastic gaze Ratsis's way and held the look as the two monks trotted off.

"Let them try," Ratsis explained. "Then we'll be back to seventh shares, even considering the expensive services of the Shifter."

Jermander snorted and didn't seem overly bothered by that possibility.

Drizzt crouched a few steps away from the trunk of the large pine tree, beneath the bending thick branches that had served as his and Dahlia's shelter for the night. He saw the coating of white between the pine needles, and he stood straighter, pulling apart a pair of the branches. The first snow had indeed fallen that night, coating the ground in glistening white under the rays of the morning sun.

With the light peeking into their natural bedroom, the drow glanced over his shoulder at the sleeping Dahlia. A single ray touched her check, but no war woad shimmered there. Dahlia had worn her softer look again that night, after a long and uncomfortable silence had trailed the couple throughout the day on the heels of their earlier argument. Her hair was back in the soft shoulder bob, her face clear and smooth.

It was the look Drizzt far preferred, and Dahlia knew that.

Dahlia knew that.

Was she manipulating him? he wondered yet again. He knew that Dahlia was a calculating woman, a clever warrior, a strategic opponent. But was it possible that she was also *his* opponent? Did she see him as a companion and a friend, or as merely a plaything and a tool for her greater designs?

Drizzt tried to shake such dark thoughts away, but he could not. Standing there at the boughs of the tree, looking back at the beautiful elf, he could not help but be drawn to her. At the same time, though, Drizzt was reminded that he did not really know Dahlia, and that what he did know of her was not so innocent a lifestyle.

Dahlia, after all, had lured Jarlaxle and Athrogate to Gauntlgrym with the intent of freeing the primordial. Even though she had changed from that malignant course in the critical moment, she still had to bear more than a little responsibility for the cataclysm that had devastated the region and buried the city of Neverwinter.

She looked so young lying there in the morning light, and so innocent, almost childlike. Indeed she was young, Drizzt reminded himself. When he was Dahlia's age back in Menzoberranzan, had he even left House Do'Urden for the warrior school of Melee-Magthere?

Still, he knew, Dahlia was in many ways much older than he. She had served in the court of Szass Tam, the archlich of Thay. She had witnessed great battles and had known more lovers than he, surely. She was greatly traveled, and deeply experienced in life.

Drizzt knew better than to allow any condescension to slip into his thoughts as he considered Dahlia. Spirited and dangerous, it would not do for anyone associated with her, friend, lover, or enemy, to underestimate her, in any way. So was she manipulating him with this soft look of hers, the alluring and more innocent cut of her hair and her unblemished face?

The drow smiled as he considered the obvious answer in light of yesterday's events. The hardened Dahlia, braid and woad, had argued with him and even invited him to leave her side. She would take care of Herzgo Alegni herself, she had proclaimed. But that would be no easy task, obviously, for Alegni was within the city, and likely surrounded by powerful allies, including Artemis Entreri.

And as the day had worn on, and Drizzt had remained at her side, though still without committing to join her, Dahlia had morphed into this alluring and gentle creature, less warrior, more lover.

Drizzt looked out at the snowy forest and chuckled at himself. It didn't really matter if Dahlia was trying to manipulate him, he supposed. Wasn't that simply the truth of relationships? Hadn't Bruenor manipulated him and everyone else, facilitating his own "death" after the battle with Akar Kessell that they might abandon Icewind Dale and head out on the road in search of Mithral Hall? And hadn't Drizzt, in truth, manipulated Bruenor into signing the Treaty of Garumn's Gorge?

The drow couldn't help laughing as his memories spun back through the years. He recalled Bruenor's deathbed drama back in Icewind Dale, when the dwarf had played out his greatest desires, so apparently lost to the winds of time. Coughing and sputtering and wheezing and obviously failing, clever Bruenor had shrunk before Drizzt's eyes, as if entering the nether realm of death, until the moment Drizzt had pledged that they would head out and find Mithral Hall. Then Bruenor had hopped up, ready for the road.

Oh, what a fine play that had been . . . but also, of course, a deep manipulation.

That Dahlia was playing some games within the context of their relationship simply wasn't that important, Drizzt told himself. He knew the truth of it, and within that truth crouched the hard fact that he could only be manipulated if he let her. It wasn't simply lust, he knew, though surely Dahlia excited him. His intrigue with the elf went far beyond physical needs. He wanted to understand her. He felt that if he could learn about Dahlia, he would learn much of himself. Her way of looking at the world was foreign to him, a different perspective entirely, and that promised him an expansion of his own viewpoints. Perhaps he was drawn to Dahlia for the same reason he seemed forever drawn to Artemis Entreri—to consider the man, at least, if not to travel beside him. For both of them, Dahlia and Entreri, were possessed of a code of honor, albeit a stilted one in Drizzt's eyes. Neither woke up in the morning with visions of creating chaos and suffering. Dahlia had shown as much with her inability to follow her master's orders and release the primordial.

So, did he want to fix them? Drizzt wondered. Did he, somewhere in his heart, believe that he could redeem Artemis Entreri and guide Dahlia to a brighter light?

He glanced back at Dahlia again, just for a moment. He couldn't deny his hubris. Likely, his desire to bring people out of darkness was part of the equation that had put Artemis Entreri in Drizzt's thoughts so many times over the decades—nearly as often as he had wondered about Wulfgar.

It was much more complicated with Dahlia, he knew. For he was indeed drawn to her in ways he could never be drawn to Entreri or Wulfgar. He couldn't deny it. No matter how many times he might convince himself that he should not be with the dangerous elf, that conviction couldn't hold against the mere sight of her, particularly when she wore her hair and face softly.

He straightened up in surprise as he felt the elf's arm slide over his shoulder and wrap around his neck. Dahlia rested her chin on his other shoulder and kissed him on the ear. "A warm bed before a journey into the cold snow?"

Drizzt smiled. His expression only widened as Dahlia added, "And then we will go and kill him."

Indeed.

He thought of Bruenor on that deathbed in Icewind Dale again and reminded himself that his bond with the deceptive dwarf had lasted more than a hundred years.

Indeed.

CHAPTER 2

THE LORD OF NEVERWINTER

C APTAIN OF THE WHITE GUARD," HERZGO ALEGNI CORRECTED, AND MANY eyes turned upon the tiefling warlord in surprise. Alegni sat at a small table along the side wall of the inn that served as their meeting house. He was opposite the hearth, about as far from the source of warmth as he could be in the room, and he had pulled open the window beside him.

Jelvus Grinch looked at him curiously. The city's leaders had just been discussing Grinch's place in Neverwinter's new ruling structure, and the Netherese lord had mentioned that Jelvus Grinch was a fine choice as the leader of the Neverwinter garrison, a role Grinch had handled for years by that point, in any case.

"The White Guard?" another in the room chimed in, voicing the question held by many in the room, obviously.

Herzgo Alegni stood up slowly, flexing his obvious muscles as he went and rolling back his shoulders to let them all witness the powerful expanse of his broad and strong chest. Slowly, taking the time to let the heels of his boots resound against the wood floor with every distinctive step, he walked to the front of the room, and even the powerfully built Jelvus Grinch seemed a meager being next to the huge and dominating tiefling warrior. Alegni's attire, black leather and metal-studded armor, and the flowing cape that reminded all of his noble station, only added to the imposing image, as did that large red blade openly hanging from his left hip. The blood red of the metal contrasted sharply with the black armor, and as Alegni dropped his naked left hand to rest atop the weapon's pommel, the sword seemed more an extension of his red tiefling skin than a separate item. It accented perfectly the red fires in Alegni's eyes, those orbs a shining reminder of his half-devil heritage. Yes, that red blade . . . a weapon that had cut through an umber hulk and left the creature writhing in its death throes on a Neverwinter street, to the amazement and cheers of so many of Neverwinter's citizens, many of whom were in this very room.

"What is the White Guard?" Jelvus Grinch dared to ask.

"The city garrison," explained the tiefling. "I think that an appropriate name."

"First Citizen . . ." Jelvus Grinch started to argue, for that was the title of honor they had bestowed upon Alegni.

"Do not call me that," Alegni interrupted, and his tone changed then, not so subtly, and more than a few in the room, Jelvus Grinch included, shifted uncomfortably.

"The White Guard," Alegni said more loudly, turning to face the larger gathering again. "It is fitting, for now Neverwinter has two garrisons, of course. The White Guard of your people," he explained to Jelvus Grinch and the others, "and my own."

"Who are to be known as . . . ?" Jelvus Grinch prompted.

Alegni considered that for a moment, then replied, "The Shadow Guard. Yes, that will do. So you will coordinate the White Guard."

He wasn't reasoning with them but rather dictating to them, something that was not lost on anyone in the room.

"And you will command the Shadow Guard?"

Alegni laughed at the notion. "I have my lieutenants in place to lead the guard."

"Freeing you up to . . . ?" prompted a red-haired woman the townsfolk called the Forest Sentinel.

Recognizing the voice, Alegni looked at her directly. "My dear Arunika," he addressed her.

"Freeing you up to assume lordship of the city," Arunika stated, and when Alegni didn't immediately disagree, the room erupted in whispered conversations, a few jeers, and several sharp complaints.

"We have scored a great victory!" Alegni addressed them in a booming voice, one that silenced the whole of the place. "Sylora Salm is dead. The fortress she was raising in Neverwinter Wood is in disarray, its magic failing. The Dread Ring itself is diminished, and greatly so."

He ended abruptly and let that stunning news—for indeed, he had not revealed any of that until this very moment—hang in the air while he reveled in the blank expressions of the city leaders.

"How can you know?" Jelvus Grinch finally managed to stammer.

Herzgo Alegni looked at him as if he had to be a fool to even ask such a question.

"The threat is diminished and will be driven forth in short order." Alegni paused and grinned. "Because of me."

"And now you claim the lordship of Neverwinter," Arunika surmised, and Herzgo Alegni smiled at her.

"Ye can't be doing that!" one man shouted from the back, and Alegni's smile disappeared in the blink of an astonished eye, and more than one in the crowd, the speaker included, ducked low under that withering gaze.

But another dared chime in, "You've not got the Crown of Neverwinter! You canno' be Lord of Neverwinter without the Crown of Neverwinter!"

"And pray tell, where is this crown?" Alegni answered in a booming, clearly threatening tone.

The room filled with murmurs, and the person who had objected sheepishly replied, "None are knowing."

"It is lost, then," Alegni declared. "And so it is time to start anew—as you all have done in coming to rebuild the ruined city."

"But if that's the truth of it, then the lord's to be one of them that's been here the years, toiling!" another man protested, or started to, for as he spoke, Alegni moved toward him, and by the time he finished the thought, he was crouched over, covering up and cowering.

"You can't be doing that!" the first protestor repeated.

"I just did it," Alegni informed them all. "You needed me, and so you need me still. And I am here, at your service."

For a moment, the whole situation seemed to be teetering on the edge of a razor, acceptance on one side and open revolt on the other, and Alegni had no idea of which way this group would fall. His right arm dropped down by his side and he flexed his hand, encased in the magical gauntlet companion of his red-bladed sword. If any made a move, Alegni intended to swiftly draw that blade and cut Jelvus Grinch in half in a single, powerful movement.

That would take the fight out of them.

"We named a bridge after you, as you wished," Jelvus Grinch replied, his voice thick with apprehension. "We granted you the title of First Citizen for your help in our struggles. Now you intend to repay us by subjugating us?"

"That is a foolish way to view this," said Alegni. "We are winning, but have not yet won. We have two forces in play. Your own, meager as it is, and mine, with resources and power far beyond your understanding. To complete the victory, we must be joined in purpose under a single voice. Do we agree on those points?"

"Even if we do, who has determined that the singular voice would be that of Herzgo Alegni?" Jelvus Grinch pointed out.

Alegni shrugged as if that hardly mattered. "Do you expect me to turn my army to your command?" he asked incredulously. "You, who cannot begin even to comprehend the power of that force, or of the Shadovar, or of the Empire of Netheril?"

"We are being conquered from within!" One woman leaped to her feet, and several shouts of agreement erupted around her.

"No!" Arunika shouted above them all. "No," she said again, staring at Alegni and bravely walking right up to him.

"Not conquered." She turned as she spoke to encompass all in the room. "Until this threat is eradicated, until the Dread Ring is fully defeated and Sylora's minions are all dead in the forest or fleeing back to Thay, Herzgo Alegni would claim the interim lordship of Neverwinter. For indeed we shall need one voice to speak out for us to those surrounding cities. It is a strong fist grabbing for power, of course." She turned a sly look upon Alegni. "But a temporary one, is it not?"

"Of course," said Alegni. He managed a lewd smile as he looked into Arunika's sparkling blue eyes. Let her believe that he desired her as a lover—what male would not, after all? But Herzgo Alegni knew the truth of this one. He had only just discovered that Arunika the Forest Sentinel was no mere human woman, that she was not human at all. And he knew much of the truth of her supposed allegiance to Neverwinter, though there was surely more to learn of this complicated creature. "Why would I deign to serve as lord of a meager city in the kingdoms of meager humans?"

Someone in the crowd started to argue, but Alegni moved with a sudden and powerful stride, shoving Arunika out of the way. "You need me!" he shouted. "You begged me for help and received that help. Without me, without my army, your town would have been gutted like a fallen cow by the umber hulks. Or your walls would have been leveled by the thunderbolts of Sylora Salm. The enemy that came against you was quite beyond you. Don't deny it! You needed me and you need me still, and I'll not be cast aside because of victories that I've brought to you. I'm no mercenary to be bought with your coin. I'm no adventuring hero to rush to your aid for the sake of my precious reputation, or for the good of all goodly men. You invited me into your home and so I came, and now I remain until I decide that it's time to go."

If the spectacle of Alegni wasn't enough to keep the city leaders in their seats, the room's back doors swung wide at that moment and in strode Effron the Twisted, accompanied by a host of armed Shadovar. Alegni noted that among that troupe walked Jermander. Jermander? Alegni knew the mercenary and knew well Cavus Dun. He made a mental note to take up with Effron that one's unexpected appearance.

Herzgo Alegni scanned the room and let some tense moments slip past. When it became obvious that none of the Neverwinter settlers would dare make a move against him, he turned to Jelvus Grinch.

"You will command the White Guard," he instructed the man. "You, and one other of your choosing, will be granted a seat at my court table, and you alone among the humans of Neverwinter will have my ear to voice the concerns of the city garrison. Do you agree?"

Jelvus Grinch couldn't help himself as he glanced down at that devastating sword. He swallowed hard and Alegni flashed him that awful knowing grin. Jelvus Grinch knew, and Herzgo Alegni knew that he knew, that a wrong answer here would leave him on the floor in two pieces.

"Yes," he said softly.

"Yes?" Herzgo Alegni stated loudly.

"Yes, Lord Alegni," Jelvus Grinch dutifully clarified.

Arunika left the meeting abruptly, not wanting to get caught in a private discussion with Lord Alegni and his band of powerful allies. The misshapen warlock had tormented her imp and had learned much of her—too much!—the red-haired succubus knew.

She moved quickly through Neverwinter's streets, constantly glancing back to ensure that she was not being followed. To create even more security, she turned down one dark, dead-end alleyway and moved swiftly to the end. There in the dark, she spread her batlike wings and flew up to the nearest rooftop, skipping along above the city.

She came down into the darkness beside a large building at the northeastern end of Neverwinter's wall. The House of Knowledge had been a thriving temple to Oghma and a flourishing repository of books and artifacts detailing the rich history of the Sword Coast. The cataclysm had changed all of that in a burst of lava and ash, reducing what had once been a holy library to a virtual refugee camp. The transition had not gone well, and the person at the tip of those decisions, Brother Anthus, had not done well. Rarely was he even at this structure any longer, preferring a secluded and abandoned ramshackle cottage across town whenever his duties allowed him a private reprieve.

With a glance around, Arunika entered through a little-used side door. Then she waited, in the dark room.

A short while later, Brother Anthus entered. He carried a single burning candle and moved toward the large candelabra near the altar at the front of the room.

"Had I known you meant to walk the city avenues backward to get home from the meeting, I would have eaten my dinner before coming here," Arunika said.

Brother Anthus barely halted in his walk, as if to prove that he was not surprised to find her here—and why would he be, given the gravity of that particular meeting? He took his time in lighting all the arms of the candelabra, bathing the room in a soft glow, then turned to regard Arunika.

"You knew this would happen," he said.

"I did not expect that Herzgo Alegni would help the city of Neverwinter out of any sense of charity or beneficence, true."

"He moved quickly," Brother Anthus replied. "Quicker than I had expected."

"He believes that the Thayans are in disarray. Given that possibility, their threat will fast diminish. By moving to secure his power now, he can continue to use the threat of Szass Tam as a bludgeon against those who would disagree." She paused and tilted her head, a wry grin on her face, and asked, "Are the Thayans in disarray?"

"Sylora Salm is dead."

"I know that!"

Brother Anthus took a deep breath and moved to sit on the bench opposite Arunika. "Valindra Shadowmantle is no minor power," he explained.

"When the insane lich is not confusing herself with her own babbling," said Arunika, and Brother Anthus nodded and shifted . . . uncomfortably, Arunika noted.

"The ambassador has helped her tremendously," Arunika prompted, referring to their contact emissary within the Abolethic Sovereignty, itself an aboleth, a fishlike mind-bending creature of great psionic power. She paused for a few heartbeats and continued to read Brother Anthus's discomfort. "But then," she added, "anything the ambassador bestows, the ambassador can take back, no doubt."

"I had thought that the Sovereignty wished to use the Thayans as foil to the Netherese, and the other way around," Brother Anthus said.

"Reasonable," Arunika agreed. "That, too, was my understanding. But who can tell with these strange creatures?"

"Brilliant creatures!" Brother Anthus corrected.

Arunika nodded, conceding the point. She wasn't in a mood to argue with the zealot.

"Do you think the ambassador will allow the Thayan threat to unravel now that Sylora Salm is dead?" Brother Anthus asked. "Will the creature bring Valindra Shadowmantle back into a state of confusion?"

"Or will the ambassador continue to twist Valindra's thoughts to the benefit of the Sovereignty?" Arunika wondered aloud, and she nodded, as that sounded plausible to her. "As long as Herzgo Alegni remains a threat, I would expect that the ambassador will keep Valindra lucid enough that her forces will cause him trouble."

"But the aboleths will never allow her the degree of lucidity to break free of their power," Brother Anthus said, completing the thought.

"Go to our fishlike friend," Arunika bade the monk. "Inform the Sovereignty of Herzgo Alegni's claim of lordship over Neverwinter. The ambassador will know how to best use Valindra to counter Alegni."

"Should the Thayans attack again?" Brother Anthus asked. "Is that your recommendation?"

Arunika considered it for a moment, then shook her head. "Alegni's forces are not so strong," she explained. "With Sylora Salm dead, I expect that he will have little leverage to garner more soldiers from his Netherese masters in the Shadowfell. Let us keep it that way. There is more afoot than the Thayans or the Netherese, and it will be interesting to see how it plays out."

Brother Anthus looked at her curiously, but Arunika let the tease stand, deciding not to tell him about the trio who had killed Sylora, and about where that dangerous group was likely to turn their blades next.

"Promise the ambassador that we will inform the Sovereignty as events unfold," she said.

"Perhaps you should travel with me."

"Nay. Herzgo Alegni suspects that I am compromised," she replied, not mentioning that Alegni knew her true devilish identity, of course, since Anthus remained oblivious to that little detail. "I would not risk leading him to the ambassador. Besides, I have other issues pressing." It occurred to Arunika that a visit to Valindra Shadowmantle might be overdue.

The light snow continued to fall, though it seemed as if it could not touch the brooding and hulking dark figure that was Herzgo Alegni as he stood on his namesake bridge in the heart of darkened Neverwinter. This was his favorite place now, a symbol of his successes, and here he believed he was invincible. Here, he was truly Lord Alegni.

"I would express surprise in seeing you," he said as a tall and broad tiefling warrior approached. "Of course, it would be feigned, for you always seem to appear where you are least wanted."

"You have not seen me in more than a decade," came a sarcastic reply.

"Not long enough."

"My Lord Alegni, I never go where I'm not invited," Jermander replied. "Indeed, I never go where I'm not paid to go."

Alegni looked past him, to the smaller form, that of Effron.

"You know why they have come," Effron answered his questioning look. "The Bounty Hirelings of Cavus Dun are more effective in dealing with such . . . problems as those which we seem to now have before us."

Alegni had been asking for more soldiers for a long while, but this group was surely not what he had in mind. For this mercenary band owed fealty to the person with the purse, and since Alegni had not invited them or hired them, that meant someone other than himself. It wasn't hard for him to figure out who that person might be.

"I am here in support of your mission," Effron said with a bow, conceding the point before Alegni could even make it.

"But not to follow my commands, it would seem."

"Draygo Quick suggested Cavus Dun," Effron retorted, once more pulling rank by invoking his powerful mentor, who was one of the few Netherese lords Herzgo Alegni feared.

Alegni moved to the rail, his customary spot, and stared out at the dark river and the distant sea. "If you get in my way, I will kill you, Jermander," he said matter-of-factly. "Do not doubt that."

"I would expect . . ." Effron started to interject, but Alegni fixed him with a threatening stare.

"You do not hate her more than I do," the twisted warlock remarked, then he spun on his heel and shuffled away.

Alegni shifted his gaze to Jermander, who did not shy from it.

"There are many moving parts," the mercenary said. "Neverwinter is akin to a gnomish contraption."

"Too many moving parts, perhaps," Alegni agreed. "And you are but one more."

With that, Jermander grinned, bowed, and walked off after Effron.

Alegni stayed on the bridge for quite a while longer, wondering how he could parlay all of this to an even greater advantage. He didn't like having Cavus Dun around, for they were too much of a wild card, but he had to admit—to himself, of course, for he would never speak aloud any such thing!—that there were indeed a very troubling number of moving parts. Dahlia was formidable, and much more so, apparently, with this drow companion fighting beside her. And Barrabus?

He put his hand on the pommel of his great blade, taking comfort in its obvious energy. Claw reassured him. The sword remained alert. Barrabus the Gray remained Claw's to command.

Still, too many moving parts spun like a giant gear works above him.

He thought of the clever Arunika, his lover, his ally with the foolish settlers, and likely his enemy. Whenever he thought of the night he had spent with the woman, and the many more he intended to spend lying beside her, he had to remind himself that she was much more than she seemed, that she, this supposedly innocent woman, was also friend to Valindra Shadowmantle, and was actually helping the lich clear her jumbled mind.

With Sylora dead, Valindra seemed to stand as Alegni's greatest rival.

What did that make Arunika?

The tiefling grinned as he considered the possibilities.

He was Herzgo Alegni, after all, Lord of Neverwinter. He would take them, any of them, as he wished, and kill any of them as needed, Effron included.

"Greeth, Greeth," Arunika muttered as she walked through the forest, and she shook her head in disgust. She had hoped that the Sovereignty ambassador had used its influence with Valindra to prepare the lich to take over where Sylora Salm had left off. The Thayans might again serve as foil to the Netherese threat, but this time with a leader who was, ultimately, under control of the ambassador.

Thus, Arunika's disappointment had been paramount upon meeting up with Valindra at the remains of Ashenglade, Sylora's fortress created out of the magical coalescing ash of the Dread Ring. As Ashenglade had diminished, its binding forces dissipating, its ashen walls crumbling, so, too, had Valindra's clarity diminished. Just a short meeting with the confused lich had shown Arunika the truth: The aboleth had abandoned Valindra, had perhaps even thrown in an added bit of jumble to the lich's already-scrambled brains for good measure. Certainly Valindra had regressed. She seemed less lucid than when Arunika had first met her, and that was before Arunika had arranged the introduction between the lich and the aboleth.

"Ark-lem! Greeth! Greeth!" Valindra had shouted, the name of her mentor, Arunika believed, or a long-lost lover, or both, perhaps.

The succubus let the thoughts of Valindra melt away as she came to her destination. Standing on the edge of Sylora's Dread Ring, Arunika found herself surprised and disappointed yet again. She knew that the Dread Ring had been injured—its weakness was apparent in the diminishment of Sylora's fortress construct—but never had she imagined so dramatic a change as this. Where once had been a field of death, a black ashen scar tingling with nether energy, now seemed more a place that had, perhaps, been witness to a recent fire. The blackness remained, the stench of ash hung thick in the air, but nothing like before, with nowhere near the intensity that promised power to challenge Herzgo Alegni's forces.

Arunika strode onto the scarred ground, something she would not have dared just a couple of days previous. For then the ring had teemed with palpable necromancy, and then the ring had served Sylora and Szass Tam. Arunika was schooled enough in the Thayan manipulation of the thin veil between life and death to understand that such a functional Dread Ring could accomplish many tasks for its masters, not just in granted power to raise a fortress or raise and control undead, or even to create implements of channeling energy to draw the life force of enemies, but the power of scrying and manipulation. For Arunika to enter Sylora Salm's functional Dread Ring was to grant Sylora and Szass Tam true knowledge of Arunika, perhaps even to strike forcefully into Arunika's mind in a manner similar to the intrusions the aboleth had waged on Valindra.

But not now, the succubus knew with confidence. There was residual power, but it posed no threat to a being as powerful as she. She continued her walk through the blackened patch until a scrabbling sound caught her attention. On her guard, Arunika cautiously approached.

It took her a moment to decipher the curious sight, for before her lay a female, dressed in torn but once-magnificent robes. Arunika gasped as she recognized Sylora Salm, or what was left of the sorceress. Several brutal wounds showed on the corpse, burns and blasted holes, but even those mortal injuries paled compared to the greater image. For Sylora had been bent in half backward, folded at the waist in reverse! It seemed as if some powerful creature, a giant or major devil, perhaps, had simply folded the woman's body over backward.

Arunika couldn't contain a giggle as Sylora moved, trying ridiculously to crawl. She got only a few inches before toppling over onto her side once more, and so the scrabbling began anew as the zombie—a pathetic undead thing animated by the residual power of the Dread Ring—tried to prepare itself for another short dash.

37

Arunika nodded and considered Valindra's present mental state in light of this new information.

She thought to destroy the undead Sylora, out of mercy, but then scoffed at the notion and simply walked off, shaking her head. As a creature of the lower planes, Arunika had little sense of, or care for, the concept of justice, but she did have a soft spot for the notion of cosmic karma. To see Sylora Salm, who had raised so many dead into a state of undead slavery, scrabbling so pathetically on the ground, pleased the succubus. Whatever the greater implications to the succubus's overall designs, good or bad, Sylora's demise, this part of it . . . pleased her.

The devil walked from the grotesque crablike zombie and turned reflexively toward Neverwinter, considering the now-dominant Herzgo Alegni. Perhaps the Thayans would return in force. Perhaps Szass Tam would appoint another powerful sorcerer, or even oversee the rebuilding of his Dread Ring personally.

Arunika shook her head, thinking that doubtful, and realizing that even if such an event were to come to fruition, it would not be in any timely manner, considering how fast things were moving in Neverwinter.

The foil for Alegni was no more.

What did that mean? What did it mean for her? She thought of the many possibilities and potential roads before her.

"It is weaker," came a raspy and familiar voice behind her.

"Invidoo," Arunika replied, speaking the true name of the imp, a name that gave her great power over the nasty little creature. She turned to face the imp and shook her head, smiling knowingly, as she considered the open sores and torn flaps of skin that still covered the diminutive devil's form, wounds suffered at the hand of Sylora Salm.

"She is defeated."

"She's dead," Arunika corrected.

"Yesss!" Invidoo replied with a satisfied hiss. "Sylora Salm is defeated and dead and gone, and Invidoo killed her."

Arunika stared at the imp doubtfully.

"I took her wand!" Invidoo insisted. The imp began to gulp in air then, manipulating its torso, rolling its thin belly under its rib cage. Then with a cough and some gagging, Invidoo vomited into its own hand, and as the acidic bile flowed through, only a small discolored digit remained. Grinning widely, showing a grate of yellow, bile-soaked pointed teeth, Invidoo held up that trophy.

"Took her wand, took her fingers!" the imp said triumphantly. "Have more, have another!" Invidoo assured Arunika, and it began to undulate and gag once more, until the succubus patted her hand in the air and bade Invidoo to stop.

"Invidoo killed Sylora!" the imp announced proudly.

Arunika didn't know what to make of the seemingly absurd claim, and didn't really care anyway. It mattered not at all to her how Sylora Salm had died, only that Sylora was dead.

"You said when Sylora dead, Invidoo go home," the imp reminded her. "Invidoo go home?"

The question reminded Arunika of her suspicions regarding some of the imp's other recent exploits, and her pretty face grew very tight as she stared hard at Invidoo.

"Had you come to me directly upon Sylora's death, I would have granted you leave," she said slyly.

Invidoo hopped into a back flip, then landed rocking back and forth from clawed foot to foot. "Had to heal."

The imp's voice trailed off and it began to upchuck again, a panicked expression coming over the little creature's face as Invidoo realized the telepathic intrusion of the succubus.

For Arunika was not without some mind-reading powers of her own, particularly regarding an imp she had taken as her familiar.

"Let me go!" Invidoo implored her. "Home! Home! Away from him!"

"Him?" Arunika asked, and she moved nearer, towering over the imp.

"The broken tiefling."

There it was, Arunika knew, her suspicions confirmed. She had guessed that Effron had played a role in informing Alegni of the recent dramatic events in Neverwinter Wood, and Invidoo's admission had just clarified for her where Effron had gotten the information.

"I should utterly destroy you," the succubus warned.

"Everyone say that!"

Arunika laughed, and almost fell murderously over Invidoo. Almost, but she reminded herself that this one might still be of use to her, particularly since she now knew that Effron might utilize the imp for his own information—or misinformation, if she played it correctly.

"You will go home," Arunika said, and Invidoo leaped into another back flip, this time spinning over twice in mid-air with barely a flap of its small batlike wings before alighting dexterously on clawed feet. But the wretched little creature's glee proved short-lived.

"Without prejudice," Arunika added matter-of-factly.

Invidoo's eyes popped open wide and his jaw hung slack, his small wings drooping. "No!" he cried. "No, no, no, no, no!" For "without prejudice" meant that it was not being dismissed from this duty, that it had not completed the terms of its indenture, and that Arunika retained the right to recall it to her side at her whim.

"You say . . ."

"And you will return to me when I call," Arunika informed it.

"No fair!" Invidoo argued. "Appeal to Glasya!"

Arunika narrowed her eyes at the threat. She knew it to be a hollow one, for Glasya, Lord of the Sixth Layer, would never side with the likes of Invidoo against her. But still, in devil society, a breach of contract was no minor issue, and even though Glasya wouldn't overrule her, likely, she might not look favorably on being bothered over so minor a detail as the indenture of an imp.

"Do you truly wish to play this game against me?" the succubus asked quietly, her tone revealing an overt threat.

"A summary task!" Invidoo insisted, meaning that Arunika should give it a way to complete its indenture without having to return to the Prime Material Plane and her side. "Invidoo demands a summary—"

"Done," Arunika agreed, smiling once more now that any thought of Invidoo going with its complaint to Glasya was off the table. All she had to do now was be a bit cleverer than the imp, and that seemed no difficult task. "Find me a replacement."

"Easy!" Invidoo said without hesitation, and with a snap of skinny, clawed fingers.

"A replacement who knows of this new force," Arunika finished.

Invidoo seemed to deflate once again, and stood staring at her. "Who knows of . . . ?"

"Drizzt Do'Urden," Arunika remarked, nodding as she formulated the plan. "Find me a replacement familiar with . . ." She paused and looked at Invidoo suspiciously, knowing full well where it would take that edict. "Nay," she corrected. "Find me a replacement *intimately* familiar with Drizzt Do'Urden, and you may transfer your binding to it."

Invidoo shook its catlike face so furiously that it nearly threw itself from its feet—indeed, only a last-moment flap of wings prevented it from toppling right over! "Cannot! Intimately? How possible?"

Arunika shrugged as if that hardly mattered to her, which it did not. "That is your summary task. You asked for one and I complied."

"Glasya will hear of this!" the imp warned.

"Do tell," Arunika replied, calling the impotent bluff.

Invidoo growled and stamped its clawed foot.

"Intimately," Arunika repeated. "Now be gone before I destroy you for betraying me, for even speaking to that wretched Effron creature."

Arunika thrust her arm out to the side and a bolt of fire flew from her hand, striking the ground and catching hold, a sizzling, wildly dancing flame gate. "Be gone!"

Invidoo squealed in fear and half-ran, half-flew to the fire, then dived in head first.

As if expecting the imp to deceive her and slip back out, Arunika was fast with her next invocation, blowing out the flames with a ferocious wave of her hand. She considered the spot on the ground, a second dark scar atop the wider carnage of the Dread Ring.

She would have to concoct some elaborate ruse for when Invidoo returned to her side, she knew, for of course she expected that the imp would fail in its task. She would have to be ready to match wits with this Effron creature, and he was one she would not underestimate.

But that plotting had to wait, she told herself, for more immediate concerns pressed in on her, not the least of which was the obvious damage done to her relationship with the dangerous Alegni.

She started for home but moved slowly, letting her thoughts carry her along every avenue of possibility.

Even though she meandered for half the night, Arunika was still quite surprised to find Brother Anthus waiting for her at her small house south of the city. His visits with the ambassador usually lasted much longer.

More surprising was the expression on Anthus's face, a look of complete confusion and even fear, as if something had truly unnerved the young man.

"They're gone," he said, barely getting the words out, before Arunika could begin to question him.

"Gone?"

"The Sovereignty," the monk explained. He rubbed his face red.

"The ambassador is gone? Has it been replaced?"

"All of them," Brother Anthus replied. "The ambassador and all of its minions. All of them have gone."

"Relocated, then," Arunika reasoned. "Perhaps they believed themselves vulnerable since Sylora's fall, and so moved to—"

"Gone!" Brother Anthus shouted, and Brother Anthus rarely raised his voice. He was frantic, though, thoroughly flustered and agitated. "They have departed the region. The ambassador left this behind." He pulled a small cloth off a vial beside him and held it aloft. Arunika looked at it curiously.

"A thought bottle," Brother Anthus explained. He held the opened vial up before his nose, closed his eyes, and inhaled deeply, then shook his head as if listening to a sad song, finally ending again with a simple, "Gone."

Arunika took the vial from him and similarly inhaled. She didn't exactly hear a voice in her head, but the message left behind was clear enough. The situation was too unstable, the Sovereignty had decided. The fall of Sylora Salm might well introduce more powerful minions of Szass Tam, or even Szass Tam himself, into the region, and that might bring a corresponding response from the Netheril Empire. Most prominent of all of the thoughts imparted was the notion that this was not the time for the Sovereignty to move on the region.

"They are not mortal in the sense that you are," Arunika explained to Brother Anthus.

"They play the long game," the monk agreed.

"They can afford to."

"As can you," the monk retorted rather harshly, and Arunika found herself surprised by his declaration. "What does it matter to you?" he asked rather flippantly, and the succubus feared then that the monk had figured it out and knew of her true identity. Had the aboleths informed him?

"Or to them?" he quickly added, seeing the devil's dangerous scowl. "What is a score of years to beings who measure their lifetime in centuries, or even millennia? What is a century?"

"Aboleths are not eternal."

"But their thoughts are. Their collective understanding, their meld, will continue through generations yet unborn."

"And you will be dead," Arunika said, somewhat callously.

Brother Anthus looked at her plaintively. "I gave them everything," he whined. "I let them into my every thought. I stood naked before them as never before, even to myself."

"Could you have stopped them from so stripping you, had you tried?" Arunika tossed out, but Anthus, wound up in his tirade, seemed to not hear.

"I believed in them!" the monk roared on. "I forsook my own order, my kin and kind. I made few inroads among the citizens of Neverwinter, gave not a thought to Sylora Salm, and have not even spoken directly with the new Netherese Lord of Neverwinter. And now they have abandoned me! And I am left with . . . what?"

"And myself?" Arunika asked, trying to get a full admission from the man.

"What do you care?" he shot back. "You did not throw in with the Sovereignty as I did. Arunika will thrive, whichever lord claims stewardship of Neverwinter."

Arunika quietly breathed a sigh of relief, now thinking that Anthus's comments referred to the little she had to lose, and not the millennia she had to live.

"Szass Tam will not come," she assured him. "I have visited his Dread Ring, and there is little left of it worth his troubles. With the Netherese strong in the region, the cost would prove too great. He'll keep his Ashmadai fools here, likely, and there remains Valindra—though believe me when I tell you that she is missing the Sovereignty more than you ever could. But Szass Tam will make no further concerted move against the region."

"There remain the Shadovar."

"With the fall of the Thayans, Alegni will get no further help from Netheril."

"He will not need it."

Arunika smiled at him slyly. "That remains to be seen."

"What do you know?" the monk asked hopefully.

"If Herzgo Alegni is to be Lord of Neverwinter, then who will come to join the settlers? What man or elf or dwarf or halfling or any other race will come in to join the glorious rebuilding of Neverwinter when it is under the domination of the likes of a Netherese tiefling barbarian like Lord Alegni?"

"What Shadovar, then?" the suddenly-cynical Brother Anthus said. "Or orcs. He will attract orcs, no doubt!"

"And invite the Lords of Waterdeep to turn their eyes and arms to the north?" Arunika replied with a laugh. "Alegni thinks he achieved a great victory with the death of Sylora Salm, but in truth, his power came from the fear of an enemy. As that enemy diminishes, so will he, do not doubt. Soon enough, he will grow bored and fly away. Or his Netherese masters will send him back into the forest in search of the artifacts, as was his original mission. Or he will overstep and invite war with Waterdeep, and he will lose."

She nodded solemnly at Brother Anthus, even rubbed the forlorn monk on the shoulder. "The Sovereignty will return in a decade or two, fear not. Few understand them, but their pattern is not to abandon a place once they have laid the base of a new home. Use these years wisely, my young friend," she advised. "Make of Brother Anthus a great name in Neverwinter, so that when the aboleths return, they will see in you a powerful ally."

The monk looked up at her and tried to nod, albeit unsuccessfully.

"I will help you," Arunika promised.

"You are staying?"

"To watch the downfall of Alegni? Surely!" She laughed, uncomfortably perhaps, but she was indeed feeling quite jovial at that moment, for in trying to bolster Anthus, Arunika had herself found a new way to view the recent dramatic developments. She wasn't sure that everything, or anything, of what she had predicted would come to pass—perhaps Alegni would remain as Lord of Neverwinter for fifty years.

But her hopes of his demise were quite plausible, even probable, she had come to realize.

And there remained an even more immediate solution, a powerful group allayed against Alegni, the same trio who had defeated Sylora, who seemed every bit the Netherese lord's equal. Perhaps they would rid Arunika of the troublesome shade.

Perhaps Arunika would find a way to help facilitate that.

As she considered the delicious possibilities, the succubus found herself feeling even more jubilant. She would survive this, as Anthus had predicted. She would survive and she would thrive, whoever proved victorious in the struggles for Neverwinter. She looked Brother Anthus in the eye, her grin from ear to ear.

"What?" he managed to ask in the heartbeat before Arunika fell over him passionately.

Not long after, Arunika walked the quiet and dark streets of Neverwinter, her edginess hardly smoothed, her passion hardly sated.

Arunika hailed from the Nine Hells, not the Abyss, and though a place no less evil, the distinction between demon and devil rested mostly in the contrast between chaos and order. Arunika liked an orderly society. Lawful by heritage, by nurture, by the very essence that gave her form and substance, uncertainty unsettled her.

It made her edgy. It made her itchy.

Poor Brother Anthus. For all of his youthful enthusiasm, he could not match or sate the passionate succubus.

She had thought the Sovereignty would give her the pleasure of order here in Neverwinter. Perfect order, demanded internally and externally. But now they were gone and so many roads had opened. Too many roads for Arunika's comfort, but she knew that it would pass as she came to better command the ultimate destination.

The agitated devil shook her head repeatedly as she followed every potential turn to its logical conclusion. What of Valindra? What of Szass Tam? What of the trio now hunting Alegni?

And most of all, what of Alegni and the Netheril Empire? Even with the potential pitfalls opening all around him, it seemed to Arunika that Alegni held the upper hand. Despite her assurances to Brother Anthus, Arunika understood that if Alegni survived the near future, he would become Lord of Neverwinter, perhaps for many years. Her meeting with Valindra had shown her the truth of the Thayans, and they would not threaten the power of Alegni and his Shadovar.

This likely outcome was not to Arunika's taste, of course, but she was of the Nine Hells. The strong imposed the rule, and the rule was more important than the ruler.

Her preference, thus, seemed irrelevant.

She glanced back to the south, where Anthus lay on her floor, exhausted beyond consciousness, then shifted her gaze just a bit to the west, to an inn on a small hill, and a room looking back toward the river and the Herzgo Alegni Bridge.

Arunika did not like the uncertainty, but she knew what she must do if she wished to remain in the region, and more importantly, if she wished to help shape those rules that would govern this tumultuous area.

Now she walked with purpose, along the boulevards running south and west.

She could battle uncertainty by situating herself properly for all potential outcomes.

That was her litany, and it did help to calm her a bit as she passed by the darkened windows of sleeping Neverwinter. Emotionally, at least, though there remained the physical agitation, which Brother Anthus could not calm.

As she neared the inn, Arunika glanced around to ensure that there were no witnesses. Leathery wings appeared on her back as she willfully minimized her disguise, and then her wings spread wide.

As much a hop as flight put the succubus on the balcony of a particular room at that fine inn, and there she folded her wings once more and leaned on the railing,

44

her back to the darkened city, her eyes watching the darkened room beyond the wood and glass door before her.

A long while passed, but she did not mind, as she worked even harder to clarify the possibilities and her potential within each.

Finally, she heard the lock click and a few moments later, the balcony door swung open and Herzgo Alegni stood before her, his expression a mixture of sly anticipation and hardened resolve.

Most of all, Arunika recognized, he was not surprised to see her. She stood on a balcony some thirty feet from the ground, with no stairway and only a locked door providing access, and yet, he was not surprised to see her.

His twisted warlock minion had extracted much from Invidoo, Arunika knew then more clearly, as she had suspected.

She answered Alegni's hard look with a disarming smile.

"Keep your enemies closer," Alegni remarked, the second half of a common warrior litany.

"Enemy?" Arunika asked innocently—so much so that she made it obvious to Alegni that she was denying nothing.

Alegni couldn't resist her expression, her posture, her playful retort, and a grin spread on his broad face.

"You have won, Herzgo Alegni," Arunika stated flatly. "What enemies remain?"

"Indeed," he replied unconvincingly.

Arunika smiled all the wider, coyly, and let her wings spread wide once more as she walked deliberately toward the hulking tiefling. "How close would you like your enemies?" she asked quietly, her voice husky and promising, and her devil wings embraced him.

"Close enough to kill," Alegni answered.

Arunika couldn't resist that tease. Where Brother Anthus failed, Herzgo Alegni excelled.

CHAPTER 3

THE SPELLSPINNER

*I*T IS NOT THE DWARF HOMELAND, JEARTH'S FINGERS FLASHED TO RAVEL XORLARRIN. The forward scouts of the expedition, a tenday and a half out of Menzoberranzan, had come upon a vast cavern, its walls tiered and worked. First word back along the lines had been promising that this might be a lower barracks or undercity of some sorts, something with which Jearth apparently did not agree.

You know definitively?

Jearth nodded, then nodded again to indicate the approach of Tiago Baenre on Byok, his famed lizard mount. "These are orc dwellings," he said aloud, including Tiago into the conversation. "The place is filthy with them, and with bugbears."

"Then we are likely nearer the surface than we believed," Ravel reasoned, and he cast a quick look to acknowledge Tiago's arrival before turning back to directly address Jearth. "We should send scouts—perhaps your friend here—along any ascending tunnels we find to see if we might break free of the caverns."

The reference to Tiago Baenre, a noble of the First House of Menzoberranzan and very likely soon to be named the weapons master of that most important drow family, as a scout drew a thin grin from Tiago. It was sourced, Ravel knew, less in amusement than in the young Baenre's desire to let him know that the comment had been appropriately marked and would be appropriately remembered.

The proud Ravel wanted to retort, but the sensible Ravel suppressed that foolish urge.

"We have scouts suited to the mission," the wiser and older Jearth replied, "already seeking such boulevards."

When Ravel started to respond, Jearth flashed him a warning stare.

Ravel hated this, hated having a Baenre along. For, like many of his family, he hated House Baenre above all. The Xorlarrins rarely admitted that, of course, usually reserving their public venom for Barrison Del'Armgo, the Second House of Menzoberranzan, and indeed, Matron Mother Zeerith's most vociferous fights at the Council of Eight usually involved the matron of Barrison Del'Armgo.

For who would dare openly speak against Quenthel Baenre?

And this young Baenre was very much cut of that one's cloth, Ravel knew. He watched Tiago closely as the young warrior gracefully dismounted, straightening his perfect clothing and silvery chain armor before he was even fully clear of the beast. His short-cut white hair was perfectly and stylishly coifed, as everything about his appearance—the bone structure of his slender face, the set and sparkle of his eyes, even the whisper of a thin white mustache, something very uncommon among the drow—showed that Baenre perfection. It was rumored that much of House Baenre's magical energies of late had been preempted for superficial reasons, to create beauty among the House's inner circle, but if such magical intervention had been the case with Tiago, it had happened long ago, at the time of his birth. For this one had always seemed to have "the right side of the mushroom in his face," as the old drow saying about luck went.

Tiago came up in a casual, easy posture, fully in control in his own mind, Ravel assumed. His hands rested easily on the hilts of the twin swords sheathed at his hips—no doubt among the most fabulous weapons in all of Menzoberranzan. The spellspinner would have loved to cast a dweomer then to determine the no-doubt abundance of magical items and implements carried by this privileged noble, and he made a note to secretly enact such a spell next time he saw Tiago coming.

He pulled his gaze from the handsome young warrior and turned back to Jearth. "Can we circumvent the chamber?"

As Jearth began to answer yes, Tiago interrupted with a resounding "no," and both Xorlarrins turned to regard him with surprise.

"Why would we?" Tiago asked.

"True enough," Jearth interjected before Ravel could speak. "No doubt the orcs and bugbears will cower before our march and would not dare try to hinder us."

"And why would we let them do that?" Tiago asked.

Ravel looked from one to the other, crinkling his face in disapproval and incredulity that they would dare have such a discussion around him, as if he was not even there.

"It is true," Jearth insisted, the weapons master obviously catching the growing and dangerous ire of the spellspinner.

"We should demand a tithing of fodder for our inconvenience of even having to ask," Ravel replied.

"No," Tiago again unexpectedly interrupted, and again, both Xorlarrins looked at him in surprise.

"It is past time for a fight," the young Baenre explained.

"We have had fights," Jearth reminded.

"With a pack of displacer beasts and a few random creatures," Tiago explained. "Nothing against an entrenched enemy, the likes of which we will surely find when we do at last come upon this place called Gauntlgrym. This is a great opportunity for us to witness the coordination of our various factions. Let our warriors see the power of Ravel and his spellspinners."

Ravel narrowed his eyes just a bit at that remark, wondering if what Tiago really meant was that he personally wanted to see how formidable an enemy Ravel might truly prove to be.

"Let us all, warrior and spellspinner alike, witness the tactics, power, and boundaries of these damned driders we have towed along," Tiago finished.

Ravel continued to stare hard at him, while Jearth gave an agreeing nod, apparently easily swayed by the young warrior's argument. Or was it that Jearth was easily swayed by any argument put forth by a Baenre? Ravel wondered.

"We need such a fight, spellspinner," Tiago said directly to Ravel, and the deference in his tone caught the Xorlarrin off guard a bit. "It will bolster morale and hone our tactics. Besides," he added with an irresistible and mischievous grin, "it will be fun."

Despite his reservations, suspicions, and general distaste for the Baenre noble, Ravel found himself believing in Tiago's sincerity. So surprising was that to him that the spellspinner briefly wondered if one of Tiago's magical items had secretly cast a dweomer upon him to enamor him of the young warrior.

"Well enough," Ravel heard himself saying, to his surprise. "Coordinate it."

Tiago flashed him a shining smile and motioned for Jearth to follow, then turned to his mount.

"I will lead the first assault," Ravel demanded, his tone changing abruptly. "I and my spellspinners will cast the first stones."

Tiago bowed respectfully and mounted Byok, then waited as Jearth retrieved his own lizard mount. In the few moments he had alone with Tiago, Ravel found that their discussion was not quite at its end.

Free yourself of your envy, Xorlarrin son, Tiago's fingers flashed at him.

Ravel looked at him suspiciously, then answered, *I know not what you mean, presumptuous Baenre son.*

Don't you? came the response, but it was flashed with an expression of honest curiosity and not consternation, minimizing the accusation.

Tiago's fingers flashed emphatically, and quickly, since Jearth was even then climbing into the saddle, and soon to return. *When our elders speak of the promising young males of Menzoberranzan, two names are most often mentioned, are they not? Tiago Baenre and Ravel Xorlarrin. Promising young students, respective leaders of their academies. Perhaps we are doomed to be rivals, bitter and ultimately fatal to one.*

His grin as he signaled this showed which of them Tiago expected that to be.

Or stronger, perhaps, would we both become, if we found common gain here. If you uncover this Gauntlgrym and tame the beast of the place, House Xorlarrin will flee Menzoberranzan. We all know this, he added against Ravel's widening eyes. *Do you believe the designs of Zeerith a secret to Matron Mother Quenthel?*

His reference to Ravel's matron without use of her title, coupled with his own reference to House Baenre's matron mother, raised Ravel's doubts and his anger, but he suppressed both as he focused on this surprising young warrior's hints and designs.

Perhaps Baenre, Barrison Del'Armgo, and the other five of the eight ruling Houses will see this as treachery, and will summarily obliterate Xorlarrin and all associated with her. You might be wise to foster relationships with some in Bregan D'aerthe to facilitate your escape in that instance, he added flippantly, for so intricate was the drow sign language that it allowed for such inflection.

Or perhaps not, and in that instance, Ravel Xorlarrin would do well to have a friend within the noble ranks of House Baenre, Tiago finished, as Jearth came riding up.

"Come, my friend," Tiago said to Jearth, teasing Ravel with the wording as he turned and started away.

Ravel watched the young man go and even whispered "well-played" under his breath. For indeed, Tiago's presentation had been believable. The young Baenre hadn't begun to indicate that he would be anything other than an enemy if House Baenre and the others decided to come after House Xorlarrin. After all, though his reference to the mercenary band of Bregan D'aerthe was more than a bit intriguing, Tiago was a Baenre. Bregan D'aerthe worked for, above all others, House Baenre.

Was there a hint, then, that should war befall House Xorlarrin, Tiago might stand as Ravel's only chance of escape?

The spellspinner couldn't be sure.

Well played, indeed.

Ravel and his fellow spellspinners could hear the murmurs beyond the wall of blackness that separated them from the main area of the immense underground chamber. Not darkness like the near absence of light so typical in the Underdark, but overlapping magical globes, visually impenetrable and absolutely void of light.

The noble spellspinners of House Xorlarrin had enacted these globes, this visual wall, just inside one of the chamber's more nondescript entrances. Another wizard had created a floating eye and directed it up above the wall of blackness, so he could function as lookout.

In went the goblin fodder, disciplined because to veer astray was to die, and to utter a sound, any sound, was to die. The ugly little creatures lined up shoulder to shoulder, forming a semicircle within the room, a living shield, while the drow spellspinners silently moved into the clear area behind them and began their work.

Nineteen sets of Xorlarrin hands lifted up high, fingers wiggling, wizards slowly turning and quietly chanting. This ritual had been Ravel's greatest achievement, a particularly Xorlarrin manner of combining the powers of multiple spellspinners.

From those reaching, wiggling fingers came filaments of light, reaching out to fellow wizards precisely positioned, equidistant to others within their particular ring, with four in the innermost, six in the middle, and eight in the outer. In the very center of the formation stood Ravel, his hands upraised and holding a sphere almost as large as his head.

The filaments crossed with near-perfect angles, reaching out and about, drow to drow, like the spokes of a wheel, and when this skeletal structure was completed, those casters in the innermost ring turned their attention to Ravel and sent anchoring beams to the strange sphere, which caught their ends and held them taut.

The eighteen went fast to their weaving, running filaments across those anchoring spokes. White drow hair tingled and rose up in the growing energy of the creation. Ravel breathed deeply, inhaling the power he felt mounting in his anchor sphere, glorious reams of energy tickling his fingers and palms, and seeping into his bare forearms so that his muscles tightened and stood rigid. He gritted his teeth and stubbornly held on. This was the moment that distinguished him from the other promising spellspinners, Ravel knew. He accepted the mounting energy into his body and soul. He merged with this, becoming one, adapting rather than battling, like an elf walking lightly over a new fallen snow, while a less nimble, less graceful human might plod through it.

For Ravel instinctively understood the nature of magic. He was both receptacle and anchor, and as the web completed, the energy mounted even more swiftly and powerfully.

But Ravel was ready for it. He heard his lessers scrambling around, glimpsed drow fingers flashing furiously, relaying commands and preparations.

He was not distracted. Slowly Ravel began to wind his hands around, and the magical web responded by beginning a slow and steady spin, the bright strands becoming indistinct as they left glowing trails behind their movement.

Ravel heard commotion beyond the wall of summoned blackness, as he had expected. Quiet as goblinkin might be, they sounded quite clumsy and raucous to the dark elves.

The globes of darkness began to dissipate, and the wider cavern reappeared to the noble spellspinner, beyond the semicircle of goblin fodder, and beyond that line, barely fifty paces away, stood ranks of orcs interspersed with taller, hulking bugbears.

Several raised voices in protest at the sight of the goblins, with the drow still mostly obscured, but with that glowing, spinning web up high above the goblin line and in clear sight. Despite his discomfort and needed concentration, Ravel managed a smile at the stupefied reactions he noted among the humanoids.

Only for a moment, though, for then the spellspinner threw all of his energy and his concentration into the rotating web. He turned with it, a complete circuit, then another and a third, and as he came around, Ravel pulled back his left arm and threw forth his right, launching forth the web in a lazy spin. It floated out past the goblins, continuing its rotation, and without the anchor that was Ravel, the magical energies contained within it began to escape the spidery structure.

The web reached forth, floating, rotating, lines of white lightning shooting down to split the stone beneath it. Orcs and bugbears, eyes widened in shock, scrambled and tangled, falling all over each other to get out of the way.

The web rolled over them. A lightning blast hit an orc full force and the creature burst into flames, screaming and flailing among its scrambling kin. The whole cavern reverberated in the thunderous reports, one after another, drowning out the screams of the terrified orcs and bugbears.

The drow spellspinners moved aside of the cavern entrance in an orderly fashion, while the goblins scrambled frantically, and less effectively—so clumsily, indeed, that as the next wave of attackers entered, several of the unfortunate goblins got trampled under clacking appendages.

Ravel held his ground, not even looking back with concern, confident that the melee battalion, Yerrininae and his warrior driders, would not dare even brush him.

And they didn't. With great agility considering their ungainly forms, the driders charged past the noble spellspinner, chitin clattering against the stone. Any stumbling goblin fodder were less fortunate, the driders taking great pleasure in stomping them down as they charged out into the cavern.

To a surface-dwelling human general, this group might have seemed akin to the heavy cavalry he would employ to dissolve the integrity of his enemy's front line defense, and given the confusion already caused by the dissipating lightning web, the driders proved incredibly effective in this role. With their bulk and multitude of hard-shelled legs cracking against the stone, the stampede alone might have sent the whole of the opposing force running, but adding in the sheer ferocity of the cursed drow creations, and armed with tridents and long spears of exquisite drow craftsmanship, the cavern's front-line defense was quickly and easily overwhelmed and scattered.

So terrified of the horrid driders, some of the orcs and bugbears retreated straightaway, inadvertently running back under the still floating energy web, running right into the midst of the continuing lightning barrage.

Ravel heard himself laughing aloud as one bugbear flew backward from the jolt of such a bolt, which split the stone floor right before it. The flailing creature never touched back down, for powerful Yerrininae thrust forth his great trident and caught it in mid-flight, skewering it cleanly and easily holding the three-hundred-pound creature aloft with but one muscled arm.

Using that trophy as his banner, the drider leader rallied his forces around him and charged in deeper, breaking ranks perfectly to circumvent the lightning web, and coming together once more on the other side, in perfect, tumultuous formation.

Ravel lifted his hands so his companions could clearly view them. *Find your place in the fight,* he instructed the spellspinners.

And what is Ravel's place? a drow hand-signaled back.

"Wherever he deems," the spellspinner answered aloud, for he wanted Tiago Baenre to hear the imperiousness in his voice.

Astride his lizard, Byok, Tiago merely grinned at that response and tipped his short-brimmed top hat to the spellspinner. Off the young Baenre rode beside Jearth and a host of mounted warriors, veering sharply to the side to go far off to the right of the thundering web. Let the brutish and ever-angry driders and the lesser fighters entangle themselves in that confusing maelstrom while the more skilled warriors strategically conquered the flanks. Shallow caves lined the side wall, with clear indications that these were barracks, some quite high above the floor, and with ladders defensively raised.

Drow mounts could quite readily climb walls. The lack of ladders offered little defense.

"It was an impressive web of power," Ravel's sister Saribel said, walking up beside him along with the other two Xorlarrin nobles, Berellip and Brack'thal, the latter looking quite miserable about it all.

"It took too long to effectively create and launch," the always-stern Berellip disagreed. "Had our enemies not been stupid thugs, they would have fallen over us before we could begin to defend."

"You deny its power?" Saribel asked skeptically.

"I deny its efficacy against any serious enemy," Berellip quickly replied, and she added a scowl at Ravel for good measure, one that stung the young spellspinner more deeply because of the added spectacle of a grinning Brack'thal staring at him over Berellip's shoulder.

"The region of devastation cannot be so easily dismissed, sister," Saribel insisted.

"So much of arcane magic is useless show," Berellip interrupted. "Because it is not divinely inspired."

"Of course, sister," Saribel agreed, for what priestess of Lolth would not accede before such a truth as that? She bowed gracefully before Berellip and followed the older Xorlarrin priestess away.

"They will find more to kill," Brack'thal decided, moving into the void beside Ravel. "Your favored ploy did little actual damage, after all. I count no more than five dead from it, and one to the spear of Yerrininae and not the lightning net."

Ravel slowly turned to regard Brack'thal, and he stared unblinkingly at the elder Xorlarrin's smile until it at last faded.

"If ever you doubt the effectiveness or power of my creations, do speak up, brother," Ravel said. "I will gladly demonstrate more closely."

Brack'thal laughed at the threat.

He could do that, Ravel understood, because Saribel and Berellip were nearby. That wouldn't always be the case.

For Ravel, coordinating the battle in the cavern quickly became more a matter of preventing Yerrininae and his drider battalion from slaughtering needed slaves than organizing any combat tactics. The four components of his strike force—spellspinner, drider, drow warrior, and goblin shock troops—hit the orc cavern so hard and so furiously that no semblance of organized defense ever materialized against them.

The young spellspinner found this quite disappointing. He had wanted to test out his battle theories and had concocted some elaborate magic-melee coordination for wiping away stubborn defenses. Besides, any clever victories he might win against opponents who proved themselves worthy would only serve to impress his miserable sisters, and even more delicious, to frighten his broken father-brother.

As the final bugbears and orcs were being rounded up for the continuing march, these creatures to serve alongside the goblins as battle fodder, Berellip took the moment to quip that the fight had hardly been worth the energy. She did so publicly, and loudly, and many eyes, including those of Yerrininae, focused on Ravel, whom she was clearly diminishing.

"And not a single drow or drider lost," Ravel countered, looking to Yerrininae as he spoke.

"To mere orcs?" Berellip countered with a laugh, as if the thought of losing a drow to such a lesser creature was unthinkable.

Her open levity attracted more drow around them, and Berellip played to them loudly.

"To a combined force larger than our own," the young spellspinner retorted, and he didn't back down a bit, judging that the respect of his forces might be wavering a bit—and surely that seemed to be Berellip's intent.

Ravel looked at his older sister directly, matching her intense stare. Then he spun away with a laugh, taking center stage, commanding center stage.

"Mere orcs?" he asked, addressing all around him now. "A most relative term, would you not agree? They are 'mere' only when measured against a superior force, and we are that, to both the orcs and the clever bugbears who ruled this cavern. And not simply superior, for if that, then surely we would have suffered losses, which we did not! They were overwhelmed from the start, because of preparation, dear sister. In a search of history, too many are quick to dismiss losers as inept, rather than attribute the crushing victory to the brilliance of the victors."

"Do tell," Berellip said with a fair amount of sarcasm apparent in her tone.

"Our easy victory here began with the selection of the force," Ravel insisted. "We have found balance, magic to sword, finesse to sheer power." He wanted to add, but didn't need to—and didn't think it wise, given Berellip's apparent challenge to his authority—that he, of course, had been the one to select the expeditionary force.

Still, Ravel couldn't resist a bit of self-aggrandizing as he added, "Our enemies were broken before the fight even began. When at Sorcere, I envisioned such a usage of the lightning web, and had hoped that such an opportunity as we found this day would arise."

"Back to that?" Berellip asked, narrowing her eyes and tightening her jaw. "A few meager orcs killed for such an expense of power?"

"A few killed and hundreds sent in flight, horrified," Ravel replied. "Is not the threat of Lolth's vengeance as effective a weapon for the priestesses as the actual manifestation of the Spider Queen?"

Ravel could hardly believe the words as they left his mouth! To invoke the Spider Queen in an argument with a priestess of Lolth!

For a moment, Ravel, like everyone around him, held his breath, staring unblinkingly at Berellip with an expectation that she would lash out at him, with her hand, her snake-headed whip, or even some of her devastating divine spells.

She wanted to do just that, he could clearly see on her tightened face. Berellip would take great pleasure in torturing him for all to see.

But the moment passed, and Berellip made no move, and only then did Ravel truly appreciate how important this expedition must be to Matron Mother Zeerith. He had pushed past all boundaries of protocol and would not be punished—not then, at least.

Mark your words carefully, young spellspinner, Berellip signed to him, her hands in close so that few other than Ravel could read the threat. The priestess turned on her heel and walked away, Saribel in her wake.

She wouldn't even chastise him openly before his minions.

Hardly believing his luck, or that it would hold, Ravel turned to the gathered drow and waved them off to their duties. He noticed Jearth as he did, the weapons master staring at him incredulously. And more than Jearth, Ravel noted Tiago Baenre, whose expression revealed the brash young Baenre's intrigue, and even a bit of amusement.

Ravel had no answers for any of that, for he was no less incredulous than the two warriors. "We will make our encampment here in this cavern," he ordered, and started away.

Jearth caught up to him soon after.

"This area is quite open and vulnerable," the weapons master explained.

"No enemies will come upon us," Ravel insisted.

"You cannot know that. And if enemies do find us, smaller areas favor our smaller numbers."

"Set the camp."

"Or face Lolth's vengeance?" Jearth remarked with a sly grin, and he was one of the few drow alive who could so tease young Ravel.

The spellspinner merely shook his head and held his hands up helplessly in reply, as if to say that he, too, could not believe that he had so challenged Berellip, and on the foundation of her very existence.

Tiago Baenre came to Ravel a short while later, to inform him that they had identified the bugbear king of the cave and had him waiting for an audience with his conquerors.

"Does he wish to negotiate?" Ravel asked sarcastically.

"To continue breathing, I would assume."

The Xorlarrin spellspinner stepped back and took a long look at the Baenre warrior. They were about the same age, he knew, and had been in their respective academies in overlapping years. They were rivals out of simple circumstance, as two of the most promising young drow males in Menzoberranzan.

Or were they?

Tiago moved to the front of the shallow cave and pointed out the abode across the cavern where the bugbear king was being held. "There is more that I would ask of you for my allegiance," Tiago warned, and turned back to face Ravel.

The spellspinner looked at the warrior suspiciously.

"I travel with you to represent my family," Tiago explained. "To report back to Matron Quenthel, favorably or unfavorably, on the progress of House Xorlarrin."

Ravel nodded. They had been through all of this before.

"And I go for personal gain, and in more ways than reputation," Tiago explained.

As Ravel narrowed his eyes, Tiago balked. "Pretend not that you expected more of me," he said sternly. "Perhaps some devotion to the greater good, or the glory of Lady Lolth, or some other such nonsense. Do not assign me such motives, for such a limited view of me would surely wound me, my friend, and never would I presume that Ravel would act outside the benefit of . . . Ravel."

Ravel had to nod his agreement of that assessment. What drow, after all, had ever achieved greatness without first seeking and demanding it? "Do tell," he prompted.

Tiago reached into a pocket in his *piwafwi* and produced a thin silver scroll tube. He held it up so that Ravel could clearly see the etching of a hammer, a bolt of lightning energy, and a pair of crossed swords, along with the name Gol'fanin.

Ravel's own decorated dagger, more a focus item than a weapon, bore that same signature, as did the weapons of many of the nobles of the ruling drow Houses.

Given their destination, given the rumors of the magic powering the ancient forge, there was no need for Tiago to elaborate further.

"I will meet you beside the prisoner," Tiago said, and started away for the prison of the bugbear king.

But Ravel called him back. "Go with me," he said, and he took care with his tone to make it more of an offer than an order.

Tiago nodded.

Ravel took his time in crossing the large cavern. He wondered if he and Tiago Baenre might have much to discuss regarding the bugbear lord, the continuing expedition, and perhaps even beyond that. He reminded himself that this was a Baenre, after all, and so he knew he'd need to sweeten every subject with *tinguin lal'o shrome'cak,* or *the promise of a fungal pie,* as the drow saying went, in reference to a particular delicacy which could induce the most marvelous of daydreams. Tiago hadn't asked about this second bargain he had just revealed, but rather had stated it as a matter of fact, not to be argued or denied.

So it would be in the presence of a Baenre, Ravel realized, and the more he might do to keep Tiago beside him, the better. It didn't take the spellspinner long to determine which fungal pie might be given at this time and in this place.

Tutugnik, the bugbear king, offered little to impress Ravel as anything other than ordinary. He was larger than most bugbears, particularly those clans which lived so deep in the Underdark, and even sitting strapped to a stone chair, he could look Ravel in the eye. Perhaps he was considered handsome for his race; to Ravel they all looked the same, other than the occasional garish scar, with their flat faces, bloodshot eyes, and broken yellow and brown teeth, all sharpened and crooked. Like all bugbears, Tutugnik's hair was greasy and dirty, matted in no particular style.

Nor was he impressive intellectually, answering Ravel's pointed demand that Tutugnik and all his minions would now serve the drow, with an uninspired, "Tutugnik is leader."

Perhaps he meant that he wished to continue to serve as leader of the slave force. Perhaps, but Ravel didn't care to find out.

He convened an audience with the whole of the cavern, drow and drider, orc and bugbear. Standing on a high and well-lit ledge beside Jearth and Tutugnik, Ravel ordered the bugbear lord brought out to stand on the other side of his weapons master. Tiago Baenre accompanied the brutish creature.

"You are conquered," Ravel yelled out simply to the orcs and bugbears, his volume magnified by a simple dweomer so that his voice boomed off every stone in the cavern. "You will fight for me, or you will die, and if you fight well, perhaps I will allow you to fight for me again." He nodded and started to turn away, as if there was really nothing more to be said, but then he paused and looked to the bugbear king.

"Leader?" Ravel asked loudly, pointing to Tutugnik, who puffed out his massive chest with pride.

Among the gathered orcs and bugbears, the response was muted, with the captives looking to one another for hints about how they should react. Gradually that direction led them to a tentative few affirmative stomps of heavy feet, even a huzzah or two.

All of which evaporated in the blink of an eye as Ravel glanced at Tiago. The young Baenre leaped and spun, drawing one of his swords too quickly for anyone to realize it, including Tutugnik, who had barely begun to glance the leaping Baenre's way before that sword sliced under Tutugnik's chin, front to back.

The bugbear's expression never even changed as his head tumbled free of his neck, so swift was the blow.

"Some of them cheered," Ravel said to Tiago and Jearth.

The warriors smiled and nodded, and started down from the ledge.

Among the prisoners, the game was quite simple: any who told of another who had cheered Tutugnik would be pressed into service. Those pointed to as Tutugnik loyalists were dragged aside and tortured to death, in full view.

"Am I to be beaten, or murdered?" Ravel asked when he answered his sister's summons to a large cave that she had taken as her own.

Berellip's many goblin slaves had already cleared the place of bugbear debris and feces, scrubbing it dutifully. The drow priestess had not traveled light, with many pack lizards devoted entirely to her comforts. Though the expedition would remain in the caverns only for a couple of days, as scouts moved around the region to determine their exact position and plot the most likely trails to this sought-after dwarf homeland, Berellip's well-trained goblins had turned the cave into a room fitting for a drow noble House. Tapestries covered nearly every wall, and plush pillows and blankets adorned every rock or ledge that could serve as bed or chair.

Saribel lounged on one such stone, far to the side of her sister, but watching Ravel quite intently. Beyond the three Xorlarrins and a handful of meaningless goblin slaves, the cave was empty.

"You ask lightheartedly, as if either would not be a distinct possibility, or quite legal, even fitting," Berellip replied.

"Because I wish to know which path you would take," Ravel pressed. "If the former. . . ." He shrugged. "But if the latter, then I suppose that I would be wise to defend myself."

"You miss the third possibility," Berellip said, her tone suddenly cold, "to join with Yerrininae."

Ravel laughed, but even though he was quite confident that Berellip was merely taunting him. The thought of becoming a drider was truly too awful for any honest levity.

"Or the fourth," he said suddenly.

Berellip looked at him curiously, then glanced over at her sister, who shook her head and shrugged, obviously at a loss.

"Do tell."

"You could accept that all of my actions, even those seeming disrespectful of your superior station—"

"Seeming?"

"They were disrespectful, I accept," Ravel conceded, and he bowed deeply and slowly, exaggerating the movement. "But they were done with no disrespect intended, and for the benefit of House Xorlarrin."

"Sit down," Berellip commanded, and Ravel turned for the nearest cushioned stone chair.

"On the floor," Berellip clarified.

Ravel looked at her with incredulity, but wiped it from his face almost immediately and plopped down to the floor as quickly as he could manage.

"For the benefit of House Xorlarrin?" the priestess asked.

Ravel took a deep breath and lifted his hand to tap the side of his head, trying to phrase his explanation precisely and carefully. But Berellip stole his thunder.

"For the benefit of Tiago Baenre, you mean," she remarked.

Ravel had to take another deep breath—and pointedly remind himself that these sisters of his were priestesses of Lolth, and surely loved her more than they cared for him. They had attended Arach-Tinilith, the greatest of the Menzoberranzan academies, and Berellip, in particular, had excelled in that brutal environment. Ravel had to take care in dealing with these two. He fancied himself smarter than almost any drow, perhaps excepting Gromph Baenre, but in a moment like this, he understood that arrogance to be more a matter of determined attitude than a true belief.

"If for Tiago Baenre, then surely for House Xorlarrin," he answered. "That one might prove important to us."

"Which is why I will bed him this very night," Berellip replied.

"And I tomorrow," Saribel quickly added.

Ravel looked from one to the other, and truly was not surprised. "Tiago is intrigued with our House."

"He is an upstart male who does not like his place in life," Berellip explained.

"And so House Xorlarrin interests him," said Ravel. "For it, above any others, expects achievement from its males, and rewards such achievement with respect."

"This is an advantage of House Xorlarrin throughout Menzoberranzan," Berellip agreed. "For in Xorlarrin alone are males allowed some true measure of respect."

"Then you understand my disrespect," Ravel said, or started to, for somewhere between the first word and the fifth, a snake-headed whip appeared in Berellip's hand. She lashed out at him, the three heads of her weapon snapping forth, fangs bared, tearing the flesh of his face.

He threw himself backward and to the floor, but Berellip pursued and struck him again and again. His main robes were enchanted, of course, and offered him some protection, but those wicked snakes found their way around it, tearing his shirt and skin alike.

He felt the agonizing poison coursing through his veins almost, even as new eruptions of fire from fresh bites assailed him.

Saribel was there then, her own whip in hand, adding two more serpent heads to the vicious beating. It went on and on, Ravel's senses stolen by the sheer agony of it. At last they stopped striking him, but still he writhed, poison assaulting his nerves and muscles, forcing him into spasms of sheer agony.

Sometime later, a bloody Ravel dared to sit up again, to find Berellip sitting comfortably in her chair, with Saribel off to the side as if nothing had happened.

"So ends our advantage with Tiago Baenre," the mage managed to gasp.

Berellip smiled and nodded to a nearby goblin, who rushed over with an armful of clothes—clothing to exactly match the now-tattered nonmagical garments.

"The end of this chamber is silenced, and you will look the same. Tiago will know nothing of this," Berellip assured him. "Dress!"

Ravel grunted repeatedly as he struggled to his feet, his joints still aflame from the wicked whip poison.

"Dear sister," Berellip teased as Ravel slipped out of his blood-soaked and ripped robes, "we are but a tenday from Menzoberranzan, and have only four more sets of replacement clothing for our dear brother. Whatever shall we do?"

Ravel's hateful stare might have carried some threat with it had he not been so wobbly, even falling back over to the ground at one point.

CHAPTER 4

A COLLISION

HE WAS NOT A MAN PRONE TO FITS OF NOSTALGIA, NOT A MAN WHOSE thoughts filled with wistful images of what had gone before, mostly because most of what had gone before wasn't worth replaying. But the small human assassin with grayish skin found himself in a strange, for him, emotional place one afternoon outside of Neverwinter.

"Artemis Entreri," he whispered, and not for the first time this day. It was a name that had once struck fear throughout the city of Calimport, throughout most of the southland. The name itself had once offered him great advantage in battle, for the reputation it carried often overwhelmed the sensibilities of his enemies. Employers would throw extra gold his way as much because of their fear of angering him as because they knew he was the best man for the job.

That notion brought a rare smile to Entreri's face. Angering him? "Anger" implied a heightened level of agitation, a state of personal maddening.

Was Artemis Entreri ever really angry?

Or then again, had he ever been not angry?

As he looked back over the years, Entreri recalled a moment he had been more than angry, when he had been outraged. He still remembered the man's name, Principal Cleric Yinochek, for it seemed more than a name to him. The title, the man, all of this creature who was Yinochek gave body and soul to the anger that was within Artemis Entreri, and for that one brief moment after he had cut Yinochek down, and after he and his companion had burned the vile man's church down, Entreri had known a taste of freedom.

In that freedom, on a cliff overlooking the city of Memnon and the burning Protector's House, Artemis Entreri had at long last looked back at himself, at his life, at his anger, and had managed to cast it aside.

Albeit briefly.

He thought of Gositek, the priest he had spared, the man he had ordered to go out and live according to the principles of his espoused religion, and not to use that religion as a front to cover his own foibles, as was so often the case with priests in Faerûn.

Gositek had followed that command, Entreri had learned in subsequent visits to the rebuilt Protector's House. Entreri's uncharacteristic mercy had been paid forward.

How had he lost those moments, those brief few years of freedom, he wondered now, staring at Neverwinter's battered, but still formidable wall? How fleeting it all seemed to him.

And how enticing.

For what might he find when he was free of Herzgo Alegni?

Entreri cast aside the memories, for he had no time for them now. Drizzt and Dahlia were coming for Alegni. He needed to find a way to get far from this place, physically and emotionally, and far from Alegni, before their arrival, for surely Entreri's undeniable anticipation would tip off Charon's Claw—and thus Alegni—to the coming attack.

He urged his nightmare steed toward the city but had gone only a couple of strides before pulling up the reins once more.

He considered then Charon's Claw and its intrusion into his thoughts—no, not an intrusion, he realized, for his years wielding the diabolical blade had made it more than that. Claw's scouring of Entreri's thoughts was more a melding than an intrusion, and so subtle at times that Entreri had no idea the blade was watching.

He couldn't fool the sword, and thinking otherwise was a delusion as surely as when he deluded himself into thinking he could get at Alegni if he just struck reflexively, without thinking.

That day on the coveted bridge when Alegni had learned that the folk of Neverwinter had named it after Barrabus, Alegni had tortured him severely, laying him low on the stones, writhing in pure agony. Entreri had struck back at the Netherese warlord, without thinking, too fast, he had thought, for Claw to intervene.

He had been wrong. Claw had known. He couldn't fool the sword.

And now he was about to walk into Neverwinter to face Alegni, to face that sword, and without doubt, to reveal that Drizzt and Dahlia were on their way.

Perhaps he had already done exactly that. Perhaps the distance out in Neverwinter Wood had not protected him from the intrusions of the sword.

Not really knowing—and that was the worst thing of all—Entreri turned his hellish steed around and galloped away from the city.

Drizzt and Dahlia walked quietly through the morning forest, though the occasional crunch of the light snow cover, the crackle of leaves and twigs beneath, sometimes marked their passage. The ground was uneven, brush and deciduous trees dotting the landscape around them in no discernible pattern. They would make the north road by midday, and there they'd bring in Andahar for the swift run to Neverwinter—right through the city's gate and onto her avenues. As rash as that frontal assault sounded, it might prove their best chance at getting anywhere near Herzgo Alegni.

Still, to Drizzt, the idea seemed preposterous. He and Dahlia hadn't yet discussed the specifics, other than "kill Herzgo Alegni," but they'd need to come up with something, he knew. The warlord was on his guard, no doubt, if Entreri had returned to his side.

The couple had gone only a few hundred yards, though, before the hairs on the back of the drow's neck began to tingle and all of his warrior sensibilities had him measuring his strides.

The forest was quiet—too quiet to the trained ear of Drizzt Do'Urden. Dahlia sensed it, too, and so said nothing as she looked curiously to Drizzt.

The drow motioned her to the side and slowly slid Taulmaril the Heartseeker off his shoulder. Likely it was just a hunting cat, or a bear, perhaps, he expected, but enemies were ever near in this dangerous land and so he wanted to take no chances.

A soft clicking sound had him glancing at Dahlia, as she carefully broke her staff down into twin poles and then into flails, which she casually sent into slow spins to either side.

The drow crouched lower, narrowing his gaze to focus on the space between underbrush and canopy. Something had caught his attention, he wasn't quite sure yet what it might be.

Slowly he brought his bow around, his free hand moving almost imperceptibly over his shoulder toward the quiver strapped to his back.

A tall strand of a bush was moving, but not in concert with the flutters of the morning breeze. Something, someone, had jostled it.

Drizzt froze, every muscle in his body preparing for the next moment, only his eyes shifting left and right, scanning, waiting.

He was not one to be caught by surprise, but when the ground beside him, the ground between him and Dahlia, lifted and lurched, a wave of energy rolling out through the brush and new-fallen snow in every direction like the ripples on a pond, neither Drizzt nor Dahlia had any response except to go with the inevitable push.

Suddenly they were twenty paces apart, rolling and dodging trees and stones, Drizzt trying to hold the Heartseeker free of any tangle. And as the magical energy dissipated, the enemy came on with brutal abandon.

Two lightly armored shade warriors, human and tiefling, leaped from a spot very near to where Drizzt had landed. Clearly, this ambush was carefully planned, and the earth-shaking spell meticulously aimed. They came in for a quick kill with their spears, planting the weapons in the ground and vaulting high to kick out, spinning and stabbing as they flew at their prey.

Drizzt could have taken one down with his bow, perhaps, but he drew blades instead, meeting the furious attacks with circling parries and defensive counter thrusts. Within the first heartbeats of the encounter, he knew that these were not mere highwaymen, nor even mere warriors of Shadowfell, for these two worked in brilliant concert, much as he had done with Entreri or with Dahlia.

The monks started to widen their approach, as if intending to flank Drizzt to either side, but when Drizzt turned his shoulders and came with a roundhouse left-hand slash, the human monk blocked it with his spear, but fell with the weight of the blow back in toward the center. Down he went in a sidelong roll, while his tiefling companion leaped up high and back the other way, clearing him, so that now the tiefling stood on Drizzt's left and the human, rolling right back to his feet, came in from the right.

The tiefling's spear thrust almost got through, picked off at the last second by a desperate backhand of that same scimitar.

Drizzt used his enchanted anklets as well—not in a sudden rush, but in a wise retreat.

With her melee weapons already in hand, Dahlia was more prepared for the close-quarters ambush than Drizzt had been, but still found herself nearly overwhelmed by the power and coordination of the two opponents who burst from the nearby brush.

On came an enormously fat tiefling male, heavily armored and whipping a flail that seemed sized for a giant in wild circles above his head as he charged. He hardly cared for the branches as he rushed for Dahlia, barreling through, his weapon not slowing in its spin, but just snapping the obstacles into flying splinters.

From the other side came a woman, tall and strong and working a hand-and-a-half broadsword with practiced ease.

Dahlia glanced back and forth, trying to determine her best course. She knew immediately that she couldn't begin to parry or block the tiefling's gigantic flail, so she had to use her speed to avoid any thunderous swings. A single staff would give her that mobility, but she didn't prefer that weapon against a long-bladed sword, where her tactics were typically to get inside the arc of any swing to strike fast with the flails.

Her thought process got no further, though, for Dahlia had no choice but to trust in her improvisation and hope it would sort out. She darted for the woman, flails spinning, but cut back the other way as the woman pulled up short. Dahlia dived into a forward roll, gathering momentum, and went in at the huge tiefling hard, falling low as she closed in to avoid a high swing of his flail.

Strangely high, she thought briefly, but she didn't question her luck and unloaded a flurry of sharp cracks against the belly and legs of the shade.

She still didn't understand why the tiefling had put the flail across above her head—and it likely would have missed her skull even if she hadn't easily ducked—until she started back the other way, to find a pair of thin but strong filaments stretching along before her, then catching on her hip and shin.

She spotted the spiders, huge, pony-sized, and hairy, to her left and right, completing the box around her.

She had to duck again as the tiefling swung even more furiously, and this time just a bit lower, forcing Dahlia down.

In a move of sheer stubborn defiance, the elf slapped up with one flail, cracking it against the massive flail, which didn't veer in the least from its determined course.

Dahlia hadn't expected it to, and was already turning as her flail spun free from the huge weapon. She worked her left hand fast, cracking her spinning pole against the warrior-woman's broad sword repeatedly. It took Dahlia three such strikes to realize that she wasn't parrying the woman's blade, for her opponent wasn't actually trying to hit her.

The angle of the warrior woman's strikes seemed more an effort to contain than to kill.

Dahlia understood that, and was not surprised to see the spiders spinning their webbing her way, filling the air around her with filaments. She felt the profound tug on her leg from one as she tried to scamper aside, then had to dive low once more as the heavy flail spun low to high to block her escape.

Dahlia worked her flails quickly, spinning them so their flying poles collided repeatedly, and she called out for help from her companion, who suddenly seemed so very far away.

From the nearby brush, Ratsis watched the encounter, Jermander and the Shifter beside him, Ambergris hidden before them in reserve to either of the two fighting groups. As soon as the Shifter had separated the couple with the initial, earth-rolling dweomer, Ratsis had called forth his pets.

Convinced that he had Dahlia tied up enough for Bol and Horrible to control her movements, Ratsis telepathically ordered his spiders to shift their angles of attack. The next filaments that came forth fired out to anchor on trees some distance behind Bol, and thus between Dahlia's fight and Drizzt's.

"You need not do that," the Shifter remarked.

Ratsis studied the fight between the three to the other side. He knew that Parbid and Afafrenfere were quite skilled, despite their almost buffoonish pride, and their companionship and coordinated movements were the stuff of legend and jokes in certain circles. Each was formidable on his own, but together, they were better than any three of equal skill.

Yet, this drow ranger's reputation, so formidable indeed, seemed to pale against his movements now. He leaped and spun, turning every which way as the situation demanded, but always did his curved blades dart out at precise angles, and with adequate power to not only repel an attack, but to send one or the other monks diving aside.

"The monks will not hold him," Ratsis started to protest to the Shifter.

"I never thought they would, but contingencies are in place," the Shifter assured him.

As Ratsis turned to look at the shade, the Shifter motioned back the other way, directing the gaze.

Dahlia was doing much better than Ratsis had expected. Every spin of her flail produced a solid strike—as often as not on the other flail—and despite the webbing grabbing at her legs, she retained enough mobility to sting Bol and his mate repeatedly—and if they backed off at all from keeping her occupied, the stubborn elf managed to wriggle looser from the few webs binding her. Neither of the warrior shades were taking it well, Ratsis recognized, given Bol's ferocious reputation and propensity to kill people as a matter of first resort.

Ratsis turned his spiders back to the main prey, needing to properly tie up the troublesome Dahlia, for her own sake.

Despite the frenetic movements of his very active opponents, Drizzt was not oblivious to the plight of his companion. He noted the spiders and caught the sunlit reflection of the few filaments between himself and Dahlia's battle, obstacles he expected he could slice with little trouble.

A spear thrust in from his right, and at the same moment, front and left, the human monk went up into the air and double-kicked.

Drizzt threw his hip out to the left, barely avoiding the stab, and twisted to lurch back and right. He heard the snap of air just before his face as the leaping monk's fast-kicking feet missed by less than a finger's breadth.

The drow straightened, turning both his scimitars against the thrusting spear, even though the kicking monk leaped once again, and this time with his weapon planted in the ground nearer to Drizzt so he could extend his attack.

Drizzt let him. He had to break this dance quickly and get to Dahlia. He drove his blades down in a cross, catching the thrust with Twinkle in his left hand, driving through with Icingdeath, and as he expected and hoped, the fine diamond-edged blade sheared through the edge of the wooden spear.

Drizzt threw his left arm up and finally started his lurch to the right, albeit far too late. He was surprised by the weight of the monk's blow. For one so slight, this trained fighter could hit like an ogre!

But Drizzt was also already surrendering the ground when the monk connected, intending to fly away to the right, and so he did, throwing himself as far as he could, tumbling and rolling, deftly tucking his right shoulder and reaching back with his left hand as he did.

He came out of the roll without his scimitars and facing back to his previous position and on his knees, but far from helpless as the tiefling with the broken spear charged in close pursuit.

Drizzt had left those scimitars on purpose, instead retrieving his bow and an arrow, and with the precision wrought by hundreds of hours of practice, of endless repetition and measurement, of pure muscle memory, he came to his knees, facing back with the Heartseeker leveled crosswise before him, an arrow nocked and ready.

The tiefling monk leaped, but not soon enough, and a lightning arrow lived up to the bow's name, blasting into the monk's chest and hurling him back the way he had come, with his feet leading as the arrow's mighty momentum laid him out. He landed flat on his face, without so much as a groan.

The second monk was in the air, though, right over his falling companion. Perhaps Drizzt, so fast and so skilled, could get another arrow in place, perhaps not. He didn't try. He scrambled forward and dived under the leaping monk, and as the small human extended his legs to touch down more quickly, Drizzt slapped Taulmaril up over the flying monk's feet, hooking him between bow shaft and string. The drow dug in and planted firmly, and tugged with all his strength, sending the monk tumbling away, though Taulmaril was torn from his grasp and went flying with his enemy.

Without the slightest hesitation, the drow improvised. Above all else, he had to get to Dahlia, and so he went that way with all speed, scooping Twinkle and Icingdeath as he passed.

A shimmer of light in the air before him warned him. He thought it spidery web tendrils, and so brought his blades slashing before him.

At the very last moment and with no time to change course, Drizzt noted that the edges of that shimmer didn't quite match the flora immediately before him.

He fell through the extra-dimensional gate, the Shifter's trap, reappearing near the edge of a high bluff far to the other side of Dahlia. He managed to skid to a stop before falling over, but only got his head and shoulders back around in time to see a tall female shade smiling widely and with her arm extended toward him.

From that extended fist, from a ring on her finger, came the ghostly, nearly translucent head of a ram, rushing through the air.

Drizzt tried to tuck and turn, but got slammed on the side, and found himself flying from the ledge into the open air.

"Go with him. Kill the drow," Jermander said to Ambergris as the enraged Afafrenfere rushed past their position, slowing only to vault the spidery filaments between him and the drow, barriers impeding his rush to avenge his partner's death.

The dwarf nodded and sped out to the right, toward the ledge from which Drizzt had flown.

"She is not yet secured," the Shifter said, nodding toward the surprisingly resilient Dahlia, who, despite a continuing filament barrage, had managed to wriggle one leg free, and despite the efforts of Bol and Horrible, continued to duck and dodge and lash out with stinging hits.

"These are the hirelings to whom you promised a full share?" the Shifter asked, her sarcasm heightened by her accent, which bit off the words in a sharp manner.

"Bol and Horrible are hindered by their orders," Jermander sharply replied. "Their weapons are lethal, their tactics designed to kill, and yet we have forbidden them from even injuring Dahlia."

"Who is formidable in her own right," Ratsis added.

"You promised me that she would be caught easily if separated from her drow companion," the Shifter reminded. "I have done so, quite expertly."

Ratsis glanced to Jermander, who rolled his eyes, then nodded toward the nearest of the huge spiders. Taking the cue, Ratsis redoubled the efforts of his minions, prodding them on with telepathic commands.

The agitated arachnids stamped their many legs and more filaments shot out at the dodging elf warrior as she continued to lash out with those metallic flails.

Lashing out wildly, Ratsis noted, her spinning weapons more often than not getting nowhere near to Bol or Horrible . . . but never hitting only air, Ratsis noted. Dahlia always seemed to twist those spinning weapons in line with each other, and every attack routine ended with them smacking together, throwing sparks.

More sparks with each hit, Ratsis realized, as if they were building energy.

"Clever woman," he started to say, but abruptly stopped as Dahlia played her hand.

Bol's heavy flail head swung around above her once more, and up slapped the woman's flail, a blow that should have barely diverted the heavy flail ball. But when the pole struck, there came a flash of lightning, a great release of energy, greater, even, than the tremendous momentum of the swinging ball.

That ball shot straight up suddenly, and the surprised Bol couldn't react other than to instinctively hold on tight to his jolted weapon.

He should have let it go, for as the ball reached the end of its chain, it continued over backward and down.

Ratsis's eyes widened as the big man's head snapped forward, Bol's face a mask of confusion. The burly warrior stumbled a step to the side, then toppled over, flail handle falling underneath him so that when he landed, the pull on the handle and chain yanked his head around, leaving him lying on his side, but face down in the dirt.

The flail's ball remained on the back of his head, secured by the spikes that had driven through his skull.

It had all happened in the blink of an eye, but now time seemed to slow greatly, so that Horrible's outraged, shocked scream went on and on, as the woman, her orders overruled by her rage, leaped in to cut down the webbed Dahlia.

Dahlia managed to turn and block that initial strike, but even then, more filaments fell over her, further enwrapping and hindering her. One arm was down now, caught fast, and though she parried brilliantly with her remaining flail, there was no energy charge remaining there, and none to be built.

Jermander shouted out for Horrible to stop, but the furious woman would not relent.

"Stop her!" Ratsis said to the Shifter, who was already lifting her fist and grinning.

Horrible leaped back from Dahlia, out of reach of the spinning flail. As Dahlia's arm came around behind her, it, too, got tangled in the webbing, leaving the woman twisted awkwardly at the hip. With both arms pinned, Dahlia stood helpless as Horrible swung her sword up over her head for a killing chop.

But Horrible jerked weirdly, then a ghostly ram's head appeared at her side and slammed her, throwing her many strides to the side. She kept moving forward when she landed, almost reflexively, and even tried to continue her overhead swing. But that long blade tangled in the branches of a tree even as she stumbled face-first into the trunk.

She fell to the side, to the ground, and lay very still.

"The spiders!" the Shifter yelled at Ratsis when he turned to her in surprise. "The spiders! Catch her fast!"

He landed with his typical grace, and might have even managed to keep his footing long enough to scamper down the steep slope and relieve some of the weight of the fall. But Drizzt's descent took him in line with the short and stabbing, sharp-edged branches of a dead tree. He touched down on the sandy hillside, the light snows and early cold having done nothing yet to solidify the loose soil, and had to throw himself around backward, desperately dodging those deadly branches.

And as he did, spinning around and throwing himself forward and low to try to catch himself, the soil gave way beneath him and in his slide, his leg hooked under an exposed tree root.

Drizzt's momentum threw him backward over that root with tremendous force. His leg bent in half as he slammed hard to the ground, and there he lay, hooked and caught and barely conscious, fully dazed by the weight of the crash. Both of his blades had flown from his hands, though he was hardly aware of it, and his leg wrapped back under him, bent tightly at the knee, the hook of it being even more pronounced and painful because of the steep slope, where Drizzt's head was much lower than his knee.

Drizzt searched for points of clarity, for anchors of consciousness through which he could grab on and hold on. Two realities came clear to him: he was in trouble, and Dahlia was in serious trouble.

That latter thought inspired him to force some clarity. He felt the keen pain in his leg, and understood instinctively that it would take him some time and great effort to extract himself, if he could even do so at all.

He brought his hand to his belt pouch, to find it open and empty. He glanced around, then back over his head, lower down the hillside, where he spotted the black shape.

"Guenhwyvar!' he called. "I need you!"

Ambergris could only hope that Jermander and Ratsis hadn't noticed her spell, her waggling fingers creating a translucent hammer in the air behind Horrible, striking hard, right through the woman's skull just an instant before the Shifter had stopped the warrior woman's killing blow even more effectively with the ram's head attack.

Running on after Afafrenfere, she took some comfort in knowing for certain that the monk hadn't noted her treachery. His vision and course narrowed by sheer outrage, Afafrenfere was seeing nothing but the straight line path that would take him to the drow.

And the dwarf wouldn't get there before him, or even with him, she realized.

She slowed her pace just enough to cast a second spell, a whispered command to "halt" that had the weight of divine power behind it. Despite his urgency and rage, Afafrenfere skidded to a stop, momentarily only, but enough for Ambergris to catch up.

"He dies!" the monk insisted.

"Yeah, yeah, don' we all?" Ambergris replied, and she grabbed Afafrenfere's arm so that he could not sprint out ahead of her.

"Hurry!" the monk urged.

"Be easy," the dwarf countered. "If ye're wantin' to jump into this dark one's face, then ye're wantin' to be dead!"

Afafrenfere tried to pull away anyway, but Ambergris had a grip to make a stone giant proud, and he wasn't wriggling free. Together they came to the edge of the cliff. Down below lay Drizzt, in clear sight, still caught and bent over backward awkwardly on the root. Below him and to the side, a gray mist was forming.

"Fly away!" Ambergris cried to the monk, shoving him to the side. Afafrenfere tried to protest, but Ambergris shoulder-blocked him hard, and both went rushing down the side of the hill, a slope not as steep as that near Drizzt, but one that still left the pair scrambling simply to keep their feet under them.

"Fly away!" Ambergris kept saying, and whenever the monk tried to argue or to slow down, the dwarf barreled into him, buckler leading, and kept him moving along.

Finally, many yards down the side, Afafrenfere managed to catch a hold on a tree as he passed and pull himself out of the insistent dwarf's way.

Ambergris skidded to a stop.

"What are you doing?" a flustered and sputtering Afafrenfere yelled at her.

"Keepin' ye alive!" she shouted back at him.

Afafrenfere responded with a growl and started to shove past her.

Up came Ambergris's Skullbreaker, smacking the monk in the face and laying him low. "Shut up, ye fool. Ye're feedin' the worms were meself not wanting a bit o' company, and to be sure yerself's th'only one o' that bunch I e'er could stomach."

She grabbed the dazed and disoriented monk roughly by the collar and tossed him up over her shoulders, then trotted off into the forest.

With Bol and Horrible out of the way, Ratsis's spiders increased their barrage, lines of webbing flying all around Dahlia, and despite her protests and frantic movements, she was becoming inexorably wrapped and trapped. One of her arms became pinned to her side, and she lost the flail in her other hand, unable to pull it free of the webbing.

With all of her considerable strength, Dahlia could not twist the weapon free, nor yank her wrapped arm free, nor could she get her legs free of the piling webs.

"Well done," Jermander congratulated and he started forward from the brush, sword in hand. He was almost to Dahlia when a form appeared, leaping down from the branches of the same tree where Horrible had fallen. The agile newcomer hit the ground with a second leap, one that lifted him right atop one of Ratsis's arachnids. He came down hard, sword set tip-down, and with expert precision, he drove the weapon right through the pony-sized spider's bulbous eye. The eight-legged beast thrashed and shrieked as goo bubbled up around the blade, but only for a moment before it crumbled down and lay still.

Jermander eyed the newcomer. Behind him, Ratsis screamed in protest over the demise of one of his treasured pets.

The newcomer, a smallish but well-muscled man, jerked the sword free and started Jermander's way. Ichor dripped from his long blade. He held a smaller dirk in his left hand.

Jermander was no cowardly commander hiding in the bushes, however. Noted for his skilled blade work, the shade didn't shy from many fights. He brought his fine silver sword up in a salute and stalked in.

"You are with Dahlia, then?" he asked as he neared, his sword waving before him.

"No," came the curt reply, the small man's sword slapping hard across to drive Jermander's leading thrust aside.

Jermander rolled his blade free deftly, re-angled, and went straight back in with the sword—only to have a backhand roll of the dirk move the strike harmlessly aside.

Which Jermander had expected, of course, and so he worked fast, suddenly—retract and stab, retract and stab, retract once more, turning the sword up and over in a diagonal downward slice. He didn't expect to land a blow, and he didn't come close, but was merely trying to get a measure of this unexpected and unknown opponent.

"Yet you leaped in to defend her?" the shade remarked.

"I don't like spiders."

"How do you feel about elf women?" Jermander said with a light grin—one that was wiped away immediately as this newcomer raged forward suddenly, his feet moving fast, his blades a blur of circling and stabbing.

Jermander worked furiously with his fine sword, and more so with his feet as he found himself in the unusual position of full retreat! This warrior of Cavus Dun was well known in many regions of the Shadowfell. Long and lanky, deceptively fast and carrying a light and thin mithral blade that glowed with magical energy, Jermander had risen high in the ranks of the hireling hunters as much for his fighting skills as his organization and leadership qualities—and more so in the beginning.

He needed every bit of that skill now to fend the speeding strikes of his adversary, and though he could hardly take the time to sit back and consider the moment, or his opponent, a thought did occur to him.

"You are Alegni's man!" he shouted between the ring of metal on metal. As he spoke the words, he knew them to be true; this one's complexion and reputation had indeed preceded him.

Artemis Entreri didn't even smile in response, just kept up his impeccable offensive barrage, kept Jermander on his heels.

Ratsis was just about to order his remaining spider to shift its webbing attack to the newcomer when he and the Shifter heard Jermander's claim that this unexpected addition to the fight was Alegni's man.

The two glanced at each other and Ratsis swallowed hard.

"We are not in accordance with the wishes of a Netherese Lord?" the Shifter whispered breathlessly.

Her answer had to wait as a low feline growl filled the air.

The Shifter's eyes widened as she looked past Ratsis, her expression prompting Ratsis to turn likewise, affording them both the view of a large black panther standing atop the ledge where the drow had flown. A large black panther seeming very intent on them.

"Guenhwyvar!" Dahlia cried, her voice somewhat muffled by the stubborn webbing.

Ratsis's gaze darted from the cat to Dahlia to Jermander and Alegni's man and back to the Shifter, who was shaking her head.

"I will expect my payment in full," she said, and she hustled away into the shadows—and back to her homeworld.

Ratsis glanced around again. Three of his mercenary group lay dead, and the value of Dahlia had therefore increased to him personally. But caught between health and wallet, Ratsis soon enough realized the price he would almost surely pay if he tried to follow the enticing course of his greed.

He sent his remaining spider to intercept the cat, but held no reasonable hope that the arachnid would slow this powerful beast.

He glanced again at Dahlia, wrapped and ready for delivery.

So close.

But not now, Ratsis realized, and he was glad that he, too, had learned the difficult art of shadow-stepping.

"Alegni's man!" Jermander yelled again, barely dodging a sword thrust that got past his own blade and almost took him in the hip.

"You keep saying that as if you know what it means," Entreri teased and taunted.

"I know Alegni!"

"You know what he wishes you to know." Across came the sword, taking Jermander's blocking weapon aside, and in stepped the small killer with a half-turn and wide slash of his dagger, and then a backhanded stab back across which almost got Jermander in the face as he tried to counter.

"Effron employed me!" Jermander argued, and he tried to keep the panic out of his voice—though unsuccessfully, he realized by the grin on the face of Alegni's champion.

"Effron employed me as well," said his opponent, "to kill you."

Jermander stared at him dumbfounded, but not before wisely backing out of reach.

"He is in love with Dahlia," Entreri explained and leaped forward, leading with a wild, circular flurry of his long sword which had Jermander flailing all around to keep up.

And the small man tossed his dirk—he didn't throw it at Jermander, but merely tossed it up before him, close enough for Jermander to snatch it from the air. The shade warrior almost did just that, but realized the diversion for what it was and protected against a sword thrust instead.

He should have protected from something else, though he couldn't know it, for indeed Entreri came forward with the expected thrust, half-turning once more, but only, Jermander soon realized, so that he could hide the movement of his free hand, down to his belt buckle and suddenly forward.

At first, Jermander thought he had been punched in the chest, and he staggered back a few steps, working his sword defensively. Only when he realized that Entreri wasn't pursuing, only when he noted the smug look on the small man's face, did he begin to understand, and he glanced down at his chest to see a small knife buried up to its hilt.

He tried to speak out, but found that he had no air in his lungs.

Jermander fought against the dizziness and breathlessness. Strangely, he felt no pain. He steadied himself and assumed a posture to continue, but as he expanded his focus once more and looked to his opponent, he saw that the man had his dirk in hand once more—had he caught it before it had ever hit the ground?—and now cocked his arm, ready to throw.

Jermander tried to clutch up into a smaller target and readied his sword for a block.

Entreri pumped his arm and the warrior dodged, then dodged again with a second fake.

Each movement brought on more dizziness, waves of disorientation. Jermander told himself that it was time to flee, and he, too, started that shadowshift, to return to the other world, the Shadowfell.

But shadowshifting took concentration, and this time, Entreri didn't fake.

Jermander felt the profound thud as the dirk plunged in beside the knife. He saw the man stalking in at him as his body went numb, and then a gray mist filled his vision.

For a moment, Jermander thought he was slipping away into the Shadowfell. The sensation and the view seemed much the same.

A blinding flash ended that thought, ended all thought, as a sword creased his skull.

CHAPTER 5

THE GENDER OPPRESSED

DRIDERS ARE NOT THE QUIETEST OF CREATURES, PARTICULARLY WHEN A SCORE of them, armed and armored and anxious for battle, scrabble along rocky cavern floors and walls.

Something was afoot, Yerrininae believed. He could feel it, and it was a tangible sensation, not just a gut instinct.

The air was colder—unnaturally colder.

The drider leader drove his charges on, rushing around blind bends in the corridor recklessly. He had sent two scouts up front, and he knew now—he just knew—that the pair were soon to encounter . . . something.

So focused was the large mutant that he nearly passed through a remarkable juncture in the otherwise unremarkable corridor.

Yerrininae skidded to a stop, his eight legs clacking and scraping on the stone. Behind him, several driders pulled up fast, frantic to avoid a collision with their merciless leader.

"What is it, my commander?" one dared ask, as the others wandered around in confusion.

Yerrininae continued to look to the wall instead of the open corridor ahead. He moved over slowly, almost reverently, and eased his great spear out wide with his left hand, the other reaching tentatively for a peculiar crease in the wall. A smile widened upon his face as the drider ran his fingers along that peculiar groove.

"My commander?" the other drider asked again.

"This is no natural crease in the stone," Yerrininae explained. "This is a worked juncture—once, long ago, likely a portal . . . a door of some sort."

The other drider dared move up, and on Yerrininae's bidding, lifted his hand to also feel the straight lines of the worked stone. "What does it mean?" he asked.

Yerrininae straightened and looked all around, considering the caverns and corridors they had traversed that day. "It means that this was the outer waypoint."

"Of?"

Yerrininae looked at the drider and grinned.

A shriek stole the moment, echoing off the stones, bouncing all around them as if a hundred drider warriors were suddenly under great duress. Yerrininae leaped sidelong down the corridor, legs working perfectly to spin him as he landed in full stride, charging along, spear at the ready.

Only a few bends later, they found their scouts, though the driders were only barely visible beneath a mound of flailing semi-translucent ghostly dwarves.

No, not ghostly, but actual spirits, Yerrininae realized, and he commanded his charges forward, into the morass.

The large drider led the way. Yerrininae was never one to view a battle from afar. He crashed into a small horde of the ghosts, his fine drow great spear stabbing and slashing every which way.

But to little effect, for these creatures were only partially bound to the material plane. He could barely hit them, with weapon or with appendage. Similarly, their reciprocating swings did not connect solidly.

When a dozen other ghosts leaped away from one of the unfortunate scouts to charge his direction, though, Yerrininae understood that those seemingly insubstantial attacks could surely combine to great effect, for that drider scout from which they had crawled slumped right to the floor, its face a ghastly mask of missing eyes and torn lips, its head all twisted around as if it had been squeezed between heavy stones. The creature lolled around, propped by the symmetry of its eight legs, but hardly alive.

"Close ranks!" the drider leader demanded.

As the valuable drider warriors fell back, Jearth ordered his shock troops past them and into the enemy.

Goblins, orcs, and bugbears surged forward along the corridor and into the wider cavern beyond, fighting every instinct in them which told them to turn around and flee—for those who did so, those who even hesitated slightly, felt the bite of a drow crossbow bolt.

"Dwarf ghosts!" Ravel said happily from the back. "Gauntlgrym! It must be! Right before us. We have found the dwarven city."

"We cannot be certain," Berellip said beside him.

"I can feel the power of the place," Ravel argued. "Primordial power." He wasn't bluffing, nor was he imagining anything due to the appearance of dwarf ghosts. The sense of bound magic was powerful and primal. He could feel it under his feet. Ravel had done a lot of work with elementals during his tenure in Sorcere. Gromph Baenre was quite fond of summoning them by the dozen, all different types, merely to torment them.

He thought to confer with his brother Brack'thal, who had reputedly been supremely skilled in the elemental arts in the years before the Spellplague. Only briefly, though, for he did not want to give Brack'thal the satisfaction.

Even without that confirmation, Ravel knew the feeling of elemental magic, and such was the tingling energy he felt in the floors and walls now, a deep resonance of the purest energy.

Along the wall to the left came Tiago Baenre, charging his lizard above the heads of the many drow crowding the area.

"The goblinkin will be of little effect," he told Ravel and the others. "These ghostly defenders are quite beyond them."

"Shall you throw a lightning net upon them, dear brother?" Berellip remarked, and behind her, Saribel giggled.

"It might prove quite potent," Ravel replied, ignoring the sarcasm.

Berellip gave an exasperated sigh and moved past him, Saribel and the other priestesses of Lolth in tow.

As soon as they had moved past Tiago, the young Baenre signaled to Ravel, *Shall I gather your wizards that you can enact a second lightning net?*

The question caught Ravel off guard, so much so that he balked and even moved back a step. He stared at Tiago for a few moments, ensuring that the warrior was serious. He glanced down the corridor; the sounds alone convinced him that his goblinkin fodder were indeed being slaughtered.

Ravel nodded. He wouldn't give his sisters the satisfaction of being saviors.

"They are a stubborn bunch," Berellip admitted to Saribel. They had hit the dwarves with a vast repertoire of spells, from shining beams of unholy light to waves of biting flames. They had used their allegiance to Lolth to compel the ghosts away and had even tried to harness the spirits to their will, to dominate them and turn some against the others.

But this was a stubborn group indeed, much more so than typical for such undead creatures.

"They are fighting for their most ancient homeland," Berellip continued, reasoning it out as she went along. "They are bound here as guardians, singular in their devotion."

"They will not be easily turned, nor easily destroyed," Saribel agreed.

"Fight on," Berellip instructed Saribel and the others, and she fell into her next spellcasting but stopped abruptly, startled when Tiago Baenre, Jearth Xorlarrin, and a host of lizard riders charged past her.

The cavalry swept into the cavern, veering to the right as they extended their line.

In came Yerrininae and the driders on their heels, reinforcing that line as it began to sweep back to the left, effectively clearing the nearest right hand corner of the cavern.

Into that void went Ravel and his spellspinners. Berellip spat on the stone and urged her priestesses on with more powerful spells. She began casting her own bursts of brilliant devastation, focused lines of unholy light, as Ravel and his wizards took their places and began their web-spinning.

Now it was a competition as priestess and wizard vied for the top honors in the ghostly slaughter.

"Damn you," Berellip cursed Tiago when he called for a retreat at precisely the right moment, drow rider and drider alike running back to the opposite flank just in time for the spinning lightning net to cross above them harmlessly.

The dwarf ghosts did not flee as the orcs had back in the cavern city, and a host of them fell under that net. The sparking, biting filaments crackled as it battered them.

Berellip and many other drow averted their sensitive eyes from the bright white energy.

When all finally settled, the number of ghosts was greatly diminished. The few remaining drifted back to narrower halls, moaning all the way.

"Secure the cavern!" Jearth's voice rang out above the din. "Huzzah for Ravel!"

A great cheer went up, and Berellip seethed.

Her visage did not soften as Tiago Baenre rode up beside her and Saribel.

"You chose sides," Berellip warned. "You chose wrongly."

"Not so," Tiago flippantly replied. "It was a coordinated effort and you and your priestesses played no small role. It would seem that I was wrong, and that priestesses have a place, after all. Other than in the bedroom, I mean."

"Blasphemy," Saribel mouthed, and Berellip stared at the upstart male incredulously.

"It was quite a beating you put on your brother over such an innocuous, and indeed a worthwhile, slight," said the confident young Baenre, who was ever so full of surprises.

"Are the Baenre sisters so used to you speaking in such a manner?" Berellip warned.

"Of course not!" Tiago said with a laugh.

"You dare?" Saribel said.

"My dear Berellip," Tiago said, unwilling to even acknowledge Saribel, other than to toss her a lewd wink, "you are a priestess of Lolth." He gave a shallow bow, hindered as he was by sitting astride his lizard mount. "And I am the son of House Baenre."

"You are a male," Berellip said, as if that alone should humble Tiago. But he only sat straighter and laughed at her.

"I understand," Tiago said with a nod. "By all conventions, you are my superior, and so you believe that to be the case. But consider, upon whose side in our battle would Matron Mother Quenthel stand? In customary terms, you are correct in your indignation, but in practical terms?"

"You're a long way from House Baenre," Berellip warned.

"Do you believe that I was selected to go along with you at random?"

That gave Berellip pause.

"Selected," Tiago said again, emphatically. "House Baenre knows your every movement, and every intention. Understand now that I alone will determine if House Baenre will allow Xorlarrin the room you desire to found your city. I alone. A bad word from me will doom Xorlarrin to a noble—excepting perhaps some spellspinners, as their powers have intrigued Matron Mother Quenthel of late. Since Gromph has retired mostly to his room at Sorcere and meddles little in Baenre business, Quenthel has come to see a growing gap in the armada of House Baenre, one that would be nicely filled by absorbing some of Xorlarrin's skilled spellspinners."

"Then she would want them obedient!" Berellip argued, and her tone made her sound desperate, and so clearly revealed that she had lost the initiative in this argument.

Tiago had easily gained the upper hand, and he wasn't about to let it go. "She will want what I tell her to want," the brash young warrior replied. "And to dispel any secret hopes you now harbor, understand that if I am killed out here beyond Menzoberranzan, Matron Mother Quenthel will hold Zeerith Q'Xorlarrin personally responsible. And of course, her daughters as well."

Berellip stared at him, not blinking, not backing down, not willing to give him the satisfaction.

"You would doom Xorlarrin to a noble," Tiago quietly reiterated, and then he smiled and signed so that only Berellip could see, *I do anticipate our next coupling*, and he rode away, as if nothing was amiss.

Not so far behind that encounter, Brack'thal Xorlarrin leaned against the corridor's stone wall, his sensitive fingers feeling the stone, his thoughts permeating the stone. Ravel had felt the tingling of elemental energy here, but that paled compared to the understanding Brack'thal had for such magic. In his day, he had been one of the strongest evokers in Menzoberranzan, a drow who could reach to the elemental planes, so it seemed, to bring forth fire and lightning and other primordial powers. Once he had commanded an entire company of earth elementals, for no better reason than to impress the masters of Sorcere.

Now he felt it, the fiery beast, the god of flaming destruction. This was why Matron Zeerith had included him in his hated brother's expedition, and now, suddenly, feeling that power, experiencing the clarity of mind which could only be brought through such a close communion with an old and basic power, Brack'thal held his curses back, and even thanked Zeerith for allowing him this journey.

He did not even watch the battle at hand before him. His sisters would win out, he fully expected, and he could no sooner turn from this stone, from the deep sensations and vibrations of the primordial beast of fire than he could from a tryst with Lady Lolth herself.

For the promise was no less.

The promise of power.

The promise of magical strength as it had been those many years ago.

CHAPTER 6

COMRADES IN COMMON CAUSE

DAHLIA FOUGHT HARD AGAINST THE STUBBORN WEBBING TO TURN HER HEAD. She didn't want to miss the demise of her tormentor, and was quite pleased when Entreri's sword split open the shade's skull.

She wriggled some more and managed to free her head almost completely, though the rest of her remained tightly bound. As she glanced around, she came to understand that she was alone—alone with this man Entreri, Alegni's champion. After a moment to catch his breath and retrieve his thrown knife, he started toward her, sword leveled her way.

Dahlia twisted and strained, struggling to free up one arm. But then she settled, knowing she could not hope to defend herself.

The sword was close.

Dahlia stared the small, cold man in the eye, trying to discern his intent.

The sword came in at the side of her neck and she stiffened and held her breath. But Entreri began to cut the webbing away.

"I am truly touched," she said sarcastically after she had recovered from the shock.

"Shut up," Entreri said as he continued freeing her.

"Are you embarrassed by your concern for me?" the elf woman quipped.

"Concern?"

"You're here, against your master's allies," Dahlia reasoned.

"Because I hate him more than I hate you," Entreri was quick to reply. "Do not presume that such thoughts shine brightly upon you."

His last words were lost in the rumble of a low and threatening growl, and Entreri froze, and Dahlia smiled—she could see six hundred pounds of muscle-rippled panther crouching right behind him.

"You have met my friend Guenhwyvar, no doubt?" she asked with a grin.

Artemis Entreri didn't move.

"Hold!" came a call from the side, as Drizzt Do'Urden, limping only slightly, came over the ridge. Whether he was speaking to Entreri or Guenhwyvar, neither Dahlia nor Entreri could be sure.

Both, likely.

Entreri dismissed the drow with a snicker and drove his sword down halfway to the ground, greatly loosening the bindings on Dahlia.

"A change of heart?" Drizzt asked when he came beside the pair. Dahlia extracted herself from the webs. Behind Entreri, Guenhwyvar remained poised to leap upon the small man.

"Easy, Guen," Drizzt prompted the cat, and her ears came up.

"Why have you returned?" Dahlia asked Entreri as she continued to pull strands from her clothing. She wasn't feeling particularly generous, and didn't much like being rescued. She intended to push Artemis Entreri, and hopefully to push him far away.

When he didn't immediately answer her question, Dahlia stopped plucking the webs. Her question had struck him hard, obviously. She was caught by surprise, for she had never expected to see him in such a pensive pose.

"Why?" she asked again, sharply and loudly, but only to pull the man from his apparent introspection.

"I don't know," he admitted.

Dahlia felt Drizzt's gaze upon her and glanced his way. His visage was cold, as if chastising her for going after Entreri so bluntly. The man had just saved her life, after all. She offered a shrug.

"Well, why did you leave us, then?" Dahlia asked, a bit more cordially.

"Herzgo Alegni carries my old sword," Entreri replied. "My old sword, sentient and telepathic, can learn things from me. Being with you endangered you, and while I care not a whit for the lives of either of you, I do not wish for you to fail in your quest."

"And yet, despite your words, here you are, endangering us."

"I know your intent," Entreri replied. "Being closer to Alegni makes it more likely that he will learn of your intentions from me."

"So we should just kill you," said Dahlia, and she kept any hint of humor out of her voice.

"You will die first," Entreri promised.

Drizzt stepped between them. Only then did Dahlia realize that she and Entreri had begun drifting together, face to face, unblinking.

"I thought to simply go away, though I could not escape Alegni if I fled Faerûn itself," Entreri explained.

"And you just happened upon us?" Drizzt asked.

Entreri shook his head. "I don't know how much I'll be able to help you before Alegni—before my old sword—lays me low on the street," he admitted. "And yet, here I am," he added, looking around at the dead Shadovar, "helping you on your way. Alegni and Charon's Claw did not hinder my blade as I struck at your enemies, whom I would have to presume serve as his allies."

He looked Drizzt directly in the eye, and Dahlia noted that they shared something, some long and deep bond and obvious respect.

"I'm not going back to serve him," Entreri stated flatly. "There is no amount of pain, no amount of torture, that will put me beside Herzgo Alegni."

To her surprise, Dahlia realized that she believed him—not only that he intended as he said, but also that this grayish man was possessed of inner power great enough to do as he had just claimed.

She stepped back and let Drizzt and Entreri have their conversation, and caught only a few snips of the dialogue, as Entreri admitted that his mere presence with them might well have compromised any hope of secrecy they might harbor, or that this attack might have been directed to this place and against them because of his previous proximity to them.

Dahlia knew from his responses and body language that Drizzt would accept Entreri as a companion on this mission, and when she let down her own stubbornness, she realized that if Drizzt did not, she would insist. She focused mostly on Entreri then, staring at him, understanding him.

She saw the pain.

She knew that pain.

"An interesting dilemma," Drizzt said to Dahlia a short while later. In the distance, they could see Entreri gathering firewood, as they had agreed.

"You doubt his sincerity?"

"Strangely, no," said Drizzt. "I have known this man for many years—"

"Yet, you have not known of him for many years," Dahlia was quick to point out.

"True enough." Drizzt nodded in deference to her obvious logic. "But in our time together, I came to know who he truly was. I saw him emotionally stripped naked in Menzoberranzan, raw and unprotected. He is many things—including many heinous traits that I cannot abide—but in a strange way, there is honor in Artemis Entreri, and there always has been." As he spoke the words, Drizzt thought about that first encounter with the assassin, when Entreri had held Catti-brie captive for days. Helpless and at his mercy—and yet the assassin had shown her great mercy in that time.

But there were other times, when Entreri had not been so kind, Drizzt thought, and he remembered a halfling's finger . . .

He looked away from Dahlia, to Entreri—a confusing link to a distant past.

"He won't willingly betray us," Dahlia said, and Drizzt spun back on her. "He hates Herzgo Alegni as I do."

"Why?" Drizzt asked.

Dahlia looked at him curiously.

"Why do you hate Herzgo Alegni?" Drizzt almost fell back a step as Dahlia's face tightened. She spat on the ground at Drizzt's feet.

"So you believe Entreri will not willingly betray us, and I agree," Drizzt said quickly, thinking it wise to change the subject. "But what about unwillingly? He has already admitted that his mere presence with us might well have tipped Alegni off to our intentions. The sword holds him, and seems to know his every thought."

Dahlia turned her gaze to the distant Entreri, and slowly shook her head. "It cannot," she said, and she seemed to be speaking more to herself than to Drizzt. "Sentient weapons do not hold such power."

"It enslaves him."

"It feels his intentions, his anger, his move to action," Dahlia replied. "That is a different matter. The sword reacts to his impulses, as Kozah's Needle heeds my call, and it is powerful enough because of their long history to overrule his demands."

"You cannot know that."

"As you cannot know that your fear is well founded," Dahlia said. "Artemis Entreri did not lead those Shadovar to us, as he was near Neverwinter while they were out on the hunt. Perhaps his presence with us allowed his sword to understand the general course of our intent, but perhaps not nearly as specifically as you believe—else why would he have been allowed to get so near to Neverwinter without a host of Alegni's guards falling over him? The sword does not know his every thought and every move. I cannot believe that, particularly when he and the sword are not near each other. It's a sword, not a god!"

"But we will get near, and so Entreri will be near to the sword, and there remains the possibility," Drizzt reasoned.

"So you would abandon this potentially powerful ally out of that fear?"

The drow thought about that for a long while, and realized that he really didn't want to walk a separate road from Entreri. Once again, this man tied him to a past for which he longed, a time when the world seemed simpler to him, and far more comfortable. Still, despite all of that, he heard himself saying, "Yes."

"Then he will seek out Alegni on his own—he won't turn from that. I saw the pain in his eyes, and he will not turn from that! So we each will strike at Neverwinter, and weaker will we both be—"

"There is a third option," Drizzt interrupted.

Dahlia eyed him curiously.

"There are ways to block such telepathic intrusions," Drizzt explained, the idea just coming to him—and it seemed one that solved many of his current problems and addressed many of his current fears. "Jarlaxle's eye patch—do you recall it? It was so enchanted. With it, the mercenary rendered himself invisible from magical and telepathic spying, and such dominance as the sword has shown over Entreri."

"So we'll go and find Jarlaxle and he'll help us?"

"He has ties to Entreri, as well—"

"He is dead," Dahlia stated flatly. "You saw him die. You saw him go over the rim of the primordial pit only heartbeats before the creature vomited its killing spew. Accept it, you fool!"

Drizzt had no way to answer. He wasn't sure that his hopes for Jarlaxle were simply a matter of refusing to accept the obvious. He had seen Jarlaxle dodge too many arrows. By all indications, Jarlaxle had died in Gauntlgrym. Who could have survived the power of the primordial erupting from inside that rim of fire, after all?

But Drizzt had once made the mistake of thinking some dear friends dead without conclusive proof, and he didn't intend to travel that fool's road again. Maybe Jarlaxle's charred remains lay on the side of the primordial's pit, or perhaps he had fallen into the fiery maw of the lava beast and nothing at all remained of him.

Or maybe not.

"So you'd use Entreri's dilemma to once again take me far from this place," Dahlia said. "To once again turn me from my quest."

Her anger was clear for Drizzt to see. "If Jarlaxle is to be found, then wonderful, for he, too, would prove a valuable ally," he said. "But the point stands even if Jarlaxle does not. There are items, or enchantments, which we might procure to protect Entreri from the prying sword."

"Do you think he has not already looked for such things?"

Drizzt wasn't sure what to say. At the very least, Dahlia's point showed that they might spend months in search of their answer. In his many decades of adventuring, had Drizzt ever encountered anything other than Jarlaxle's eye patch that might provide the needed shield, after all? And even that eye patch had failed Jarlaxle against the mind-bending manipulation of Crenshinibon, the drow reminded himself. He looked back at Entreri, who was approaching now, and gave a resigned sigh.

"So will you send me away or accept my help?" Entreri asked when he got to them, and he dropped an armful of kindling on the ground beside the small fire pit the drow had dug.

"Are we that obvious?" Drizzt asked.

"It's the discussion I would be having were our situations reversed," said Entreri.

"And you would send us away."

"No, I would cut out your heart," the assassin quipped, and he went to sorting the firewood. "Makes things simpler, you see."

"Would you settle for having your skull crushed?" Dahlia asked, and if she was joking at all, her voice didn't reflect it.

Entreri dropped a piece of kindling and rose, turning slowly to face the woman. "If it were that easy, I would have been killed already," he said, expressionless. "And you will not turn me away. I've made my choice now, and my road is for Neverwinter, beside you or not."

"We fear the sword," Drizzt explained. "Should we not?"

Perhaps it was the simple honesty of that statement, Drizzt thought, or maybe it was because he wasn't questioning Entreri's word, but simply addressing influences that might prove beyond the assassin's control, but Entreri seemed to relax then.

"Is there a way we can protect you from the intrusions? Do you even know when you are being scoured?"

"Idalia's Flute," Entreri replied, and it seemed as if he was looking far, far away then. He snorted and shook his head.

"A magical item?" Dahlia asked.

"One I possessed for some time," Entreri explained. "If I had it now, I'm sure that I could defeat the call of Charon's Claw, or at least offer some resistance."

He looked into Drizzt's questioning expression.

"Jarlaxle has it," Entreri explained. "He repaired it, used it to lure me back to his side, then took it from me when he sold me into slavery to the Netherese."

"Ah, then we should find Jarlaxle and seek his help," said Dahlia, and Drizzt felt the bite of her sarcasm keenly.

Entreri stared at her incredulously, obviously not appreciating her sarcasm.

"How complete is Claw's understanding of your thoughts?" Dahlia asked, her tone changing suddenly then, as if she were truly interested, as if she had an idea.

"You assume that I know when Claw is in my thoughts," Entreri replied.

"Tell us everything you know about Neverwinter's defenses," Dahlia said with a wry grin, as if her desire to learn of those defenses—surely authentic—was only part of her reasoning.

Entreri looked to Drizzt, who, after studying Dahlia, recognized her plan and matched her smile. He looked back at Entreri and nodded.

With a shrug, Entreri explained the layout of the city, and detailed the wall's strong points and its weaknesses. He knew where Alegni slept, and where the tiefling could usually be found. He told of the various Shadovar encampments around the city, as well, and as he moved along in his recounting, he too began to smile.

Drizzt nodded again, this time at Dahlia and her clever ploy to determine if Claw was then within Entreri's thoughts, which, given the level and detail of the information he was providing—information that could prove fatal to Herzgo Alegni—the sword likely was not.

"Neither of you are schooled in the ways of wizards," Dahlia said when Entreri was done.

"Enough so to kill them when they annoy me," said Entreri.

"I have studied the magical arts," the elf explained. She held up Kozah's Needle. "Particularly those aspects that affect the creation of magical items. I am no novice to such weapons—to be so ignorant while wielding this weapon would be dangerous."

"And your point?"

"It is not likely that this sword, Charon's Claw, remains in your thoughts," Dahlia explained. "More likely, the sword reacts to those forceful commands you make to your muscles."

Entreri screwed up his face, clearly skeptical of the reasoning, or not understanding it.

"Kozah's Needle knows when I need it to release its energy," Dahlia said.

"Because you dominate the staff, as I once dominated Charon's Claw," Entreri replied.

But Dahlia was shaking her head. "Sentient weapons, all but the very greatest, are not separate beings. They have pride and demand of their wielder—such is part of the magic imbued within their metal or wood. But they aren't conscious beings, plotting and conniving for personal gain. Charon's Claw has come to dominate you through your long affiliation. All that truly means is that Charon's Claw recognizes your action cues. It knows when you mean to strike and how you mean to strike, and what you wish its role to be in that strike, were you wielding it. Now, it retains that clear recognition of your action cues, and so it can react to them faster than you can counter the reaction."

Entreri's expression showed him to be less than convinced.

"What properties does the sword possess?"

"The ability to trail an opaque veil of ash," Entreri replied hesitantly, not sure where this was going.

"And how quickly can the sword create this trail if called upon by its wielder?"

"Instantly," said Entreri, and he suddenly seemed more intrigued.

"And would the sword ever put forth this ashen trail without your call?"

The assassin thought on that for a moment, then shook his head, but without much conviction.

"Your bond with it was so strong that you are not even sure if you consciously had to call upon it any longer," Drizzt reasoned. "And so now you presume, logically, that the sword is reading your thoughts."

"You don't understand the pain this sword can inflict upon me," Entreri answered.

Dahlia shrugged.

"The sword can dominate him," Drizzt reminded her.

Entreri added, "And so just having me with you might compromise your mission, as I said."

"And if Charon's Claw was in your mind," Dahlia asked the assassin, "would it have allowed you to kill that shade warrior and free me from the web? For surely Herzgo Alegni would have me brought to him in bindings."

"So it is not a constant intrusion," Drizzt said. "But how will we know?"

Dahlia broke Kozah's Needle into two four-foot lengths, then. She regarded them for a few moments—and it seemed to Drizzt that she was communicating with the weapon—then tossed one length to Entreri.

"Certainly Kozah's Needle will recognize the intrusion of a different sentience," she explained.

Entreri stared at the length of metal, then put it up as if testing its balance.

"Do not even think to wield it as a weapon," Dahlia said. "And at the first signs of any battle, return it immediately! But as we travel, let this serve as our sentry. If your sword attempts to infiltrate your mind, that bo stick you carry will know of it, and the one I carry will inform me."

Drizzt and Entreri exchanged looks then, and both could only nod in admiration of the resourceful elf woman.

On a high turn along the southern coastal road, Drizzt and his two companions looked down upon Neverwinter. Nestled within the wider ruins of the old city, the newer construction and wall were clear to see—at least, those parts of the wall that were not obscured in shadow.

It wasn't the shadow from any trees, or the angle of the sun behind any of the nearby hills in the region, that hid the wall, but a dull haze—a magical shadow, a fog brought forth from the Shadowfell itself.

"The Netherese have reinforced," Dahlia stated, her tone aptly expressing what all three realized as they looked down upon Alegni's stronghold. She turned a suspicious eye upon Entreri and remarked, "Perhaps the wretch does know of our plans."

"If every setback is to be pinned to my cloak, then tell me now," Entreri replied.

Drizzt couldn't help but smile at the perfect timbre in Entreri's voice, conveying the man's apparent boredom and just a bit of a threat. He was ever calm, and so there was always that threat, Drizzt understood. He looked at Dahlia to see if she had caught it, and her expression, a mixture of anger and only slightly-hidden surprise, confirmed the drow's suspicion.

"How many, do you think?" Drizzt asked, thinking it wise to deflect this conversation.

"Perhaps he fears that we're coming for him—surely he knows of Sylora Salm's fate," Entreri reasoned. He dropped down from his nightmare steed and climbed atop a large stone to get a better vantage point. Drizzt and Dahlia slipped down from Andahar and moved to join him.

"Several score, at least," Entreri explained when they arrived. He pointed out a handful of Shadovar encampments just outside the city wall. "Alegni has tightened his defensive ring, as well."

"If he knows of Sylora, then perhaps he believes that the Thayans will strike out recklessly, at least initially," Drizzt said.

Entreri nodded his agreement. "Whether against our threat or that of the Thayans, Herzgo Alegni has prepared his city for defense."

"Perhaps, then, we would do well to shrink back into the forest and let the time of potential crisis pass," Drizzt offered, and no sooner had he gotten the words out of his mouth when Dahlia joined right in.

"Your advice on every development is to wait and hide," she retorted sharply. "How you ever earned a reputation for being anything more than a coward eludes me, Drizzt Do'Urden."

Drizzt's eyes widened, particularly given the adventures he and Dahlia had already shared in their short time together. In addition to the assault on Sylora's fortress, they had gone to Gauntlgrym side by side and battled a lich and a primordial.

He didn't know how to respond, but Entreri did. It wasn't often that Drizzt or anyone else had heard Artemis Entreri laugh aloud, but he was surely doing so then.

Drizzt stared hard at Dahlia. A part of him wanted to strike back at her, for he found that he didn't much like being mocked, and found, to his surprise, that he truly did not like being mocked in front of Artemis Entreri. That last revelation did surprise him more than a little, but he couldn't deny it.

"And you would throw yourself in front of any danger, because you foolishly believe yourself immortal," he said, though it took him a long while to find his voice.

"Or she simply does not care," Entreri replied before Dahlia could, and the assassin and Dahlia exchanged a look then that set Drizzt back on his heels.

Entreri understood something about her that he did not, Drizzt realized. Yes, he too had wondered about exactly what Entreri had just claimed, but even though he might recognize the possibility, Drizzt knew from the glance his two companions had shared that Entreri understood this part of Dahlia on a much deeper level than he ever could.

Again to his surprise, and there were many that morning on the high road, Drizzt found that the revelation bothered him more than a little.

"How would you have us get into Neverwinter, then?" the drow asked, bringing the conversation back to the point. "You know their defenses," he said to Entreri. "Where are they weak?"

"I *knew* their defenses," the assassin replied, glancing back down at the city. "It would seem they are much stronger now."

"Too strong?" Drizzt asked.

"No," Dahlia replied.

Entreri shrugged. "They have weaknesses. Jelvus Grinch, perhaps the leading citizen among the settlers, is no friend to Herzgo Alegni. Their alliance—one that I created—was wrought of mutual hatred of the Thayans, and from the beginning, the citizens of Neverwinter have been wary of the Netherese. They are much like the folk of Ten-Towns."

Drizzt nodded eagerly, appreciating Entreri's attempt to bring this to a better level of his own understanding, and indeed, his own limited experiences with the folk of the new Neverwinter somewhat confirmed the assassin's comparison.

"They intend to pick their own rulers," Entreri finished.

"And they wouldn't choose the Netherese," Dahlia reasoned.

"Would you?"

Dahlia spat on the ground.

"How can we exploit this?" Drizzt asked. "I know Jelvus Grinch—how might I meet with him and enlist his aid?" Even as he spoke the words, though, Drizzt began entertaining doubts regarding that course. As he looked down at Neverwinter, the deep pockets of shadow gave him pause. If he enlisted Grinch and others in this personal vendetta of Dahlia's, would he not, perhaps, be creating a possible massacre within Neverwinter?

Even as Entreri began laying out some manner in which he might arrange such a liaison, Drizzt was shaking his head.

"If your old sword notices one instant of our plotting, and that plotting includes Jelvus Grinch, many in Neverwinter will be killed," Drizzt interrupted.

"Then how?" Dahlia demanded. "If I must fight my way through that garrison, then so be it, but I will not turn aside."

Entreri began to smile immediately, as a thought obviously came over him.

"What do you know?" Drizzt prompted.

"When the river flowed as lava and the hot ash piled deep on Neverwinter, I was trapped under that bridge," he explained, pointing to a distant structure, one that had been known as the Winged Wyvern Bridge. "I had no idea how I would ever get out of there, and yet I could not stay. The heat from the river . . ." His voice trailed off and he shook his head.

Drizzt recalled his own experiences when the volcano blew, when he watched from afar as the mountain crumbled into a river of roiling stone and ash, when the shock wave rushed across the forests, leveling ancient trees as if they were insignificant strands of grass. The power of the spectacle had brought Drizzt to his knees. What must it have been like to be in Neverwinter that awful day, to see the devastation up close, to hear the screams of men, women, and children as they were burned and buried alive?

"How did you survive?" the drow prompted somberly.

"I crawled off the bridge," Entreri replied, "and to the street, but it was too deep in ash—hot ash—for me to plow along it. And the stones were falling thick. I saw more than one person crushed under a fiery boulder. The buildings, strong as they seemed, provided no shelter. Those who hid inside were buried under rubble or chased out by the fires—everywhere were fires. The air was too thick to breathe."

"So you died and the sword brought you back," Dahlia reasoned, but Entreri shook his head.

Drizzt solved the riddle by remembering the layout of Neverwinter, whose streets he had walked several times. He, too, had often been drawn to the bridges, to the river that served as the city's heart.

"You couldn't pass along the street, so you went back to the river, near the bridge," he said.

"To swim in the lava?" Dahlia mocked.

But Drizzt just shook his head and kept looking at Entreri.

"There was an opening along the bank, above the level of the river," the assassin explained. "And the water flowing from it was relatively cool."

"You crawled out of Neverwinter through her sewers," Drizzt reasoned. "Do you think they remain open?" He watched Dahlia as he spoke, and noted that her smirk disappeared.

Entreri pointed down to the south of the city, to where the great river meandered into the Sword Coast. "It's possible."

CHAPTER 7

SHADOWS, ALWAYS SHADOWS

E FFRON CONTINUALLY LOOKED OVER HIS SHOULDER, PEERING THROUGH THE ashen mists and endless shadows of the Shadowfell. He wasn't supposed to be there, and Draygo Quick would punish him severely if the weathered old battle mage discovered his breach of etiquette and station.

But he had to know.

This involved Dahlia. He had to know!

Despite his desperation, Effron didn't dare travel anywhere near the Cavus Dun guildhouse, nor did he dare speak with any of the leaders of that organization. Nay, they would rush straight to Draygo, he knew, for they would not protect the confidentiality of a mere ascendant noble like Effron when weighed against the potential ire of Draygo Quick.

He knew that he had only a matter of hours, however, and when he could not locate Jermander or Ratsis at their usual haunts—and more troubling, when he learned that Ratsis had indeed been spotted that very day in the Shadowfell—he went to a secluded boulder tumble, set with a small cottage that never seemed to stay in the same place for more than a moment or two.

Effron waited for a shift, then sprinted for the door and reached out to grasp . . . nothing.

Smiling, appreciating the cleverness of the home's owner, the twisted warlock waited and watched, trying to discern some pattern to the illusionary games. When he thought he had it figured out, he quietly began a spell, timing it for another house jump.

The cottage disappeared and popped back into view between a pair of large boulders. Into the ground went the wraithlike Effron, slipping through cracks in the stone, sliding down and popping up again right where the house should have been.

But it was across the way, beside a different stone entirely.

"Clever," Effron whispered under his breath. "Was it ever really in this place?"

"What do you want?" came a sharp reply from right behind him, and the startled Effron jumped around so violently that his limp arm went into a great pendulum swing behind his back.

"Shifter," was all he could gasp as the spectacle of the imposing woman stood before him—or, he reminded himself, *appeared* to stand before him.

"What do you want?" she snapped at him again, biting each word short with her harsh accent. "I do not appreciate uninvited visitors."

"I am Effr—"

"I know who you are. What do you want?"

"You went with Jermander."

"You assume much."

Effron straightened and cleared his throat, then politely rephrased, "Did you go with Jermander's band?"

"Again," the Shifter reiterated, and then she was gone. Effron thought to spin around, guessing that she would be standing right behind him, but he decided against that course.

"I hired Jermander of Cavus Dun—"

"Mentioning that group, admitting that you paid them, speaking of them at all, will likely get a person killed," came the reply from right behind him. "Assuming, of course, that such a person or such a group even exists."

Effron realized that in his desperation and fear of Herzgo Alegni—or was it his fear of disappointing Herzgo Alegni, he wondered—he was getting very sloppy.

"I need to know the fate of Dahlia," he said simply, resisting the urge to add any details that might hint at Cavus Dun, Jermander, Ratsis, or anyone else.

"Dahlia?" the Shifter asked. Effron suddenly wondered if Jermander had indeed subcontracted the Shifter. But then she unexpectedly added, in a whisper, "Alegni's man."

Effron wasn't sure if the Shifter was referring to him or to Barrabus the Gray, but the way she spoke the words led him to believe it to be the latter, and made him think that it was directly related to whatever had happened, or had not happened, regarding Dahlia.

He turned around to face the woman. "Whatever you can tell me, whatever you can learn for me, will be much appreciated."

She looked at him skeptically.

"And richly rewarded," he added.

A smile widened on the Shifter's pretty face. "Five hundred pieces of gold," she said flatly.

Normally Effron would have argued, even to the point of refusing the transaction, so outrageous was the price, but again the specter of Alegni hovered over him and he brought forth a bag of coins and handed it to the Shifter.

Of course, that was just an image of the disorienting woman, and he felt a sudden pull from the side as the invisible lady snatched the purse, which seemed to dematerialize into nothingness as it left his hand.

He heard the clink of coins off to the other side and started to turn, but just held his ground and laughed helplessly. Maybe she was there, maybe not, for this clever sorceress could certainly misdirect sound as easily as she created the visual discrepancies.

"You did not tell Jermander that Alegni's man would defend Dahlia," she said.

"Defend her? Or did he wish to claim the kill as his own?" Effron replied.

"Either way, Jermander is dead."

Effron swallowed hard, suddenly understanding that there would likely be a great price to pay for this unfolding catastrophe.

"And Dahlia?" he managed to ask past the lump in his throat.

Herzgo Alegni felt like a prisoner in his own city of Neverwinter, and it was a feeling he did not like at all.

"I would see the result," he stated flatly, and started for the door.

"You would not," Draygo Quick rasped back at him.

Alegni paused and composed himself, not looking back at the withered old warlock. Draygo Quick's news that Jermander and some others of Cavus Dun had been killed was not unwelcomed by Alegni, nor was it surprising, for he had figured from the first time he had seen Jermander in Neverwinter that Effron had hired out the mercenaries, and that Effron would be bold enough to try to strike at Dahlia despite his orders to the contrary.

For the twisted and broken young warlock, it would be, after all, a double victory.

"Don't you think they are coming for you?" Draygo Quick asked. "Or lying in wait, should you ever leave the defenses of this place?"

Alegni shrugged as if it hardly mattered. It wasn't as if Barrabus the Gray could actually hide from him, after all, though he did wish that his magical link to the dangerous man was more informative and more continual.

"Do you not think they will come into the city after me?" he asked.

"Do you?"

"I count on it," Alegni said with a grin. "I hope for it."

"Don't underestimate—"

"I do not underestimate anyone," Alegni interrupted. "Even you."

It was not often that Draygo Quick could be put back on his heels in a conversation, but Herzgo Alegni had obviously done just that, and the warrior tiefling did well to hide any gloating at that moment.

"Effron is young," Draygo Quick said, and Alegni could hardly believe that the stubborn and fierce warlock was actually changing the subject. "He is full of promise."

"And full of conflict," Alegni added.

"Indeed," said the warlock. "Particularly in this delicate situation."

"I didn't bring him here," Alegni reminded. "I didn't want him here." He paused and stared hard at the withered warlock for just a moment. "I do not want him here."

He thought that he might have pushed just a bit too far, though, when Draygo Quick stiffened and hardened his gaze.

"And yet he is here," the warlock stated flatly. "And he remains here by my command."

Alegni's face tightened, but there was no room for debate in Draygo Quick's tone.

"There are proper punishments and there are excessive punishments," Draygo Quick warned. "I take it personally when one of my minions is excessively punished."

"And there are reparations," Herzgo Alegni offered, and Draygo Quick cocked his head curiously. He seemed so decrepit and withered that, had he been reclining, Herzgo Alegni might have thought that he had just died.

"Sylora Salm is dead and the Thayans in disarray," Alegni explained. "But they are not yet fully defeated. And there are other interests in the region, including these Neverwinter citizens I have subjugated, and some agents, I presume, of other interested parties. Now is the time for a full show of force."

"You're asking again for more soldiers."

Alegni shrugged. "It would seem prudent."

"The best thing you might do to secure your hold here is to destroy these assassins who hunt you," Draygo Quick replied.

"That will be done," Alegni assured him, and he instinctively grasped Claw's hilt, though the sword had offered him little of late regarding Barrabus the Gray. "But still . . . to minimize the damage done by Effron . . ."

"A hundred," Draygo Quick agreed.

"Three," Alegni started to bargain, but Draygo Quick cut him short with a sharp reiteration.

"A hundred."

After a courteous—and wise—bow, Herzgo Alegni took his leave.

"You understand your role?" Draygo Quick spoke in the apparently empty room.

From behind a tapestry stepped an elf Shadovar, dressed in fine breeches and an expensive waistcoat, and with a flat top hat adorned with a ribbon of gems. He wore his blousy white shirt open to the waistcoat, showing a shapely neck and a small tattoo to the right of his windpipe: the letters CD, for Cavus Dun, intertwined.

"We have a great opportunity here," Draygo Quick said.

"And a great risk," the elf, Glorfathel, replied, his words carrying more weight in light of the recent losses Cavus Dun had realized.

"You are my hedge against that," said the old and powerful necromancer.

The elf bowed low. "How will I know?"

"I trust your judgment," Draygo Quick assured him. "This region of Toril, Neverwinter Wood particularly, is of importance to us, no doubt, but not with the urgency that drives Herzgo Alegni. And I will not be embarrassed by chasing that hot-humored tiefling on a fools' errand."

"I understand."

"I knew you would."

"Did you think it would be any different?" Arunika asked Jelvus Grinch when she found him with some other prominent citizens of Neverwinter, all standing with hands-on-hips, staring dumbfounded at various points along the city walls. Portions of the wall were cloaked in deeper gloom. For at those locations, shadowy magical gates had appeared, like doorways into the void, and Netherese soldiers, shades one and all, were coming through.

"Is it an invasion?" Jelvus Grinch asked the red-haired woman.

"If it is, then ye'd be wise to be thinkin' o' leaving," answered a voice from the back, and a female dwarf, quite dirty from the road, stepped out into the open.

"And who might you be, good dwarf?" Jelvus Grinch asked.

"Amber Gristle O'Maul, at yer service," she said with a low bow. "O' the Adbar O'Mauls. Me and me friend just come in from the road to yer fine city."

"Your friend?"

"Sleepin', " Amber explained.

"Came in from where?"

"Luskan, and what a mess that place's become!"

"A paradise compared to Neverwinter," another man remarked, and several laughed—but it was an uneasy bit of mirth, to be sure.

"Aye, ye got some problems, and I'm thinkin' that me and me friend'll be wandering on our way quick as can be done."

"You should be on your way now," Arunika said, rather coldly. "This is none of your affair."

The dwarf eyed her curiously for a few heartbeats, then just bowed and walked off.

"Why would Herzgo Alegni invade that which he already owns?"

Grinch turned an angry look over Arunika. "You played no small role in his ascension," he reminded. "Early on, when first he came to us, you teased with words that he might be our great hope."

"We could not have foreseen the fall of Sylora Salm," Arunika admitted. "Not in the manner in which it happened, at least. With the counterbalance of the Thayans removed—"

"There remain only Alegni and the Netherese," Jelvus Grinch finished.

"That is not necessarily true," said Arunika. "There is more to play out, I am confident."

"When you decide that I am worthy to hear your information, do tell," Jelvus Grinch sarcastically replied.

Arunika didn't bother answering the man, and she really had nothing definitive to tell herself, never mind tell him. She believed that Dahlia and this drow ranger, Drizzt Do'Urden, were coming for Alegni, perhaps with Alegni's own champion in tow, but she couldn't be sure. And even if they did come after him, she mused as she watched the dozens of new Netherese recruits pacing the city walls, what might three do against this force? For unlike the overconfident Sylora in her forest fortress, Alegni was obviously on his guard now.

Patience, the succubus reminded herself. The Abolethic Sovereignty was gone for now, but they would likely return. Or would they?

Her own thoughts gave Arunika pause. She had assured Brother Anthus that the Sovereignty's departure would prove a temporary thing, but how could she know anything for certain regarding those strange, otherworldly fishlike creatures? They would come and go as they pleased.

And did she even truly want them here? Arunika thought that she had figured out the Sovereignty, at least to the point of understanding their passion for order, one that even outdid her own. But there was something else here, something more, and the succubus couldn't deny a bit of relief that the aboleths had apparently departed the region. For within their promise of order loomed the threat of enslavement—perhaps even for a being as powerful as Arunika.

The succubus considered the cityscape around her. She had invested much here, years of her time on the Material Plane. Glasya had only grudgingly allowed her to come to this place and remain for so long, and only because of Arunika's passion and insistence that the desperate settlers of the ruins of Neverwinter could be subtly coerced toward the will of Glasya through the teachings of Glasya's loyal Arunika.

But where was she now, with any of that? The changes in the region could prove quite dramatic, and after all, would she even be around to witness them? For while Arunika found the movements of soldiers and the shifting power of the region tantalizing, perhaps she was, after all, growing a bit bored with it all.

Why was she interested in opposing Herzgo Alegni in the first place? Jelvus Grinch's claims were true, and she had teased this bold tiefling warrior into a more solid footing of power in Neverwinter. And though that had honestly been, as she insisted, more to provide a counterbalance to the threat of the Thayans, what benefit to Arunika if Jelvus Grinch and his fellows once more regained supremacy in Neverwinter at this time?

None of them could please her in the way Alegni did, after all. None of them could aspire to any real position of power and influence, within or without Neverwinter, as Alegni had and would no doubt continue.

She could become a consort to Alegni, perhaps, and help usher him to new heights of power and more brazen demands, on the city and the region. Perhaps she could use him to get the attention of Waterdeep, and thus unleash upon Neverwinter an even greater struggle, one that would pit the Netherese Empire directly against the Waterdhavian lords.

It could be perfectly delicious.

Still, the succubus couldn't quite manage a smile. Such bold actions would bring powerful opposition. Too powerful, likely. Suppose she proceeded only to find that the Sovereignty had returned and were not pleased by her choices, by her helping Netheril to gain a strong foothold here?

But still. . . .

"The Thayan Dread Ring is continuing to animate corpses," Alegni said to Effron late that night.

"Sylora Salm is dead and the ring's power is greatly diminished," Effron assured him, and the young warlock tried hard not to look too curiously at Alegni, though he suspected from the hulking tiefling's tone that Alegni was hinting at something.

"But still functioning."

Effron shrugged and tried to look unconcerned. What did it matter, after all?

"Including our own Shadovar fallen, who stand once more, this time in opposition to Netheril," Alegni said.

"So it has been."

"A curious zombie came against us this very day. I think you would know him."

Effron swallowed hard and when he looked at the hulking warrior, he knew the truth of Alegni's implication: Jermander.

"You struck out against Dahlia without my permission," Alegni bluntly accused.

"T-to capture her only," the tiefling warlock stammered. "She was not to be harmed."

"Your Cavus Dun mercenaries were sophisticated enough to make such a distinction?"

Alegni said with obvious, mocking skepticism.

"They were!" Effron insisted, hardly taking a long enough breath to consider the words before he blurted them. "I employed Ratsis and his spiders. And the Shifter! Even the Shifter . . ."

He almost finished before Herzgo Alegni backhanded him, launching him across the room to crumple hard to the floor. The tiefling warlord stormed over and gathered Effron up by the collar, hoisting him to his feet before he could begin to recover from the swat.

"You are not an independent entity," Alegni warned. "You are mine, to do with as I please."

Effron managed to squeak out, "Draygo," but that only got him a violent shake that had his limp arm flapping wildly and his teeth chattering. When it ended, Effron was gasping for breath, but he managed to say "The Shifter," one more time, this time plaintively.

Alegni tossed him down into a chair.

"It was a powerful band," Effron said as soon as he had composed himself. Alegni had gone to his balcony door by then and stood staring out over Neverwinter, toward the bridge that bore his name.

"It would have been a gift to you," the young warlock added after several more silent moments passed.

Herzgo Alegni swung around on his heel, an incredulous glare aimed Effron's way.

"Had my hirelings killed the drow and delivered Dahlia," Effron tried to explain, his voice rising as he expected the angry Alegni to rush over and swat him, or likely worse.

"You sought to capture Dahlia for my benefit?" Alegni asked skeptically.

"You wish her captured, surely!"

"You did it for yourself!" Alegni yelled at him, the warrior's booming voice overwhelming any pathetic attempts to deny the obvious truth of the matter. "You seek vengeance on Dahlia—your craving for it outweighs my own!"

"I . . .I . . ." Effron shook his head and looked down, unable to deny any of it. He knew that his eyes were moist and he didn't know whether to simply squint or to reach up and wipe them to ensure that no tears rolled down his slim face.

Herzgo Alegni would surely not accept tears.

The large tiefling didn't advance, and Effron realized that Alegni's posture had softened, as had his scowling visage. "I cannot blame you."

"I thought the win assured," Effron admitted. "The Shifter, Jermander, Ratsis the Spider Farmer—and with more warriors and monks beside them." He took some heart that Alegni nodded in recognition, for most important Netherese from their region of the Shadowfell surely would know those names. "It was no meager band assembled, nor did they come cheaply. These are expert hunters."

"And yet, Dahlia and her new companion defeated them," Alegni replied.

"Perhaps they had allies," Effron reasoned, and he noted that Alegni put his hand to Claw's hilt at that suggestion. Neither was saying it aloud, but they both knew that Barrabus the Gray had likely been involved.

"They won't find enough allies to help them into the city," the tiefling warrior proclaimed.

"You parlayed my actions into reinforcements," Effron realized, and he dared smile. "You turned my error into gain in your continual bargaining against Draygo Quick."

"You would do well to keep your reasoning to yourself," Alegni interrupted, and that scowl returned tenfold. Effron's eyes widened and he shut his mouth, realizing then that he was walking down a dangerous road, and remembering then that he was dealing with Herzgo Alegni, who, despite any understanding of Effron's motivation, was not the forgiving type, nor particularly merciful. But Alegni seemed distracted.

Slowly the young warlock rose from the seat into which Alegni had dropped him, eyeing the hulking tiefling with every movement, and ready to drop back down in an instant if he thought he was angering the volatile warrior. Even after he got to his feet, Effron moved tentatively, but if Alegni had any residual desire to punish him, the tiefling wasn't showing it.

Effron started slowly for the balcony door. Alegni fixed him with a stare and he froze, expecting an attack.

But Alegni's expression was surprisingly sympathetic. He stared at Effron, slowly nodded, and said, "We will get her."

After her run-in with Jelvus Grinch, Arunika was in no mood for the sour Brother Anthus who came rapping at the door of her cottage south of the main city late that evening.

"Arunika!" he called loudly, and banged hard on the door.

Arunika pulled open the door, catching the young monk in mid-swing. "Arun—" he started, and stopped abruptly.

"Do announce our liaison at this late hour to the world," Arunika replied, every syllable dripping with sarcasm. She grabbed Anthus by the wrist and tugged him hard. "Get in here," she ordered, and she slammed the door behind him.

"You said that he would get no further help from Netheril!" the monk growled, and pointed his finger at Arunika's face.

It took all of the tired and angry devil's willpower not to bite that digit off.

"It didn't seem likely."

"You were wrong!"

Arunika shrugged and held her hands up as if that hardly mattered for anything.

"Had I foreseen Herzgo Alegni's reinforcements, would we have been able to change anything?" she asked. "What actions would you have taken, would you have had me take, to prevent Alegni from strengthening his hold?"

"We could have gone to the ambassador earlier," Anthus fumed, almost incoherently. "We could have convinced the Sovereignty—"

"Of nothing!" Arunika interrupted. Her patience had reached its end.

"No!" Anthus flew backward through the air, launched by an open-palmed thrust into his chest. He slammed hard against the back wall, and were it not for the wall, he surely would have tumbled to the ground.

Gasping for breath, Anthus stared back at Arunika, whom he had known as merely a simple human woman—daring in her subterfuge and espionage and surely forceful sexually—but no more than a human woman.

He was wondering about that right at that moment, Arunika realized. She'd hit him hard—harder than any human woman of her stature ever could.

Had she just compromised her true identity?

For a moment, Arunika thought it might be prudent to walk over and simply snap the fool's neck.

Just for a moment, though. Brother Anthus might be a fool, but in the end, he was her fool. His contacts with the aboleth ambassador had saved her from any personal dealings with the otherworldly creatures. She could easily manipulate him and control him. That counted for something.

"We could have done nothing had we guessed correctly that the Netheril Empire would strengthen Herzgo Alegni's forces," she said calmly. "With the Thayans in retreat and the Sovereignty gone, we have little leverage against the Netherese."

"Then what are we to do?" Anthus asked, or tried to, for he had to repeat himself several times until his breath at last came back to him. He pulled himself up and straightened his robes. "Are we to simply allow this dominance of the Netherese?"

"If they overstep, they will attract the attention of Waterdeep," Arunika said, and she knew she sounded less than convincing. "But there are other possibilities afoot," she quickly added when Brother Anthus started, predictably, to argue.

He looked at her, clearly intrigued and clearly skeptical.

"So for now, we are to observe," Arunika instructed. "There will be holes in Alegni's defenses—there always are, after all. Find those holes. Find his weaknesses. When his enemies make their appearance, whoever those enemies might prove to be, let us, you and I, be ready to help them exploit those weaknesses."

"What enemies?" Anthus demanded.

"That, too, is for us to learn," Arunika said cryptically, unwilling to play her hand fully in the fear that the weakling Anthus would break to the interrogation of Alegni, should that come to pass. And given his screaming at her door and his open agitation, it did seem quite likely to Arunika that the fool might well turn unwanted curious gazes his own way soon enough.

As if to prove that very point, Anthus started to growl and yell at her again, even coming forward a stride, but again, Arunika had tolerated too much already. She didn't strike out at him physically this time, but reached out with her mind, assaulting Anthus with an overpowering blast of willpower, imparting images of her tearing his beating heart right out of his chest, and other such pleasantries, and the monk stumbled to a stop, staring at her incredulously.

"I too have learned some tricks from the Sovereignty," Arunika lied. "Herzgo Alegni has made temporary gains in a game as fluid as the sea. The waves will again crash against him."

"You underestimated him," the obviously humbled Anthus said quietly.

"You underestimate me," Arunika warned. She said it so forcefully, the succubus almost believed her bluff. Alegni might win here, or he might lose, and while Arunika preferred the latter, simply in case the Sovereignty did return, she intended to find her preferred place in either instance.

She moved to her door and swung it open. "Get out," she instructed. "And do not ever come back here with your ire directed at me, unless you desire a fast journey to the end of your days."

Brother Anthus turned sidelong as he moved past her, as if not daring to let her out of his sight while he remained in striking distance. He was barely out the door, though, when he spun around. He lifted one finger and started to speak out.

Arunika slammed the door in his face, and reminded herself repeatedly that Anthus was an idiot, but a useful one. It was the only thing keeping her from opening the door once more and tearing out the young monk's beating heart.

"No, you cannot!" Invidoo said with a hiss and a sneer, and snapped its poison-tipped tail up over its shoulder.

Only a deft dodge from the other imp prevented that stinger from taking out an eye, and still it tore the imp's large ear substantially.

"Through the length of the Nine Hells and the Abyss I sought you out!" screeched Invidoo, and the diminutive devil stumbled to the side, grasping at the torn ear. The poison wouldn't bother the imp, of course, but the gash was real enough, and painful enough. "You cannot deny!"

"You put your indenture on me! No!" screamed the imp, but then, just before a full brawl erupted in the smoky ash of this hellish land, a larger voice interrupted.

"No," said the large demon. "I do."

The angry imp scrunched up its face, a low growl of utter frustration issuing between its pointy teeth, for yes, this imp understood the inevitability of this, given its master, from the moment it had learned of Invidoo's inquisition. The imp began to shake its head, growling all the while, as the huge demon continued.

"You will replace Invidoo as Arunika's servant," the great beast instructed. "This, I desire."

The poor imp relaxed then and stared hatefully at Invidoo. The creature was helpless. Its master had spoken.

And it all made perfect sense, of course, given the history.

CHAPTER 8

NOT QUITE THE UNDERDARK . . .

AHLIA BROUGHT HER HAND OVER HER FACE AS SHE SPLASHED DOWN INTO the shallow water outside the metal grate. "We're crawling through that?" she asked with disgust.

Before her crouched Artemis Entreri, tugging at one of the bent bars to move it to the side. He had almost created a large enough opening for them to squeeze through.

Beside her, Drizzt understood her reluctance, for the smell was indeed overwhelming, wafting out on visible gases escaping the dark tunnel.

"We need not," he said to her, and he nodded his chin to the north. "We could take the road to Luskan instead. Or past Luskan to Ten-Towns, though we'd not beat the onset of winter in Icewind Dale."

"Or the eastern road to Mithral Hall," Dahlia retorted, clearly not amused.

The bar came free in Entreri's hand, which seemed to surprise him. He stared at its rusted end, then tossed it aside to splash into the water. He crouched lower and washed his hands in the salty liquid. "Decide now," he said. "This way lies Alegni."

Dahlia pushed past him and hopped up into the tunnel on her bare knees, then quickly rose into a standing crouch as she glanced back at the other two. "Light a torch," she instructed.

"It will blow up in your face," Entreri replied with a derisive snort.

"We'll need a light source," Dahlia argued, because she needed to say something at that point. Artemis Entreri had just gained the upper hand on her, had just diminished her in front of Drizzt. Dahlia could not let that stand.

"I came through without one," the assassin replied glibly, and Dahlia could only scowl.

She put her hands on her hips and glared at the man, but Drizzt drew forth Twinkle. The magical sword answered his call and glowed a soft blue-white hue. The drow hopped up into the tunnel and squeezed past Dahlia, the blade out before him, dimly lighting the way.

Cut unevenly through the stone, the sewer was sometimes high enough for Drizzt and the others to stand straight, but often they crouched as they moved along. The floor was concave, lower in the center, and a flow of dark water trickled past, sometimes pooling ankle deep or even past their knees, which was quite alarming. Everywhere, just at the edges of their vision, critters slithered or crawled or scurried aside.

At first the sword light seemed meager, but as they got deeper into the tunnel system—a maze of angles, turns, and indistinguishable stones—and the daylight receded behind them, Twinkle's glow seemed brighter by far. More rats huddled in the shadows at the side of the tunnel, more snakes slithered away into the water, and a multitude of insects, flying and stinging and spidery things hanging on slight webs, looked on.

None of the three spoke the obvious truth: the sword could illuminate a few feet around them, but to someone or something far away, it no doubt shined like a warning beacon.

Drizzt, born and raised in the near lightless Underdark, was most conscious of this, of course. A drow carrying a light source in the corridors around Menzoberranzan would soon enough be murdered and robbed. Holding the glowing blade now was anathema to everything he had learned as a young warrior. With his superior vision, he could navigate these tunnels well enough without the glow.

"I can see in the dark," Entreri said behind him, surprising him, and he turned on the man.

"You wore a cat's eye circlet," Drizzt agreed, and he held up Twinkle, confirming that Entreri was not wearing any such thing at that time.

"Innate now," the assassin explained. "A gift from Jarlaxle."

Drizzt nodded and moved to sheathe the sword, but Dahlia caught his arm. He looked at her curiously, and she shook her head, her face a mask of discomfort.

"I don't like snakes and I don't like spiders," she said. "If you sheathe that, then know that you'll be carrying me."

That brought a laugh from Entreri, but a brief one, as Dahlia, deadly serious, fixed him with a glare telling him in no uncertain terms that he was crossing a dangerous line.

Drizzt started away, and Dahlia splashed along behind him. "A gentleman would carry me," she muttered under her breath.

"Because you're such a lady?" Entreri asked from behind.

Up in front, Drizzt stopped and took a deep breath. An image of the two locked in a passionate embrace flitted through his thoughts and he nearly growled aloud as he dismissed it.

With the light of Twinkle leading the way, the trio moved farther along the main passageway, and soon enough came to a honeycomb network of more impressive and hand-worked side tunnels. They knew that they were underneath the outskirts of the city—the old city, at least. Their choices were limited at first, for these were still much smaller tunnels, almost all impassable and with a couple that they might have traversed by belly-crawling . . . something none of them wanted. But a short while after that, they came to a network of passages larger still, many as navigable as the one they now traveled and a couple even larger than that.

"Do you remember the way?" Drizzt asked Entreri. He whispered the words, for other sounds echoed across the wet and slimy stones.

Entreri moved up beside the drow, who stood at a five-way intersection, and surveyed the area. Hands on hips, he at last shook his head. "It was long ago."

"Not so long," Dahlia argued, clearly impatient.

Both Entreri and Drizzt looked at the elf woman.

"When I last came through here, I simply followed the water's flow," he explained. "I cared for that which was before me, not behind."

"You would have been far cleverer had you marked your passing, or at least, had you returned and mapped it after you had escaped," Dahlia continued.

Entreri stared at her hard. "I didn't intend on returning through this route. Ever."

Dahlia waved at him dismissively. "You disappoint me," she said. "A true warrior always prepares."

Drizzt studied Entreri closely, expecting the man to explode and to fall over Dahlia in a murderous rage. But he just stood there, staring at her for a bit longer, before turning back to face Drizzt and look to the tunnels once more. "Left, I would guess," he said. "The river is to our left and I entered the sewers along its bank. It is the source of the running water that flushes these passages, and so . . ."

"Flushes?" Dahlia prodded a thick pile of muck and feces with the half-staff she carried, her face a mask of disgust.

The pile shifted aside and out from under it came a serpent, black and thick and coiled, and easily as long as Dahlia was tall. It flew out from its position, lifting into the air, so fierce was its strike at Dahlia.

Dahlia recoiled and tried to fall away as the snapping toothy maw closed for her face.

A descending line of light flashed before her, but more importantly to her at that time, the bulk of the snake crashed into her. How she screamed and thrashed! All discipline flew from her as she worked purely in reaction to get that horrid thing away from her. And even after it fell aside, it took the woman quite a few heartbeats to sort it all out, to realize that she had not been bitten, to understand that the light marked the descent of Drizzt's scimitar, and that she had been met by nothing more than the snake's headless body flying from momentum and thrashing in its death throes.

Drizzt grabbed Dahlia and held her arms by her sides, trying to calm her as Entreri walked by.

"Did it pierce me? Am I poisoned?" she asked over and over again.

"Perhaps, and no," Entreri answered, and both looked at him, and Dahlia's face crinkled with disgust. He held the severed snake head, stuck on the end of his sword. "It is a constrictor, not a venomous serpent," he said. "It won't kill you with a bite, but would wrap you instead and crush the breath out of you, all the while trying to swallow the top of your head."

Now it was Drizzt's turn to flash a glare at Entreri. "It is—was not poisonous," he said calmly. "And it did not bite you, in any case."

That seemed to steady Dahlia a bit more. She kicked the thick, strong body of the snake farther away from her, and the body jerked spasmodically once more. Dahlia gasped and hopped away.

"You really don't like snakes, do you?" Entreri said, and he flicked his blade, launching the snake head far away. He walked back past Drizzt and Dahlia. "Come along, then. The sooner we are out of these smelly sewers, the better."

Neither Dahlia nor Drizzt was about to argue with that statement and they rushed to catch up, Drizzt again taking the lead—but this time, Dahlia stood right beside him.

Entreri handed her the other half of Kozah's Needle. Dahlia looked at it doubtfully, not taking it.

"If it serves as we had hoped, then it has shown me no contact by Charon's Claw in the time I have carried it," he explained. "If the sword has sought me and found me, then your weapon didn't notice. Either way, better for you to be armed now."

"What do you know?" Dahlia asked.

"That," Drizzt answered, and when Dahlia and Entreri turned to him, he thrust his sword out before him, and in the light farther along the tunnel, more snakes writhed, some taking to the water, some crawling over others, and all looking back at them.

"Let's leave this place," Dahlia said.

"We're trying to do just that," Entreri reminded.

"Back the way we came," Dahlia insisted. She joined the ends of Kozah's Needle back together, forming a singular eight-foot length. It wasn't very practical for fighting in a narrow tunnel, of course, but when Dahlia stabbed the staff diagonally into the water before her, Drizzt understood that she wanted her weapon to keep these slithering creatures as far from her as possible.

"They're not poisonous," Entreri replied. "They know they cannot swallow us and have no means to kill us. They'll likely retreat."

"Like the first one?" Dahlia sarcastically replied, and she backed down the corridor a few steps.

"You startled it. It attacked out of fear," Drizzt answered. He was a ranger, and well versed in the ways of the wilds. He moved forward—or started to, until a serpent threw itself through the air at him. Up flashed his arm to block, and he intercepted the snake's opened maw closing on his forearm, grabbing tight, its body immediately slapping around his torso as it tried to gain a hold and begin its crushing squeeze.

The strength of the creature surprised the drow, its every muscle working in perfect coordination. Noting movement to the side, he glanced at Entreri, at first thinking that the assassin was rushing to his aid. Not so, he understood, when he realized that Entreri had his own problems.

On came the strangely aggressive snakes, slithering through the water, sliding along the walls, throwing themselves through the air.

With a growl, Drizzt lifted his bitten left arm, extending the snake out before his right shoulder, turned and wriggled enough to free his other arm, and brought a quick backhand of Twinkle to cut the creature in half. Immediately, the lower torso loosened around him and dropped with a splash to the floor, but that head held on, stubbornly. Too concerned with drawing his other blade—a bit awkwardly since Icingdeath, which he usually carried in his right hand, was sheathed on his left hip—Drizzt let the half-serpent hang there.

His focus remained before him, as it had to, slapping, slashing, and kicking to fend off the onslaught.

Beside him, Entreri worked with equal fury, his dirk swiftly deflecting leaping serpents, his sword scoring kills.

But behind them, there came a long series of dull raps, and in one of the infrequent moments of pause, Drizzt glanced back, as did Entreri, to see Dahlia straddling the water, her staff presented horizontally before her and she rapidly shifted it up and down, out left and out right, cracking it against the stone walls.

"Hit the snakes, you idiot!" Entreri yelled at her, and he was nearly toppled at the end of that sentence as one of the serpents slithered through his defenses and wrapped around his legs, tugging him powerfully.

"Dahlia!" Drizzt implored her.

But the rapping continued and so did the onslaught of serpents—there seemed to be no end to them! Entreri freed himself only to get hit again, and Drizzt nearly had Icingdeath pulled from his grasp when one snake took hold.

The corridor began to flash, not from the waving of Drizzt's glowing scimitar, but with sharp spikes of light, crackles of lightning.

Entreri kept cursing at Dahlia and growling at the snakes, and swinging and stabbing and kicking. And just when Drizzt thought he had gained some measure of momentum, a serpent appeared on the ceiling before him. He threw himself back and low into a crouch and the snapping jaws rent the air, just missing his left ear. The snake retracted before his blade could decapitate it, then threw itself at him, slamming him hard and nearly knocking him from his feet.

To fall was to be overwhelmed, Drizzt knew. The water shimmied, alive with serpents.

"Dahlia!" he cried for help.

This time she answered him, not with words, but with thunder. She thrust Kozah's Needle through the water to slam against the floor, and there she released the energy her rapping had imbued within it. The retort jolted all three of them into the air, though all three held their footing as they landed. The water churned and sizzled, a stinky steam lifting from it so thickly that it obscured their vision.

Drizzt tried to respond, to say something, but found his jaw clenched from the energy pulsing through him.

Then it was over, as unexpectedly and abruptly as it had happened, and an eerie stillness replaced the fury of the previous moments.

Snakes dropped from the walls and ceiling, or hung in place, their lengths looped over a natural beam or a jag or jut. Snakes lay on the floor in various poses, like living runes or glyphs. Snakes floated in the water, sliding down to bump against a leg or foot.

Perhaps dead, perhaps stunned. That latter, very real possibility had Drizzt more than a little alarmed.

Beside him, Entreri slashed down on one reptile, and its convulsion as his blade struck home told the ranger that it had indeed been alive until cleaved.

"Be gone, and quickly!" Drizzt cried. "Leave them, there are too many!"

"Out the way we came!" Dahlia said.

"Alegni is that way," Entreri reminded, pointing ahead. "And it's shorter."

They didn't have time to think it through. They didn't have time to consider the unusual behavior of so many ordinary creatures. They simply had to react. Perhaps it was the carrot of Alegni, which Entreri had dangled before Dahlia, but whatever the reason, Drizzt was surprised when the woman splashed up behind him, prodding him and Entreri to move on.

He noted that Entreri crouched and reached into the water and pulled something forth before scrambling to pace him, but took no further note as the three zigzagged their way through a maze of stunned serpents.

Fortunately, the magical energy of Kozah's Needle had reached far enough along the corridor to get most of the snakes, and they passed beyond that point in short order, and even more fortunately, so they presumed, the corridor widened a bit more, and heightened, and they could press on with more urgency.

Except that they had to wait for a moment as Entreri pulled up to a rock and sat down, and only then did Drizzt understand what the assassin had stopped to retrieve from the water: one of his low boots.

Dahlia's jolt had lifted him right out of his shoe.

With a few muttered curses and a shake of his head, Entreri pulled the smoking boot back on and stood straight. He looked hard at Dahlia and said, "You owe me a new pair."

"I saved your life," she retorted.

"If you had just bothered to join in the fight, it wouldn't have needed any saving, would it?"

Again Drizzt watched the two and their verbal sparring with something less than amusement, but he couldn't really focus on it at that moment, because something about their encounter with the bed of serpents was now, in retrospect, truly bothering him.

"Why were all of those snakes exactly the same size?" he asked when they had started on their way again.

"Why wouldn't they be?" Dahlia asked.

"Snakes shed their skins and grow quickly, and continually," Drizzt explained.

"So they were all the same age," the elf woman replied, her tone showing that she hardly saw the point of this conversation.

Drizzt shook his head. "Snakes don't herd."

"That was a herd of snakes," Dahlia quickly retorted.

"A bed of snakes," the ranger corrected, but half-heartedly, for her point was well taken. Drizzt shook his head, not quite accepting it. Snakes did collect in the winter, of course—the drow had found many such dens in his travels, some containing thousands of the creatures. But he had never seen such a hunting pack as they had just encountered, and had never heard of a coordinated snake attack!

"Magically conjured?" Dahlia asked, and that sounded right to Drizzt, until Entreri chimed in.

"Babies."

"Babies?" Dahlia echoed doubtfully, stating the obvious, for how could a six-foot snake be a baby?

But it was the way Entreri had said it that had both Drizzt, and Dahlia, despite her argument, turning his way, then following his gaze.

To the mother.

In a small room lit by a single candle, Brother Anthus sat cross-legged on the bare floor. His eyes were closed, his hands resting on the cool stone beside his legs, palms facing upward. Softly, the monk chanted, moaned even, as he focused on his deep inhalation and exhalation, using that rising and falling movement of his belly to clear his swirling thoughts, to find a place of deep peace and emptiness.

This was his only refuge, and even it, at first, seemed not a place of serenity.

Should he travel to Waterdeep and alert the lords that the Netheril Empire was gaining a stronghold just north of them?

Images of that road, fleeting glimpses of the trouble he would have slipping away unnoticed, or of the consequences should Herzgo Alegni's many soldiers capture him before he got away, assailed him. And if he went, of course, he could not return to Neverwinter unless and until Alegni had been thrown down and the agents of Netheril routed.

One by one, Brother Anthus patted down those thoughts.

He felt the rise and fall of his belly.

And what of Arunika? Where had the woman found such strength as he had witnessed firsthand at her cottage? How could a small woman survive so casually outside the city walls, anyway? The region was full of wild things, and evil things, coordinated like the Thayans, or rogue bandits, goblinkin, or owlbears.

Brother Anthus saw the image of Arunika and gradually pushed it away.

He felt the rise and fall of his belly.

What did Herzgo Alegni think of him? Did the warlord even know who he was? And what of Jelvus Grinch—what of value might Anthus bring to Jelvus Grinch to get the man to properly introduce him to the Netherese warlord?

In his mind, Alegni and Grinch stood side by side, smiling back at him, but not a grin of friendship. More likely, he knew, they were mocking him and would allow him no ascent within the ranks of the city, for what of value might he offer, indeed?

But those two, too, receded, pushed back by the deepening emptiness of Brother Anthus.

He felt the rise and fall of his belly.

And that was all. There was no more. He had chased away the thoughts, the tumult, the uncertainty.

Now he simply was.

An empty vessel, at peace and contented, and the outside world didn't matter. Time didn't matter, and didn't register to him.

Just the rise and fall of his belly, the cool emptiness.

Then he felt the twinge.

It was not a memory, not an internal thought, not a question needing to be answered.

His belly rose softly, and the cool darkness of his mediation saw a flash, a flicker, an intrusion.

Brother Anthus had seen this before, of course, and now he fought hard to maintain his detachment, to mute the noise. This was a state of reception, with his involuntary filters and noise shut down. But it wasn't that easy, for he had felt this type of twinge before and he knew what it meant, and knew its source, generally, at least.

He had to stay in his purely receptive state to keep hearing it, he knew, but how could he, given the implications that he had heard it at all?

And if he followed that line of reasoning on those implications, and the potential, he would lose it all.

You are deceiving yourself, his thoughts scolded. You want it too badly.

But no, it was there, one more time, and he knew what it was.

The Sovereignty.

An aboleth!

Brother Anthus's belly rose and fell more quickly, then, as he began to gasp for breath. His eyes opened wide and he unwound his legs and quickly scrambled to his knees, hands coming before him in a motion of supplication.

Give me this, he silently prayed to his god, for he wanted the Sovereignty back, needed it back.

Mentally he reached out for the signal, but now his thoughts were spinning again, full of implications and possibilities.

Many heartbeats passed, and so desperate was Brother Anthus to hear the creature's telepathic music once more that he couldn't even register the pain the stones of the floor were causing to his bony knees.

"Please," he whispered aloud, then more insistently and loudly, "Please!"

He shook his head vigorously in denial against his growing fear that he had wanted this to happen so badly, he had tricked himself into hearing it. He struggled to his feet, his knees popping, and he staggered stiff-legged for the doorway to exit the small chamber.

He burst out into the temple's main chapel, holding the door jamb for support, his gaze wildly darting around the dimly candlelit room as if expecting a visitor to be waiting for him.

But it was just him in the chapel. And now, too, it was just him, alone in his thoughts.

Denying that obvious reality, with his eyes wet with tears, Anthus rushed for the outer door. "Please!" he said over and over again, and he stumbled out onto the street, wearing nothing but his loincloth, in the cold air and sparkling stars of a late autumn Neverwinter night.

Brother Anthus wandered the streets aimlessly, begging and pleading, crying and wailing, shaking his fist and shouting of betrayal, and whether out of fear that the man had gone mad, or simply through lack of care, not a shade or a citizen went to retrieve him.

More than once, he thought he heard the sweet sound of an aboleth's voice again, though it seemed to be about him and not directed at him, and Anthus folded up and fell to his knees once more, right in the middle of a wide, four-way intersection.

Apparently oblivious of his surroundings, of the many curious gazes that came his way, Brother Anthus began to chant.

He felt the rise and fall of his belly.

"I need more," Herzgo Alegni implored the red blade. He had felt a sensation, a flicker, a feeling that his assassin was somewhere around, not too far. Claw's hold on the man known as Barrabus was, in truth, limited, and was curtailed even more by distance. Fortunately for Alegni, the dangerous little man had never caught on to this truth.

In those situations that truly mattered, where Barrabus wanted to strike out against Alegni, Claw was quite effective. It could warn of, and react to, Barrabus the Gray's strikes before Barrabus the Gray ever made them. The span of time between thinking of a strike and executing it was exceedingly small to an outside observer. But Claw observed from the inside, and those fleeting fractions of a heartbeat were much longer within the universe of thought in which Claw resided.

The sword didn't answer Alegni's call just then, and that brought a frown to the hulking tiefling's red-skinned and devilish face.

"Where is he?" the warlord asked directly. "Where is your slave?"

In reply, the tiefling was given the impression that Barrabus was near, but he felt something else, then, something more.

In the distance, Alegni heard screaming, a desperate plea of "Please!" shouted over and over again in the Neverwinter night. He dismissed it as unimportant— likely one of the new shade soldiers had encountered one of the pathetic citizens, to bad end for the citizen. He focused once more on the red-bladed sword and this other sensation.

There was energy in the air, he understood. Telepathic energy.

Herzgo Alegni leaned back in the chair on his balcony, suddenly concerned. The idea of Barrabus—Artemis Entreri—coming back into the city didn't bother him at all, even if the man was accompanied by Dahlia and that drow ranger who had joined by her side. To Alegni, they might prove an inconvenience, but more likely an opportunity. Not Dahlia, of course. She would have to be captured and tortured, and likely killed, but as long as he held this sword, Barrabus couldn't hurt him. Of that Alegni was sure.

But what of this other power? He was sensing it now because Claw was sensing it. What might it be? Who or what was coming to threaten his hold on Neverwinter?

He got nothing more from the sword, then, and eventually gave up and slid the red blade back into its loop on his belt. He considered going to Effron— surely a necromancer would be more attuned to such mystical energies as he had sensed—but only briefly, for how could Alegni be sure that the source of this energy was not the twisted warlock himself?

In the end, the tiefling simply sighed and let it go. He glanced at the decorated pommel of his wondrous sword, and wondered if he had even really sensed something external to Claw at all. Perhaps it had been Claw's energies, reaching out in search of Barrabus, that he had inadvertently intercepted. He looked out at the wider city, at the multitude of checkpoints and sentry positions he had enacted about Neverwinter. Barrabus and his new friends, if they were indeed Barrabus's allies, weren't getting past that wall without Alegni knowing about it.

He scanned the darkened city, eyes roving from firelight to firelight, torch to torch. Nothing seemed amiss or out of the ordinary.

Alegni nodded, satisfied, collected his sword and the boots he had just removed, and went back into his room, hoping to get a half-night's sleep before the dawn.

The huge serpent, its body as thick as a large man's chest, lifted its massive head off the floor to stare into the eyes of the three invaders to its sewer realm.

"Fan out," Drizzt told his companions, Entreri to the right of him, Dahlia to his left. "Widen out. We have to flank that maw."

He ended with a gasp as the giant snake head snapped at him, lightning fast. His first thought was to block with his blades, but how ridiculous that notion seemed to him in the face of the opened maw, a mouth large enough to swallow him whole, flying at him with the power of a charging horse! Instinct took over and the drow desperately dodged aside, and the air rippled as the snake head snapped past him so powerfully that the shock alone nearly knocked Drizzt from his feet. He held his balance, but the snake recoiled too quickly for the drow to strike it on its retreat.

"We cannot fight that," Dahlia whispered, and Drizzt caught more than pragmatism in her defeated tone, and when he glanced at the fighter, at this elf who reveled in battle, he saw her arms slipping down helplessly, as if in surrender.

He looked back to the giant snake, to the huge head swerving tantalizingly side to side, to the black eyes looking back at him, looking right through him, mocking him with their power.

Many heartbeats passed. It occurred to Drizzt more than once that Dahlia was correct here, that they couldn't fight this great creature. The snake was far above them, far too great a foe.

And it didn't want to kill them.

That truth seemed obvious, and made perfect sense—until Drizzt managed to step back from the obviousness and actually think about it.

Only then did the drow widen his view around the great serpent, to see a half-dozen other people flanking the snake, contentedly.

Contentedly.

There they were, human citizens of Neverwinter, along with a pair of Shadovar, all unarmed and standing beside the serpent as if it was their friend.

Or master.

Drizzt glanced left and right. Dahlia had dropped Kozah's Needle, and stood shaking her head helplessly, and Entreri, perhaps the most fearless man Drizzt had ever met, a warrior who only got angrier and more ferocious when faced with a seemingly hopeless situation, rolling his sword and dirk nervously and hardly even looking at the giant creature.

Drizzt knew then that there was no need to fight this creature. Indeed, they couldn't hope to win, or even survive, if they engaged in such a futile battle. Nay, the better course was to simply surrender to its obvious godlike qualities, to accept the reality of their inferiority and live happily beside this living deity.

There would be pleasure and peace.

Drizzt felt his scimitars slipping down by his sides. He was lost. All was lost.

Her thoughts were pried open and flying free.

Dahlia recognized this, but it seemed natural, and the intimacy created in such a shared moment seemed somehow warm and inviting. This creature before her, this god, understood her. It saw her deepest pain and greatest fears. It stripped her naked before it, for it and all to see, and there, open and without secret, she felt . . . free.

This was no enemy.

This was salvation!

Her pain lay bare before her, the rape, her guilt, her terrifying and evil choice to murder her child, the source of her rage, the multitude of dead lovers—and wouldn't Drizzt sit atop that pile of corpses?

Or wouldn't he be strong enough to kill her instead, and free her? That was the point, after all!

But perhaps, she realized now, she didn't need that extreme, that suicide-by-lover approach to ending her pain.

Perhaps the answer was here, before her, within reach, in the dark eyes of this knowing, brilliant creature.

His thoughts were pried open and flying free.

Entreri recognized this, but it seemed natural, and the intimacy created in such a shared moment seemed somehow warm and inviting. This creature before him, this god, understood him. It saw his deepest pain and greatest fears. It stripped him naked before it, for it and all to see, and there, open and without secret, he felt . . . free.

This was no enemy.

This was salvation!

Entreri, ever guarded, instinctively recoiled, though. How could he not? He, who had lived a life of lies, even from himself, he who had lived in the shadows of fabrication and denial, suddenly found an abrupt reversal—and not just from this creature, as he had with Charon's Claw, but opened to all within the collective "family" the creature was now offering to him.

His guards went up without a conscious thought to them.

His memories floated before him anyway: the childhood betrayal by his mother, the ultimate betrayal of his uncle and those others, the dirt of Calimport's streets.

He felt a violation, as he had known as a child, of the most intimate and damaging sort. He faced it again, or tried to, but he realized something . . . something quite unexpected.

Entreri lost his own contemplations to a moment of surprise, and glanced over at Dahlia, and she at him.

Naked, joined, with no place to hide.

His thoughts were pried open and flying free.

Unlike his companions, though, Drizzt Do'Urden knew this type of intrusion, and recognized almost immediately the subtle trickery, the willing slavery.

During his days wandering the Underdark, after abandoning Menzoberranzan, Drizzt had been seduced in just such a manner—logical promises and wondrous carefree visions of life in Paradise—by the illithids, the wretched mind flayers. Obediently and lovingly, Drizzt and his companions had massaged the hive mind of the illithid community.

He had traveled this same road before, had fallen victim to it, his identity stolen away. Determined never to face such slavery again, Drizzt had trained himself to resist—with a wall of anger. In light of that terrible experience, it wasn't hard for Drizzt to build that wall once more, almost instantly.

He slowly and subtly reached into his pouch and grasped the onyx figurine, quietly calling for Guenhwyvar, and like his subdued companions, he lowered his blades and began to walk slowly and unthreateningly toward the mesmerizing beast. Every step proved a labor, for the intrusion was strong here, truly powerful. Drizzt had learned painfully how to battle it, and still he doubted he could resist.

Or perhaps even worse, that he could resist without tipping his hand.

He saw the many images floating around him, and had he found a moment free of the demands of discipline, he might have been surprised to glimpse the deep secrets of his companions, particularly those of Dahlia, particularly the one that had him lying dead atop a pile of the corpses of former lovers.

But to go there and take in the view would have meant that his thoughts, too, floated free, and thus, that he, too, would be trapped by the telepathic web.

He stayed behind the wall, strengthened it with every step. He remembered his terrible experience with the illithids. Only one thing had saved him then.

He felt himself beginning to slip, felt the tendrils of another mind, this godlike snake's mind, reaching into his deepest thoughts.

He thought of Catti-brie and Bruenor, of Belwar and of Clacker, of Zaknafein and of Regis and Wulfgar, of lost friends and those who had given him his identity. This intruder would steal all of his memories, he told himself repeatedly, strengthening the wall of anger.

For without those memories, Drizzt Do'Urden had nothing.

His walk slowed to a halt, his blades dipped because he could not raise them. Out of the periphery of his vision, left and right, he noted that Entreri and Dahlia had begun eyeing him suspiciously, even threateningly.

This deity had recognized his resistance and his deception, he knew, and would turn his own companions upon him.

"No!" Drizzt yelled, one last act of defiance, and he fell back and forced his blades to the ready. Both Dahlia and Entreri turned on him, weapons moving as if to strike, and Drizzt had to face the possibility of killing his lover, and of killing Entreri, this one tie to a past he desperately missed. It all happened so quickly, though, that those thoughts barely registered as anything more than fleeting regrets, and purely on instinct, the drow struck hard, Twinkle backhanding away a stab of Kozah's Needle, Icingdeath keeping Entreri at bay.

He could win, for they were not fighting as Entreri and Dahlia, but as controlled shells of those magnificent warriors, as mere pawns to the god-snake.

He could not win, he realized immediately after, for in addition to these two, there remained the other slaves, and worse, the giant snake itself, a foe he doubted he could beat.

A foe he knew he could not beat.

A foe so far beyond him that it mocked him for even thinking he could defeat it, or even resist it!

The subtle web closed in as Entreri and Dahlia backed off, and Drizzt lost again, and would be lost, fully so, as he had been to the illithids as a young rogue, a century before.

All the discipline, all the rage, could not win.

Not against a god.

Besides, Drizzt then realized, life would be good in the service of this all-knowing creature. Life would be peace and calm and satisfaction in seeing to his master's needs.

He sighed and let down his guard before the great snake . . .

He was the first of the slaves to cry out a warning as the black form of Guenhwyvar leaped atop that huge creature. Drizzt shrieked first in outrage and then again in surprise as he saw that the snake wasn't a snake at all, but a fishlike, horrid looking thing, and how it screamed, both in an audible watery voice and in Drizzt's mind—so brutally in his mind that it knocked him from his feet, to join Dahlia, Entreri, and the others on the wet floor.

There was a giant snake, lying dead to the side, and this strange creature had taken its identity and place and image. But no more. Guenhwyvar's attack had stripped away that illusion, leaving a creature that appeared far less formidable.

Drizzt leaped up immediately and charged, pausing only long enough to knock Entreri aside and kick the staff from Dahlia's hands, for he knew then that he was free, but did not know if the others had broken from their bonds.

Certainly the six slaves who had accompanied this strange creature had not thrown aside their allegiance. A pair of humans scrambled and leaped for Guenhwyvar, who kicked out with a rear claw, driving them both away, cutting one grotesquely, chin to shoulder.

The other four charged past to intercept Drizzt, who spun to his right, coming around to plant the pommel of a scimitar right on the nose of one pursuing man, dropping him in a heap. He didn't want to kill this group, understanding that they did not act of their own will, but when a shade following that human leaped in with a deadly sword thrust, Drizzt's instincts had him parrying and responding before he had even realized the instinctive riposte. He did shorten his strike, taking the shade under the ribs but not driving the blade home, but when that didn't even slow the attacker, who apparently felt no pain in his possessed state, Drizzt had no choice but to strike again, harder and repeatedly.

He had no time to dawdle, and down went the shade, and when the human stubbornly rose against him once more, the drow laid him low by cutting his legs out from under him with a great swipe of his scimitars. He tried not to dig in the blades too deeply, and winced with a bit of regret, but could do little than that when he saw the blood spilling.

Hoping that he had inflicted no permanent damage, Drizzt joined Guenhwyvar at the aboleth—for indeed, this was one of those strange and little-understood creatures, a young aboleth left behind by the Sovereignty as a sentry and scout for a place they had not abandoned forever.

Drizzt struck hard and he struck fast, and even more so when he rolled around the fishlike beast and caught a glimpse back at his friends. Guenhwyvar's attack had freed them, and the two of them worked brilliantly and ferociously against the remaining slaves. Drizzt tried to keep his focus on the creature before him. It was physically weak, true, but with the potential to fell him, or paralyze him at least, with one suggestion. He had to keep his mental guards up and had to drive his blades home quickly.

He couldn't help but grimace when Dahlia, flails spinning in perfect coordination, came face to face with one of the Shadovar slaves. He knew what was coming, and could only look away, renew his focus on the aboleth, as Dahlia's deadly weapons cracked repeatedly against the slave's skull, tearing skin and cracking bone, and bashing the shade's brains to pulp.

Entreri was no more merciful, reminding Drizzt keenly of the true disposition of this man he viewed as a link to his past, shattering any nostalgic notions floated before him by the reappearance of his old nemesis. The drow gasped audibly when Entreri's sword came right through the torso of one human slave, stabbing out the man's back. Entreri retracted the blade almost instantly, but fell into a sudden spin that brought it back around and down, across the falling man's throat.

Even with the threat defeated, the vicious Artemis Entreri could not resist that killing blow.

Too many doubts pressed in on Drizzt then, doubts about his road and his companions, but he pushed them away, even told himself that these were mere implantations by the insidious psychic beast. He turned that disappointment, rage even, into more focused anger on his oppressor, the aboleth.

Down came Twinkle with a smash, crunching bone, and down came a stabbing Icingdeath right behind, plunging through that opening to find the creature's brain.

Always the brain, the source of the beast's strength.

Drizzt leaped astride the struggling, flopping creature, alternately plunging his scimitars into the opening, and when one went in deep, the drow turned his wrist and slid it out to the side, left and right, severing the internal connections.

He saw the remaining slave, a Shadovar, rushing at him in a last desperate attempt to save its beloved master.

But too late. Guenhwyvar continued to tear and rend and Drizzt's blades found their mark.

The aboleth flopped to the stone fully, and lay deathly still.

The approaching Shadovar skidded to a stop and stared at Drizzt in abject confusion, and the drow immediately wondered if he might have found an ally in their quest to get past Alegni's defenses; he could well understand the profound sense of gratitude anyone in such a state of slavery might feel toward his rescuers.

Before Drizzt could even explore that, though, before he could even further study the Shadovar's face for hints, he was distracted by a form rushing up from behind the freed slave.

"Dahlia, no!" he shouted, but between his words came the crack of Dahlia's flail spinning in from the side to cave in the Shadovar's skull. That powerful strike alone would likely have proven fatal, but Dahlia left little to doubt as she followed with a barrage of heavy blows.

"Did you even pause to consider that he might have supplied us with important information?" Drizzt asked the elf.

Dahlia seemed unimpressed. She looked down at the dead Shadovar and spat on him for effect. "He's a Netherese dog," she said, as if that explained everything. "He would have simply lied to us anyway."

"He might have known Alegni's defenses," Drizzt argued. "We do not know how long he was enslaved . . ."

"What's done is done," Entreri said. When Drizzt and Dahlia glanced his way, he motioned to two of the humans, the one Drizzt had dropped and one other. They were both alive, though wounded, but neither injury appeared mortal. A third, too, seemed alive, though her wounds looked far more grievous.

Drizzt pulled off his pack and rushed to the wounded woman first. He produced some bandages and a poultice of mixed and mashed herbs and quickly stemmed the blood flow. As soon as he had the bleeding under control, he looked to his companions, both staring at him incredulously.

"Tend to the others!" he scolded.

"They attacked us," Dahlia reminded.

"The . . . that creature attacked us, through them," Drizzt retorted. "Tend to them!"

Dahlia glanced at Entreri skeptically, and to Drizzt's dismay, it seemed that Dahlia was being more stubborn and less merciful than Artemis Entreri.

"Tend to them or we—or I—will remain with them," Drizzt warned, and that broke the stalemate. He threw his pack to Entreri.

Six individuals started along the tunnels a short while later, the two minimally wounded humans, a man and a woman, half-carrying, half-dragging their other female companion in a makeshift litter Drizzt had constructed from a cloak and the bones of the fishlike creature that had enslaved them. They were citizens of Neverwinter, or had been.

"I was raised outside of Luskan," the woman, Genevieve by name, explained to Drizzt as they walked. "My family farmed there."

She went on to describe the fall of that region, but Drizzt already knew the sad tale well.

"Did you know a family Stuyles?" he asked.

"Aye, the name sounds familiar," Genevieve replied. "But 'twas a long time ago. I been here many years. Before the ruin."

"But you survived," Drizzt said, and he looked to Entreri as he did, and the assassin wore an expression of interest, at least.

"We all did," the man on the other side of the litter replied. "Because of that thing back there."

"Aye, we been down here for years and years," Genevieve added. She winced and seemed quite pained as she tried to sort it all out. "A couple of times after the ruin, we went up. To spy, I expect, though I hardly remember it."

"Seems like you'd make a fine spy, then," Entreri said sarcastically.

"Was the fish creature looking through us," she explained. "Oh, but it could do that. It could do almost anything."

"Killed the great snake and controlled her brood with little trouble," the man added.

"They *were* babies, then," Drizzt remarked, and he shuddered to think that Neverwinter's sewer might soon be home to a thriving community of gigantic constrictors!

He left the trio, then, to rejoin his companions at the lead.

Drizzt wanted to speak with Entreri on that journey, to help him to recognize the intrusion for what it was, to learn from the dominance of the aboleth so that he might use those lessons as he tried to resist any such dominance from his old sword. But the drow found that he couldn't talk to the man at that time, or to Dahlia, and he quickly fell back, following the three wounded humans, helping them where he could, while Entreri and Dahlia led the way, the assassin once more holding half of Dahlia's staff to ward against any unwanted intrusions. They didn't need Twinkle's glow any longer, for the sun was rising outside, and peeking in at enough junctures—through cracks up above, or grates—to provide enough light for the two, with their lowlight vision, to navigate.

They chatted as they walked, and Drizzt could catch only bits and pieces of their conversation, which frustrated him even more. After only a few twists and turns in the sewer, even those pieces of conversation were lost to him, drowned out by the sound of flowing water, for they were then paralleling the river, very nearby.

Still he watched them, feeling very distant to them, so suddenly.

Feeling very lost.

"Soon," Entreri whispered to Dahlia, up in front of the others.

Dahlia looked at him curiously, not quite understanding. Was he talking about them getting out of the sewers soon? Perhaps, but she suspected something more, particularly given the strange intermingling of personal secrets.

Entreri nodded, and there was so much in that simple gesture, a recognition of things far deeper than the practical implications of the single word he had spoken.

"Soon," he was saying, meaning that Dahlia would find a proper resolution "soon."

"Soon," he was saying, as if to indicate that some moment of peace was "soon" before her.

"Soon." He was hinting, Dahlia understood, that the resolution of her greatest tragedy and greatest moment . . .

The elf warrior looked away, not willing to let him see the moisture in her blue eyes, not willing to let this stranger, this former, and perhaps still, adversary, look into her soul yet again.

Or was it just shame?

CHAPTER 9

THE FOOTHOLD

THEY OWNED THE FORGE.

That stunning notion hovered around Ravel Xorlarrin's shoulders as he made his way to his scheduled meeting with his sisters and some of the other leaders of the expedition.

They owned the forge.

The other chambers they had taken since entering the Gauntlgrym complex had offered them hope, both in the joyous shock of realizing their destination in the first place and in coming to know that they could build some measure of security and defense against the stubborn ghostly guardians of the ancient dwarf homeland. But none of that would have mattered one bit without the grand prize.

They owned the forge.

Ravel had to hold back his elation as he entered that very room, the ancient forge of Gauntlgrym, to face the gathering. He met the eyes of each, starting with Berellip, who sat grim-faced, and moving quickly to Saribel, whose clear uneasiness showed the cracks in their meaner sister's unrelenting glare. Saribel understood the gravity of this moment, and she understood, obviously, that the victory was Ravel's most of all.

The poor priestess didn't seem to know how to react, and she was simply not as skilled as Berellip in covering everything up with anger.

Emboldened by Saribel's quandary, Ravel glanced at Tiago, who sat beside Jearth, and there he found allies. Tiago even nodded and smiled.

If his sisters' unease had bolstered him, the salute from House Baenre had him standing even taller.

Behind the two weapons masters, the drider Yerrininae squatted on eight bent legs, and he, too, seemed eager—and why wouldn't he be, for this was the promise to an existence with dignity and possibility.

They owned the forge.

Ravel paced slowly past the group, including the other House wizards and a few of the more important melee squad leaders, on his way to the nearest in the line of actual forges, a large firebrick oven, taller than Ravel. To the drow warrior, it looked like any other forge, but he had been told differently, and he understood now as he examined the oven.

There was no place to load fuel to burn.

Behind the forge loomed what seemed like a chimney, stretching floor to ceiling, of thick bricks, mortared with workmanship so amazing that the centuries seemed to not have touched them. After a cursory glance at the loading and cooling trays, Ravel found himself drawn to this chimney. He ran his hands along the stone, feeling the integrity.

He looked down the length of the large chamber, the row of similar forges, the line of similar chimneys.

"Untouched by the millennia," he said, coming around to face the group once more.

"They will need minor repairs, likely," Yerrininae replied. "But yes."

"Where is Brack'thal?" Berellip interjected, her tone sharp, unyielding and prideful, as always.

Ravel smiled, the look of a displacer beast as it closed in on its prey, and moved toward the group, looking to his fellow wizards.

"Have you figured out the workings?" he asked.

"We've found the source," the spellspinner started to reply, but was cut short by Berellip.

"Where is Brack'thal?" she demanded.

"He is doing his job," Ravel curtly replied.

"He should be among us."

"The perimeter chambers must be secured before our work begins in earnest," Ravel countered. "That is no small task."

"It is a task for that one," Berellip replied, pointing to Jearth. "And his Baenre friend. And the driders—why are they even here?"

Tiago laughed aloud at the priestess's flustered pronouncements, and Ravel understood that he had done so for Ravel's benefit. Yes, the Xorlarrin son had a powerful ally here, and one who would not blink before Berellip's intimidating glare.

"My dear sister, I am Xorlarrin," Ravel replied. He looked to Jearth and bowed in what seemed like an apology as he finished, "I would not trust such a critical duty to a mere warrior."

For a moment, he thought Berellip might swallow her lips, so tight did her face become.

"Nor would I trouble you and your priestesses, who have far more important duties in ensuring that this place, this city of Xorlarrin, will prove suitable to the goddess we all hold dear," he added, looking more to Tiago, who nodded his approval.

For the time being, Ravel had disarmed his sister.

"We have much to do," Jearth interjected. "My scouts have assured me that this complex is huge, even without the miles and miles of mines running beneath and beside it. There are other groups here in addition to our forces and the stubborn dwarf ghosts. We have found dire corbies—they will need to be cleaned out."

"Seems a minor distraction," said the usually quiet Saribel, and her look to Berellip as she spoke tipped Ravel off to her true purpose, that of pleasing their dominant sister.

"Many of the interesting chambers we have discovered are unsound," Jearth went on with hesitation, for he, like Ravel, had perfected the art of ignoring the annoying Saribel. "This place was wracked by the cataclysm of recent years. There may be untold treasures and secrets lying around, defenses we might put to our use, side chambers that will provide better quarters for the nobles."

Saribel moved as if to interject, but Jearth pressed on before her. "There may be a source for these bothersome ghosts, as well, a temple to a dwarf god, and that we cannot abide in any place House Xorlarrin might come to call home."

The younger of the Xorlarrin sisters slumped back at that remark.

"We have much to do," Jearth reiterated, and there would be no arguments coming forth in reply.

"Yes, much," Ravel agreed, and he glanced down the line of forges to the great and huge oven that centered the room's rear wall. "And first we must discover how to fire these ovens." He wore a sly look as he made the comment, hinting that he knew more than he was letting on, which, of course, he did.

"The source is nearby," Berellip said. "It must be, along with the fuel . . ."

"The source is there," Ravel said, pointing to the wall near the large forge, to an archway which they had not explored, as the passage it indicated had been bricked up and sealed.

"How can you know?"

"I am a spellspinner," Ravel replied. "You do not believe that a pile of stones could block my way, do you?"

He focused on Tiago, the most important one in his audience, and watched the young Baenre warrior, obviously intrigued, glance from the archway back to him and back again.

"Are you to keep us waiting?" Berellip asked angrily after many heartbeats slipped past in silence.

"To explain what lies beyond would not do it justice, I fear," said Ravel. "Assemble a team of goblin diggers to clear the tunnel—it is not long—and let us travel together to better appreciate our good fortune." He glanced at Jearth and nodded, and the weapons master moved off immediately to gather some slaves.

As the informal meeting disbanded, Tiago found his way to Ravel's side. "You have raised expectations," he said quietly. "Do not disappoint, lest you return the upper hand to your sister. And that, we cannot have."

"Disappoint?" Ravel echoed incredulously. "Behind that wall lies a god. A trapped god. The power of Gauntlgrym."

Tiago grinned. "The fire beast?"

"The primordial," Ravel confirmed. "The fire beast my matron mother determined as the source of the cataclysm. Indeed it exists, right before us, trapped as it has been for millennia." He paused as his grin widened even more. "So near the magical forge."

Tiago's look, his responding smile as he stared at the distant archway, showed his appreciation of this moment. Across Faerûn, the weapons of ancient Gauntlgrym had remained legendary for their craftsmanship and imbued powers; even those who refused to admit the existence of this rumored dwarf homeland could only dispute the origin, and not the wonder, of those ancient artifacts.

"I will have the first two master items created when the forges are re-fired," Tiago said.

"That was part of our deal, so you have informed me," Ravel replied with only a hint of sarcasm. "Your servants have brought the needed materials, I assume."

Still looking at the archway, at the promise, the young Baenre nodded. "If one would consider Gol'fanin a servant."

That had Ravel back on his heels! "Gol'fanin?"

"You have traveled from Menzoberranzan to one of the most famed forges of the ancient world. Please do tell me that you, a mage of high reputation, are too intelligent to be surprised by this revelation."

Put that way, of course, Tiago was right. But Ravel found himself indeed surprised, more by the planning that had gone into this expedition from the Baenre side than by the secret accompaniment by one of Menzoberranzan's most accomplished blacksmiths. Suddenly the spellspinner found himself doubting every detail of this expedition, even that it was an undertaking of House Xorlarrin. How much influence, how much subterfuge, had House Baenre exerted here?

"You understand that this part of my bargain with you will come at a great cost to me," Ravel said when he managed to properly compose himself. "With Jearth, I mean."

"You understand that I don't care," came the instant response, a reply surely worthy of a Baenre.

The chamber thrummed with energy and waves of heat rose from the oblong pit that dominated the room. That heat was overwhelmed, however, by the mist in the air, and the low fog that clung to the stones.

Standing at the edge of that pit, Ravel and the others could not but appreciate the sheer power of the beast below: a frothing, roiling, primordial power chewing stones into lava and burping gouts of heavy slag upward.

But no less impressive was the containment of that volcanic monster, a cyclone of thick watery power spinning around the sides of the pit from the lip all the way down to the primordial. More water ran down continually from the high ceiling, thin lines, perhaps, but no doubt keeping the equilibrium of the room intact.

"Elementals," Brack'thal Xorlarrin breathed. "Scores of them."

Ravel looked at his older brother skeptically, but did not challenge his words. He knew better than to do so, for Brack'thal was a student of the old schools of magic, primarily engaged in summoning this very type of beast to his side. His powers had decreased tremendously with the Spellplague and the fall of Mystra's Weave, but in his day, he had often been seen wandering the ways of Menzoberranzan, a watery or fiery companion at his side and leaving a trail of droplets or smoke through the streets.

The younger spellspinner looked to his sister as Brack'thal finished, and Berellip merely nodded, seeming unsurprised. Only then did Ravel come to fully comprehend why Matron Zeerith had insisted that he take Brack'thal along on the expedition, and why Berellip had recalled him from his other duties as the tunnel to this room was being cleared by the goblin slaves.

Once again, as with his last conversation with Tiago, the young spellspinner felt as if he were standing on sand rather than stone. So much of this expedition, *his* expedition, seemed to be comprised of people plotting around him and above him. Why hadn't Matron Zeerith simply explained to him why she thought Brack'thal might prove to be a worthy addition? Why hadn't Tiago Baenre simply explained to him the presence of Gol'fanin, so that the blacksmith might walk openly among the ranks, in a position of proper respect and station, instead of as a mere commoner?

Ravel looked into the pit, down through the cyclonic watery turmoil to the fiery eye of the godlike beast, and laughed at his own foolishness. Why? Because they were drow, after all, and knowledge was power, and power was not, was never, to be willingly shared!

"They are done," he heard Berellip say, and when he looked up, he realized that she was speaking directly to him. She guided his gaze down to the right, where a stone bridge had once stood. With giant mushroom planks hauled along from the deeper Underdark, goblin and orc workers had already reconstructed a walkway across the pit. It was comprised only of four long and thick pieces, interlocked so that it was triple thick in the middle and singular at either end.

Saribel had overseen the project, along with Jearth, and now the two prodded a group of heavy bugbears across the walkway, testing its integrity. It didn't even bow.

Tiago Baenre and one of his "servants," who was, of course, really Gol'fanin, joined the Xorlarrins in their march across the way, to a low archway and a second, much smaller chamber set with a single large lever in its floor. Blood stains showed on the handle.

"These are not so old," Saribel said of the stains after casting a minor divination.

"Someone put the primordial back in its hole," Brack'thal announced, and all eyes turned his way.

He peered back under the archway and pointed up toward the high ceiling over the fiery pit, where water continued to flow into the primordial chamber. Then he pointed back at the lever. "This released the elementals into their guardian position."

"You cannot know that," Berellip said, but Brack'thal continued to nod against her doubts.

"I have already seen the channels that bring them in, like great roots throughout the tunnels of Gauntlgrym," the elder wizard replied. He pointed to the lever again. "The primordial is contained. Someone has completed our major task for us."

"Need we free the beast again to refire the forges, then?" asked Tiago.

Five sets of Xorlarrin eyes stared at him incredulously, and even his "servant," old Gol'fanin, dared a bit of a laugh at his expense.

"If you intend to do so, then please alert me first," Brack'thal said, "that I might be well on my way to Menzoberranzan to inform your Matron Mother Quenthel that we found Gauntlgrym, but you decided to blow it up."

Tiago straightened. Tiago was not amused.

A sudden look of panic crossed Brack'thal Xorlarrin's face, as he realized, as everyone around him realized, that he had gone too far in mocking the proud Baenre. "There will be another room, another control," he stammered, "to channel power to the forges. For surely this beast is the source of their legendary powers—what else could it be?"

"Then find it," Tiago said evenly, and he didn't blink. Had he leaped over then and lopped off Brack'thal's head, no one in the small room would have been the least bit surprised.

"Now," he added when Brack'thal hesitated and dared look away from him to Berellip.

Berellip wisely nodded, but Brack'thal was already moving anyway, out of the room and across the mushroom stalk bridge.

Tiago followed soon after, motioning for Gol'fanin to follow, and casting a stern and threatening glance Ravel's way as he went.

"Cursed Baenres," Saribel muttered with open contempt when he was out of the primordial chamber.

In his thoughts, Ravel Xorlarrin felt the floor shift under his feet just a little bit more.

They found the second room soon after, as Brack'thal had predicted, beneath a secret panel in the flooring of one of the forges in the line. This particular forge was not a forge at all, but a clever disguise to hide the sub-chamber.

It didn't take the skilled blacksmith, Gol'fanin, long to decipher the multitude of levers, cranks, and wheels in the steamy room. Each group of three led to one of the forges in the long line, and a combination of throwing a lever switch and turning the crank and wheel would determine how much of the primordial's heat and sheer energy would be allowed into the respective forge. A double set of larger controls across from the others was obviously for the main forge.

"Fire up the minor ovens first," Gol'fanin advised Ravel, who joined him, Jearth and Tiago in the lower chamber. "One at a time and slowly. That will reveal to us how contained the primordial beast truly might be."

Ravel looked to Jearth first, his grin telling, and Jearth, after a brief shake of his head, could only return the look.

"No," the spellspinner said. "The main forge will be the first fired."

"We do not know if the chimney to that forge and through that forge is intact," Gol'fanin argued. "It would be best to allow any escape of primordial power through a narrower chamber, would it not?"

"In the short term, perhaps," said Ravel. "But I prefer to gain an advantage where I find it."

"And if a substantial portion of primordial energy is released to wreak havoc?" Tiago asked.

"We blame Brack'thal," Ravel replied without hesitation.

"He takes the blame, but you take the credit," Tiago remarked.

"As it should be," said Ravel, and he started for the metal ladder leading back to the forge room. He paused before the first rung, though, and turned back on the others. "Not a word of this," he said.

"I like you more than I like Berellip, though that bar is, admittedly, low," Tiago replied.

"And I need the main forge," Gol'fanin added.

They all assembled in the forge room soon after, more than a hundred dark elves and even a few of the driders.

Ravel nodded to Gol'fanin, having decided to let the blacksmith have the honors, though few knew the true identity of Tiago's "servant." The older drow stooped low, entered the oven of the false forge, and climbed down the ladder.

Moments later, the forge room reverberated with a series of bangs and even small explosions, and the sound of heavy stones sliding across each other.

A gasp beside Ravel turned his gaze to the main forge, and the sudden glow that shined deep in its thick recesses. The spellspinner licked his lips and moved closer as the flames within began to mount. He bent low, but stood up straight in surprise when he noted several small, impish creatures of pure fire begin dancing within the forge.

And several became a score, and a score became a thousand, and all the room gasped loudly as the light and warmth poured forth, many drow shielding their sensitive eyes. And it was more than the light and the strength of the flames that had brought the response, for Ravel felt it clearly: There was magical energy in there. It wasn't just a fire that needed no fuel, wasn't just a hotter fire that could better melt all alloys. No, this fire was different. This fire was truly alive, magically alive, with a thousand elementals ready to lend their magical energies to any implements created within.

Returned from the sub-chamber, Tiago Baenre came up beside the mesmerized spellspinner, Gol'fanin close behind.

"Is it what you expected?" Ravel managed to ask Gol'fanin.

"Beyond," the old blacksmith breathed.

"My weapons will be the envy of Menzoberranzan," Tiago remarked, and Ravel glanced at him, then at Gol'fanin, whose awe-stricken expression showed that he did not disagree with that statement.

Ravel instinctively glanced across the way, to Jearth, and wondered what price he might have to pay for his bargain with Tiago.

"This is working as designed," Gol'fanin said, drawing him back. "Quite ingenious and perfect in its simplicity. The primordial hungers to be free, and so it embraces these channels, these little specks of freedom. It gives a bit of its life to those pieces that escape to the forge oven, and look how they dance!"

"And the lines are holding?" Ravel asked.

Gol'fanin gave a noncommittal shrug. "The valves are open, though not fully. If the primordial could break free, it would do so—would likely have already done so."

"And the other forges," Ravel prompted. "We must fire them."

"One at a time until we are certain of their integrity," the blacksmith advised.

"See to it," Ravel answered. He waved Jearth over to join them. Brack'thal came, too, which Ravel did not question. Indeed, at that time and with what was before them, perhaps even his idiot brother might prove of some worth.

"Explain to them what they might need do if any of the forges fail," Ravel instructed Tiago, though both knew he was really addressing Gol'fanin, who seemed to understand what was going on better than anyone.

Most of the drow and all of the driders were dismissed then, back to their work in the other halls, exploring, flushing out ghosts and other unwanted creatures, and fortifying the defenses, and throughout the rest of that long day, the forges of Gauntlgrym flickered to life, one after another. Only one of the two-score in the room had any problems initially, and a host of tiny elementals found their way into the room and caused quite a commotion, spitting stinging fireballs at any who ventured near and lighting lines of flame with sudden bursts as they ran this way and that.

But the drow wizards controlled it quickly, and particularly effective was Brack'thal, once a master of elemental summoning and control. While Tiago and Jearth and their charges destroyed the nasty little creatures, Brack'thal brought them to himself, and controlled them, and willed them to merge, and by the time

Ravel, Berellip, and Saribel came back into the forge room, their planning session interrupted by shouts of the commotion echoing down the halls, Brack'thal had quite a formidable fire elemental standing beside him.

As expected, the stares of the two Xorlarrin spellspinners locked, and it occurred to Ravel that Brack'thal had gained a significant upper hand over him in that moment, just in that one moment. He pried his gaze away and noted particularly the wry grin on Berellip's face, and knew that she agreed with that assessment, and seemed a bit too pleased with it for Ravel's liking.

"Destroy it," Ravel ordered his brother.

Brack'thal looked back at him skeptically.

"Put it in the main forge, then!" Ravel demanded.

"Yes, the main forge," Brack'thal answered, and he turned to regard it. "I wonder what pets I might pull from there."

"Brother," Berellip warned.

Brack'thal turned back at the sound of Berellip's voice. "It is an intriguing thought, you must admit," he said, and he started to wave away his pet elemental, which stood as tall and twice as wide as he.

But he stopped short. "No," he said, looking back to Ravel. "I think I will keep this one for now. It will be of great service in my duties in the outer halls."

"Your duties are here now," Ravel replied. "We have many more forges yet to light."

"Then perhaps when I am done, I will have an even larger escort to the outer halls," Brack'thal said slyly, and he walked off toward the as yet unlit forges. "Do tell your lackey to continue, young Baenre," he said. "All is under control."

Ravel's eyes narrowed and he began whispering, as if in spellcasting, as if he meant to punish his obstinate brother then and there.

But a look from Berellip dispelled that foolish notion.

She wasn't any more comfortable with Brack'thal playing with fire than Ravel was, the spellspinner understood, but he recognized, too, that Berellip was truly enjoying his discomfort.

With a wicked little laugh, Berellip signaled Saribel and Ravel back to their private meeting.

Ravel was the last of the three out of the room. He paused at the door to regard Brack'thal, to regard Brack'thal's elemental. This day had been the pinnacle of his achievement to date, even greater than the initial discovery of Gauntlgrym. The promise of those forges, he knew, would stand as the cornerstone of House Xorlarrin's plans, for they needed more than an empty dwarven complex if they truly wished to break free of the stifling ruling Houses of Menzoberranzan. They needed the magic of Gauntlgrym, the promise of magnificent arms and armor and implements. They needed Tiago to return to Menzoberranzan armed with swords that would make every drow warrior drool with envy.

But they were playing with fire, and so this day had also been the scariest of the journey thus far.

Much as he had done when the main forge had fired, Ravel licked his lips and went to his sister's command.

CHAPTER 10

THE WALK OF BARRABUS

H E IS DOWN THERE," THE IMP TOLD ARUNIKA.
"You're certain?"

The petulant little creature gave a great harrumph and crossed its deceptively skinny arms over its scrawny chest, its barbed tail whipping back and forth behind it like a cat waiting for a cornered mouse to emerge from under a bureau.

"I know him," the imp answered. "I smell him."

"Drizzt Do'Urden?"

"In the sewers, moving to the bridge. Hunting Alegni, as I was hunting him, and where else, where else?"

"With his two companions?"

"The two the warlock hates, yes."

"And have you told Effron that Dahlia and Barrabus have returned to Neverwinter, my dear little untrusted slave?" The succubus saw a look of curiosity on the little one's face then that comforted her greatly. Effron had compromised Invidoo, she knew for certain—the wretched little fellow had even admitted it to her. But this was not Invidoo, after all, despite the remarkable physical similarities.

"I speak to you," the imp said at length. "To you only in this world. I would be gone soon—poof! Now, I be gone, if you will let me."

"Not yet, but perhaps indeed soon, my little pet," Arunika promised. Her thoughts were spinning then. The trio had come for Alegni, as expected, and quite cleverly and efficiently, it would seem. And if they were heading for the bridge, they would probably find the tiefling warlord. He went there every morning, after all, and the sun was beginning to rise. Dare she hope that they would, perhaps, kill him?

Then what? She, they, had to be quick.

"Hide," she instructed her minion. "Do not leave this room. I will return presently." With that, Arunika grabbed her night coat and rushed out of her small cabin. She didn't even worry about her disguise, spreading her devil wings and flying away with all speed, only folding them and taking her human disguise when she landed before the side doorway to the room of Brother Anthus's in the large temple.

She pushed through and roughly woke the man, blabbered out her plans immediately, and sent him on his way.

And she went on hers, again taking to the night sky, and this time landing before the house of Jelvus Grinch.

They had to be ready. This would be their one chance to break free, and Jelvus Grinch had to understand that. She paused before entering, though, and weighed again the possibilities, both if Alegni remained as lord of Neverwinter and if he was thrown down.

The latter scenario proved more promising, and certainly would afford her more power.

She had to warn Jelvus Grinch, and from him, to spread the word.

He was the key.

"What do you know?" Effron asked Alegni, his voice thick with suspicion as the hulking warlord drew his red-bladed sword and lifted it before his eyes, the glow of the face making Alegni appear even more diabolical than usual.

"They are here," Alegni informed him.

Effron glanced all around, in near panic, as if he expected Barrabus and Drizzt and that most-hated Dahlia to spring from the shadows and throttle him at that very moment.

"Clever," Alegni remarked, and Effron realized that he was talking to the sword.

Effron almost said something, but thought better of it. Eventually, Alegni turned back to him.

"They saw our reinforcements, it would seem," Alegni informed him. "And so our sneaky enemies evaded the wall entirely." As he finished, he flipped the sword in his hand and plunged it down into the floorboards. Alegni was on the second story of the inn on the hill, and the mighty sword drove right through, cracking through the ceiling of the room below him, and drawing a gasp and cry from the occupants.

"They could not come over the wall without being spied," Alegni explained. "So they went under the wall."

Effron looked down at the floor, not quite sure of what the hulking tiefling was implying.

"Under the city, where the waste drains to the river."

"The sewers?" Effron asked, and crinkled his face.

"A fitting place for that traitor Barrabus, wouldn't you say? And more fitting

134

indeed for Dahlia; I cannot think of a better road for her to walk."

"Or a better place for her to die," Effron replied, but Alegni shook his head.

"No need. They have come for me. Barrabus knows where to find me."

"Here?"

Alegni shook his head again. "They'll not escape the sewers before dawn's light," he explained.

"The bridge," Effron breathed.

"Go to our minions," the tiefling warlord instructed. "Block every escape route from the bridge."

"You intend to meet them?" Effron asked.

"I intend to enjoy this spectacle to the fullest," Alegni replied.

"They are three to one against you," the warlock warned.

"Are they?" Alegni asked with a wry grin as he pulled his sword out of the floor. "Are they indeed?"

"I would help you kill Dahlia!" Effron demanded, and even he was a bit surprised at the stridency in his tone.

"I suppose that you have earned that," Alegni replied, and Effron held his stern gaze, but was truly relieved, having feared that his outburst would get him punished yet again by the merciless brute. "But first, you will help me to get her companions under control. If we are careful, we might get Dahlia alive."

"She dies!" Effron insisted. The words surprised him, though, particularly the conviction he heard in his own voice. For a long time, he had been telling himself that he wanted to speak with this elf woman, wanted to ask her questions that only she could answer. But then, in the moment of truth, he had felt no sense of mercy.

"Eventually," Alegni replied.

That thought, so obviously pleasant to Alegni, strangely had Effron off his guard. He wanted Dahlia to die—more than anything in the world, Effron wanted to be the one to deliver that killing blow—but now the notion of something more than simply killing her, of capturing her and torturing her . . .

It should have been a pleasant thought to him, and yet, surprisingly, it was not.

"Go!" Alegni said to him, and when he looked at the tiefling and considered the explosive tone, Effron realized that Alegni had repeated that command, likely several times.

Effron ran from the room, almost tripping down the stairs and almost running over a trio on the first landing, a man and woman dressed in nightclothes and the owner of the inn.

"Here now, is there trouble?" the innkeeper demanded.

Effron glanced back up the stairs to Alegni's door. "Go ask him," he said, and he laughed.

For he understood Alegni's agitated state, for he shared Alegni's agitated state, and he knew that if the innkeeper and these other two fools went up there to complain about the broken ceiling, Herzgo Alegni would cut them into pieces.

The eastern sky was just beginning to lighten, but already it was promising to be a lovely and memorable day.

"The sun is soon to rise," Drizzt remarked from around the corner of the crawl tunnel he had entered. The others could barely hear him, for the sound of the rushing water echoed all around them.

"He will be at his bridge, then," Entreri said. "He is always at the bridge at sunrise. He faces the sea to the west and casts a long shadow upon the river. It probably makes him feel dominant over the city, or some other foolish symbolism."

Dahlia didn't reply, didn't even look at him, just started up to the tunnel, whose entrance was chest-high to her. To her obvious dismay, she had to back out immediately as Drizzt slid back to them. He came out feet-first, settling on the wider corridor beside them.

"Do you think you can get him through?" the drow asked the three former aboleth slaves.

The two bearing their badly-wounded companion looked doubtfully at each other.

"They don't need to," Entreri interjected. "I remember this region now. If they just follow this wider tunnel, they will find an easy exit, farther along and near the city's northern wall."

Drizzt looked at the assassin curiously, but Entreri didn't wait to return that gaze and slipped up into the crawl tunnel.

"We go with them, then," the drow said. "There are other dangers down here—"

"You go with them if you so choose," said Entreri, who sat on the lip of the crawl tunnel, looking back. He offered his hand to Dahlia, who took it without a second thought, and sprang up without hesitation as Entreri pulled her into the small entrance beside him, even let her into the crawl tunnel before him.

"This is our chance at Alegni," he said. "Likely our only chance to find him without a powerful escort."

"We cannot leave them on their own."

"I can," Entreri replied. "Dawn is coming." He glanced down the tunnel, and indeed, even though he wasn't around the bend, it was clearly lighter in there. "And coming fast. Alegni will wait for it and then he will leave. We haven't the time to travel underground all the way to the north wall and double back to catch him, nor could we exit up there and not draw the attention of a dozen Shadovar sentries."

"They have no weapons," Drizzt complained.

"Then give them yours," Entreri growled back, and he started down the crawl tunnel after Dahlia.

Drizzt looked to the three humans.

"Go," the man bade him. "Do what you must. You have done enough for us already, and know that we are grateful and will not forget."

"We'll make it out," Genevieve added.

The drow rubbed his face and looked deep inside, seeking some alternative. Ultimately, though, he jumped up into the crawl tunnel and rushed along.

Had he known that Entreri was lying, that the assassin had no idea of the layout of this region, including the wider tunnel along which he had just directed the three, Drizzt might have chosen differently.

The crawl tunnel led to an old iron grate, with several of its bars torn out or twisted wide.

"I came through this very grate," Entreri whispered to the others, but loudly enough so that he was heard over the melodic and continual song of the river beyond, "on my escape from the volcano." He tapped one of the bars with his long sword, pulled it free at the bottom, and yanked wide out to one side. "My doing."

"Apparently, the lava did more behind you," Drizzt noted, for only a pair of the eight bars on the grate remained intact, and the one Entreri had indicated as his handiwork would not now allow the easiest passage. Black stone lay where once had been clear ground, narrowing the vertical height of the opening, and the river channel was tighter now because of that cooling lava rock, like natural levies, forcing the water up nearer the grate than in years past.

Still, it was not hard for Drizzt to slip though, using the grate itself as a hand hold as he came onto the riverbank.

The winged wyvern that marked Alegni's bridge loomed above him and to his immediate right as he exited, the path to its entrance clear to see. A bit of brush along the bank provided ample cover for him to get to the base of the bridge unseen.

Though she was the most anxious to get on with this confrontation, Dahlia was also the last out of the tunnel and onto the riverbank, and she did not press the others to move more quickly toward the bridge.

This was the fight she had wanted for all of her adult life, the chance to truly repay this rapist and murderer. But now she found herself strangely ill at the mere thought of it, caught somewhere between the bile of hatred and the tears of memory, the longing to exact revenge and her unspoken fear, one she had barely admitted to herself, that the taste might not be sweet.

And if that taste did not heal her broken heart, what might be left for Dahlia?

It took all the elf warrior's focus to carefully position herself as she hunched and crawled along the brush. It was not until Entreri tapped her on the shoulder and nodded his chin to direct her gaze that she even noticed the solitary hulking form standing at the center of the winged wyvern's long expanse.

Dahlia recoiled. Suddenly, she was once more a helpless child so easily pinned beneath the great bulk Herzgo Alegni.

Her mother fell dead again before her mind's eye.

She held a baby in her arms, the wind in her face as the ravine opened wide before her . . .

She had no idea how many heartbeats passed, then, but knew it to be many, for not only was Entreri prodding her but so was Drizzt, having come back from his lead position.

Dahlia quickly lifted a hand to wipe the tears from her eyes. She could not hide them from these two, sitting so close, their gazes intent, expressions confused and sympathetic.

The elf woman took a deep breath, a small growl escaping her lips. She sublimated her pain to her rage, and with a grim face, motioned for the two to move along.

She had to stay behind them, she told herself, had to use them as a shield against the base outrage that threatened to launch her headlong at Alegni, and no doubt, headlong to her death.

The city was mostly still asleep, most windows still dark and not a soul to be seen, other than the one figure standing at the rail at the center of the gently arcing bridge. The eastern sky glowed, the first rays of dawn soon to reach above the trees of Neverwinter Wood to cast long shadows at the nearby Sword Coast.

Drizzt looked to Entreri, his fingers moving slowly and deliberately in the drow sign language as he silently asked the assassin if this kind of empty early morning was typical in Neverwinter.

Entreri, with only rudimentary understanding of the language, shrugged noncommittally, and then became distracted as Dahlia crept up behind him.

It seemed too easy to the cautious drow ranger, too pat. He regarded Entreri once more, and wondered if perhaps Dahlia's desire for this fight had clouded both their judgments. Had Entreri led them into a trap?

Drizzt shook the thought away almost as soon as it had come to him. The pain on Entreri's face was all too real; the man wanted Herzgo Alegni dead almost as surely as Dahlia desired that outcome.

Sometimes, indeed most of the time, things were as they seemed.

The drow stepped out of the brush, standing to his full height, and walked onto the bridge. He drew Icingdeath in his right hand and dropped his left hand into his pouch.

Entreri was beside him in a heartbeat, Dahlia scrambling out behind, and the three started their stalk.

They were only a few steps onto the bridge when the tiefling warlord noticed them. He turned and straightened, staring at them. At that very moment, the first rays of dawn shot the length of the bridge, past the three intruders and shined upon the warlord as if it was intended for him alone. That glow revealed a strange grin on Alegni's face, visible to them even though they were still thirty strides away.

Alegni had been expecting them.

No matter, Drizzt realized, and he paused and produced the onyx figurine as Entreri stopped beside him.

Not Dahlia, though. She rushed between her two companions, knocking them both aside, her reassembled long staff carried like a javelin. She had left her hesitation and her tears back in the brush, it seemed.

"Guenhwyvar, come to me!" Drizzt commanded, and as soon as that call was heard, he replaced the statue and brought forth his second blade, following Entreri into his charge.

Up ahead, as Dahlia closed in, Herzgo Alegni calmly reached to his hip and drew out his huge red-bladed sword.

But Dahlia didn't slow, coming in furiously, with a powerful stab at the tiefling's face.

Across came Charon's Claw, turning aside the weapon.

Drizzt put his head down and called upon his magical anklets to speed him past Entreri and up to Dahlia. He had to get there, he could tell that his lover was too eager, and too forceful in her assault on the dangerous tiefling.

Alegni would cut her down!

He sprinted around Entreri, or almost did, until the assassin's sword flashed out to the side, stabbing Drizzt hard in the left shoulder.

The drow threw himself aside, nearly falling from his feet. He tried to turn and set a defense, but his left arm would barely rise and it was all he could do to prevent Twinkle from falling from his failing grasp.

Artemis Entreri, Barrabus the Gray, was on him, sword and dagger flashing.

It had been so easy!

Herzgo Alegni could hardly contain his laughter as he watched this fool elf's two companions battling halfway back to the bridge entrance. With a mere thought, his prized sword had once again defeated Barrabus, had turned the man against himself! For truly Alegni could sense that one's hate toward him, toward the sword.

And truly, Alegni understood, there was nothing Barrabus would ever be able to do about it.

Barrabus already had the drow, this legendary ranger who had attached himself to Dahlia, under control, it seemed, and so Alegni, who of course had other allies lying in wait, was left to focus on this one.

On pretty young Dahlia.

She kept up her barrage of thrusts and wild swings, and Alegni didn't even try to counter, instead blocking and misdirecting the blows, or dodging aside to prevent any solid strikes. He let her rage play out through many movements, then, as she seemed to be slowing, he added a new twist to the dance.

Dahlia's staff stabbed in at his midsection and across came Claw to drive it out harmlessly wide. But this time, the red-bladed sword trailed a line of ash, an opaque barrier.

Alegni stepped back and to the side, and when the staff came back into view, predictably stabbing right back through the ash cloud, he took up Claw in both his hands and drove down hard, thinking to ruin the weapon.

Except that the head of the staff dipped too quickly, and at an unexpected angle, and for a heartbeat, Alegni thought that the elf woman must have leaped up impossibly high to clear the ash barrier.

When Dahlia herself exploded through that barrier, though, he understood— understood the unexpected movement of the staff head, if not the manner in which this transformation had occurred, for now the elf held in her hands not a single long staff, but a pair of exotic flails, spinning and crossing at every conceivable angle.

Alegni fell back to regroup, but Dahlia was too close. The tiefling warrior flailed Charon's Claw wildly side to side and straight ahead, to block, to drive her back, to score some hits, perhaps. He winced as a flying pole cracked hard against his shoulder. Only his thick horns saved his skull as Dahlia's diagonal downstrike jarred and staggered him.

Back he stumbled and on she came, her jaw locked in a mask of fury. She banged her sticks together as she pursued, sparks flying with every hit.

Alegni saw his chance and thrust his blade out at her, knowing it would be slapped aside. In that parry, a blast of lightning energy shocked Claw, flowing from Dahlia's weapon to Alegni's blade and up to his hands.

His left hand surely stung from that magical bite, but his right, gloved in the gauntlet that served as sister to Claw, accepted the blast easily.

Dahlia came on; she thought her clever trick would defeat him, of course.

As he had expected.

Across came Claw in a brutal backhand slash, and Dahlia, obviously surprised that Alegni still gripped the blade with such strength, threw her hips back desperately.

But still Claw tore her shirt and her flesh, a line of blood erupting across her belly, a flash of agony twisting her pretty face. Claw's bite was more than that of a mere piece of sharpened steel. Claw's bite was charged with the powers of the netherworld, the essence of death itself.

Alegni continued his swing out wide to the right, even letting the blade turn him as it went.

For he knew that Dahlia's rage would outdo even that profound agony, knew that she would come right in at him despite the wound.

He continued to turn, and as he went, he lifted his trailing right leg in a perfectly-timed kick. He felt Dahlia's flails smacking around his hip and thigh, but more than that, he felt the whoosh of breath leaving Dahlia's body as his heavy boot connected.

He came around in a defensive posture, hardly hurt by the strikes, denying them with his sheer muscle and brawn.

Dahlia wasn't on him, though. His kick had thrown her back several long strides, where she sat upon the ground, clearly stunned and pained.

"You think I will kill you?" he taunted as he stalked in. "You will soon enough pray for such an outcome, pretty girl. I will hurt you, oh indeed! And then I will tie you down for years to come, and fill you with my seed and tear from your loins my progeny!"

"Fight it!" Drizzt implored Entreri, but he hardly got the words out as he twisted and turned and stumbled aside, dodging the assassin's flashing blades. He managed to glance back along the bridge, to see the gray mist of Guenhwyvar beginning to take shape. If he could only hold out for a few heartbeats, Guen would free him of the crazed Entreri.

And none too soon, he realized as he glanced ahead, just in time to see Dahlia flying backward and to the stone, to see the hulking form stalking in at her.

"Guen!" Drizzt cried.

He felt the blood rolling out of his burning shoulder, but he stubbornly tightened his left hand and fought the pain. Down went Icingdeath to pick off Entreri's low thrust, then up again, swiftly and horizontally to force the assassin to cut short his clever dagger follow-up, thrusting, perhaps even thinking to throw the dirk into Drizzt's face.

A growl from the end of the bridge brought Drizzt little hope, for in that call of the great panther, he clearly heard pain. He worked around to the side, between Entreri and Dahlia, looking back the way they had come, looking back at Guenhwyvar.

The panther spun and bit furiously as dark bolts filled the air around her. Wafts of smoke still trailed from her black form, though she was fully substantial now, the gray mist completely coagulated.

Those awful bolts burned at her, Drizzt understood, and he followed them to their source: a twisted and malformed tiefling in purple and black robes, flicking a wand her way. As she had become corporeal, this one had intervened, assaulting her before she had even taken in the scene around her, distracting her and paining her greatly, so it seemed.

As Guenhwyvar tried to go to Drizzt's call, the tiefling warlock filled the area before her with a black, sizzling cloud, and the panther shrieked and snarled.

"Kill your tormentor!" Drizzt ordered the panther.

He couldn't rely on Guen. Not then.

He batted aside another strike, and slid one foot to the left, circling. He had to get to his fallen scimitar, had to deny the pain and the blood and fight with both hands against Artemis Entreri. There was no other way.

He darted side to side, using his speed to keep the assassin from any straightforward attacks. Icingdeath spun out before him in tight circles, the blade humming as it gained momentum—but never too much momentum for Drizzt to interrupt the flow suddenly and stab it out, ahead or to either side, as he did often.

Now he was facing Dahlia again, and to his relief, she was back to her feet, flails spinning. She leaped and somersaulted out to the side, landing lightly and charging right back in at the hulking figure.

But then she retreated at once as the great red-bladed sword swept across.

Drizzt sucked in his breath, and got stuck in the forearm for his distraction.

This was Artemis Entreri he was facing, and the man had lost nothing of his skill in the decades since last they had battled! Drizzt told himself to focus, reminded himself repeatedly that he could be of no use to Dahlia if he could not first win out here.

He moved Entreri out toward the right-hand rail of the wide bridge, away from the fallen scimitar.

"Resist it," he implored the assassin between parries. "Alegni will kill Dahlia. Resist the call of Claw."

In response, Entreri gritted his teeth and let out a cry of pain. His knuckles whitened as he grasped his weapons and he fell back a step.

"Fight it!" Drizzt implored him, and indeed, Entreri seemed locked in some inner battle, some great torment.

That was the moment for Drizzt to leap in and cut him down, a moment when the assassin could not defend. A stride forward, a single stab, and Drizzt could move to help Dahlia.

She focused on the last moments of her mother's life. That horrible image flitted through Dahlia's thoughts again and again, alongside all the other painful memories.

The thought of this beast atop her and inside her filled her with fury, but it worked against her, Dahlia realized almost immediately. For amid her rage at that ultimate violation, there remained too much guilt, too much vulnerability. If she let her mind take her back to those awful moments, she would paralyze herself.

But she had no such conflicting emotions concerning the fate of her mother.

Just rage.

Pure rage.

No guilt, no vulnerability, no fear.

Just rage.

Her belly burned from the poisonous cut of Claw, but Dahlia transformed that profound sting into energy, and yet more rage. She leaped and darted all around, keeping Alegni turning, his blade cutting the air only a finger's breadth behind her—and yet, always a finger's breadth behind her.

Her flails always spun in too short to strike Alegni. And his smile showed that he knew it, and knew that Dahlia was expending far more energy than he, since she ran around while he merely turned in tune with her.

She rushed away to the right, diving into a roll, came to her feet, planted her right foot, and turned in at him as he pursued.

And in that clever move, Dahlia wiped the smile off Alegni's face, for as she executed her roll, her hands worked independently, each contracting the respective flail into a singular four-foot length, and as she rose up, so did she connect those poles together as one, only for the blink of an eye before breaking Kozah's Needle into two pieces again, this time joined by a length of magical cord.

When Dahlia's left hand snapped out at the trailing Alegni, it was not with a shortened flail, but with a much longer reach. The first pole snapped into place, the trailing free end whipping around, past the surprised tiefling's defenses to crack him across the face, and Dahlia, of course, used that moment to let loose the lightning energy.

Herzgo Alegni staggered backward, a black line of charred skin down the left side of his face, just beside his eye socket all the way to his chin.

On came Dahlia, her staff reassembled to one piece, thrusting spearlike before her. She knew that she had stunned the tiefling; she could see it in his eyes.

Those hateful eyes.

Even dazed, even outraged, though, the warlord kept up his defenses, his sword slapping hard against each thrust of Kozah's Needle.

"Your drow friend is dead," he remarked at one point, laughing, but even there, Dahlia saw the grimace of pain behind his fake grin.

She hardly registered his words. She hardly cared.

At that moment, all she cared about was her mother, about exacting revenge at long last.

Her belly burned, her arms should have slumped from exhaustion, so furious had been her routines.

But she fought on, ignoring the pain and oblivious to the weariness.

The pain assaulted the panther's senses, and worse, one of those black bolts had transported creatures within it, and now Guenhwyvar clawed furiously at a line of spiders burrowing under and crawling out of her skin.

Maddened, she spun and rolled, and scratched that shoulder so hard with her rear claw that she tore open her own skin.

"Guen!" she heard, plaintively, from far away. "Guen, I need you!"

That call captured Guenhwyvar. That so familiar voice, that dear voice, brought her through her pain and confusion just enough so that she could see the next magic missile flying her way.

Guenhwyvar charged at it, flew over it with a great and high leap, and descended from on high upon the source of her agony: the twisted necromancer.

She was the essence of the panther, of the hunter, primal and pure, and she knew the look of her prey, the look of life at its end.

This tiefling wore no such expression.

As Guenhwyvar came down upon him, so did he descend, as if his form had become that of a wraith, to slide into the cracks between the cobblestones!

Guenhwyvar landed hard, her great claws scratching on the stones. She spun around furiously to see the necromancer reforming some dozen strides away. How her legs spun on the hard stones, digging for traction as she propelled herself at him once more.

Another stinging bolt came forth, drawing a roar from the panther in mid-air, and again, the wily necromancer slipped down through the stones just ahead of killing claws.

Guenhwyvar's claws screeched on the cobblestones, and she threw herself all around, seeking her prey. It took her too long to spot him this time, she knew, and she got hit harder, a more substantial dweomer.

Maddened by the pain, the burn and the feeling of crawling things under her skin, the panther leaped away, driving the necromancer underground yet again.

She heard a cry, distant and desperate, and knew it to be Drizzt.

But Guenhwyvar couldn't turn away from this magical threat. To do so would surely doom her beloved master.

Much of her fur hung ragged now, but off she sprang yet again, landing on stone and scrabbling around, panting heavily, but ready to leap and charge once more.

The opportunity was there, but Drizzt didn't take the kill.

He wasn't sure why, wasn't sure what instinct or subconscious plan, perhaps, stayed his hand. Dahlia needed him and all that stood between him and her was this old nemesis, Artemis Entreri, who had betrayed him once again here on this very bridge and in this very moment.

His words had given the assassin pause, a moment to fight back against the intrusions of Claw, and in that pause came a moment of vulnerability.

But Drizzt didn't take the kill.

He leaped aside instead, rolling low and scooping his fallen scimitar.

He came back to his feet at the ready, but with his left arm hanging low, still burning, still bleeding.

Yet the drow managed to defeat Entreri's pursuing attack, sword and dirk, for the moment of hope had passed and Entreri had lost his struggle against Charon's Claw.

Now Artemis Entreri fought with fury, and so Drizzt growled and ignored the pain and returned the barrage, and heard again a song they both expected long lost: the continual ring of metal on metal as these two ferocious warriors played through their turning, twisting dance, as they had so many times before.

She rotated her arms violently, and with both hands down low on Kozah's Needle, the top few feet of length began to spin over and over. She wanted to lure Alegni into trying to keep up, and every so often stabbed out, the angle changed by the staff's bend instead of by re-aligning her arms. Despite Alegni's size advantage and the large sword he carried, Dahlia had a substantial reach and her remarkable quickness, and she needed to use both, she knew, to have any chance at all.

Such tactics did not come easily to her at this time, not against this opponent.

All she wanted to do was throw herself at him and tear him apart.

She sated some of that hunger when one of her thrusts slipped past Alegni's late block and jabbed him hard under the ribs, and the grimace on his face was a good thing, she thought.

But then he responded, and no more did he even try to parry her staff, instead coming on wildly, that deadly sword flashing down and around like a pendulum to drive her weapon away, and every stride bringing him a bit closer to Dahlia, who was now frantically backing.

She might hit him fifty times, she realized, and get hit in return but once.

And still she would lose.

Again the elf warrior suppressed her rage in lieu of tactics. Alegni was almost on her, his sword slashing across powerfully.

Dahlia spun back just out of reach and darted ahead and to her left, and Alegni, of course, whipped Claw back the other way with a mighty backhand, either to cut her in half or at least to drive her back yet again.

But Dahlia did not run out of reach, nor did she try to block the blow. As soon as she had passed Alegni's flank, the elf planted her staff and threw herself up high in the air atop it, and as Alegni turned, his blade whipping through the air just short of her carefully planted pole, she came down from on high with a double kick, perfectly timed and perfectly aimed.

She felt her foot crunch into the tiefling's face, felt his nose crumble under the weight of that blow.

Dahlia landed lightly, a wild and elated look coming upon her as she noted the splatter of blood on Alegni's face. Hunger overtook her and she broke her staff in two, and two into four as she threw herself at the hulking tiefling, flails spinning with fury.

But so too was Alegni full of fury and he countered with short, heavy cuts, more than willing to trade several hits of Dahlia's weapon against one of his own.

And Dahlia couldn't accept that trade. Instinct alone overruled her rage, and she deftly turned aside right before they came together in the middle of the great expanse.

She started to spring, felt the close pursuit, and daringly skidded to a fast stop, turning hard and throwing her elbow up high.

If Alegni had been able to put his sword in line, Dahlia would have been skewered then and there—and she knew it—but her guess paid off, and instead of feeling the tip of that awful sword, she instead felt Alegni's broken face once more, this time with her elbow.

She expected that the tiefling had staggered back under the weight of that blow, and it was indeed a heavy strike, and so she turned, setting her weapons to spinning.

Or started to.

Herzgo Alegni, so powerful, had held his ground, and he swatted Dahlia with a backhanded slap, his free hand catching her under the shoulder as she started her turn.

She was flying then, across the bridge and to the stones, and she rolled in hard against the metal railing.

He was too strong, too powerful.

She could not beat him. Not with pure rage and brute force, and not with tactics.

So suddenly, Dahlia felt once more like a helpless little girl.

Her mother's lost voice cried out to her.

146

It became a battle of guessing, and much like the one with Dahlia and Alegni, one had to guess correctly simply to survive, while the other, guessing wrongly, would merely be stung. Thus, the twisted tiefling necromancer held the temporary advantage, but Guenhwyvar understood the deeper matter.

She was wearing his spell power down. She had taken the worst he could give and had survived it. He could continue to sting her, all day and longer, but if she managed to get to him just once, she would tear his head from his skinny neck.

And so whenever Guenhwyvar landed from one futile leaping attack, she sprang away again, in a different direction. The necromancer couldn't see such a leap from his underground travel, of course, and so only luck alone could keep him from reappearing right under her leap. Only luck alone could keep him alive and from her tearing claws.

The panther tried to determine a pattern to the necromancer's movements. He was trying to move her farther from the bridge and the other combatants.

She went flying again, thirty feet with ease, glancing all around as she went. When, guessing wrong, she located the necromancer popping up from a crack in the cobblestones, she landed, re-directed and flew off again immediately.

On one such spring, the tiefling came up not far to the side, and Guenhwyvar saw then that her tactics were indeed unnerving him, clearly saw the look of fear on his face. When she landed, barely two strides separated her from the necromancer, who didn't even think to sting at her with one of his black energy bolts, but melted away at once.

And Guenhwyvar was in the air again immediately, flying beyond his last position, but not so far. She suspected that her enemy would instinctively move straight back, or that he might even come right back up to his previous position with an expectation that she would have leaped beyond.

He did go back, but to the side just a bit, and Guenhwyvar, with her shortened leap, was able to spring again without much scrabbling to reverse momentum, and by the time the necromancer reappeared fully, clever and deadly Guenhwyvar was already high in the air, descending upon that very spot.

He favored his left arm with his attacks, but had no such luxury with his defenses, as Entreri, sensing the advantage, pressed him hard. In came the assassin's sword for Drizzt's left flank, a strike that called for an easy parry, center-out, of Twinkle. But Drizzt used his right hand instead, cutting Icingdeath all the way across to bash the slashing sword harmlessly wide.

In came the assassin's dagger from the other side, and instead of simply backhanding with Icingdeath to block, now Drizzt did use his left hand, Twinkle darting across in a movement that seemed a mirror image of his last parry.

Against the lighter dagger, the block did not profoundly sting Drizzt's wounded shoulder, and more than that, because of the shorter reach of the dagger, now Drizzt was closer as he turned.

He reached up and over with his right hand, stabbing straight for the assassin's face, and Entreri had to desperately throw himself back to avoid that cut.

Drizzt felt as if he had been propelled back in time, to a place and mind of simpler truths. He was on the mountain ledge again outside of Mithral Hall! He was in the sewers of Calimport, battling Regis's kidnapper!

He couldn't deny the exhilaration. Even with Guenhwyvar desperately struggling behind him and his lover in dire peril before him, this was the life Drizzt had known, the better life Drizzt had known, purer in morals and with a clear distinction of right and wrong. And this was the very man Drizzt had battled, so many times, in so many places.

And Drizzt understood that this man, Artemis Entreri, was indeed a worthy foe.

Predictably, the skilled assassin reversed and rushed right back upon him, right hand thrusting, sword reaching back for Drizzt's face even as the drow retracted his own blade.

Now he needed to use Twinkle, and met the thrust with a solid block, and how his shoulder ached for that effort!

Entreri didn't let up, launching into a spinning reverse circuit around to his right.

Drizzt instinctively mirrored the move, and only halfway through his own turn did he realize his mistake. For as he came around, as Entreri came around, the assassin did not lead with a backhand of his dagger, as Drizzt might have done with his own leading, longer blade, but Entreri cut in tighter and quicker, bringing his sword to bear with a powerful forehand slash.

Drizzt had no choice but to meet that with Twinkle, with his left arm, and the numbing wave of pain nearly toppled him with dizziness and nausea, and he nearly dropped his scimitar to the stone once more.

On came Entreri aggressively, and Drizzt had to work furiously to counter, with both arms.

He couldn't keep up the pace for long, he recognized.

"Fight it!" he implored the assassin as he managed to disengage for a heartbeat by jumping straight back. "You are no man's slave!"

He saw a hint of hesitation, just a hint, but Entreri growled through it and came on.

"You are no weapon's slave!" Drizzt insisted, but this time there was less in the way of a pause from Entreri, for this time, the heat of combat, the ring of metal, drowned out any reasonableness in the words.

Suddenly Drizzt understood the opposing needs, realizing that this battle was feeding Entreri's insanity. The instinctive and necessary aggressiveness of such a brutal fight made so much stronger the intrusions of Charon's Claw. Drizzt jumped back, using his anklets to buy him some room, and called out to Artemis Entreri, "Do you remember when we two fought side by side beneath the chambers of the dwarven halls?"

Entreri, fast in pursuit, stutter-stepped and seemed torn for just a moment.

Drizzt didn't back down, and met the assassin's attacks with a series of blocks and deflections and dodges, and in the midst of that encounter, emphatically reiterated, "Do you remember when we two fought side by side beneath the chambers of the dwarven halls?"

No hesitation at all by Entreri, no look of doubt in his eye.

The heat of battle worked against Drizzt.

In his own distraction as he considered this revelation, Drizzt suddenly found himself pressed hard. He thrust out Icingdeath, only to have Entreri roll his sword over it, drive it out wide to Drizzt's right, then press forward with a thrust of that sword.

Drizzt's only block came with Twinkle, and the heavy collision of blades sent a shiver of agony through his torn shoulder.

Entreri did not relent, and moved out to Drizzt's left, forcing him to keep using that blade, that injured arm, to defeat blow after heavy blow.

Drizzt stumbled and tried to turn even with the man, to bring Icingdeath more into play, but Entreri countered every movement and struck again, and again.

Drizzt could hardly feel the scimitar in his left hand, and stubbornly told himself to hold on. Finally he got his right arm across enough to pick off that thrusting sword, but even as he took some satisfaction in the block, he came to realize that it, too, was a feint, that in that fleeting moment, Entreri managed to get his dirk up and under the upraised Twinkle. With a flick of his wrist, the assassin sent the blade flying from Drizzt's hand.

Now he pressed Drizzt ferociously, but the drow met him and more with Icingdeath. Surprisingly, freed of the blade, or more pointedly, freed from the pain of holding the blade, Drizzt tucked his left arm and found new energy, enough to beat back the assault, and even to work his remaining scimitar into strikes that put Entreri back on his heels.

His elation proved short-lived, though, as he saw Dahlia go flying into the air before him. He glanced back to call for Guenhwyvar, only to discover that the panther was many, many strides away then, across the square at the end of the bridge. And worse, now other Shadovar loomed there, closing in!

He couldn't possibly defeat Entreri in time to get to Dahlia, if he could defeat Entreri at all, which he doubted, for the blood continued to flow from his shoulder and the pain continued to wear at him.

He had found a temporary respite, and nothing more.

And even if he somehow managed to beat Entreri, it would come far too late for Dahlia.

He jumped back. "Are you Artemis Entreri or Barrabus the Gray?" he cried.

The pursuing assassin straightened as if slapped.

But again it was only a temporary reprieve.

Drizzt leaped back again and sprinted away, and Entreri went in pursuit.

He had bought the distance he needed, but now Drizzt needed to find the courage to execute his last hope. In that eye-blink of time, his mind whirled through all that he knew of Artemis Entreri, of the man's capture of Catti-brie, of fighting against him and fighting beside him.

In the end, though, it came down to the simple truth that Drizzt had no choice. For Dahlia's sake, for Guenhwyvar's sake, Drizzt had no choice.

He dropped Icingdeath to the stone and held his arms out wide before the approaching killer.

"Are you Artemis Entreri or Barrabus the Gray?" he yelled again. "Free man or slave?"

The assassin kept coming.

"Free man or slave?" Drizzt yelled, and it sounded almost like a cry of final despair in Drizzt's ears as his tone turned to a near-shriek, as the assassin's sword came in fast for his heart.

Every swing of that red-bladed sword had Dahlia moving desperately, diving aside, ducking or leaping.

He was laughing at her.

Herzgo Alegni, her rapist, her mother's murderer, laughed at her.

She kept slapping her flails together between blocks, during dives and leaps, trying to build a powerful charge, trying to find something, anything, to bring this foul tiefling to his knees.

The sword slashed down at her left, then up and over and down past her right side, and both cuts filled their path with a veil of black ash.

Dahlia went forward, even managing a slight strike on Alegni by flicking her wrist and throwing one flail out straight before her.

It hardly bothered him, though, and he rushed aside, his sword slashing every which way, bringing in veils of ash.

"You are alone, little girl," he taunted, and Dahlia understood that he was creating the ash fields not for any tactical advantage, but simply to add to her sense of despair.

Was he giving her a chance, she wondered? Was he shaping the battlefield to better suit her advantages of speed and agility?

She burst through a hanging sheet of ash, diving down low, then leaped up through a second one, and there Alegni stood before her, but not facing her directly. She rushed in, flails spinning, striking, one after another.

But his single elbow jab as he turned weighed more heavily on Dahlia than her handful of strikes had inflicted on him, and once more she found herself bursting through sheets of hanging ash, but this time involuntarily, launched yet again through the air. She landed in a roll and came up once more right before the railing of the bridge, turning and setting herself for the incoming Alegni, preparing her stance to send her out to the right or left as needed.

But she couldn't see him behind the remaining ash walls.

She took a deep breath, or started to until she felt the sharp pain that doubled her over.

She knew then that she had a broken rib.

She knew then, once more, that she could not win.

Drizzt Do'Urden hardly dared to breathe.

"Free man or slave?" he asked in a whisper, Entreri's deadly sword touching his chest and with no way for him to prevent the assassin from plunging it into his heart.

He saw the struggle on Entreri's face.

"Are you Artemis Entreri or Barrabus the Gray?" Drizzt asked.

Entreri winced.

"I know you. I remember you," said Drizzt. "Deny the call of Herzgo Alegni. No mere sword can control you; no artifact can steal that which is yours."

"How long have I wanted to kill you," the assassin stated, and Drizzt recognized that he was trying to justify that which the sword compelled him to do.

"And yet you paused, because you know the truth," Drizzt countered. "Is this how you would kill me? Is this what would satisfy Artemis Entreri?"

The assassin grimaced.

"Or would it, instead, perpetuate Barrabus the Gray?" Drizzt asked.

Entreri spun away, and Drizzt nearly swooned with relief.

And disbelief, for before him, shaking his head with every stride, Artemis Entreri walked up the bridge expanse, sword and dagger turning over in his hands, determinedly toward Herzgo Alegni and the maze of ash walls.

The drow started to follow, and only then did he understand how badly he had been wounded, how badly that wound had drained him, for he stumbled down to one knee and had to fight hard to collect his balance.

The warlock didn't even fully materialize—to do so would have given Guenhwyvar the certain kill. He faded straight back into the stone and came up far away, running for the Shadovar reinforcements, flailing his good arm, his broken one swinging of its own accord, and crying out to Glorfathel to help him.

Guenhwyvar had sprung away as soon as her claws screeched on the empty stones once more, and had leaped back the other way, toward the bridge. In mid-flight, she heard the warlock's cries, far back the other way, and knew that she had guessed wrong.

And now before her knelt Drizzt, wounded, and perhaps mortally, it seemed, for Artemis Entreri had left him there.

To die?

He thought of the days of his youth, running the streets of Calimport—running freely because he was respected, even feared.

He was feared because of a reputation earned, because he was Artemis Entreri.

That was before Barrabus, before the betrayal of Jarlaxle and the enslavement by Charon's Claw. Rarely could Artemis Entreri recall those days now, particularly when he was around Alegni and that awful sword. Claw wouldn't allow it.

Claw had told him to kill Drizzt.

Now Claw insisted that he turn around and kill Drizzt.

His steps came more slowly. He couldn't believe that he had denied the intrusion this long, but even pausing to be incredulous at that thought cost him ground.

In a daring move, Entreri had allowed the citizens of Neverwinter to name this bridge "The Walk of Barrabus." How that had infuriated Herzgo Alegni! And how Alegni had punished him for his insolence!

Punished him through the sword.

He remembered that pain keenly now.

He used that memory of pure agony in a manner opposite its intent. The punishment had been to warn him, but now Entreri used it to reinforce his hatred of Claw and of Alegni, and most of all, to reinforce his ultimate hatred . . . of Barrabus the Gray.

"The Walk of Barrabus," he whispered aloud.

"The Walk of Barrabus."

He transformed those four words into his litany, a reminder of the agony Alegni had inflicted upon him, and a reminder of the man he used to be.

Claw screamed protests in his head. He shook with every step.

But Artemis Entreri said, "The Walk of Barrabus," and stubbornly put one foot in front of the other.

He burst through the ash wall, sword stabbing and slashing with power and abandon, and had Dahlia not guessed perfectly, rolling aside at the last possible second, she surely would have been cut down.

Alegni pursued, creating more visual barriers as he went, laughing at her, mocking her, certain that he was fast cornering her.

Dahlia couldn't disagree, particularly when she rolled through one ash wall to slam hard into the bridge rail, for she was closer to the edge than she had believed.

Through the cloud of swirling blackness she had left behind, she noted the confident approach of Alegni.

Too close!

She glanced left and right, looking for an out, and on that turn to her left, the woman noted a curious sight. Her gaze apparently tipped off Alegni, as well, for as she rose to her feet, now looking back at the man, she saw that he, too, was glancing that way.

"Barrabus?" he asked, and his voice showed a lack of confidence that Dahlia had not heard before.

The elf leaped to her feet, thinking an opportunity before her, but Alegni turned on her immediately and rushed in.

She couldn't hope to dive out to the left, nor to the right, nor could Dahlia begin to parry or block the mighty tiefling with her back against the rail.

So Dahlia took the only course remaining: she jumped over the rail.

Alegni charged in and swept his blade across as Dahlia fell away, then growled in anger at his clean miss. The river was low, so late in the autumn season, the fall considerable, the jagged rocks plentiful, and her desperate escape would likely be the end of her, he knew.

But that seemed an empty victory indeed, considering the pain and torture he had intended to inflict on Dahlia. Perhaps his minions might find her alive, he dared hope, and they could nurse her back to health enough for him to play with her.

He dismissed all thoughts of Dahlia at that, and turned on Barrabus.

Barrabus!

No, not Barrabus the Gray, but Artemis Entreri, he realized as Claw informed him that the foolish man was somehow resisting.

"Impressive," he said loudly enough for the man to hear.

Artemis Entreri did not acknowledge the words, but merely kept walking, head and gaze steady, his lips forming some words, some mantra, that Alegni could not quite catch.

Herzgo Alegni reached to his belt and produced the tuning fork.

"You should rethink your course," he warned.

Artemis Entreri roared and leaped forward in a sudden rush.

Alegni banged the fork against the blade, the vibrations sending forth the bared power of Charon's Claw.

How close Entreri came! Barely a stride away, the wave hit him and stopped him, as if every muscle in his body was suddenly on fire. He staggered, he growled, he managed to spit "The Walk of Barrabus!" one last time before he found himself on his knees.

"Oh, a pity," Alegni teased, and he snarled and cracked the fork against the metal blade again.

Entreri grimaced, veins standing clear on his forehead as he battled the disrupting energy. He almost fell to the stones—it seemed so much like that time when Alegni had heard of the bridge's intended name!

But he didn't fall flat. Not this time. The waves would likely destroy him in his stubbornness, but he didn't care. He knelt and he even managed to look up at Alegni, to let the man see his hate-filled eyes, to let the man know that he was not Barrabus!

He was Artemis Entreri, and he was a slave no longer!

Herzgo Alegni's eyes went wide then as he considered the sight before him. Entreri could not break free of the physical pain prison enacted by Claw, perhaps, but the man had resisted the mental entrapment.

The man had resisted.

"Ah, you fool," Alegni said, deep regret in his voice. "I can never trust in you again. Take heart, for you have found your freedom, and your death."

Herzgo Alegni knew that he was losing the best associate he had ever commanded, and it pained him greatly, but he knew, too, that Barra—Entreri, had at last found his way through the maze of Claw's machinations. Indeed, he could never trust this one again.

He stepped forward. Entreri tried to lift a sword against him, but Alegni easily kicked it from his grasp. Then he banged the tuning fork once more and the waves of agony knocked the dagger, too, from Entreri's hand.

Alegni grabbed Entreri by the hair and roughly pulled his head aside.

Up went Claw.

At the end of the bridge, Drizzt Do'Urden watched it all helplessly. He did not know what had happened to Dahlia, only that she was gone, for his view had been obscured by walls of floating ash. But he could clearly see the end of Artemis Entreri as the red blade went up high.

A strange sensation of deep regret came over Drizzt.

He was alone again?

No, not alone, he realized as Guenhwyvar, battered but still very animated and obviously angry, bounded up to him.

"Go!" he yelled, pushing the cat along, and surely hope sprang anew within him, but when he turned back up the bridge, he knew that it was too late. "Kill the Shadovar!" he ordered. "Kill him, Guen!"

The recognition that this would be mere vengeance, though, for surely Entreri was doomed and Dahlia nowhere to be seen, and likely already dead or gravely wounded, filled Drizzt with anger, and that rage brought strength back to the torn drow and he forced himself to stand.

Herzgo Alegni saw the cat coming fast, but he kept his concentration—Entreri was too dangerous for distraction!

He twisted the assassin's head farther as Claw went up, opening an easy target, and down came the blade.

Almost.

A shadow appeared on the ground beneath them, and before Alegni could even register it, a great form crashed up against him, a giant raven, battering him with its wings and pecking him hard—right in the eye!—with its powerful beak.

He staggered to the side and thrust his sword out before him to fend the beast, but then it was a beast no more, but an elf warrior.

A young elf woman.

And in her hands, Dahlia held not a long staff, and not flails, but a tri-staff, spinning and sparking with power, and before the hulking tiefling could properly orient himself, she was before him, then beside him, striking him hard across the fingers with the handle-pole of her weapon. The tri-staff swung down and under, then back up again with its third length, that last pole nearly clipping him in the face and forcing him even farther off balance.

Dahlia didn't pursue. She ran directly away from him and tugged with all of her strength, and the tri-staff unwound, Kozah's Needle releasing its considerable lightning energy at that very moment, and the force of the twist and the blast tore Claw from Alegni's grasp and sent the sword flying high over the far rail of the bridge.

Herzgo Alegni roared in protest, and leaped upon her, catching her by her skinny throat and squeezing with all his strength. But then he felt a profound sting as a spinning dagger caught him in the gut, and he noted the betrayer, Entreri, picking his sword from the bridge stones.

And past that formidable enemy came another, the panther, up in the air and flying down from on high.

Alegni threw Dahlia down to the stone, but there was nowhere to run.
So Herzgo Alegni didn't run.
He stepped instead.
Shadow-stepped.
Guenhwyvar hit him halfway through, and went with him through the gate into the Shadowfell.

CHAPTER 11

WHAT PRICE FREEDOM?

"WE SHOULD HAVE GONE IN EARLIER," GLORFATHEL THE WIZARD LAMENTED as the battle on the bridge turned sour. He started forward, but a strong dwarf hand grabbed his shoulder. He turned to regard Ambergris.

"Nay, it's as I told ye it'd be, and if ye went in, all ye'd've done is get us all killed to death," Ambergris replied. "Townsfolk're watchin', don't ye doubt!"

Glorfathel glanced around, and indeed, most shutters around the area were open, a bit at least.

"As I told ye," the dwarf said, and she pointed to a distant street corner, where some townsfolk—armed townsfolk—had gathered. "They're smellin' their freedom and coming to take it."

"Draygo Quick will not be pleased."

"Less pleased if ye lose half yer force. Lord Alegni chose his own course, always. He demanded the fight and he got it." The dwarf looked up the bridge just as the panther leaped upon Alegni. "Oo," the dwarf groaned. "Aye, he got it!"

Glorfathel considered his Cavus Dun cohort and nodded.

Artemis Entreri straightened immediately, his pain gone, his enslavement broken. He staggered back from the receding mists of Alegni and Guenhwyvar, trying to sort it all out, trying to regain his composure.

No such ambivalence slowed Dahlia. She leaped back from the bridge stones, ignoring the cuts and bruises, and threw herself with abandon at the spot where Alegni had been, thrashing the air with helpless fury, and crying out for the tiefling to "Die!"

A cry of "Guenhwyvar!" from back down the bridge turned Entreri, to see Drizzt stumbling toward him, the onyx figurine in one hand.

Entreri grew concerned—that Drizzt might come for him after his earlier betrayal. But any thoughts about the drow did not hold for the assassin, for the sight beyond Drizzt demanded his attention.

"Dahlia," he said somberly. "Dahlia, the fight isn't over."

Beyond the bridge in the square stood Effron, his twisted form shaking with outrage. And next to him loomed the Shadovar forces, five-score and more.

"Dahlia!" he said again, more insistently, and she at last paused in her furious outburst to notice him.

"I will kill every one of them," she promised under her breath.

"Get your unicorn, drow," Entreri remarked, and he produced the enchanted token that would bring his nightmare steed to his call. As Drizzt slowed to regard him, he pointed past the ranger.

Drizzt looked over his shoulder, then back at Entreri, showing the man the onyx figurine. Truly Drizzt seemed a broken person in that moment, a flash of hopelessness evident against the mask of stoicism he typically wore.

"We have to go," Entreri said.

Drizzt didn't move, just looked at the statuette.

"Later," Entreri promised.

Drizzt finally nodded and reached for his whistle, but paused and asked, "The sword?" and ran to the side of the bridge.

"Take Dahlia with you!" he instructed. "I will meet you in Neverwinter Wood!"

And with that, Drizzt sprinted along toward the far end of the bridge, then went over the rail and dropped from sight.

"I will take myself," Dahlia growled, and she threw her cape up over her head and became a giant raven, then issued a great cawing cry to those approaching Shadovar, a cackle of challenge.

"Just flee, you idiot," Entreri said to her, and he threw down his token and brought forth his nightmare steed. He gathered his sword and leaped onto the hell horse's back. He reflexively looked for his dagger for just a moment, before taking satisfaction in the memory of his throw, in knowing that his dagger had gone to the Shadowfell with Alegni, had gone to the Shadowfell lodged in Herzgo Alegni's gut.

"Perhaps you should ride with me," Dahlia the Crow said, her voice sharper and more brusque in tone in that bird form. As she spoke, she indicated the far end of the bridge, and the host of Shadovar gathering there, as well. "It would seem that Herzgo Alegni has ultimately trapped us and not the other way around."

Artemis Entreri ignored that last remark, considering his options. He could get into the river safely with the nightmare easing the fall, as it had done in leaping out of Sylora Salm's treelike tower.

Or he could indeed go with Dahlia—but did he trust that she would actually fly away? Her rage bordered on insanity. The way she had thrown herself at

Alegni, the spittle in her every word now . . . there was something more here, some profound scar that Entreri had not yet deciphered.

But one that seemed all too familiar to the man.

He was about to dismiss his mount and fly off with Dahlia when the decision was made for him, for in the square back the way they had come, a great commotion arose, a blowing of horns and cries of battle.

Both Entreri and Dahlia turned around to witness the spectacle, as on came the citizens of Neverwinter, Jelvus Grinch at their lead, weapons bared and fists pumping.

"Revolt," Entreri mouthed. He turned back to Dahlia, but she was already away, taking flight and soaring for the battle.

Entreri kicked his nightmare into a gallop, fiery hooves clicking loudly on the bridge stones. Perhaps Herzgo Alegni's final moments had escaped him, but more importantly, he had escaped Herzgo Alegni!

Effron glanced around in shock as the folk of Neverwinter descended upon the square, tearing into the flanks of his force before they even understood that an enemy was upon them.

How could the citizens have known of this moment? How could they have been so prepared to seize this unexpected opportunity?

It made no sense to him.

He surveyed the scene, trying to gauge whether he could lead the Shadovar to victory.

Then he noted the approach of the crow—of Dahlia!—and with that dangerous assassin close behind. And there was that drow, standing on a stone in the low river, picking his way to the edge of the bridge abutment and carrying Alegni's sword.

Too many variables, he thought, shaking his head. Too much chaos and unpredictability. He looked at the giant crow, now descending his way, and he so badly wanted to lash out at her with his magic.

But that wretched panther had taken so much out of him.

Effron stepped into the shadows, back to the Shadowfell.

The wizard Glorfathel glanced to the dwarf at his side.

"Not worth the losses," Ambergris said. "Draygo'll be waiting to hear yer explaining."

Glorfathel agreed with a nod, then motioned to the other Shadovar nobles, the commanders of this force, offering his permission.

Only Netherese nobles and warriors of high standing had been granted the shadowstep, but those who possessed the ability used it, and they were, invariably, the leaders of the various brigades, the commanders and the champions.

The commoner shades left behind found themselves sorely outnumbered and disorganized—and battling a group of hardy folk who were fighting for their homes.

And on came the man many knew as Barrabus, once their leading champion, and now cutting them down with abandon.

And on came Dahlia, once their opposing champion, sometimes a ferocious giant crow, other times the elf warrior they had once and still so greatly feared.

Had Alegni prevailed on the bridge, the city would be theirs. Had Effron and the others not fled, they might have had a chance.

Glorfathel recalled Draygo Quick's instructions, and the decision was not a difficult one. He didn't shadowstep, as had Effron, but instead enacted a gate in the middle of the square, a purplish-black glowing door inviting his charges to flee the battle.

"Meself'll call 'em in," Ambergris assured him.

At that point, Glorfathel hardly seemed to care, and indeed, he was the first to use his dimensional gate.

But certainly not the last.

Many shades died, many fled through the gate or even out over the city's walls, and many others, particularly those on the far side of the bridge, surrendered as the battle of Neverwinter quickly became a rout.

Fighting on the side of the Neverwinter garrison was Amber Gristle O'Maul, of the Adbar O'Mauls, for with a simple roll of one of the black pearls on her enchanted string of pearls, the dwarf had turned the appearance of shadowstuff into the dirt of the road. She knew who would win, obviously, and Ambergris always preferred to be on the winning side.

In the middle of the battle stood Arunika, sword in hand. More than one Shadovar leaped at the unremarkable woman, thinking her an easy kill, only to fall dead a heartbeat later.

As she watched the ranks of shades crumbling, the succubus knew that she had played this perfectly.

The Thayan threat had been defeated, and now the Shadovar had been run off.

It would not be long before the Sovereignty returned, or even if they did not, Arunika knew that she could find a place of dominance.

Shaking, and surprisingly free of bloodstains, Brother Anthus stumbled up to her, tears streaking his cheeks. For a moment, Arunika looked him over, wondering if he had sustained some grievous wound.

But no, these were tears of joy, she realized.

"I was a fool to doubt you," the monk sputtered.

Arunika flashed him a cute smile, then knocked him from his feet with a heavy punch.

"Never make that mistake again," she warned.

"Hear now, woman, haven't we enough enemies to battle?" came a voice behind, and Arunika turned to see the approach of Jelvus Grinch. Unlike Anthus, this one had indeed seen battle this day—quite a bit of it, judging from the spattering of blood all around his form.

"Neverwinter is free," he said. "Because of you."

"Hardly," Arunika answered, and she truly did not wish to be seen as the instigator of this revolt, or as a major player in the defeat of Alegni at all. The Netherese, after all, might well return in force!

She glanced over toward the bridge, directing Jelvus Grinch's gaze, to see Alegni's former champion standing near the edge, with the drow ranger moving toward him and carrying Alegni's mighty sword. As they watched, a giant crow swept down, reverting to the form of Dahlia.

"Because of them," Arunika corrected.

In his right hand, Drizzt held the red-bladed sword by one neck of its decorative crosspiece, the metal thickly wrapped with bandages. In his other hand, the drow held the onyx panther figurine. He was still calling to Guenhwyvar when Entreri rode his hellish steed over to join him.

Calling futilely for Guenhwyvar, the drow knew, for he could sense that the panther was beyond his reach, beyond the call of the figurine.

Dahlia swooped down beside them and reverted to her elf form. She was not happy, clearly. Drizzt didn't need to ask her why, for he understood that she had not seen the actual death of Herzgo Alegni. Worse, Drizzt wondered, Herzgo Alegni might have escaped their attack with his dematerialization. If that thought unsettled him, and it did, what might it be doing to Dahlia, whose hatred of Alegni was more profound than anything Drizzt had ever seen?

"You should have left that thing in the river," Entreri said, and he was shaking his head, obviously torn and obviously afraid.

"Where a common citizen of Neverwinter might have happened upon it?" Drizzt asked.

"The blade would be beyond him."

"The blade would eat him," Drizzt said. "Or it would enslave him . . ." The drow cast a stern gaze at Entreri, letting his disappointment show. "You would so sacrifice an unwitting person?"

"I would be free of that wretched sword, however I could!"

"It wouldn't let you go," Drizzt countered. "Whatever other slaves Claw might find, it would come back to you, and would force you back to it."

"Then I should take it now and wield it?"

Drizzt looked at him, but instinctively pulled the blade farther from him. He knew a bit about sentient weapons, artifacts of great power and great ego, and he understood that Entreri, after decades of enslavement, could not begin to control Charon's Claw, whether he held the blade or not.

Entreri knew it, too, Drizzt realized when the assassin laughed at his own absurd question.

"Destroy it, then," Dahlia offered.

"And then I will be dust," said Entreri, and with conviction. He gave another laugh, sad and resigned. "As I should have been half a century ago."

Dahlia looked alarmed at that, and her expression stung at Drizzt more than it should have.

"Destroy it," Entreri agreed. "You could not do me a greater service than to release me from the bondage of Charon's Claw."

"There must be another way," Dahlia said, almost frantically.

"Destroy it," said Entreri.

"You presume that we can," Drizzt reminded him. Powerful artifacts were not so easily gotten rid of.

But even as he spoke the words, Drizzt found his answer. He looked at Dahlia and knew she understood it too.

For she, like Drizzt, had witnessed a force more powerful than Charon's Claw, with a magic and energy older and more primal than even the dweomers imbued upon this magnificent, evil blade.

PART II

II

COMMON DESTINY

My thoughts slip past me, slithering snakes, winding and unwinding over each other, always just ahead, coiling and darting, just out of reach.

Diving down into dark waters where I cannot follow.

One of the most common truths of life is that we all take for granted things that simply are. Whether a spouse, a friend, a family, or a home, after enough time has passed, that person, place, or situation becomes the accepted norm of our lives.

It is not until we confront the unexpected, not until the normal is no more, that we truly come to appreciate what once we had.

I have said this, I have known this, I have felt this so many times . . .

But I find myself off-balance again, and the snakes slide past, teasing me. I cannot catch them, cannot sort through their intertwined bodies.

So it is with the ill person who suddenly must face mortality, when the paralyzing shackles of the concept of forever are sundered. As time diminishes, every moment crystallizes into one of importance. I have met several people in my travels who, when told by a cleric that they had not long to live, insisted to me that their disease was the greatest event of their existence, insisted that colors became more vivid, sounds more acute and meaningful and pleasurable, and friendships more endearing.

The shattering of the normal routine brings life to this person, so paradoxically, considering that the catalyst is, after all, the imminence of death.

But though we know, though we are seasoned, we cannot prepare.

I felt this rippling of the serene lake that had become my life when Cattibrie became afflicted by the Spellplague, and then, even more profoundly, when she and Regis were taken from me. All of my sensibilities screamed at me; it wasn't supposed to be like that. So many things had been sorted through hard work and trial, and we four remaining Companions of the Hall were ready for our due and just reward: adventures and leisure of our choosing.

I don't know that I took those two dear friends for granted, though losing them so unexpectedly and abruptly surely tore apart the serenity of calm waters I had found all about me.

A lake full of tumultuous cross-currents and slithering snakes of discordant thought, sliding all about. I remember my confusion, my rage, helpless rage . . . I grabbed Jarlaxle because I needed something to hold, some solid object and solid hope to stop the current from sweeping me away.

So too with the departure of Wulfgar, whose choice to leave us was not really unexpected.

So too with Bruenor. We walked a road together that we knew would end as it ended. The only question was whether he or I would die first at the end of an enemy's spear.

I feel that I long ago properly insulated myself against this trap of simply accepting what was with the false belief that what was would always be.

In almost every case.

Almost, I see now.

I speak of the Companions of the Hall as if we were five, then four when Wulfgar departed. Even now as I recognize my error, I found at my fingertips the same description when I penned, "we four."

We were not five in the early days, but six.

We were not four when Wulfgar departed, but five.

We were not two when Catti-brie and Regis were taken from us, but three.

And the one whom I seldom consider, the one whom I fear I have too often taken for granted, is the one most joined to the heart of Drizzt Do'Urden.

And now the snakes return, tenfold, twisting around my legs, just out of reach, and I stagger because the ground beneath my feet is not firm, because the sands buckle and roll beneath the crashing waves, because the balance I have known has been torn from me.

I cannot summon Guenhwyvar.

I do not understand—I have not lost hope!—but for the first time, with the onyx figurine in hand, the panther, my dear friend, will not come to my call, nor do I sense her presence, roaring back at me across the planescape. She went through to the Shadowfell with Herzgo Alegni, or went somewhere, disappearing into the black mist on the winged bridge of Neverwinter.

I sensed the distance soon after, a vast expanse between us, too far to reach with the magic of the idol.

I do not understand.

Was Guenhwyvar not eternal? Was she not the essence of the panther? Such essence cannot be destroyed, surely!

But I cannot summon her, cannot hear her, cannot feel her around me and in my thoughts.

What road is this, then, that I find myself upon? I have followed a trail of vengeance beside Dahlia—nay, behind Dahlia, for little can I doubt that it is she who guides my strides. So do I cross the leagues to kill Sylora Salm, and I cannot consider that an illegitimate act, for it was she who freed the primordial and wreaked devastation on Neverwinter. Surely defeating Sylora was a just and worthy cause.

And so back again have I traveled to Neverwinter to exact revenge upon this tiefling, Herzgo Alegni—and I know not the crime, even. Do I justify my battle with my knowledge of his enslavement of Artemis Entreri?

In the same breath, can I justify freeing Artemis Entreri? Perhaps it is that his enslavement was really imprisonment, atonement for a life ill-lived. Was this Alegni then a gaoler tasked with controlling the assassin?

How can I know?

I shake my head as I consider the reality, that I have as my lover an elf I do not understand, and one who has no doubt committed acts beside which I would never willingly associate myself. To delve into Dahlia's past would reveal much, I fear—too much, and so I choose not to probe.

So be it.

And so it is true with Artemis Entreri, except that I have chosen simply to allow for his redemption, to accept what he was and who he was and hope that perhaps, by my side, he will make amends. There was always within him a code of honor, a sense of right and wrong, though horribly stilted through the prism of his pained eyes.

Am I a fool, then? With Dahlia? With Entreri? A fool of convenience? A lonely heart adrift in waters too wide and too wild? An angry heart too scarred to linger on hopes I now know to be false?

There's the rub, and the most painful thought of all.

These are the questions I would ask of Guenhwyvar. Of course she could not answer, and yet, of course she could. With her eyes, her simple glance, her honest scrutiny reminding me to look within my own heart with similar honesty.

The ripples, the waves, the wild cross-currents, lift me and drop me and twist me all around, and I cannot set my feet and direction. I should fear that unexpected winding, these turns left and right to places not of my own choosing.

I should, and yet I cannot deny the thrill of it all, of Dahlia, more wild than the road, and of Entreri, that tie to another life, it seems, in another world and time. The presence of Artemis Entreri surely complicates my life, and yet it brings me to a simpler time.

I have heard their banter and seen their glances to each other. They are more alike, Entreri and Dahlia, than either to me. They share something I do not understand.

My heart tells me that I should leave them.

But it is a distant voice, as distant, perhaps, as Guenhwyvar.

—Drizzt Do'Urden

CHAPTER

12

ARTIFACTS

D RIZZT WINCED AND REFLEXIVELY PULLED AWAY. HE HADN'T BEEN EXPECTING Dahlia's touch, particularly not on his wounded shoulder. Stripped to the waist, he sat on a stool in a room at the inn in Neverwinter. Outside Drizzt's window, the sounds of battle could still be heard, though intermittently. The few remaining Shadovar in the city had been cornered.

"It is a salve to clean the wound," the elf explained. Perturbed by his inattentiveness, Dahlia grabbed Drizzt's arm none too gently and straightened him where he sat.

That had to hurt, she knew, but the drow didn't flinch. She braced his shoulder then, keeping it still, and moved his arm out to the side and back, separating the wound, opening it wide.

Still Drizzt didn't blink. He sat staring at the onyx figurine set on the table before him, as if it were his long-lost lover. A combination of disgust and anger filled Dahlia's thoughts.

"It's just an artifact," she muttered. She wore her hair in the bob now, her braid and the warrior woad were gone. She had become softer for the wounded Drizzt, and all he did was stare at that onyx figurine.

Still, Dahlia couldn't suppress some degree of sympathy as she examined the wound. Entreri's sword had slipped under the short sleeve of the drow's mithral shirt and had penetrated fairly deeply. With the blood now washed away and the arm tilted back, she could see right through the layers of flesh to the torn muscles within.

Dahlia shook her head. "That you could even lift your weapon again after this cut is remarkable," she said.

"He betrayed us," Drizzt said without turning to look at her.

"I told you to kill him in the forest or to send him away at least," Dahlia snapped back, more angrily than was called for, certainly.

"And in the end, he saved us," Drizzt said.

"I wounded Alegni," she said. "And I took his mighty sword. Even without Artemis Entreri on that bridge, Herzgo Alegni would have died."

Drizzt turned to look at Dahlia, and his expression, so full of sarcasm, made the elf want to thrust a finger into his open wound, just to bring him to his knees.

Instead she roughly applied the salve-covered cloth, pressing it tight. When Drizzt didn't wince, Dahlia pressed it more tightly, and finally, one lavender eye did narrow in pain.

"The priests will be in presently," Dahlia said, trying to cover her rough handling as a pragmatic matter.

Drizzt wore his stoic expression again. "Where is Entreri?"

"In the other room with that red-haired whore," Dahlia said. The drow tilted his head and his expression turned sly, if somewhat annoyed.

Her animosity toward this citizen, Arunika, was uncalled for, she knew. And yet, there it was, hanging in the air between them and worn clearly on her unblemished face.

She tied off the bandage and let go of Drizzt's arm, then reached for the onyx figurine.

He caught her by the wrist.

"Leave it."

Dahlia pulled back, but Drizzt would not let go.

"Leave it," he repeated, and then he released her.

"I was only trying to learn if I might sense the cat," she said.

"I will sense the return of Guenhwyvar before any others," Drizzt assured her, and he pulled the figurine in closer to him.

Dahlia heaved a great sigh and turned her attention to the other artifact in the room, the red-bladed sword standing against the wall.

"Is it a mighty weapon?" she asked, moving toward it.

"Don't touch it."

Dahlia stopped short and swung around to face the drow, cocking her head.

"So you command?" she asked.

"So I warn," Drizzt corrected.

"I'm no novice to sentient weapons," said the wielder of Kozah's Needle.

"Charon's Claw is different."

"You carried it from the river," said Dahlia. "Did it steal your soul in that journey, or merely your humor?"

That brought a smile to the drow's face, albeit a small and brief one.

Dahlia walked right beside the weapon, and even dared to touch the counterweight ball at the base of the pommel with one finger.

"Do you think it still controls him? Entreri?" she asked, purposely acting quite pleased by that possibility.

"I think that anyone who lifts that blade will be consumed by it."

"Unless they are strong enough, like Drizzt Do'Urden," Dahlia added.

The drow half-nodded and half-shrugged. "And even one strong enough not to be so consumed would invoke the wrath of Entreri."

"The sword controls him."

"Only if the wielder of the sword knows how to make the sword control him," Drizzt warned. "If not, one who tries would likely be dead long before she learned how to make Entreri her puppet."

Dahlia laughed as if Drizzt's reasoning were absurd, and most especially at his use of the female pronoun in his warning.

But she did move away from the sword.

A loud rap turned them both in time to see the door swing open and a dirty female dwarf march in.

"Amber Gristle O'Maul, o' the Adbar O'Mauls," she said with a bow.

"So you have told us every time you enter," Dahlia replied dryly.

"Good for ye to hear," the dwarf answered with a laugh. "Folks know o' Drizzt Do'Urden, and having me name tied to that one's good for me own reputation, haha!" She grinned widely in response to Drizzt's widening smile.

The drow's smile didn't hold, though. "How does she fare?" he asked, and both Dahlia and the dwarf knew of whom he was speaking: the woman who had been dragged from the sewers on a litter.

"Better!" Ambergris declared with a toothy grin. "Didn't think it when first I seen her, still covered in sewer muck and dirty wounds, but she's to live, don't ye doubt!"

Drizzt nodded, with obvious relief.

"Got me a platter o' healin' spells for yer wound this day, ranger," Ambergris said with an exaggerated wink. "We'll get ye on the road soon enough, where'er that road's to be!"

"I have no wounds, you fool," Entreri said to the red-haired woman who held a steaming mug of some medicinal tea or other herbal remedy.

"You staggered from the bridge," Arunika replied, "Herzgo Alegni wounded you greatly with that foul blade of his."

She presented the mug near to the man and he tried to push it away.

But he might as well have been trying to shove a stone building aside, for Arunika's arm did not budge in the least.

"Drink it," she ordered. "Do not act like a child. There is much still to be done."

"I owe this city nothing."

"Neverwinter owes you, and we know it," Arunika replied. "That is why I am here with medicinal tea. That is why the healers come to tend to your friends, and to you, if necessary."

"Unnecessary."

The red-haired woman nodded, and nodded again when the stubborn man at last took the mug and began to drink.

"Tell me of your story, Barrabus the Gray," she prompted. "Truly I was surprised to see you betray Alegni—I had thought you his squire."

Entreri's face grew tight.

"His champion, then, if that description less wounds your foolish pride," Arunika said with a laugh. "But do tell me of your travels and how you became such a champion of a Netherese lord, for you are no shade, though your skin is a shade too gray for your human heritage."

"Tell you?" Entreri echoed with a laugh. "You bring me tea and think yourself my ally? Did I ask for such allegiance?"

"The best allies are often unexpected and uninvited."

Entreri considered those words in light of the two companions he found beside him on the bridge against Herzgo Alegni, and he chuckled yet again.

"I need no allies, woman," he said. "Alegni is gone and I am free for the first time in a long, long while."

"He was your ally," the woman protested.

Entreri glared at her.

"What, then?" she asked. "I would know."

Artemis Entreri suddenly felt a compulsion to tell her all about his relationship with Herzgo Alegni. He almost started, but then recoiled, feeling much as he had on those many occasions when Charon's Claw had invaded his thoughts.

He looked at Arunika with more scrutiny, as he might consider a sorceress.

"Herzgo Alegni swept into Neverwinter through your actions," Arunika quickly replied. "He would never have found such a dominion here in the city had not Barrabus the Gray become a hero to the folk." The timbre of her voice changed abruptly, evoking sympathy and making Entreri feel foolish for his suspicion. "And now Alegni is no more, and I'm tending your wounds at the behest of the leaders of the city," Arunika went on. "I would be remiss, and betraying my duties to my fellow citizens if I did not ask—and why should we not know?"

"He was my slaver and nothing less," Entreri replied before he even realized that he was speaking the words. He looked curiously at Arunika, but just for a moment, before concluding that she was a trustworthy and sympathetic listener. "And now he is gone. For most of my life, my ally was me and me alone. I prefer that, and need no alliance with you or anyone else in this town."

He tried to sound defiant, but really didn't.

"Then not an ally," Arunika said. She moved her face before Entreri's and said in a suggestive tone, "A friend."

"I need no friends."

Arunika smiled and moved even closer.

"What do you need, Barrabus the Gray?"

Artemis Entreri wanted to assert that Barrabus the Gray was not his name. He wanted to tell Arunika again that he didn't need her. He wanted to move away even as she moved forward.

He wanted to do a lot of things.

Drizzt flexed his arm and stretched it upward as he moved to Entreri's door. The healing salve and the visit by the cleric had helped, no doubt.

Physically, at least.

In his good hand, the drow still held the onyx figurine, and he still called out silently for his friend who would not answer.

Entreri's door opened before the drow reached it, and the red-haired woman called Arunika walked out. She paused and flashed a disarming smile at Drizzt, then threw a wink at Dahlia, who stood behind him.

Drizzt caught Dahlia's gaze with a questioning stare.

"She is a strange one," Dahlia remarked.

"One of the leaders of Neverwinter, I believe."

Dahlia shrugged as if it did not matter and pushed past Drizzt and into Entreri's room.

The assassin stood at the room's small bar, stripped to the waist and looking quite exhausted as he poured some fine brandy into a small glass. This had been Alegni's room during his brief tenure as Neverwinter's self-appointed lord, and the tiefling warlord had decorated it and stocked it quite well.

Dahlia entered the room before Drizzt, and the drow was given pause by her sudden stop. She turned and looked back over her shoulder at the receding Arunika, then, barely muting her scowl, turned back on Entreri.

Drizzt winced.

"You are . . . healed?" the elf woman asked, her voice dripping with sarcasm.

"Ready for the road," Entreri answered, and he downed the brandy in one swig.

Drizzt moved to the bar and took a seat. Entreri poured himself another drink and slid the bottle Drizzt's way, staring at the drow intently.

That surprised Drizzt for just a moment, before he realized that Entreri wasn't staring at him, but at the great sword strapped diagonally across his back, in a harness given him by a leatherworker of Neverwinter.

Drizzt blocked the sliding bottle and left it sitting idle, but Dahlia was fast to the stool beside him, and quickly grabbed the brandy and another glass.

"Ready for the road?" she echoed. "And what road does Artemis Entreri desire?"

Entreri took a sip of his drink and nodded his chin toward the sword.

"Gauntlgrym?" Dahlia asked.

"Of course."

"You will be free?"

"I will be dead, I am sure," Entreri said. "So, yes."

Dahlia shook her head. "How can you know?"

"I am tied to the sword," Entreri answered. "My longevity is due to the sword—it alone has kept me in a state of perpetual youth . . . or middle age, perhaps. I have known this for a long, long while."

"And still you would destroy it?" Dahlia said.

"I will find no peace until Charon's Claw is no more."

"You will be dead!"

"Better that than enslaved," Entreri said. "It is long past time for me to be dead." He looked past Dahlia to Drizzt and smiled wickedly. "You would agree, of course."

Drizzt didn't respond in any way. He did not know whether he preferred such an outcome or not. Entreri was his tie to a past much missed. Just having Entreri around brought him a strange sense of peace, as if his friends were out there, waiting for him to return home.

But was that enough? He knew Entreri's deadly history, and expected that this killer's reputation would remain well-earned going forward.

It was the same dilemma Drizzt had faced with this particular man in the past, such as when they had walked out of the Underdark side by side. On more than one occasion, Drizzt could have killed Entreri, and never had he been confident that staying his blade had been the correct choice. What about Entreri's victims, if there were such, after Drizzt's acts of mercy, after all? Would they appreciate Drizzt's eternal optimism, and his rather foolish hopes for redemption?

"We do not know that the primordial will destroy it," Dahlia warned.

"At the least, we know that it will be someplace where no one can retrieve it," Drizzt said.

"Sentient weapons have a way of being found, and wielded," said Dahlia.

"The primordial will destroy it," Entreri replied with conviction. "I sense the sword's fear."

"Then we go, straightaway," Drizzt said.

"Are you so interested in killing this man, then?" Dahlia accused, turning sharply on Drizzt.

The drow leaned back, caught off guard by the elf woman's intensity.

"I am," Entreri interjected, and both turned to regard him.

Entreri shrugged and drained his glass, then moved to retrieve the bottle.

"There is a time for all of us to die," Drizzt said, matter-of-factly, callously, even. "Sometimes, perhaps, past time."

"Your concern is touching," Entreri remarked.

"It is, of course, your choice to make," Drizzt offered. He tried to keep the coldness out of his tone, but he couldn't. Drizzt silently berated himself. He was angry and agitated about Guenhwyvar's absence.

And there was more to it than that, Drizzt knew deep in his heart, whenever he glanced at Dahlia, to find her staring at Entreri.

He felt irrelevant, like there was some bond between these two greater than his own bond with Dahlia.

And without Guenhwyvar, what did he have left other than his companionship with Dahlia? Drizzt took a deep breath.

Entreri suddenly threw his glass against a wall across the room. The assassin scooped up the brandy bottle and took a long swallow.

As surprising as that was, Drizzt surprised the others and himself even more when he stepped back from them and drew Charon's Claw from off his back.

The powerful sword bit at him immediately, releasing energy into his hands. The first concentrated attacks came at the core of the drow, at his heart and soul, as Charon's Claw tried to utterly obliterate him—and it had the power to do that to most who tried to wield it, Drizzt understood without the slightest bit of doubt.

But Drizzt Do'Urden was not so easily dominated or destroyed. Nor was he inexperienced in the ways of sentient weapons. The sword Khazid'hea, the famed Cutter, had once similarly attacked him, though not nearly as powerfully as this particular blade, he had to admit. And in the drow academy for warriors, Melee-Magthere, students spent many tendays studying the powers of sentient weapons and pitting their wills against dominating magical implements.

The drow doubled down on his own concentration then and fought back, demanding fealty from the blade.

The blade fought back.

Gradually, Drizzt altered his counterattack, promising the sword a glorious joining. He would wield it well.

Charon's Claw teased him with power. It directed Drizzt's thoughts to Artemis Entreri, who was now, the sword assured him, his slave.

And indeed, when Entreri protested the drawn blade and took a step toward Drizzt, Charon's Claw laid him low.

Dahlia cried out and broke Kozah's Needle into her flails, putting them into motion immediately.

But Drizzt held up his left hand and motioned her to patience. He told the sword to free Entreri, and when it did not, he demanded that the painful vibrations cease.

"Now!" he ordered aloud.

Artemis Entreri staggered to the side and gradually straightened. He walked straight back from Drizzt, never taking his eyes from the drow, never blinking, though the pain had obviously ceased.

He believed that this was a betrayal, Drizzt saw clearly from his angry expression. "Free him," Drizzt told the sword.

Charon's Claw went at the drow's soul again, even more ferociously, and Drizzt groaned and staggered once more. Images and thoughts of obliteration, of nothingness, filled his mind, as Charon's Claw tried to use fear to weaken his resolve.

Drizzt had lived too long, had been through too much, to give in to such despair.

He won the fight, but only to a draw. Charon's Claw would not release Artemis Entreri, and there was no way Drizzt would ever get through that angry wall. Perhaps Drizzt could prevent the sword from inflicting, or at least from sustaining, any torture upon the man, but he could make no progress past that point.

He turned to the sword's own tactics.

Now the drow's thoughts were back in Gauntlgrym, at the pit of the primordial. Entreri had said that he could sense the sword's fear at such a prospect.

Drizzt saw it, too, felt it keenly.

He redoubled his concentration, picturing the sword dropping down, down to the waiting fiery maw of the godlike beast.

This was no deception, and despite his desperate struggle, a smile widened on his face. Charon's Claw was deathly afraid.

Charon's Claw recognized its doom.

The sword went at him again, wildly.

Drizzt changed the image in his mind to one of Entreri wielding Charon's Claw once more, presenting the blade with a clear choice: the fire or Entreri.

Charon's Claw calmed immediately.

Drizzt slid it away into its scabbard. He shook his head and looked back at his companions, and nearly fell to his knees from sudden weakness, thoroughly drained by the battle.

"Are you mad?" Entreri growled at him.

"Why would you do such a thing?" Dahlia added.

"The sword fears our course," Drizzt explained, and he cast a sly look at the assassin as he finished, "It would prefer your hand once more above a journey to the mouth of the primordial."

"You can control it," Dahlia said breathlessly.

Entreri never looked at her, his gaze fixed on Drizzt.

"As I said, the choice is yours," the drow said.

"You would trust me beside you with that blade in hand?" Entreri asked.

"No," Drizzt said, even as Dahlia started to say yes.

Entreri stared at the drow for a long, long while. "You wield it," he said at length. "I cannot."

"Because you know it will turn on you," Entreri reasoned. "You have not the accompanying glove, and cannot maintain your discipline indefinitely at so high a level. And that sword is relentless, I assure you."

"Then you cannot wield it, either," the drow replied.

Entreri started to drink from the brandy bottle, but just laughed helplessly and retrieved another glass from the bar, pouring himself a modest amount. He set the bottle down, held his glass aloft, and said, "To Gauntlgrym."

Drizzt nodded grimly.

Dahlia's chortle sounded more like a gasp.

They heard their names called out ahead of them as they moved to the common hallway on the inn's second floor, and from there to the stairs, and before the trio ever reached the exit, the cheering on the street outside began to mount.

"Hailed as heroes," Dahlia remarked.

"They are truly pathetic," Entreri was fast to respond.

Drizzt studied the man, looking for a clue that perhaps he was enjoying this notoriety more than he would let on. But no, there was nothing to indicate any such thing, and when Drizzt considered Entreri in light of the man he had once known, he wasn't really surprised.

Neither Drizzt nor the assassin cared much for such accolades, but for very different reasons. Drizzt didn't care because he understood that the community was stronger than the individual. In that same vein, he accepted the cheers in the knowledge that they would do the community well.

Entreri, though, didn't care because Entreri didn't care—about applause or sneering, or anything else regarding his place in the world and the views of those around him. He simply didn't care, and so the enthusiasm with which they were greeted when they exited the inn brought a scowl to Entreri's face, one Drizzt knew to be sincere.

Dahlia, though, seemed quite pleased.

Drizzt didn't know what to make of that. She had just exacted revenge—her most desperately wanted revenge—upon a tiefling who had apparently haunted her for most of her young life. Drizzt hardly understood the visceral level of hatred he had seen this elf woman exhibit, but truly that battle had meant quite a bit to her, and on a very deep and primal level. Even her obvious fears for Entreri's impending demise now seemed to wash away as she basked in the excitement of the crowd.

And indeed, the citizens of Neverwinter exuded excitement and joy at this time. Nearly the entire population of the settlers had gathered along the streets outside the inn, and among their front lines stood Genevieve and the man who had helped her drag their wounded companion from the sewers.

That sight gave Drizzt profound peace. Perhaps the death of Alegni and the retreat of the Shadovar was a bigger gain for the future of Neverwinter, but personalizing such a victory to the level of the three saved aboleth slaves settled well on the shoulders of Drizzt Do'Urden.

Weapons and fists lifted into the air defiantly, a cry of freedom regained. When Drizzt considered the recent history of this settlement, he came to understand and appreciate the exuberance.

He had come through Neverwinter beside Bruenor not so long ago, before the revelation of the Thayan and Netherese presence even, and had found the citizens besieged by the strange, shriveled zombie victims of the cataclysmic volcano. They hadn't known the source of the threat, of the Dread Ring then, and the nefarious powers behind the unsettling and dangerous events.

But now it had played out and the Thayans were in disarray, perhaps even gone from the region. And Alegni and his Netherese had been driven from the city, the beast beheaded.

Had the prospects for a new Neverwinter, post-apocalypse, ever looked any brighter?

Perhaps they were laying that victory too much onto the shoulders of Drizzt and his two companions, the drow thought, for it was the work of these many folk that had really won the day. Drizzt and his companions had defeated Alegni and had kept that twisted necromancer at bay, but the bulk of the fighting had been done, and won, by the people now cheering. When Drizzt considered his own role in it all, mostly trying to simply stay alive against a possessed Artemis Entreri, it seemed laughable to him that he would be viewed on such a figurative pedestal.

But to no harm, any of it, the drow knew from decades of similar experience. He had seen this type of celebration in Ten-Towns, surely, and in Mithral Hall, and across the lands. It was a collective expression of relief and victory, and whatever symbols—Drizzt and his two companions, in this instance—were purely irrelevant to that needed emotional release. He looked directly at Genevieve and nodded, and her beaming smile back at him warmed him indeed.

"Well met again, Drizzt Do'Urden," Jelvus Grinch said, stepping out ahead of the crowd and moving right before the trio. "I trust your dwarf companion is well."

Drizzt didn't wince at the reference to Bruenor, whom Jelvus Grinch had met briefly under an assumed name. For a moment, his reaction surprised him, and when he thought about it, his reaction pleased him. He missed Bruenor sorely, but he was indeed at peace about the dwarf.

He merely nodded to Jelvus Grinch, not wishing to go into detail over something the man didn't really care about anyway.

"Once before, I asked you to stay with us," Jelvus Grinch said. "Perhaps now you understand how great your value to Neverwinter might prove . . ."

"We're leaving," Artemis Entreri coldly interrupted.

Jelvus Grinch fell back and looked at the man curiously.

"Now," Entreri added.

"We don't know how far the Shadovar have retreated," Jelvus Grinch pleaded. "Many went through the gates their wizards enacted—and perhaps they can come back through those same gates!"

"Then you should remain vigilant," Entreri replied. "Or leave."

"You know more about them than we do," Jelvus Grinch shot back, now with a hint of anger in his tone.

"I know nothing of them or of the dark place they call home," Entreri spat back at him before he could gain any momentum. "They're gone, Alegni is dead. That's all I care about."

"And you have his sword," Jelvus Grinch said, glancing over at the weapon strapped diagonally across Drizzt's thin back.

Artemis Entreri laughed, a condescending and mocking tone clearly telling the Neverwinter man that he couldn't begin to understand the implications of his last words.

"We must go," Drizzt interjected calmly. "We have urgent business that cannot wait. Keep your guard strong, though I doubt the Netherese will return anytime soon. From what I have seen, they are obedient to strong leaders, and with Alegni gone, would any other Netherese lord deem to replace him in a place so dangerous and hostile as Neverwinter?"

"We cannot know," Jelvus Grinch said.

Drizzt dropped a hand on the man's strong shoulder. "Hold your faith in your fellow citizens," Drizzt advised. "The region is full of dangers, as you knew when first you returned."

"And you'll remain?" the man asked hopefully.

"Not too far for now, I expect," Drizzt assured him.

"Then don't remain a stranger to the folk of Neverwinter, I beg. You, all three, are ever welcome here."

A great cheer arose behind him, affirming the sentiment.

The gathering followed the trio across the city, across the winged wyvern bridge.

"We will name it again the Walk of Barrabus!" Jelvus Grinch proclaimed, and the cheering renewed.

"Barrabus is dead," Artemis Entreri replied, cutting Grinch's grin off short. "I killed him. Don't remind me of him with your foolish names."

It sounded as a clear threat to everyone who heard it, and Entreri followed it by staring hard at Jelvus Grinch, by silently letting the man know that if he named the bridge as he'd just promised, Entreri really would come back and kill him.

Drizzt noted it all. He knew that look—frozen, utterly uncaring, uncompromisingly removed from sympathy—from a century before, and the poignant reminder of the truth of Artemis Entreri slapped the drow's romantic nostalgia quite decidedly, and shook him profoundly in his current time and place.

Drizzt looked to Jelvus Grinch to view his reaction, and the way the blood drained from the strong man's face revealed that Artemis Entreri had lost none of his charm.

The First Citizen of Neverwinter cleared his throat several times before mustering the courage to resume speaking, this time to Drizzt. "Have you found better fortune with your panther?"

Drizzt shook his head.

"I suggest you speak to Arunika," said Jelvus Grinch. "She is investigating this, at my insistence. The woman is quite wise in the ways of magic, and knows the workings of the various planes."

Drizzt glanced at his companions, who offered no obvious opinion.

"Where do I find her?" he asked.

"We're ready for the road," Artemis Entreri remarked.

"We can wait," Dahlia said.

"No, we can't," said Entreri. "If you wish to go and find the red-haired woman, then do so, but we'll be on our way up the northern road. I trust you'll ride hard to find us."

Drizzt turned to Jelvus Grinch, who indicated the inn behind him. "Arunika has been given a room there, that she could better tend to your companion."

The drow turned and regarded Entreri and Dahlia one last time, to see Entreri's harsh expression and obvious agitation at the thought of any delays, and conversely, Dahlia's almost frantically-darting eyes, as if looking for some way to forestall this expedition. Drizzt had never expected anything quite like that from Dahlia, whether she wore her hard-visage braid and woad, or the softer image she now painted upon her pretty face.

Guenhwyvar's plight was more important, and he rushed into the inn. He had barely said the name "Arunika," before the innkeeper directed him to a room down the first floor hallway.

Arunika opened the door before he had even knocked, and he understood the reception when he entered, for her room looked out on the gathering in the street and the window was open. Even as Drizzt noted that, Arunika moved over and closed it.

"You believe that throwing the weapon into the mouth of the primordial will destroy it," she said.

"I came to speak of Guenhwyvar."

"That, too," the red-haired woman agreed.

Drizzt found himself quite at ease as he regarded her disarming smile . . . truly disarming, with freckled dimples and a sweetness that went beyond all reason.

He determinedly shook that curious, and curiously stray, thought away.

"I agree with your assessment of the sword," Arunika said, and she eased back into a soft cushioned couch, casually tossing her long and soft red hair from in front of her face.

"And our course?"

"Artemis Entreri thinks that destroying the blade will destroy him."

"He does not fear . . ." Drizzt started to say, but he stopped short and stared hard at Arunika. How had she come to know Entreri's real name? To everyone else in the city, save himself and Dahlia, the man was still known as Barrabus the Gray, and as far as he knew, none of them had uttered any hints of the assassin's real identity.

"Oh, he fears it, of course," Arunika replied, apparently missing the drow's shocked response—or ignoring it. "He just has too much hatred within him to admit it. Everyone fears death, ranger. Everyone."

"Then perhaps some simply fear living more."

Arunika shrugged as if it did not matter. "If you deign to destroy Charon's Claw, your best path is to the primordial, I agree," she went on. "Oh, there are better ways—surer ways . . . the breath of an ancient white dragon comes to mind—but I expect that time is not your ally. Charon's Claw is a Netherese blade, and those unbearable despots will go to such lengths to protect and retrieve their artifacts that would impress any githyanki zealot."

Drizzt wasn't quite sure of the analogy. He had heard of the githyanki. They were sometimes seen in Menzoberranzan and the few he had viewed did seem to possess unduly decorated armor and weapons. The reference seemed clear enough, though.

"Since I know of no cooperative ancient white dragons in the area, my advice to you would be the primordial in Gauntlgrym."

"You seem to know quite a bit of quite a bit," Drizzt replied. "Charon's Claw? Gauntlgrym? Even the assassin's real name. I expect that little of that information is general throughout Neverwinter."

"I survive by being smarter than those around me," Arunika replied.

"And you have ways of seeing things others cannot discern, no doubt."

"No doubt," the woman replied, and she patted the cushion beside her on the couch.

Drizzt grabbed a wooden chair instead, and set it before her, drawing a cute—too cute—little laugh from Arunika as he did.

"Does my insight, or perhaps, my other-sight, disappoint you?" she asked coyly.

Drizzt considered that for a moment, and then answered, "Not if it aids me."

"Your beloved Guenhwyvar," Arunika stated. "May I have the figurine?"

Before he even considered the movement, Drizzt produced the onyx statuette and reached it out toward Arunika, hesitating only when she similarly stretched to retrieve it from him. Few had held this figurine, few would the drow trust to ever touch it, let alone take it from his grasp. Yet here he was, giving it to a curiously knowledgeable woman he hardly knew! His grip instinctively tightened.

"If you wish my advice and insight, it would be better for you to allow me to study it properly," the woman remarked, and Drizzt perked up as if coming out of a slumber and handed Guenhwyvar over.

"It will take some time for me to properly inspect the aura around the magical statue," Arunika explained, rolling it over in her hands before her sparkling, pretty eyes.

Incredibly pretty, Drizzt thought, and it wasn't until her words registered that he was able to get that thought out of his mind.

"I have little time," he said. "My friends have already departed Neverwinter, likely, and I will not leave without Guenhwyvar."

"Without the statue, you mean," Arunika corrected, and the reality of that stung Drizzt profoundly.

"You're welcome to stay and watch," the woman said. She rose from the couch and moved to a desk at the side of the room, pulling open the largest, lowest drawer and producing a satchel. She placed it on the table and rummaged through it, bringing forth assorted candles and powders, a silver bowl, a phial of clear liquid, and a silvery scroll tube.

Drizzt watched from across the room and said not another word as Arunika set up her scrying table. She chanted under her breath as she lit the candles, spacing them appropriately around the bowl, then began a different incantation as she poured the liquid into the bowl, splashing it over the onyx figurine in the process.

She set her hands on the table, palms up, tilted her head back, and let her eyes roll up as she began to chant louder and more insistently.

It went on for a long, long while, and Drizzt constantly glanced out the window to try to gauge the passing hours. He knew that Dahlia and Entreri couldn't go into Gauntlgrym without him—he had the sword, after all! But the thought of them out on the road alone bit at his sensibilities in no good way.

The sun was low in the sky when Arunika abruptly stood up from her seat and rubbed her eyes. Casually, she tossed the onyx figurine back to Drizzt.

"What do you know?" he asked, not liking that almost dismissive toss, or the resigned look on the woman's face.

"I sense no connection to the creature you call Guenhwyvar," Arunika admitted.

"What does that mean?" Drizzt asked, trying to keep the desperation out of his voice, though a primal scream was surely bubbling within him.

The red-haired woman shrugged.

"That the magic has been dispelled?" Drizzt demanded. "Or that the panth—or that Guenhwyvar has been destroyed? Is that even possible?"

"Of course," Arunika said, and Drizzt swallowed hard.

"She is the astral essence of the panther, akin to a goddess," Drizzt protested.

"Even gods can be destroyed, Drizzt Do'Urden. Though we do not know that such is the case. Somehow, some way, the connection between the panther and the statuette has been severed—understand that they are not the same thing! Artemis Entreri carries the token of the nightmare, indeed you wear one of a unicorn, but these are magical creations affixed to magical implements. Your whistle is your steed. To destroy the whistle would be to obliterate the magical construct you call Andahar. The same is true of Entreri's mount. These are not life forms, but enchantments cleverly disguised as such. Without the disguise, you could ride your whistle across the leagues, though I doubt your sensibilities would find much comfort in that, to say nothing of your arse."

Drizzt could hardly keep up with her, given the enormity of the woman's proclamation regarding Guenhwyvar. His blank stare brought Arunika over to him, where she dropped a comforting hand on his shoulder.

"Guenhwyvar is different from your whistle," she explained. "Different from Entreri's hell steed. Guenhwyvar is a living, breathing creature of another dimension, an essence not captured by the statuette, but one called by the statuette. It is an old enchantment—one from the days of the great mythals, I expect!—and one not easily replicated by any living mage, not even Elminster himself."

"You think her dead," Drizzt remarked.

Arunika shrugged and patted his shoulder again. "I think we cannot know. What we, what I, know, is that there is no connection I can sense between your statuette and that creature, Guenhwyvar. Your figurine still radiates magic—that much I can easily see, but it is a beacon without a viewer."

Drizzt swallowed hard and slowly shook his head, not wanting to hear it.

"I'm sorry, Drizzt Do'Urden," Arunika said, and she went up to her tip-toes and kissed Drizzt on the cheek.

He pulled back. "Keep looking!" He thought back to a fateful day in Mithral Hall, so long ago, when he had grabbed Jarlaxle by the collar and similarly implored him, only on that occasion, to find Catti-brie and Regis.

Arunika just fixed him with that sympathetic, calming smile and nodded.

Drizzt stumbled out of the room and the inn and back onto the street, where only a few folks milled around, all looking his way curiously.

"He's been to the red-headed one's bed," one woman snickered to her friend as they hustled by, clearly mistaking the drow's wobbly gait.

"Guenhwyvar," he whispered, rolling the onyx statue over in his hand. A burst of rage came over him. He blew into his silver whistle, and leaped upon Andahar's strong back as the unicorn thundered up to join him, then urged the mighty steed away at a full gallop.

He needed the exertion; he sought exhaustion. Only in action could he find solace at that dark moment.

He thundered out of Neverwinter's main gate, Andahar's hooves churning the northern road, the wind bringing moistness to the drow's lavender eyes.

Or maybe it wasn't the wind.

"I thought that *I* hated Alegni," Entreri said, standing across the small cooking fire from Dahlia. Prudence dictated that they should have no such firelight out in the unsettled wilds of Neverwinter Wood, but these two didn't often listen to such moderate voices; or perhaps it was that very voice that compelled the two troubled souls to light such a beacon, inviting danger and battle.

"You did not?" the elf sarcastically replied.

Entreri laughed. "Of course I did, with all of my heart, so I believed—until I measure my hatred of him to your own."

"Perhaps your heart is not as big as mine."

"Perhaps my heart is not as dark as yours." The assassin managed a little grin as he uttered the quip, expecting a rejoinder from the quick-witted woman. To his surprise, though, Dahlia simply looked down at the fire and stirred it a bit with a stick she had retrieved. She poked and prodded at the embers, drawing bursts of small flames which made her eyes sparkle in their dancing and darting reflections.

There was pain in Dahlia's pretty eyes, along with a simmering anger—no, something more than anger, like the purest outrage crystallized into a sharp and stabbing point of light.

Artemis Entreri recognized it, had felt the same, and when he, too, was very young.

"You presume much," Dahlia said. "We went to kill Alegni, and so we did, and you attacked him no less than I."

This, too, this avoidance, Entreri knew well.

"I had no choice. I had no escape from the man," he said. "He carried the sword and the sword owned me. My choice was to fight—"

"To die," Dahlia interrupted.

"Preferable to what came before."

The woman looked up, her eyes meeting his, but only for a heartbeat before she turned again to the safety of the distracting firelight.

"This was the easier, and the safer path," Entreri said. "A prisoner attempts to break free, or he accepts his servitude. But not so for you. Herzgo Alegni had no hold over Dahlia, yet you drove us there, to that bridge and to that fight."

"I pay back my debts."

"Indeed, and what a great debt this must have been, yes?"

She glanced at him again, but this time, not in shared recognition, but with a warning scowl. And again, she returned her gaze to the firelight.

"And when all seemed lost, Alegni's army closing in around us, Drizzt downed by my own sword, and myself helpless beneath Alegni's blade, Dahlia was free."

She did look up, then, and stared at him hard.

"Free to fly away."

"What friend would I be . . .?" she started to ask, but Entreri's quiet snicker mocked her.

"I know you better than that," he declared.

"You know nothing," she said, but without conviction, for as she stared at Entreri and he at her, the connection between them could not escape either.

"You did not fly back onto the bridge out of loyalty, but out of something so deep within you and so dark inside that you could not leave. I said I would die before returning to my servitude, but Dahlia was no less captured than I. I by a sword, and you by . . ."

Dahlia looked away abruptly, her gaze to the fire, where she kicked at it to send a rush of embers into the air, obviously needing the distraction, the change of subject, anything.

"A memory," Artemis Entreri finished, and Dahlia's shoulders slumped so profoundly that she seemed as if she would simply topple over into the fire.

And despite himself, despite everything he had spent nearly a century and a half perfecting, Artemis Entreri went to her, right beside her, and put his arm around her to hold her steady. Her tears streamed down her face and dropped to the ground below, but he did not wipe them away.

She tensed, and inhaled deeply to steady herself. As she stood straight once more, Entreri took a step to the side. He looked at the fire, giving her this moment of privacy as she passed through the darkness.

"You hated him more than I ever could," Entreri admitted.

"He's dead," Dahlia stated flatly.

"And a pity that he fell through the dimensions as he breathed his last," said Entreri. "I would have tied his corpse to my nightmare and dragged it through the streets of Neverwinter until the skin fell from his broken bones."

He felt Dahlia looking at him, though he did not return the stare.

"For me?" she asked.

"For both of us," he replied. Given what he knew now about Dahlia, such an act might have brought him a deeper peace from a more profound scar—with Herzgo Alegni substituting for one who betrayed him so many decades before.

Dahlia managed a little chuckle then, and said, "I would have liked watching that."

In the brush not so far away, Drizzt Do'Urden couldn't make out many of the words the two exchanged. He had dismounted and dismissed Andahar far back, when first he had spotted the fire. Somehow, he knew that it would be the camp of Dahlia and Entreri.

And still, Drizzt had not openly approached. He tried to tell himself that he wasn't sneaking up on them.

He had watched their discussion for some time, and could have moved closer without being detected, perhaps close enough to hear their words.

But those words didn't seem to matter. Drizzt found himself more interested in their movements, particularly the way they looked at each other, and more poignantly, how they looked away from each other.

There was nothing sexual between them, no hint that Entreri had made a cuckold of him or anything of the sort.

Strangely, Drizzt had a feeling that such a crude revelation might have stung less profoundly.

For he knew now what he had long suspected: Artemis Entreri knew something of Dahlia, understood something of Dahlia, which he did not and could not. Some cord wound between them. In her tears and in her quiet chuckle, Dahlia had shared more with Artemis Entreri then she had with Drizzt in all their nights of lovemaking.

How could it be that this quiet conversation about a campfire in the nighttime forest felt more intimate than making love?

It made no sense.

But there it was before him.

CHAPTER 13

WHERE THE SHADOWS NEVER END

THE WOUNDS WERE CONSIDERABLE," THE SHADE PRIEST EXPLAINED. "HE WILL be many tendays in repair."

"Then get more priests to tend him," Draygo Quick answered sharply. "He does not have tendays."

The priest rocked back, surprised, obviously, at being treated so. He and his brethren had just pulled the tiefling from the very edge of the grave, after all.

"Few had thought that Lord Alegni would survive, though your great action in destroying the vicious feline was brilliantly performed," the priest replied, a stinging rebuttal, though one couched, prudently, with proper compliment to the powerful Netherese lord.

The words were true enough—regarding Alegni at least, Draygo Quick had to admit. The tiefling's skin had been hanging in tatters, after all, and one of his eyes had been plucked from its socket, left hanging by a cord on his cheek.

And those had been the least of his wounds.

"I need him, quickly," Draygo Quick demanded.

"He will live," was all the priest could respond.

"He must do more than live," the warlock warned. "He must return to Faerûn in mere days to retrieve that which he has lost."

"The sword."

"Our sword," the withered old warlock replied.

"You could send others . . ."

"It is not my responsibility. It is Herzgo Alegni's. Summon other priests—as many as you can find. Mend every wound and stand him up."

The priest looked at him doubtfully.

"For his own sake," Draygo Quick answered that stare. "Now be gone."

The priest knew better than to argue with the likes of Draygo Quick, and he bowed curtly and hustled away.

Draygo Quick took a wheezing breath. He had sponsored Herzgo Alegni to a position of great power in Netherese society. He was not responsible for the tiefling, of course, but Alegni's actions—his victories and his failures—surely played upon the well-guarded reputation of Draygo Quick.

Herzgo Alegni had lost a Netherese artifact, a powerful and prized sword, and one that Draygo Quick had given to him. Herzgo Alegni had to get it back. That would always be the case in Netherese custom and law, but it was even more poignant this time, Draygo Quick knew, for the recent history of Alegni had not been one of shining triumph. His expedition to the region known as Neverwinter should have been secured years before. True, the unexpected cataclysm of the volcanic eruption had occurred at a terrible time, but excuses could only carry one so far among the strict and demanding Netheril Empire.

Now the loss of the sword seemed even more profound, because it had come at a time of even higher expectation and because it had not been the only loss. Despite Draygo Quick's controversial decision to send scores of reinforcements to Alegni's Neverwinter garrison, the city of Neverwinter itself had been lost to the Netherese.

Even with the Thayans in disarray and on the run, the city had been lost.

Draygo Quick had heard the whispers that morning, hints that he had given too much—in terms of gifts and responsibilities—to a failed leader. He had even overheard a pair of powerful nobles questioning his own abilities, wondering if perhaps age had dulled his mind, for would Draygo Quick had ever made such a terrible misjudgment in his earlier days?

They had to get Herzgo Alegni on his feet, and Alegni had to go and retrieve that sword in short order. Neverwinter was lost to them, but so be it.

The loss of Charon's Claw was another matter entirely.

The long room glowed with firelight and teemed with magical, primal energy, as two-score primordial-powered forges glowed with hot life. The sound of hammers rang clear, echoing about the stones.

"Thinking in the past?" Tiago Baenre remarked when he caught up to Ravel, who stood with eyes closed, as if basking in the more subtle sensations. "Or considering the potential, perhaps?"

"Both," the spellspinner admitted. "This is how Gauntlgrym must have sounded and smelled and seemed at the height of dwarven power."

"You approve of the height of dwarven power?" Tiago asked with sly grin.

"I can appreciate it," Ravel admitted. "Particularly now that said power works for me."

That drew an awkward look from Tiago, and he directed Ravel's gaze to the main forge, the central oven, where a drow bent over a silvery blade lying on a table, a large backpack of ingredients—magical powders and elixirs—close at hand. Not far to the side rested a djinni bottle. Looking at it, Tiago couldn't help but lick his lips eagerly. What blades might Gol'fanin create for him with such implements, and in such a forge as this magnificent creation?

"Now that it works for House Xorlarrin," Ravel corrected, but not correct enough for Tiago, who nodded again toward that particular drow, Gol'fanin, Tiago's own assistant in this journey.

"Perhaps I consider you an honorary member of my family," the spellspinner offered.

"Would that not be a tremendous step down?"

Ravel's smile disappeared in the blink of an eye, but Tiago's laughter diffused the tension before it could truly begin to mount.

"How goes the fight for the outer halls?" Ravel asked.

"Your older brother and his pet elementals are proving quite effective," Tiago answered. "They drive the critters, the corbies, and even the dwarf ghosts, before them. We have found a pocket of orcs, as well, and are . . . negotiating."

"Do we really need more slaves?"

Tiago shrugged as if it did not matter. "The more hands who serve us, the more quickly the corridors will be bolstered and secured." As he finished, he glanced over at the outer forges, both ends, where goblins and orcs and even bugbears worked the metal hard, building crude beam supports and thick iron doors, and most importantly, new rail lines and long pegs for the ore carts. Other slaves carried the finished products from the room to the appointed corridors and chambers.

Nearer in toward the central forge, drow craftsmen worked the fires, creating the finer items necessary for refurbishing the infrastructure of the vast complex. Sensitive drow fingers sheared at hot metal to create intricate locks and delicate-looking but strong sections of stairway they could assemble in the larger chambers above, where the previous stairs had been destroyed by the rage of the rampaging primordial.

Tiago's words resonated with Ravel, the young Baenre could clearly see. It would take years to restore Gauntlgrym, and to secure the chambers, and that was assuming an ample supply of metal. The forges needed no fuel, and that was a tremendous advantage indeed, but the raw materials were not so easily found in tunnels teeming with dwarf ghosts or dire corbies or other untamed monsters.

"Patience, my friend," Tiago said. "You have exceeded even your own wildest hopes thus far."

"True enough," Ravel admitted.

"And now you have something to lose, and so you tremble," Tiago said, and Ravel nodded.

"Who trembles?" came another voice, and the pair turned to regard the approach of Berellip.

"I was speaking figuratively, priestess," said Tiago.

Berellip gave Ravel a dismissive glance. "Were you?"

Tiago laughed, but Ravel didn't follow his lead.

"We were discussing the slow work," Tiago said. "The long process and road ahead for House Xorlarrin if you mean to proceed with your dreams of creating a city to rival Menzoberranzan."

"Why would we ever think to do such a thing?" Berellip replied with feigned surprise. "A rival city? That would not please Lolth."

"It would please Zeerith," Tiago quipped, again purposely leaving off her title, daring either of the children of Xorlarrin to call him out on his indiscretion, which neither did, though Berellip narrowed her eyes and offered a quiet sneer.

"You know why we journeyed here," Ravel remarked. "Matron Mother Quenthel knows, as well, as does Archmage Gromph."

"Have you reservations now, young Baenre, since we have succeeded more than you could have imagined?" Berellip added.

"Nay," Tiago replied easily. "Quite the contrary. I am pleased by what I have learned and seen. Your progress has been remarkable, and this place—these forges, this source of power, the resonating strength of this complex—is beyond anything I would have imagined. You have the beginnings of a proper sister city."

Berellip stared at him and seemed unconvinced of his sincerity.

"I would recommend that you send word back to Menzoberranzan," Tiago added. "You will need more hands, and quickly."

"Baenre hands?" Berellip asked, her voice full of suspicion. "Will Matron Mother Quenthel send her legions to aid us?"

Tiago laughed at her, thoroughly mocking her with his easy tone and manner, and Berellip stiffened even more. "You do understand that you're here at Matron Baenre's suffrage?" he asked. "If we were truly interested in establishing this place for ourselves, then why would we have allowed you to journey here so freely? Why would we not have sent our own expedition to this place?

"Because we do not wish to dissuade House Xorlarrin of its ambitions," he answered when the Xorlarrins did not. "Matron Mother Quenthel is willing to grant to you this place and your dreams, as we have made clear by our actions, and even more so by our inactions. With the advent of the Netheril Empire, the world has become too dangerous a place for the Houses of Menzoberranzan to so continue their incessant in-fighting, and House Xorlarrin is among the worst of those offenders, even you must admit."

Despite her stoic posturing, Berellip swallowed hard at that obvious truism.

"And so we'll allow you to migrate to the outskirts of Menzoberranzan's domain and influence."

"As long as our city strengthens Menzoberranzan," Ravel stated.

"Of course. Were you to rival us instead of working in accordance with our needs, we would utterly destroy you," Tiago said matter-of-factly, and he had said the same before in other words, of course. He had never made a secret of it to either of these two.

"But you think we should call for more drow to bolster our ranks now," Berellip remarked, as if seeing the contradiction.

"I never said drow," Tiago corrected. "The Clawrift could spare a few hundred kobolds, a thousand even. They are clever little wretches and surprisingly adept at mining and working metal. Such a gift from Menzoberranzan would help you greatly here and would hardly diminish Menzoberranzan, of course, since the rats breed like . . . well, rats, and they would quickly replenish their ranks in the corridors of the Clawrift. And driders! Indeed, you should ask for more driders, for I have no doubt that many in Menzoberranzan would be rid of the whole lot of them were we able! Such wretched things.

"Bring them in to your side, I say, and grant them some outer sections to secure and call as their own home."

"Driders are driders for a reason," Berellip dryly reminded.

"The Spider Queen would not be pleased?" Tiago asked sarcastically. "Better to put them into service for her, would you not agree?"

"That's not the point," Berellip argued.

"It's entirely the point," Tiago said, and he dismissed all semblance of being reasonable. "That is the only point . . . to any of this! You're here, in these halls, to serve the Spider Queen. You'll be allowed to construct a sister city to Menzoberranzan, if you can succeed, for no purpose other than to serve the Spider Queen. Matron Mother Quenthel allows you this because she serves the Spider Queen. There is no other reason, there is no other purpose. Once you truly appreciate that, Berellip Xorlarrin, you will better understand my counsel, and only if you do come to truly appreciate that, Priestess Berellip, will you and your family have a chance of surviving this daring 'escape' from Menzoberranzan. I should not have to school a priestess of Lolth in these obvious truths. You disappoint me!"

With that, Tiago took his abrupt leave, moving to join Gol'fanin, who had started the long task of creating the coveted blades.

Herzgo Alegni stubbornly pulled himself out of the bed and stood to his full, imposing height. The many bandages he wore fought against him as he straightened, but the proud tiefling just pressed through their binding, obviously determined to show no weakness before the withered old warlock. Still, he stumbled a bit, disoriented by the fact that he no longer had a working right eye.

"When will you be ready to return to the land of light?" Draygo Quick asked him curtly, and without even a casual hint that he cared about Alegni's health in the least—which of course, he did not.

"When I am ordered to do so," Alegni replied.

"Even this moment?"

"I will leave at once, if you so desire."

Draygo Quick couldn't suppress his smile. Alegni was a stubborn one. He could barely stand, his legs wobbly, his shoulders shaking from the strain as he tried to keep them squared.

"You know that you must return, of course."

Alegni looked at him curiously.

"You left something behind."

Still the tiefling seemed confused.

Draygo Quick was not surprised by the reaction, doubting that Alegni remembered much of anything of the last moments of that brutal fight. When he'd come into the Shadowfell, so near to death, the great panther tearing at him and biting deep into his flesh, his every action had been reflexive and desperate, his every sound filled with the most profound timbre of agony.

Suddenly Alegni's one uncovered eye popped open wide and he glanced all around desperately. "Claw," he muttered.

"They have it."

Herzgo Alegni turned back to face his master, and his shoulders slumped. This was his failure, of course, and one that was typically accompanied by the most profound and extreme punishment. Netherese lords lived and died, the saying went, but weapons were eternal.

They were supposed to be, at least.

"They live?"

"All three, yes. Indeed, they seem to be doing quite well among the grateful citizens of Neverwinter."

The tiefling screwed up his face. "Your soldiers failed!"

"My warlord, Herzgo Alegni, failed me, so it would seem."

Alegni stiffened at that unavoidable truth. "They were three against one," he explained.

"Four against two," Draygo Quick corrected. "By your prideful choice."

"And all of the Shadovar remained at bay!" the hulking warrior insisted.

"Lord Alegni, you are not appealing when you whimper like a child," Draygo Quick warned. "Your charges—*your* charges—acted as they had been ordered. You were certain that Barrabus the Gray would be brought under your control, and that your deception would put you alone with Dahlia for your long-desired victory. It would appear that you were not quite correct."

"Three against one!" the tiefling insisted.

"Four against two," Draygo Quick again corrected. "Would you so easily forget the drow's panther companion? Or Effron, who battled the beast for a long while as you played out your folly on the bridge?"

Alegni's face tightened at the mention of Effron. Alegni wanted to argue, to throw some insult or threat the twisted warlock's way, Draygo Quick recognized, for how many times had he seen that look?

"You have no one to blame but Herzgo Alegni," the withered old warlock insisted. "Accept your responsibility. You know what must be done."

"I must retrieve the sword."

Draygo Quick nodded. "Back to your rest. The priests will be along, one after the other. Accept their healing and their nourishing spells, for you will face that dangerous trio again soon."

"I have learned from my mistakes."

"Good, then I'll not have to tell you to take others along with you."

"I'll need a new weapon . . ." Alegni said, or started to say, for Draygo Quick was done with him and the old warlock turned on his heel and simply walked away.

He pulled the door closed as he left Alegni's room, and quickly lifted his finger to his pursed lips, indicating that Effron, who had been waiting outside the room, should remain quiet until they were away from the room.

"Will I accompany Lord Alegni to retrieve the sword?" Effron asked many steps later—a bit too eagerly for Draygo Quick's liking.

He stared at the young warlock.

"I'll go with him?" Effron asked again.

"You will go . . . near him," Draygo Quick corrected. "Herzgo Alegni likely walks to his death." He started to go on, but paused, gauging Effron's response.

"How does that make you feel?" he asked.

Effron gave one of his twisted, awkward shrugs, trying futilely to dismiss the notion as if he didn't care—but of course, he most certainly did.

"He's reckless now," Draygo Quick explained.

"Because of the sword, the urgency in retrieving it," Effron surmised.

"Partly, but mostly because of Dahlia's involvement. That, and the betrayal he feels at the hands of Barrabus the Gray."

"Artemis Entreri," Effron corrected.

Draygo Quick chortled at that, as if it hardly mattered.

"The human was his slave for decades," Effron said. "Surely Lord Alegni could have expected no fealty there!"

"There's always a strange dynamic at play between master and slave," Draygo Quick explained. "An unexpected one, to be sure. Not unlike father and son." He tilted his head in a curious manner at Effron as he spoke that thought.

"So I'm to shadow his movements," Effron said. "And?"

"You are to retrieve Charon's Claw," Draygo Quick instructed. "Nothing else matters."

Effron nodded, but there remained something less than convincing in his expression.

"Nothing else," the old warlock reiterated. "Not the fate of Herzgo Alegni, nor that of Dahlia."

Effron swallowed hard.

"Oh yes, I know how deeply you hate her, twisted one, but that is a battle for another day. One I will grant you, on my word—but not until Claw is safely back in Netherese hands."

"Likely I will have to destroy them to retrieve it," Effron said.

"Will you?"

Now it was Effron's turn to curiously regard the master.

"We have a bargaining chip," Draygo Quick explained. "One the drow will not readily ignore." As he spoke, he reached into an extra-dimensional pocket in his voluminous robes and produced a small cage, one that easily fit in his palm, of glowing blue light. Inside it, in quarters too tight to pace, stood a tiny black panther, ears flattened, teeth bared.

Despite the gravity of the situation and the dangerous road ahead, Effron laughed aloud. "It was said that you destroyed the beast."

"Destroyed? Why would I destroy something as beautiful . . ." he paused and brought the cage up before his wrinkled face, and the cat's ears flattened even more and she gave a tiny growl, ". . . something as valuable as this."

"I would truly love having such a companion as that," Effron said, but he bit off the last word and swallowed hard when Draygo Quick flashed a hard stare at him.

"You could never control this one, not even if you possessed the statuette the drow carries," Draygo Quick assured him. "She is more than a magical familiar—much more. She is tied to that drow now, bound by a hundred years and a thousand adventures. She would no sooner serve you than she would the drow's worst mortal enemy."

"Perhaps we are one and the same."

"Is that your answer for everything? Your unrelenting anger at any creature in your path?" Draygo Quick didn't try to keep the disappointment out of his voice.

"Am I to retrieve the sword or am I not?"

Draygo Quick held up the panther once more for Effron to see. "Which is more valuable to the drow, do you suppose?"

CHAPTER 14

HUNTING SIDE BY SIDE

"Y"OUR STEP HAS BECOME HALTING," ENTRERI WHISPERED TO DRIZZT, SO SOFTLY that Dahlia, who was only a couple of steps behind them, had to crane her neck to hear.

"You sense it, too?" the drow asked.

"Not as clearly as you do, obviously."

"Sense what?" Dahlia asked.

"We're being tracked," Drizzt replied. "Or more fittingly, we're being shadowed."

Dahlia straightened and looked all around.

"And if they're watching, they now know that we know," Entreri said dryly and he looked at Dahlia and shook his head and sighed.

"There is no one about," the elf woman replied, rather loudly.

Both Drizzt and Entreri stared at her, the drow shaking his head helplessly. He, too, heaved a sigh and moved off to the side, deeper into the forest brush.

"You think there are Shadovar? Or Thayans?" Dahlia asked Entreri.

"He thinks so," the assassin replied, nodding his chin toward the drow, who was then crouched beside a bush inspecting the leaves and the ground. "Shadovar, it would seem."

"And you trust his judgment over your own?"

"It's not a competition," Entreri replied. "And don't underestimate the woodland skills of our companion. This is his domain—were we in a city, then I would take the lead. But out here in the forest—to answer your question—yes." He finished as Drizzt came walking back over.

"Someone was here not long ago," the drow explained. He glanced back the way they had come, leading their eyes to a fairly clear vista of the trails and roads along the lower ground they had left behind. "Likely watching for our approach."

"Shadovar, Thayans, or someone else?"

"Shadovar," Drizzt answered without hesitation.

"How could you know such a thing?" Dahlia asked, again with her voice full of obvious doubt.

"I know that we are being trailed."

"Even so, have you seen our pursuers?"

Drizzt shook his head, and as he did, he stared hard at Dahlia.

"Yet you conclude that they are Shadovar," Dahlia pressed. "Why would you believe such a thing?"

Drizzt stared at her, seeming quite amused, for some time, before saying, "The sword told me."

Dahlia, a retort obviously at the ready on the tip of her tongue, started to reply, but gulped it back.

"It's excited," Drizzt said to Entreri. "I feel it."

Entreri nodded, as if such a sensation from Charon's Claw was not unknown or unexpected. "The young and twisted warlock, likely," he said.

"What do you know of him?" Drizzt asked.

"I know that he is formidable, full of tricks and spells that cause grievous wounds. He does not panic when battle is upon him, and seems much wiser than his youth would indicate. He's deadly, do not doubt, and doubly so from afar. Worse, if it is Effron shadowing us, then expect that he's not alone."

"You seem to know much of him," Dahlia remarked.

"I hunted your Thayan friends beside him," Entreri replied. "I killed your Thayan friends beside him."

Dahlia stiffened a bit at that remark, but relaxed quickly, for really, given her parting of the ways with Sylora, how could she truly be angered at such an admission? She, too, had killed many Thayans of late.

"He was very close to Herzgo Alegni," Entreri went on. "At times, it seemed as if he hated his fellow tiefling, but other times, they revealed a bond, and a deep one."

"A brother?" Drizzt wondered aloud.

"An uncle?" Entreri replied with a shrug. "I know not, but I'm certain that Effron is not pleased at our treatment of Alegni. And he's an opportunist—an ambitious one."

"Regaining the sword would be a great boon to his reputation," Drizzt reasoned.

"We don't even know if it is him," Dahlia remarked. "We don't even know if there are Shadovar hunting us. We don't even know if *anyone* is hunting us!"

"If you keep speaking so loudly, we'll likely find out soon enough," Entreri replied.

"Is that not a good thing?"

Dahlia's stubbornness drew another sigh from Drizzt, and a second from Entreri, as well.

"We'll find out," Drizzt assured her. "But not on our hunter's terms. We'll find out in a place and time of our choosing."

He turned on his heel and walked off along the path, slowly scanning the forest left and right and ahead, searching for enemies, for ambush, and for a place where they might turn the pursuit.

"Must we always play this game?" Effron asked, and though he tried to resist, he found himself spinning around to see the latest incarnation of this strange illusionist—or perhaps it was really her this time, he dared to hope.

But the Shifter's voice replied to him from behind, yet again.

"It's no game," she assured him. "Many are my enemies."

"And many are your allies."

"Not so."

"Perhaps you would find more allies if you were not so cursedly annoying," Effron offered.

"Allies among people like yourself, who wish to employ my services?"

"Is that so outrageous?"

"But are these allies not also soon to be my enemies when I am employed by one opposed to them?" the Shifter asked, and as Effron turned, her voice turned with him, always remaining behind the flustered young tiefling.

Effron lowered his gaze. "Perhaps both, then."

"Better neither," the Shifter replied. "Now tell me why you have come."

"You cannot surmise?"

"If you're expecting that I will return to Faerûn to steal back Herzgo Alegni's lost sword, then you are a fool. That realization would sadden me, for always have I thought your foolishness because of your age, and not a defect in your reasoning powers."

"You know of the sword?"

"Everyone knows of the sword," the Shifter replied casually, her tone almost mocking Effron's seriousness. "Everyone who pays attention to such things, I mean. Herzgo Alegni lost it to those whom you hired Cavus Dun to hunt. Your failure led to his failure, so it would seem."

"My failure?" Effron asked incredulously. "Did I not send you, along with Cavus Dun—"

"*Your* failure," the Shifter interrupted. "It was your mission, designed by you, and with the hunting party selected by you. That you did not properly prepare us, or did not send enough of us, rests heavily on the broken shoulders of Effron."

"You cannot—"

"You would do well to simply acknowledge your mistake and move on, young tiefling. Cavus Dun lost valued members to this unusual trio. They have ordered no vengeance or recriminations upon you . . . yet."

Effron surely needed no trouble with the likes of Cavus Dun! He doubted the Shifter's description of the ramifications, doubted that any among Cavus Dun's hierarchy were holding him responsible—they had given their blessing for the hunt, after all, and had assured him that his money, no small amount, had been well spent. More likely, he knew, the Shifter was bargaining for a better position in whatever deal Effron might offer her, and was also acting under orders from Cavus Dun to keep him back on his heels, as she had done, so that no blame for the failures in Neverwinter, from the disastrous battle against Dahlia and her cohorts to the loss of Charon's Claw to the near-death of Lord Alegni himself, could ever be whispered in their direction.

"Let's talk about future gains instead of past losses," the tiefling offered.

The Shifter's laughter echoed all around him, as if without a point of origin. Just floating freely in the air—or was it even audible, he wondered? Might she be imparting the chortles telepathically?

Effron looked down again, trying to find his sense of balance against this interminably aggravating associate.

Many heartbeats passed before the laughter subsided, and many more in silence.

"Talk of them, then," the Shifter finally prompted.

"What glory might we find if we regain the sword?" Effron asked slyly.

"I don't desire glory. Glory brings fame, and fame brings jealousy, and jealousy brings danger. What glory might you find, you mean."

"So be it," Effron said. "And what treasures might you find?"

"That's a more interesting question."

"Five hundred pieces of gold," Effron announced.

The Shifter—the image of the Shifter—did not appear intrigued. "For a Netherese blade as powerful as Claw?" she scoffed.

"You are not creating it, merely retrieving it."

"You forget that I have dealt with this trio of warriors before," she said. "With powerful allies beside me, some of whom are dead, and none of whom would wish to return to face those three again. Yet you expect me to do so alone, and for a paltry sum."

"Not to face the three," Effron corrected. "Just one."

"They are all formidable!"

"While it pleases me to see you afraid, I am not asking you to do battle. Not against three, not against one."

"To simply steal a sentient sword?" Again her tone was incredulous, which made sense, of course, given such a proposed task as that!

"To simply make a deal," Effron corrected. He reached into his pouch and produced a small glowing cage of magical energy, one that fit in his palm, one that contained a tiny likeness of a panther the Shifter had seen before, right before she had fled the fight in the forest.

"No, not a likeness," the Shifter said aloud, and she leaned in to better inspect the living creature trapped within the force cage—and it was indeed her, Effron realized at that moment, and not an image.

"Magnificent," she whispered.

"You cannot have her."

"Better her than the sword, I expect!"

"Except that she is untamable," Effron explained.

"You are quite young and inexperienced to be proclaiming that so definitively."

"So said Draygo Quick."

The mention of the great warlock lord had the Shifter standing straight immediately, and staring hard, not at Guenhwyvar, but back at Effron.

"You come to me with the imprimatur of Draygo Quick?"

"At his insistence, and with his coin."

The Shifter swallowed hard, all semblance of that confident trickster flown away. "Why didn't you tell me that when first you contacted me?"

"Five hundred pieces of gold," Effron stated.

The Shifter disappeared, then reappeared beside him—only it was again an illusion, he suspected, as was confirmed when she answered from the other side as he turned to face her image.

"To trade the panther back to the drow in exchange for the sword?"

Effron nodded.

"Herzgo Alegni has already taken his hunters after the blade," the Shifter explained.

Again Effron nodded, for he knew of Alegni's departure for Neverwinter Wood, a posse of Shadovar beside him. He wasn't too concerned about that, however, for Alegni had told him that they were merely going to pick up the trail. Herzgo Alegni was no fool, and after the beating he had received on his coveted bridge, one given despite his trickery with Artemis Entreri, he would not soon again take such a risk where Dahlia and her cohorts were involved—particularly not while they held Charon's Claw. For more than a few, Draygo Quick included, had warned Alegni that the weapon might not so easily forgive his failure, and might even go over to the side of Artemis Entreri against him.

Could Claw control Alegni the way it had tormented the man known as Barrabus the Gray?

The thought proved not as amusing to Effron as he had suspected and so he pushed it away quickly, returning to the situation at hand.

"The drow's friends might not appreciate such an exchange, particularly Lord Alegni's former slave," the Shifter remarked.

"If I thought they would, I would go to them myself," Effron replied. "You are clever enough to find a way, and to get away if the need arises."

The Shifter, her image at least, seemed intrigued. Effron and others always thought that the current image's expressions and posture matched that of the host, though, of course, none knew for certain. As she considered the information, a long while passed before she said, "One thousand gold if I return with the sword."

"Draygo Quick . . ." Effron started to reply.

"Five hundred from him and five hundred from Herzgo Alegni," the Shifter interrupted. "It's worth at least that to him, is it not?"

Effron didn't blink.

"Or did you think to exact that sum from him for yourself?" the Shifter asked slyly.

"I have no desire for the coins."

"Then you are indeed a fool."

"So be it."

"So be it? That you are a fool, or that you agree to my terms?"

"One thousand pieces of gold."

"And five hundred if I return without it, for my troubles."

"No."

The image of the Shifter faded away to nothingness.

"One hundred," Effron quickly said, trying hard, but futilely, to keep the desperation out of his voice. "If you return with the panther."

The image of the Shifter reappeared.

"If you lose the panther, but do not regain the sword, then you will find no gold, but surely the wrath of Draygo Quick."

"And if I bring back both?" she asked.

"The wrath of Draygo Quick, who desires no conflict with this or any other drow," Effron said. "Make the deal."

"Ah, the ever-present wrath of Draygo Quick," the Shifter said. "It seems that you have added a measure of danger to the bargain." Her image suddenly grabbed the cage from Effron's hand, but it did not appear in that image's hand, but rather, seemed to simply disappear. "How, then, can I say no?"

Effron nodded and watched the image melt away again to nothingness, and then he knew that he was alone.

He collected his wits, always so scattered after dealing with this annoying creature, and started away, hoping that Herzgo Alegni would not claim the prize first.

Because to Effron, Charon's Claw was not the prize. He would procure it and use it to prompt Herzgo Alegni to the true victory, the one he and the tiefling warlord both badly wanted: Lady Dahlia, helpless before them, in all her shame, to answer for her crimes.

Drizzt Do'Urden sat in the crook of a thick branch, tight against the trunk of a large tree, trying to make himself as small as possible. He pulled his ragged forest green cloak around him as tightly as possible, and told himself that he would need to replace this garment soon enough, perhaps with some elven cloak, or another drow *piwafwi* if he could find some way to procure one.

That thought, of course, led him back to the last time he had seen Jarlaxle, when the drow had gone over the lip of the primordial's pit after Athrogate, only to be obliterated, so it seemed, by the primordial's subsequent eruption.

Drizzt closed his eyes and forced himself to let it all go. Too many questions accompanied thoughts of Jarlaxle, as they did with Entreri. Too many inconsistencies and too many needed excuses. The world was much easier when viewed in black and white, and these two, Jarlaxle most poignantly and pointedly, surely injected areas of shadow into Drizzt's view of the world as it should be.

So did Dahlia, of course.

Below Drizzt's perch, Entreri and Dahlia went about their business, acting as if they were putting together a camp for the night. They moved half-heartedly, hardly playing their roles, as the time dragged along.

Finally, Drizzt spotted some movement in the shadows a short distance behind them.

No, not a movement in the shadows, he realized, but a movement of the shadows. Arunika's warning about the Netherese and their fanatical grip on their artifacts rang clear in his mind.

The drow gave a little whistle, a series of high-pitched notes like the song of a wren, the previously agreed-upon signal. Both Entreri and Dahlia glanced up toward him, and so, fearing that the Shadovar might be close enough to view any arm waving, he whistled again to confirm.

While the two went back to the camp-building, more determinedly and convincingly this time, Drizzt quietly slipped the Heartseeker into position and set his magical quiver on a web of branches in easy reach. Even as the first arrow went to his bowstring, the drow picked out the advancing forms again, noting at least three of the gray-skinned pursuers.

Their determined and clever movements told him that they knew of his companions at least.

Drizzt whistled again, this time a longer chain of wren-song, to communicate this new observation, and ended with three short tweets to let the others know the enemy count.

He tweeted a short fourth whistle, then a fifth and sixth, as more Shadovar, or at least, as more movement indicative of approaching Shadovar, came visible to him.

The drow licked his lips, his eyes scanning intently. If these enemies meant to attack from afar, by spell or by missile, then he would provide the only warning and the only initial defense for Entreri and Dahlia.

Behind the approaching shades and beside the magical gate that had brought them to this place, Herzgo Alegni paced anxiously. He badly wanted to lead this charge, but he had not yet fully recovered from the beating on the bridge. He could not lift his left arm, and he knew no healer with the power to restore his right eye. He wore an eye patch over that broken orb now.

Another trio of shades came through the gate, and Alegni directed them forward—and it took all of his willpower not to rush off after them.

How he hated these enemies! How he hated Dahlia and her heinous betrayal! How he hated Barrabus and his treachery!

He hoped that those two would be captured alive, so he could torture them until they begged for the sweet release of death.

Another shade came through, a wizard, and one very loyal to Effron, Alegni knew. With a curt and almost dismissive nod to the tiefling warlord, he hustled away to join the impending battle.

A low growl escaped Alegni's lips. He needed to get the many priests working harder, needed to be back in the fight, back in command, in short order. Out of stubbornness, he tried to lift his arm, and growled louder through his grimace.

He looked to the distant hillock, atop which his enemies prepared their camp, and muttered, "Soon, Dahlia, very soon," and then again, substituting the name of Barrabus.

The first shades burst into the opening, two charging in with leveled spears, the third with an axe spinning up above his head.

But the elf and human were not unprepared. As the shades had appeared, both turned, weapons in hand, to meet the charge.

From up above, Drizzt watched as Entreri swept aside the spears with a sudden rush across from Dahlia's left to her right, and Dahlia waded in behind him expertly, her flails smacking at the weapons, so that the spear-wielders had to retreat a step and reorient. As her spinning weapons drove the blades out wider with backhanded movements, the elf warrior spun them around and over, then in fast figure-eights before her to hold the axe-wielder at bay.

Drizzt lowered his bow, looking for a clear shot to take out the woman holding the spear to Dahlia's unprotected left flank, but he pulled up fast when he saw movement from a bush not far away. It was just the flicker of a hand that had come visible, but a telling one.

It was a spellcaster, he realized, and up came Taulmaril and off went a silver-streaking arrow, then another, and more in rapid succession, each burrowing through the brush like a lightning strike, leaving wisps of smoke, even small fires on the branches as they drove through. Sparks exploded from behind, for the spellcaster had obviously enacted some magical wards against such attacks.

But Drizzt kept up the barrage, confident that Taulmaril would prove the stronger. More missiles whipped through, and the spellcaster staggered out backward, coming into clearer view. Other shouts rose up around him, and Drizzt knew that he'd be facing arrows and spells as well soon enough.

But he kept up his devastating rain of lightning arrows, and the sparks came fewer and the mage's screams came louder. He staggered back, now with wisps of smoke rising from his robes, and tried to turn and run off, clutching at his belly, clutching at his burning leg.

Drizzt's next arrow caught him just under the ear and lifted him from the ground, throwing him down on his face in the dirt, where he lay very still.

The drow rolled around to the other side of the tree trunk, and just in time to avoid a line of magical fire from a second sorcerer. He came up shooting again, but not in a concentrated manner this time, for he could not afford that, as shade archers and spearmen began to launch their missiles his way.

In the heat of battle, his own situation worsening by the heartbeat, Drizzt still managed to glance down at his companions. One spearman was down, writhing on the ground with blood spilling from his side, but two other shades had joined the battle.

Entreri, in particular, seemed hard-pressed.

Drizzt started to lower his bow for a shot at one of the shades below.

But he didn't, and focused instead on the distant enemies.

Their precision and coordinated movements had only grown in the days since the fight at the bridge in Neverwinter, with both of these fine warriors coming to understand each other better, both physically and emotionally.

Artemis Entreri knew when he went spinning across to defeat the initial spear thrusts that Dahlia would be ready to step into the void left in his wake, and ready to take full advantage of their off-balance opponents. And so she had, driving back the axe-wielder and ably keeping the spearwoman over to the left fully engaged.

That left Entreri one-against-one with the other spearman.

He drove the spear out to his right even farther with a backhand slash of his sword. His opponent did well to hold on, and even to cleverly reverse his momentum, lifting his leading left hand up over his shoulder and punching out with the right down low in an attempt to butt Entreri hard with the back end of the spear.

It would have worked, too, except that Entreri's dagger came across right behind the sword's backhand to catch the spear's shaft down low, and with Entreri's arm at such an angle to hold his opponent's weapon firmly in place.

Entreri looked the shade straight in the eye, then pressed upward with the dagger.

The shade should have leaped back to disengage, and likely would have had he understood the skill of his opponent, but he stubbornly pressed on, even trying to reverse once more and bring the spear tip slashing down from on high.

But Entreri had it securely locked with his dagger, rolling the blade deftly to prevent the disengage, and turning it to use the shade's momentum to his own favor, driving the spear up slightly.

Enough so that he was able to slip the tip of his sword under the butt of the weapon.

Still staring into the shade's eyes, Entreri put on just the hint of a wicked grin and thrust his sword upward, catching the shade just under the ribs. The shade let go of the spear with one hand, trying desperately to spin away, but the assassin's sword dug in, tearing through flesh and into a lung.

The shade fell away—and Entreri smiled wider when Dahlia, deep into her spinning dance and keeping the other two engaged, managed to crack the fool across the head as he tumbled, just for good measure.

Entreri understood the level of satisfaction the elf woman took in delivering that blow.

Though he noted two more enemies charging in, he crossed by Dahlia, sword slashing in a wide angle to drive the axe-wielder back a few steps, then crossing down hard to crack into the shaft of the thrusting spear, catching it just below the tip and nearly shearing that blade off.

Dahlia responded perfectly, intercepting the two newcomers with a barrage of spinning flails that surely defeated their momentum—and likely their appetite for this fight.

Entreri noted that, and marveled at it, and silently congratulated the woman for the clever move.

The magical bolt, green energy smoking with anger, whipped in at Drizzt too quickly for him to duck aside. He took it in the shoulder and his grip wavered, but only for a moment.

Then he responded back at the mage with a new stream of lightning arrows. One after another, they blasted into the tree behind which the mage had dived, chipping bark and cracking into the hardwood. Drizzt grimaced against the burning pain running through his arm, but he stubbornly held on and kept up the barrage, telling himself that if he let up, the mage would come out and lash at him again.

A slight movement to the side caught his attention and he swiveled the bow reflexively and let fly.

Good fortune more than skill aided him in that moment, he silently admitted, for his arrow flew true, throwing a shade archer to the ground, a line of smoke rising from the hole in her chest.

Back toward the mage went the bow, more arrows flashing away, thundering into and all around the tree, throwing sparks and wood chips.

An arrow clipped the tree very near to Drizzt's face. He hadn't even seen it coming, and from the angle of the shot, he recognized that he was vulnerable. He let up on the mage and turned quickly to the new threat, down and to the side and just past the continuing fight on the ground below him. Another arrow whipped in, missing badly, and Drizzt spotted the archer. Off went the silvery flash of Taulmaril's next arrow, exploding into a large stone.

Up from behind that stone appeared not one, but two archers, both ready to let fly at Drizzt.

But he beat them to it, skipping his next shot off the stone between them, the flash stealing their eyesight, the resounding retort stealing their nerves. One never even got off her shot before she yelped and ducked, and the second missed so wildly that his arrow didn't even cross within the wide reach of the tree's branches.

Drizzt couldn't count that as a victory, though, not with the wizard likely crawling out from behind his tree barricade and preparing the next magical assault. He started to turn, thinking to unleash another volley that way, but paused.

Down below he noted the fight, noted the back of Artemis Entreri, open and inviting. He could lower the Heartseeker but a finger's breadth and let fly and be rid of Entreri once and for all.

It would be so easy.

And wouldn't the world be a better place without this murderer? How many lives, perhaps innocent lives, might Drizzt save with just that one shot?

He had actually started to draw back on the bowstring when the magical bolt struck him hard in the side, blasting the breath from him and nearly knocking him from the tree.

And up came the two archers behind the stone, both letting fly.

Drizzt, eyes hardly open as he squinted against the pain, pumped his arm repeatedly, sending a near-solid line of lightning their way. He scored one hit, he believed, from the pitch of the ensuing cry, but he knew not how solid.

He expected that he would die up there, then, in the nook in this tree.

But couldn't he take Artemis Entreri along with him?

And wouldn't the world be a better place if he did?

More enemies appeared.

Between parries, Entreri managed to glance at Dahlia and mouth, "Go."

205

The elf was already moving, with her hands at first, turning flails into four-foot bo sticks, then, as she rushed forward, deftly striking with them to align them properly for a full joining. Her long staff returned, Dahlia continued her charge, then abruptly planted the end and leaped over the surprised shades, landing lightly behind the pair and sprinting off into the thicker brush.

Reflexively, stupidly, the shades spun around and followed—or one followed, as the other stumbled, Entreri's belt knife driving deep into his kidney.

The pursuer, apparently oblivious to her companion's fate, kept running, until the end of Dahlia's staff appeared, lined up perfectly just below her chin. She couldn't stop, and Dahlia had reversed direction and was coming at her anyway, and the combined momentum drove the long staff spearlike against the soft skin of the shade's neck. Her legs flew out from under her as she tried futilely to recoil, and she landed hard on her back, gagging and choking and gulping for air that would not come. She flailed pathetically, but Dahlia just leaped past her, back toward Entreri.

None of this was lost on the two Entreri battled. The swordsman to the left of the assassin motioned for his companion to hold back Dahlia.

He should have kept his focus on the assassin instead, for as his friend turned, Entreri charged in at him. Obviously startled by the sudden boldness of the move, the shade leaped and scrambled back.

But Entreri veered and caught the turning shade instead, and that axe man heard him coming and whipped around with a mighty sidelong swing.

One that went high as Entreri skidded low to his knees, his sword disemboweling the shade.

The remaining swordsman leaped for the vulnerable assassin, and caught instead a furious Dahlia, now with flails once more, spinning and cracking him all around the head. He got pummeled a dozen times in that flashing moment, but really only felt the first burst of fiery pain as his skull shattered.

Dahlia hardly slowed as she ran past, moving through the camp and out the back side, as Entreri used his sword to drop the axe man off to the right, between him and the new group just coming through the brush. He sprinted almost directly opposite Dahlia, to where she had gone after her vault, bending, not pausing, only to yank his belt knife from the wounded Shadovar male.

He crashed through the brush in a full run, turning left as he knew—just knew—that Dahlia would spin right, that they could link up once more deeper into the woods.

More arrows flew off from Taulmaril. Drizzt scored a hit, a kill, and then a second kill in rapid order as the companion of his first victim tried to get up and run off.

Still the drow grimaced in pain, his muscles clenching against the burns of the two magical bolts, but at least he had lessened the missiles flying in at him. Below him the fight intensified. Out of the corner of his eye, he saw Dahlia springing away.

Which would leave Entreri even more vulnerable to him, he realized.

Another arrow skipped through the branches, narrowly missing Drizzt's face, and stealing all thoughts of the battle below. He wheeled around to spot the archer, who was diving behind a fallen log, and drew back, but out of the corner of his eye, Drizzt noted the pesky sorcerer, casting yet another spell. Before he could train his bow on the shade, a pea of flame left the mage's hand, soaring his way.

Drizzt knew all too well what that foretold.

He let fly the arrow, missing badly, for he was already moving, scrambling up from his perch, as he let go of the bowstring. In truth, he let fly the arrow as much to clear it from the bow as anything else.

He rushed out along the branch, nimbly balancing as he flipped the magical quiver and then the bow over his shoulders, and by the time he got out on the limb, the thinner wood beginning to bend under his weight, he had his scimitars in hand.

The tree exploded behind him, the mage's fireball turning twilight into noon-time. It was not a concussive blast, though Drizzt wished it had been, for the air around him instantly began to simmer and sting with licks of flame. Now he used the elasticity of the branch, springing up and away with abandon.

Only his magical anklets had saved him from grievous wounds from the intensity of the blast—no novice, this mage! Without the magic speeding his steps, that fireball would have caught him fully, to no good end.

Though he had escaped the bulk of that blast, he found himself more than twenty feet in the air, flying free and clear of the branches, with nothing to grasp and only the hard ground to cushion his fall.

He took some comfort, or enjoyment, in the look of horror upon the mage's face as he descended from on high. He noted the terrain, and took heart that it was mostly clear before him.

The drow turned himself over in mid-air, landing in a forward roll, coming up with a desperate swing as he passed by the mage before going into another forward roll, and a third to absorb the momentum. He crashed through some brush, painfully, but managed to come up to his feet relatively unscathed.

The same could not be said of the mage, who spun around in circles with blood spurting from the gash Drizzt's scimitar had sliced across his throat.

Drizzt tried to orient himself, to figure out where his companions might be. An image of his blades diving in at Entreri's back flashed in his mind, and brought forth a surprising amount of anger—rage he quickly focused on the situation at hand. He charged off at full speed, moving from cover to cover, from tree to brush to boulder, then even up into the lower branches of another tree.

Shouts rang up all around him as the enemy tried to get a bead on him, tried to coordinate against him.

He reversed his course, then cut out again, springing from the tree branch to a clearing behind some underbrush, then speeding through at full speed to surprise a pair of Shadovar who were still pointing at the tree he had climbed, yelling out directions.

They almost got their weapons up to block.

Drizzt ran on, leaving the two writhing on the ground. Anger grew with his speed, fueled by images of Entreri and Dahlia sharing that intimate moment.

He heard a cry from in front and knew he had been spotted, knew that those ahead would put up a better defense—against his scimitars, at least.

So he sheathed the blades as he sprinted and drew out his bow, and burst into sight of the trio. One, two, three went his arrows, blowing one shade away, lifting him into the air, cutting a second down with a glancing blow that still opened her skin from shoulder to shoulder, and sending the third diving away in panic.

Drizzt rushed through, crossing their position and disappearing into the brush so quickly that the unwounded shade wasn't even sure where he had gone.

"We cannot catch him," the Netheril commoner admitted to Lord Alegni when he rejoined the tiefling at the magical gate. "He moves like a ghost—into the trees as quickly as we run along the ground."

"You have sorcerers," Alegni replied, and he looked past the soldier to a few other shades now approaching, more than one of them glancing back over his shoulder with clear alarm.

"Two are dead, slain by the drow!" the shade replied, and as his voice rose, he could barely suppress his terror.

"What of the other two?" Alegni asked—asked all of them as the others came scurrying up. "Tell me that you fools have killed Dahlia or Barrabus!"

It was all bluster, for Herzgo Alegni didn't believe any such thing, nor did he desire any such thing. Not here, in this time or place or manner. The tiefling found himself a bit surprised by his feelings concerning this obvious abject failure. The lords of Netheril, after all, were never easy or merciful regarding failure.

"Nay, my lord," the commoner admitted. "I fear they have eluded us."

"The sword," Alegni asked. "Did Barrabus wield my sword?"

The commoner considered that for a moment. "The drow carried it, but on his back. He fought with smaller blades."

Alegni didn't quite know what to make of that. Why had the trio fled into the wilds? He looked to the northeast, toward a broken mountain, the same one that had blown up and buried the old city of Neverwinter a decade earlier.

"Where are you going?" he quietly asked the empty air.

"My lord?" the commoner asked.

Alegni waved him to the portal. There was no use in trying to turn the Shadovar around for another futile fight. They had failed.

But this wasn't *his* failure. He had argued loudly against this course of action, begging Draygo Quick and some others that they would do well to wait until he had recovered enough to personally see to this. He had argued, more subtly, that he would need many times this number, and in a place more of his choosing.

He would likely be admonished for this failure, certainly, but not in any way that would damage his designs.

He would still be the one tasked with retrieving the sword, and he felt confident that he could convince Draygo Quick to let him do it his own way.

As these ragged and defeated shades returned to the magical portal empty-handed, other than their dead comrades they couldn't simply leave behind, Draygo Quick would find himself enmeshed in what had been wholly perceived as Herzgo Alegni's failure.

Yes, the tiefling wasn't upset as the rest of the defeated band returned to him, and he had to work hard to keep any measure of sarcasm or enjoyment out of his voice when he ordered them to return through the gate.

But he was worried, quite so, when he thought of that broken mountain and the beast he knew lurked beneath its battered slopes. He felt a silent call on an unseen breeze, as if Claw was reaching out to him, pleading with him. He didn't know if that was actually the case, or if it was simply his imagination, but he suspected the former.

Claw was calling to him, because Claw was afraid.

With a last look to the north, the forest where Dahlia, Barrabus, and the drow had once again escaped, Herzgo Alegni, too, returned to the Shadowfell.

Taulmaril in hand, Drizzt rushed around a thick briar patch, cutting back between two wide-spreading elms. He knew that the shade fled before him, he could hear the panting, could smell the woman's desperation. Confident that she would not turn back in ambush, Drizzt sprinted on almost recklessly, his focus purely on covering ground.

He crossed through a pair of large, half-buried boulders, like stone sentinels framing the entrance to a great building, that structure being a grassy ridge line. A great leap brought him atop that ridge, where he at last spotted his quarry.

He leveled the Heartseeker, his arms turning slowly to just lead her movement as she scrambled along, running and falling and crawling on all fours until she could regain her footing. She moved up the side of a hill and when Drizzt let his gaze move out to anticipate her course, he understood her route, for there sat a shimmering black sphere, lined in magical purple—a gate, he knew, and he could guess easily enough where it would lead.

Drizzt lowered Taulmaril, forgetting about the shade woman and staring at that portal.

Guenhwyvar had traveled through such a gate, and had then been lost to him. Might he go through? And if he did, would that re-establish the connection between the panther and the figurine?

Could he do it? Enemies would await him, in droves, likely. But might he rush through, summon Guen, and return at once with her at his side?

He was startled from his contemplations as the shade woman rushed into view, then was gone, diving through the shadow gate.

It was worth a chance, Drizzt decided, and he dropped a hand reflexively to the pouch that held the figurine and sprinted off for the hill. He had barely gone ten strides, though, when he pulled up, for he had lost sight of the gate. He stood there and glanced all around, wondering if the angle had changed.

But no, he recognized the tree beneath which the shadow gate had been.

He ran to the side to change his viewpoint, but there was nothing to be seen. He was too late—the gate had closed.

With a resigned groan, Drizzt closed his eyes and steadied himself, then started back the way he had come, glancing over his shoulder every few steps. His resolve to go through such a gate if one could be found again only grew as he continued on his way.

If Guenhwyvar couldn't come to him, he would go to her. Would she do any less for him if the situation was reversed?

The words of Arunika rang in his ear, though. The red-haired clairvoyant had thought Guenhwyvar dead.

Drizzt glanced back one last time, staring up to where he had seen the magical gate. If he went through and there remained no connection to Guenhwyvar, then what?

Perhaps he wouldn't go through.

Drizzt stopped and paused at that errant thought, and wound up laughing at himself. He had played such a fool's game once before, when he was out in the wilds around Mithral Hall, not daring to return to the dwarf homeland because he was nearly certain that his friends had been killed in the collapse of a tower.

He would not make such a mistake ever again.

He picked up his pace, returning back near the tree where he had been perched. Smoke still poured from several spots along its blackened trunk, and orange embers glowed in more than one recess.

He heard voices and moved slowly through the fake encampment, and silently through the first bit of brush.

He recognized Entreri's voice, speaking quietly, and he moved up beside a tree and peered around.

There stood the assassin, his back to Drizzt, Dahlia beyond him and to the side.

Drizzt clutched Taulmaril, his other hand going to an arrow in the magical quiver.

An easy shot, and one he could explain. All he need do was draw out that arrow and aim true. One shot, and Artemis Entreri would be no more, and the world would be a better place, and Dahlia . . .

Drizzt shook it all away, surprised by how his mind had wandered—yet again. If he meant to kill Entreri, then would it not be more honorable to challenge the man openly and be done with it?

He imagined that—and it was not an unpleasant thought—but as the battle played out in his mind's eye, Dahlia intervened . . . on behalf of Entreri.

Drizzt grabbed an arrow and nearly drew it.

"Drizzt!" Dahlia called, noting him.

Artemis Entreri turned around and motioned to him, and the assassin and Dahlia walked over.

"A few less Shadovar to trouble the world," Dahlia said with grim satisfaction.

"And a few more will follow," Entreri added. "They will return. They want the sword."

"Perhaps next time, we will see them before they see us," said Drizzt, and that brought a puzzled look to both his companions.

"We did," Entreri said.

"I mean, before they are even on our trail," Drizzt said. "That we might learn their point of entry."

Still the two looked confused.

"A shadow gate," the drow explained. "I almost got to it, but it dissipated."

"A door to the Shadowfell?" Entreri asked skeptically. "Why would . . . ?"

Drizzt held up his hand, in no mood to explain.

Dahlia came over to him, then, and gently touched the wound in his side. "Come," she said, taking his hand. "Let's tend to those."

"Wizards," Entreri muttered, shaking his head.

They set their camp not far from that point. Drizzt and Dahlia sat off to the side, across the low-burning, shielded fire from Entreri, and behind some brush as well. The drow was stripped to the waist, Dahlia tending his several wounds with a cloth dampened with water and a healing salve.

Soon enough, the stars glittering above them, Entreri snoring from across the way, her touches became more intimate and suggestive.

Drizzt looked into her pretty eyes, trying to measure her emotions. She still wore her hair in the soft shoulder cut, her face still clear of the woad. Even in the fight, she had remained in this guise.

But even wearing her softer appearance, Drizzt recognized something in his heart, and his eyes only confirmed it. She was not looking at him with the warmth of love, but with the heat of passion.

Would she have been any less aggressive with any attractive partner, he wondered? Did it matter that it was him? Was there more of a bond here than the satisfaction of physical needs?

He felt himself a plaything at that moment. That bothered him, but what bothered him even more was that he felt Dahlia a plaything, as well, as if he was using her for her obvious charms.

She bit him on the neck then, lightly, then leaned back and stared at him, smiling mischievously. He noticed that her white shirt was unfastened, quite low and revealing.

Drizzt pushed her out to arms' length. He tried to say something, to explain his feelings, his confusion and fears. But all he could do was shake his head.

Dahlia looked at him curiously at first, then with disbelief as she pulled back from his grasp with a clear edge of anger.

"When I caught up to you outside of Neverwinter, you were engaged in a serious conversation with Entreri," Drizzt said, glad to move along to some other issue, one likely related to his emotions, but still removed from the immediate sense of rejection. "What were you talking about?"

Dahlia stepped back even farther, out of his reach, staring at him incredulously, and asked, "What?" sounding as if she had just been slapped.

Drizzt swallowed hard but knew that he had to press on. "I came out from Neverwinter to your camp, and from the brush, witnessed your discussion with Entreri."

"You were spying on us? Did you expect me to throw him on the ground and ravish him?"

"No," the exasperated drow replied, his thoughts spinning as he tried to figure out how to better communicate the turmoil within him.

"I didn't even want him along!" Dahlia snapped at him, harshly and loudly, and across the way, Entreri's snoring broke cadence as if her words had disturbed his slumber. She paused for just a moment, waiting for the rhythmic breathing to resume, but never let her glower leave her face. "You invited him, and then accepted him back again after he deserted us—and for all we know, he betrayed us in his time away."

Drizzt shook his head.

"How do you know?" Dahlia asked skeptically. "He was gone and suddenly we were found."

"And he returned to aid us when we needed it," Drizzt reminded.

"Or he set the whole thing up so he could become a hero to us."

She was deflecting him, he realized, and he shook his head forcefully and waved his arms before him, at last silencing her. "We were beaten by Alegni on the bridge," he stated flatly. "It was not deception that brought Artemis Entreri back to us, but his own hatred of Herzgo Alegni."

His mention of the tiefling, his reminder of the tiefling's demise, seemed to calm Dahlia down a bit.

She looked at Drizzt slyly, as if it had been her intent all along to bring him around in this circle. "Now you defend him?" she asked.

The simple question made Drizzt's initial statements—accusations?—toward Dahlia seem rather idiotic.

He brought his hands up to his face and took a deep and slow, steadying breath, feeling very much off guard. Entreri's snoring distracted him. It occurred to him that if he crossed the camp and hacked the assassin to death in his sleep all of his concerns here would be resolved.

Yes, a dozen strides and a single swing, and he and Dahlia could go along their way without a worry, without the need to return to Gauntlgrym, the tomb of Drizzt's dearest friend, a place he did not wish to go.

A single swing—perhaps with Entreri's own sword!

He shook the thoughts away and refocused on Dahlia, to see her refastening her shirt, her expression showing many shifting emotions, but surely nothing amorous.

"You had a serious conversation with a very dangerous man," Drizzt pressed anyway. "I would like to know about it."

"Be very careful not to press too far into places that are none of your concern," Dahlia replied, and walked away.

Drizzt stood there in the dark for a long while, watching Dahlia as she moved near to the low fire and settled, half-sitting, half-reclining against a log. She lowered her wide-brimmed black hat over her eyes and crossed her arms over her chest.

What was it between them, Drizzt wondered? When they entwined, was it lovemaking or recreation?

And if it was not lovemaking, then why did he care so much about her seemingly intimate conversation with Artemis Entreri?

Because it was Entreri?

Perhaps Drizzt's nostalgia for what once had been could carry him only so far in his dealings with the assassin. Perhaps their long battle, the taking of Regis's fingers by Entreri's dagger so long ago, the many innocents Drizzt knew Entreri had wounded and killed . . . perhaps all of that dark past of Artemis Entreri was now invading on that wistful nostalgia, reminding Drizzt that, while his personal circle might have been greater in the time that had been a hundred years before, the world at large was not so kind a place.

Once again, it occurred to Drizzt that he might be doing an act of great good for the world if he crossed the encampment and put an end to Artemis Entreri.

Once again, his desire for such violence surprised him and revolted him.

But there it remained, hovering within his consciousness.

CHAPTER 15

HOPE FROM THE DAYS OF OLD

THE BALL OF LIVING FIRE CHARGED AT THE TRIO OF GOBLINS, KNOCKING ONE of the creatures flat and rolling over him, muffling his screams with the crackle of biting flames. The other two goblins shrieked and fell back. One threw its arms up in front of its face and the sleeve of its shirt burst into flame.

Cries echoed through the great forge area, and heightened when more of the little elementals appeared.

The first came off the goblin, unfolding, and rose upright, standing about half the height of the scrambling goblins, but with wide, flaming shoulders and arms that left a trail of flames in the air whenever it swung around. It focused on one of the standing goblins and charged, and with a scream, the goblin rushed away.

The elemental left a line of fire in its wake as it glided across the stone floor, angry little living and yapping flames sparking and biting at the air. Other elementals crisscrossed the path, creating a pattern of burning lines.

Goblins ran every which way and drow nimbly leaped atop the various forges, reacting far more calmly and reasonably in the face of this otherworldly threat.

For this was not the first time over the last few days that such outbursts of raging, free-running elementals had swarmed the forge area.

It was expected—this was the power of a primordial, after all, and the forges and supporting lines were old and often in need of repair, in ways that visual inspections could not reveal. The breaches revealed them, but only when pipes and joints had deteriorated enough to let the little beasts free. And in those instances, the elementals poured forth in a frenzy. The thing's chaotic power strenuously resisted any attempts to harness it. From that fiery chaos of primordial belching came forth these pseudo-elementals, these fire-kin, unthinking, raging little expressions of freed fire.

"Spellspinners!" more than one drow craftsman yelled. These artisans were all more than capable of defending themselves, and whenever a fire-kin ventured too near, it was swatted away with a finely crafted, heavily enchanted weapon.

But the artisans didn't prefer such tactics, for those elemental-kin were a part of the magic and pure energy of the primordial beast, and to strike at them was to assault the essence of creation itself.

"Spellspinners!" The call echoed throughout the large hall and down the myriad nearby tunnels and the main drow camps.

In one such camp, farther into the Underdark the way the expedition had come, Ravel Xorlarrin took note.

"Not again," he muttered.

"Again," Jearth remarked, coming up beside him.

"Where is Tiago?"

"In the upper halls, pressing to the top level."

Ravel didn't hide his disappointment in that news, giving a harsh snort and slapping a fist against the side of his leg. When he composed himself and regarded Jearth, and the weapons master's amused grin, he realized that he was showing a bit too much petulance.

"I will need the two of you beside me to resolve this," he explained.

"They are elementals, and stinging fiery little wretches," Jearth replied. "More a play for the spellspinners than warriors."

"For mages, you mean," Ravel replied with obvious, unhidden frustration, and he let his sour expression remain for some time, that the other spellspinners, too, could view it.

They all understood the truth of it anyway: The breakdown of the forges and the multitude of dangerous elementals running free had come as a blessing for Elderboy Brack'thal, whose pre-Spellplague techniques were proving far more effective in dealing with the fire creatures than anything Ravel and his spellspinners could offer.

Berellip was taking note, they all knew, and Ravel, particularly, knew.

"I have put my trust in you and in Tiago," Ravel remarked.

Jearth shrugged noncommittally.

Ravel's expression became more sly as he continued to look at this drow he considered a friend, as he reminded himself that while Jearth might be exactly that, he was also drow, and also a weapons master. Jearth's primary concern was Jearth, of course, else he would have long ago felt the bite of a drow blade as some younger warrior tried to steal his position in the House hierarchy.

Among the Xorlarrin, spellspinners were held in higher regard than warriors, many higher even than the weapons master, but they were all merely males. The priestesses, the sisters of Xorlarrin, still were held in the highest regard. So if Brack'thal climbed above Ravel in Berellip's eyes, would it not follow that Jearth would make a new friend in Brack'thal at the earliest opportunity?

The thought unsettled Ravel for just a moment, then reminded him of who he was and to what he aspired.

Brack'thal's outdated magical repertoire had served Ravel's rise in status quite well, but Brack'thal was the Elderboy of House Xorlarrin, the first-born son of Matron Zeerith, and it was said that in the days before the Spellplague, he was held in highest regard throughout Menzoberranzan, even in the eyes of Archmage Gromph.

If Brack'thal could prove valuable, even heroic, along this most important mission, what might that mean for Ravel?

Nothing good.

"You cannot do it," Jearth said, and Ravel looked at him with confusion.

"Goad your brother into an open battle," Jearth clarified. "You cannot do it. Berellip would not tolerate it."

"Berellip walks with great care around me," the spellspinner countered. "She knows that I have the allegiance of Tiago Baenre. She understands the power of House Baenre."

Jearth's annoying chuckle scraped at Ravel's sensibilities.

"You doubt . . . ?" Ravel started to ask.

"Sometimes I doubt that you understand the play," Jearth interrupted. "Tiago is your ally because he sees you as in the favor of Matron Zeerith, even though you are not in the favor of Berellip or Saribel."

Ravel puffed up a bit at that spoken truth.

"Do not believe for a heartbeat that it follows, therefore, that Matron Zeerith favors you over either of the females, or above your other sisters. I have seen that folly many times within Menzoberranzan."

"You just said—"

"In favoring you, Matron Zeerith irks her daughters," Jearth explained. "They are older, and remember well the glory of Brack'thal, and the glory he and his minions brought to House Xorlarrin. Most of those minions died in the Spellplague, that is true, but if you're not careful, and thus give Berellip—particularly that one!—the kindling she needs to brighten Brack'thal's fire in the eyes of Matron Zeerith, you will find the fleeting truth regarding the loyalty of your people."

"This is my expedition, and so far it has been successful beyond all expectations," Ravel argued. "We have restarted the forges. We have harnessed the power of the primordial, as has not been done since the days of Gauntlgrym!"

"For the glory of Matron Zeerith and the hopes of House Xorlarrin," Jearth reminded. "Not for the glory and hopes of Ravel Xorlarrin. If Brack'thal proves the better play going forward, your sister, with your mother's blessing, will use that play and quickly discard Ravel, do not doubt."

"Because of me, Gol'fanin brings forth and executes the ancient recipes, long regarded as artifacts of a lost age."

"Because of Brack'thal, he can continue his work," Jearth quickly countered. "Which do you suppose is more important to those who would cast you aside at this time, your initial contributions or those current actions that move the dreams of House Xorlarrin forward?"

Ravel licked his lips and nervously stepped from foot to foot. "Tiago Baenre has made of me his ally, and works House Baenre's desires here through me."

"You are more important to Tiago Baenre than those weapons Gol'fanin now crafts for him?" Jearth asked, his knowing grin revealing the sarcasm masked within the rhetorical question.

"He has already bought the simmering anger of Berellip," Ravel replied.

"While he twines with her, and she, willingly and often, with him," came the response. "Imagine were she to become thick with Tiago's child."

The thought hit Ravel so powerfully that the wind from a small bellows would have knocked him from his unsteady feet! He wanted to lash out at Jearth then, to scream at the warrior and even strike at him.

But he calmed, wisely telling himself that Jearth had done him a great service by starkly reminding him of the true nature of kin and kind.

"*Abbil*," he said, the drow word for friend, though in drow culture, that concept of friendship typically meant little more than an affirmation of a temporary alliance, as Jearth had just reminded him regarding Tiago.

"We need to make a plan," Jearth said quietly.

"Brack'thal grows more powerful with every breach of the forges, with the appearance of every fiery elemental," Ravel agreed. "I cannot deny his proficiency in dealing with the creatures."

"It is a lost art rediscovered, like Gol'fanin's recipes."

"What else might be rediscovered along with it?" Ravel remarked, referring to his brother's former status among the Xorlarrin clan.

By the time they, leading Ravel's loyal spellspinners, reached the forge room, a huge and hulking beast of living fire stood back from the main forge. It appeared quite agitated, armlike appendages out wide as if wanting to engulf someone or something, anyone or anything, and with clawing fingers of fire clenching repeatedly, little bursts of flame puffing out of either side.

Several drow near the beast, however, revealed the truth of the moment. They milled around, ducking low and peering behind this forge or that in search of more of the smaller fiery creatures. This large elemental was fully under control—under Brack'thal's control. Ravel understood at once that this monstrosity was a creation of his older brother. As Ravel watched with concern, Brack'thal flushed out another of the smaller fire creatures and sent it rushing toward his behemoth. A line of fire burned behind the speeding creature, and like a wizard's fireworks lifting into a night sky, the small elemental sprang away, flying up, throwing itself into the torso of Brack'thal's monster.

Great fiery arms closed around the smaller creature, engulfing it, hugging it, absorbing it.

Then it was gone, and Brack'thal's elemental stood a little taller and a bit wider.

Ravel looked over at Jearth, who could only hold up his hands, unable, obviously, to deny the beauty of the magical display.

Ravel, though, was not so resigned. He stared at his brother. He knew of the old spells, even though he had not mastered them—what would be the point of that painstaking practice, after all, given the reduction of their power? Yet in this particular endeavor, with this particular challenge, Brack'thal seemed to be not reduced in the least. Confident and smooth in his movements, almost casual in his mannerisms as he contained yet another of these increasingly frequent breaches, the mage soon enough swept out of the room, heading for his assigned corner of the complex, and now with a formidable fire elemental in tow to help him in clearing the pesky previous inhabitants aside. For rats and goblins alike, and even the annoying dwarf ghosts, were not faring well against Brack'thal's continuing assortment of pets.

Ravel watched him depart, and the light in the room diminished greatly as soon as the drow mage and his pet had gone, which was a good thing for the sensitive drow eyes. Ravel swung his gaze back to see his sisters Berellip and Saribel standing side by side, both looking at him with obvious scrutiny and obvious judgment.

"Shut down the outer four forges on either end," Ravel said to Jearth.

Jearth looked at him with surprise. "That will slow our progress. Many doors must be created, and blockades and stairwells and locking bolts, to say nothing of the armor and arms."

"We lose more time and workers with these disruptions," Ravel added, motioning with his chin toward a trio of dead goblins lying on the floor, their clothing still smoking. "Let us proceed more cautiously for a while, until we can properly understand and repair the feed systems that fire the forge."

As Ravel looked away, he heard Jearth's knowing chuckle. Ravel wasn't trying to reduce the interruptions or the minor inconvenience of a few dead slaves. His order was meant to slow the momentum of Brack'thal's ascent.

"Your sisters will not be fooled," the weapons master quietly warned as he walked by to execute Ravel's order.

True enough, the spellspinner knew, but he had to do something to buy some time until he could figure out Brack'thal's secret.

Brack'thal hustled down the corridor in the halls above the forge room, the region brightening because of the presence of the mage's new pet. The large fire elemental eagerly followed the mage, hungered by Brack'thal's promise that it would find fuel, living fuel, for its hungry fires.

The wizard had a lot on his mind. He knew that he was caught in a desperate game. His brother had been forced to bring him along on this expedition, but

Brack'thal held no illusions about the level of control his sisters, or even Matron Zeerith, could hold over the young spellspinner. Ravel had no intention of allowing Brack'thal to survive this journey.

But good fortune was on Brack'thal's side, in the form of an item he possessed from that time before the Spellplague. On his finger, he wore a ruby band, a ring that allowed him to communicate with, and exert tremendous influence over, the very creatures spawned by the power of the primordial. That item, a ring controlling fire elementals, more than anything in his own spell repertoire, had given him the edge now—a critical edge if he hoped to outmaneuver and survive his dangerous younger brother.

The mage slowed his pace, noting a decrepit doorway on the right side of the hallway, another of many he had investigated over the last few days.

Brack'thal waved his hands and whispered a spell, summoning a floating orb, a wizardly eye, which he sent toward the door with merely a thought.

He saw through that eye as it came up on the broken door, peering through openings of missing, rotted planks.

In the room beyond the door, he noted a movement. The chamber beyond wasn't very wide, but it went deep into the stone. The first part was crafted with smooth walls and bricks still tightly mortared as a testament to dwarven crafting. The back half, though, seemed a more natural cavern, and it occurred to Brack'thal that the tumult here in Gauntlgrym, the earthquakes and eruptions caused by the primordial, might have toppled the chamber's back wall, thus connecting it to a natural cavern beyond.

He had seen this before in this part of the complex, and this only reinforced his respect for the primordial.

A second movement caught his eye, a smallish humanoid scrambling behind some makeshift barrier.

"Kobolds," he whispered, and he wondered whether he should try to enslave this group—the notion of creating his own counter army flashed in his mind—or whether he should simply obliterate them.

The magical eye moved through the broken doorway but it dissipated almost immediately, and Brack'thal recognized that he had waited too long while pondering the possibilities.

He focused on his magical ring instead and sent forth the elemental. Eagerly, it swept down the corridor and blasted through the flimsy doorway, sending splinters of burning wood and embers flying all around. An instant later came a second cacophony, this time one of kobolds crying out in alarm before the obvious power of this mighty foe.

Brack'thal began rolling his fingers, deliberately sorting through the verbal component of a dweomer he believed might soon prove important. Pragmatism told him to abandon the attempt, to simply use the fiery evocation his ring could bring forth to protect him if need be.

The mage overruled that commonsense notion, for in his gut he felt up to the task at hand without the aid of the ring.

In the room, the sounds of battle grew: flames sweeping over the kobold barricades; kobolds screeching as deadly fires bit at them; crashing stones and other missiles as the diminutive kobolds tried to battle the mighty creature of fire; footfalls, so many rushing footfalls!

Predictably, a bevy of kobolds scrambled out of the destroyed portal, tumbling into the hall, falling all over each other in a desperate effort to get away. Some charged toward the mage, others ran the opposite way.

Brack'thal lifted a small metal bar before him and completed the spell, trying to remain confident that something, some magical energy would come forth.

The lightning bolt filled the hall with a blinding burst of white light, and Brack'thal, surprised by the intensity, surprised even that he had accomplished the evocation, fell back with a shriek of his own.

He composed himself quickly, but kept shaking his head, for the level of power that had flowed through him in that spellcasting reminded him of a time long lost. Was it his work with the ring, he wondered?

As his eyes readjusted to the darkness, Brack'thal noted the image of the corridor before him, and mostly, the stillness of that hallway. More than a dozen kobolds lay dead before him, not a writhe or whimper to be found among them. He had thrown a lightning bolt that would have made him proud in the days before the Spellplague, a burst of magic that had fully overwhelmed the kobolds, taking their lives instantly.

Another pair of the creatures came out into the hall, and a quick glance had them fleeing the other way down the corridor. A third emerged and similarly ran away.

Brack'thal, too intrigued by his surprising show of magical strength, paid them no heed. It wasn't until the fire elemental returned, until he sensed the beast's wild and unsatisfied hunger, that the mage realized he would do well to put his thoughts aside and focus on the situation at hand. Indeed, the beast was advancing toward him, ill intent clear in its brightening, excited flaming coat.

Brack'thal reached through the ring, calmly reminding the beast that it was better served with him as its ally, and when that line of thought showed only a moderate slowing of the charging fiery humanoid, the mage got more insistent and demanding, willing the creature to stop, willing it to turn around that they could resume their hunt.

The mage constantly reminded himself to focus on the task at hand, to keep a tight hold on his dangerous companion as they moved deeper into the unexplored reaches of the vast complex.

The fire elemental demanded no less than that level of attention, even with the powerful ring aiding him.

It proved a difficult task, though, for Brack'thal could not ignore the implications of his lightning bolt, perhaps the most powerful evocation of magic he had achieved since the Spellplague a century before.

He tempered his elation, rightly so. He had thrown lightning bolts, magic of the old and diminished schools, in the last decades, of course, and had sometimes surprised himself by the intensity of other dweomers he had achieved. The fall of magic as they had known it was not complete, nor was it consistent. This lightning bolt in this corridor might well be no more than a result of Brack'thal's elevated state of urgency, or of his repeated usage of the ring, itself an artifact from another time.

How grand would it be if that were not the case. How wonderful if the mage's lost powers returned to him.

In that event, Brack'thal would be rid of his troublesome little brother in short order.

CHAPTER 16

HE KNEW

THREE OF THE SHADES DID NOT RETURN THROUGH THE PORTAL WITH HERZGO Alegni. From a hilltop not so far away, Glorfathel stood before a scrying pool, the dwarf Ambergris and the monk Afafrenfere flanking him on either side. Neither dwarf nor monk looked much like denizens of the Shadowfell at that time, though, due to the magical dweomers of Ambergris's black pearl necklace.

"They are formidable," Glorfathel remarked.

"Aye, I told ye as much," said the dwarf.

"I will kill the drow," Afafrenfere vowed.

"I'm thinkin' ye better find him sleeping," Ambergris replied, and Glorfathel joined the dwarf in a bit of laughter at the monk's expense.

"You were right," Glorfathel admitted to the dwarf. "I would have expected them to remain in Neverwinter, or travel the open road, were they headed north or south."

"The drow is a ranger," Afafrenfere offered. "He likely thinks himself safer in the forest."

"Still, they could be all the way to Port Llast by now, if that is their destination."

"It ain't," Ambergris assured them both, and with seeming certainty. With stares from both of her companions upon her, Ambergris added, "And why'd anyone be wantin' to go to that pit of Umberlee monsters? They're makin' for Gauntlgrym."

"For what?" Afafrenfere asked, but Glorfathel, more familiar with the recent history of the region, spoke over him.

"Why would you believe that?" the elf asked.

"Because I'm knowin' o' this Drizzt the ranger," Ambergris said. "He's got a problem. His friends' got a bigger problem. Sword's the problem, so he's off to be rid o' the sword."

"To hide it in this place, Gauntlgrym?" Afafrenfere asked.

But Ambergris turned to face Glorfathel as she answered. "To hide it, yeah," the dwarf said, her sarcasm showing that she had a different understanding of what that might mean. "To hide it where it canno' be found."

"Follow them," Glorfathel commanded, his tone turning grim as he caught on to Ambergris's meaning. "I will check in with you often." He stepped to the side, where another black portal to the Shadowfell lingered. "Herzgo Alegni will pay well to know their location. No doubt he is even angrier now, and Draygo Quick will grant him all that he needs to finish this task and retrieve the sword."

He started into the portal, but paused and looked back one last time, focusing his gaze on Afafrenfere. "Make no move against them," he warned.

"Not now," Ambergris agreed. "But ye make sure that when Alegni's catching them, me and me monk friend here'll be beside him."

"I will kill the drow," Afafrenfere vowed again.

"We'll be there," Glorfathel assured them. "I've already secured payment from Effron, that we might aid in the final battle."

With a nod, he disappeared, and the portal thinned then dissipated behind him.

"If we take them and get the sword, we will be hailed as heroes," Afafrenfere said as soon as they were alone.

Ambergris put her hands on hips, shook her head, and snorted. "Ye just don't understand, do ye?" she asked.

Afafrenfere crossed his strong, slender arms over his chest.

Ambergris just laughed and started away.

"To the hunt?" the eager monk asked.

"To see what we might find o' worth on the dead shades," the dwarf corrected. "And might be when ye see how many dead shades're lyin' about that ye'll finally understand."

"Understand what?"

"Understand that I ain't hoping to be lying dead beside any o' them anytime soon," said the dwarf as she stomped away.

Drizzt, Dahlia, and Entreri came above a ridge line, looking down a long and steep descent to a region of stone and boulders. Drizzt and Dahlia knew the place well—they had charged down that very slope into a battle with the Thayan forces of Sylora Salm.

"We're not far," Drizzt remarked, and pointed down to the left.

"Not far from the outer tunnels," Dahlia corrected. "We'll hike for hours more to get to the entryway of Gauntlgrym, if it even remains."

Her tone was combative, and Drizzt gave her an appropriately disconcerting look—one Dahlia returned tenfold.

"Better to be underground, out of the exposure of the open road," Drizzt said.

"Do you fear another fight with the Netherese?" Dahlia shot back.

"Better to be done with all of this," Entreri muttered, and started moving, without looking back.

Drizzt felt like a fool—he could only assume that Dahlia held similar feelings—for Entreri had just diminished their lovers' spat in all of its ridiculousness. The animosity and argument between Drizzt and Dahlia was obviously the by-product of some other issue between them, and given the gravity of their mission as they neared their goal, Entreri's poignant mockery had silenced them both. They were near to Gauntlgrym, thus near to the primordial, thus near to destroying Charon's Claw, an act that would mark the end of Artemis Entreri's enslavement at the price of his very life.

Next to that, how petty did Drizzt and Dahlia's jealousy and quarreling seem?

Humbled, Drizzt started off after the assassin. He had gone many steps before Dahlia followed, far back in his wake.

They found the tunnel entrance easily enough and moved deliberately and silently along the darkened pathway toward the grand cavern that housed the entryway to Gauntlgrym. All three marched with practiced steps, not a footfall to be heard among them, and with equal skill and experience, all they needed to guide them through the corridors was the meager light of Drizzt's scimitar, Twinkle.

That soft blue-white glow illuminated a very small area before the drow, who took up the lead, and no doubt it marked them, him at least, as a target for any monsters or goblinkin that might be lurking in the area. That proved to be of little concern, though, for all three of the companions itched for a fight, any fight. To Drizzt's thinking, if they didn't soon find a common enemy, they would probably be battling each other.

Once again, images of cutting down Artemis Entreri flitted through his mind, along with the reminder of that intimate conversation between the assassin and Dahlia. They shared something, Drizzt knew, something deeper than the bond between himself and Dahlia. He imagined making a fatal blow—one made, curiously, with a red-bladed sword.

"How near are we?" Entreri asked a long while later, jarring Drizzt from his thoughts in the quiet of the tunnels, an eerie hush broken only occasionally by the distant sound of dripping water, or the harsh crack of something hard against the stone.

Drizzt stopped and turned around, waiting as Entreri and Dahlia closed up behind him. He looked to Dahlia for an answer, but the elf shrugged, her memories apparently as hazy as his own.

"Halfway, I would guess," Drizzt replied. "Perhaps less."

"Then let's set a guard and rest," said Entreri.

"I thought you were eager to die," Dahlia snapped at him.

"I'm eager to be rid of the sword," he answered without hesitation. "But I'm not eager to engage more Shadovar when my legs are weak from the long hike."

Dahlia started to respond, to argue, but Drizzt beat her to it. "I agree," he said, ending the debate, though his siding with Entreri brought him a scowl from

Dahlia that likely signaled the start of another debate, he knew. "We must be on our best guard when we enter Gauntlgrym. We don't know what we'll encounter in her dark and broken halls.

"You suggested it," he said to Entreri. "So I suspect that you've discovered a place you think suitable for a camp—or do you propose that we just pause in the middle of the tunnel?"

Entreri turned to look over his left shoulder and pointed up at the top of the cavern wall, right where it rounded into a ceiling. Following that lead, Drizzt moved over and held Twinkle up high. The scimitar's glow revealed a small tunnel winding up and to the side of the corridor.

"There was a second one back a few dozen paces," Entreri explained, "running up the other way. I expect they join."

"If either is even passable," Dahlia remarked sourly.

Drizzt sheathed his blade and leaped up, catching the lip of the smaller tunnel. He pulled himself up to peer into it and paused there, allowing his eyes to adjust to the absence of any substantial light. His drow heritage helped him, greatly so, as the shapes within became clearer. The drow wriggled his way in and crawled along, coming to a landing of sorts, a level and open area large enough to hold all three comfortably. He found two other exits from that small chamber, one rising higher and the other winding back down the other way—likely the opening Entreri had noted earlier in the corridor.

To make certain, the drow went down that way, and soon came to the tunnel exit, just above the corridor he and his friends had already traversed. He rolled himself out of the crawl tunnel, back to the main corridor, and rushed back to rejoin Entreri and Dahlia.

"Suitable," he said.

Dahlia started to argue against breaking their march at that point, but Entreri moved right to the wall and leaped up, catching a hold and disappearing into the crawl tunnel without a glance back.

"He acts as if it's his expedition, and we're just minions to do his bidding," Dahlia said to Drizzt.

"He has the largest stake in this journey," the drow reminded.

Dahlia snorted and looked away.

"You wish to turn away, that he will not be killed," Drizzt whispered.

"I wish to be done with this and be away from here."

"Not true," Drizzt replied. "You wish to be away, but now, before we confront the primordial, before we destroy the sword, and so, before the sword destroys this man who so intrigues you."

Dahlia looked at him for a long while, quietly laughing, and shaking her head slowly, as if in disbelief. She spun around and leaped up along the wall, following Entreri into the crawl tunnel.

Drizzt leaped up right behind her and caught her by the ankle, forcing her to glance back. "I go to scout, before us and behind," he whispered. "To ensure that we weren't followed or seen."

He dropped back down and started off, back the way they had come, intending to double back quickly many yards to search for any sign that they had been trailed. A few dozen paces back along the corridor, it occurred to him to climb up into the second tunnel, to crawl in silently that he could spy on these two.

Then he might know the extent of their bond, after all.

Then he might know of Dahlia's deceit and infidelity.

Then he might kill Entreri, or kill them both, with a clear conscience.

The line of thinking jarred Drizzt as he hustled past that second opening to the upper chamber. He increased his pace even more, wanting to put this area far behind him, wanting to put those angry impulses far behind him.

Dahlia crawled into the low chamber at the apex of the two entry tunnels. Like the other tunnels and many of the Underdark corridors, this one was quietly lit by various lichens. She could see only half of Entreri, as he was standing up into the third opening, the tunnel climbing up from the chamber. He soon crouched back down and fell into a sitting position beneath the opening.

"Impassible," he explained. "The way up is blocked by some rocks."

"So if our enemies assemble around the two lower exits, we're trapped," Dahlia replied, and with much sarcasm, added, "Wonderful planning." She made sure to reflect that sarcasm fully in her inflection, for she knew that Entreri couldn't make out much of her features in this dark place.

"They won't find us," Entreri countered.

"Because there are so many places for us to hide in these few narrow tunnels?" Dahlia asked, her sarcasm unrelenting. And quite boring, she had to admit, even to herself.

Artemis Entreri shook his head and turned his gaze away from her. "Where's Drizzt?"

"He backtracked to ensure that we weren't followed," she replied, and Entreri nodded his agreement with that course. "Perhaps he's already been captured by the Shadovar and tortured into revealing our position, if it would take even that."

Entreri swung his head back to regard the woman. She met his stare with a glower, but he didn't give in to that apparent challenge, and merely continued to look at her, as if measuring her emotions.

"Have you hated for so long that you don't know how to not hate?" he asked with a wry grin.

Dahlia stared at him, at first angrily, but then with a bit of confusion.

"You got your revenge on Herzgo Alegni," Entreri pointed out. "Yet your mood is fouler now than before we met him on that Neverwinter bridge."

Dahlia didn't blink.

"Might it be that revenge tasted not as sweet as you expected?" Entreri posed. "Was the anticipation of revenge a more calming meal, perhaps?"

"And you're the assassin-philosopher?" Dahlia asked.

"You've been running from it for all of your life," he said.

"From it?"

"From whatever it was that Alegni did to you."

"You don't know anything."

"I know that my words have you shifting in your seat."

"Because it is a stupid seat in a stupid hold-out," she spat back. "Were we to be found here, how would we even defend ourselves? You can't even stand up in this hole unless you stick your head into the chimney! I thought I was traveling beside capable warriors, and I find myself put in this compromised position?"

She kept ranting, and Artemis Entreri kept grinning at her, which, of course, only had Dahlia growing more and more agitated.

"You killed your own excuse," Entreri said.

Dahlia looked at him with obvious confusion. She tried to reply but sputtered, just staring at him.

"Your excuse for anger," the assassin explained. "You got your revenge, yet your mood has soured. Because you're lost now. You've lived your life acting out in your anger, and does dear Dahlia have anything to be angry about now?"

She looked away.

"Are you afraid to take responsibility for your actions?"

"Are you truly the assassin-philosopher?" she retorted, turning around to glare at him.

Entreri's shrug was the only response he would offer, so Dahlia looked away once more.

An uncomfortable silence followed, for a long while.

"What about you?" Dahlia finally asked, her voice startling Entreri from private contemplations.

"What about me?" he echoed.

"What sustains your anger?"

"Who claims that I'm angry?"

"I know of your recent past," Dahlia argued. "I fought against you. I witnessed your work against the Thayans. Those were not the actions of a contented man."

"I was a slave," Entreri replied. "Can you blame me?"

Dahlia tried to argue, but again fell short.

"How did you get past it?" Dahlia asked quietly many heartbeats later. "The anger, the betrayal? How did you find your calm?"

"I helped you kill Herzgo Alegni."

"Not that betrayal," Dahlia said bluntly.

Entreri rocked back against the wall. He glanced around, this way and that, and for many heartbeats seemed truly at a loss.

"By caring not a damn," Entreri replied at length.

"I don't believe that."

"Believe it."

"No," she said quietly, staring at Entreri until he at last had to return the look.

"It was my uncle," he admitted for the first time in his life, "and my mother."

Dahlia's expression revealed her confusion.

"He . . . he stole from me, and she sold me into slavery—to others who wished to . . . steal from me," Entreri explained.

"Your mother?" Dahlia clearly seemed at a loss.

"You loved your mother, as I, once, loved mine," Entreri reasoned.

"She was murdered, beheaded by Herzgo Alegni after . . ." Her voice trailed away and her gaze fell to the floor between her boots.

"After he stole from you," Entreri said, and Dahlia looked at him sharply.

"You know nothing about it!"

"But you know that I do," Entreri replied. "And you are the first person to whom I've ever admitted any of this."

Her expression softened at that revelation.

Entreri laughed. "Perhaps I have to kill you now, to keep my secret."

"Try it," Dahlia replied, bringing a wider smile to Entreri's face, for he knew by her tone that his trust in her had lifted a great weight from her shoulders. "I have enough anger left in me to defeat the likes of you."

Artemis Entreri rolled up to his knees, to the side, so that his face was very near the woman. "Well, do it quickly," he said, and pointed back down the tunnel Dahlia had climbed to get into this hide-out. "For that way lies Gauntlgrym, not so far, and there resides the beast of fire and the end of Charon's Claw, and the end of Artemis Entreri."

Dahlia slapped him across the face, surprising them both.

Entreri laughed at her, so she slapped him again, or tried to, but he caught her by the wrist and held her off.

They stared at each other, their faces barely a finger's breadth apart. Entreri nodded and managed a smile, while Dahlia shook her head, her eyes moistening.

"It is time," Entreri said to her. "Trust me in this. It is long past time."

A thousand questions chased Drizzt Do'Urden back along the corridors, paramount among them the continuing lack of purpose for his present course. Why was he even there?

He had no answers, though, and so he kept pushing the doubts aside, and took care not to revel too deeply in the continuing stream of images of Artemis Entreri dead at his feet, pleasant as they were.

While these surroundings weren't fresh in his thoughts, they were familiar, and they brought him back to his previous journey here, the good parts. He remembered Bruenor's face when first they had glanced upon the entrance of Gauntlgrym, the high stone wall, like that of a castle, except that it was tightly encased within a subterranean cavern.

He thought of the throne, just within the great entry hall, and again recalled Bruenor's beaming face.

"I found it, elf," Drizzt whispered in the dark corridor, just to hear the sound of those words once more, for they, more than anything Drizzt had ever heard, sounded like sweet victory.

His mood brightened as he moved farther from his encamped companions. How could it not, with the ghost, the memory, of Bruenor Battlehammer so near?

"Is your heart heavy, Drizzt Do'Urden?" an unexpected, unfamiliar voice, a woman's voice, asked of him from the darkness.

Drizzt immediately fell into a crouch, moving closer to one corridor wall for the cover it provided. He glanced all around, his hands near to his scimitars, which he did not dare draw for fear that Twinkle's light would more fully expose him.

"I knew I would find you alone," the woman continued, her accent strong, biting off her consonants so abruptly that it jarred the drow. He did not know her. He did not even know of her possible origins. "It is not hard to find Drizzt Do'Urden alone in these times, is it?"

Thinking he had located the source, the direction at least, Drizzt edged out a bit, putting himself in line for a charge if necessary.

"Be at ease," the woman said, as if reading his mind. The voice came from a completely different area of the darkened corridor than the previous remarks, and there was no way anyone could have moved between those particular points without him hearing or seeing it.

Perhaps it was a matter of cloaking spells, like invisibility, but more likely, she was utilizing magical ventriloquism.

A sorceress, then, Drizzt thought, and he knew that he needed to be doubly careful.

"I have not come to do battle," she explained. "Nor to harm you in any way."

"Who are you, then? Thayan or Shadovar?"

Her laughter started behind him, but quickly came from the original spot, before him. "Need it be one or the other?"

"Those seem to be the people most interested in me of late," he said.

She laughed again. "I am from the Shadowfell," she admitted. "Sent by one who is not your enemy, though you have something he wants."

Drizzt straightened. Given Arunika's warning, he knew where this was leading. "The sword," he stated.

"It is a Netherese blade."

"A vile one."

"That is not my judgment to offer. We would like it back."

"You cannot have it."

"Are you sure?"

The question struck him curiously and put him a bit off balance.

"Does it mean so much to you?" the woman asked, and she was behind him again, and given his last response, he was fast to turn and set himself defensively. Could she move quickly enough to steal Charon's Claw from its scabbard on his back? "Do you have such loyalty to the man you call Artemis Entreri?"

"Do you ask me to return a sword, or a slave?" Drizzt retorted.

"Does it matter?"

"Of course."

"This is your friend, then, this Artemis Entreri?" the woman asked, and her voice came from an entirely different place then, farther along the corridor back the other way. "A loyal companion, like a brother to you?"

Her tone, even more than her curious words, made it clear that she was mocking him, or at least mocking the notion that he and Artemis Entreri might be the best of friends.

"Would he have to be any such thing for me to know what is right and what is wrong?" Drizzt countered, fighting hard to suppress his antagonism toward Entreri.

"Right and wrong?" she asked, her voice going from behind him to back in front of him between the words. "Black and white? Are you so simplistic as to believe that there is only one answer to such a question?"

"Which question?" Drizzt shot back. "That seems to be all you offer: questions."

"Nay, my friend," she replied immediately. "Had I nothing to offer, I would not be here." As she finished, she came out of the shadows—or simply materialized in the corridor, Drizzt could not be sure—and slowly approached him.

"You have nothing to offer against the clear morality of such a choice," Drizzt insisted.

"Are you sure?" Her smile, so confident, so knowing, unnerved him. She stopped only a few strides from him and said simply, "I want the sword."

"You cannot have it."

Her hand came up slowly, palm facing upward and holding a curious item. For a moment, Drizzt didn't understand the movement or the item, and his hands went fast to his scimitar hilts, the blades coming out just a bit. He wondered if she was casting a spell of some sort, or if this item, a very small box lined with glowing blue lines of energy and magic, would strike out at him with some unknown force.

After a moment, the item in her hand shifted.

No, he realized, something contained inside the item had shifted, something inside the small cage she held had moved around.

Drizzt peered more closely as the reality began to dawn on him. He felt the strength drain from his legs, felt his heart pounding in his chest.

Guenhwyvar.

Dahlia kept one eye cracked open, and stared out the corner of it at her companion. Entreri was sitting, his legs tucked up tight against him, his head back against the wall, eyes closed. She doubted that he was asleep at that point, and she didn't want Entreri noticing that she was staring at him.

Staring at him and measuring him.

The woman felt naked before this man. It seemed to Dahlia that he knew more about her emotional turmoil than she did. But what did that mean for her? Entreri was sympathetic to her pains. He knew her trauma—not the specifics, perhaps, though that, too, was possible, she realized, since he had been with Herzgo Alegni for so many years. Certainly he had recognized the scars, because he shared those scars, or so he'd strongly hinted. But did he, truly?

It screamed out in Dahlia's thoughts that Entreri might be using her dark secret as a cynical way to gain some level of control over her, or to gain her trust for his own eventual gain. That he could speak to her so intimately, as if he was a kindred spirit, certainly forced her to let down some of her ever-present guards.

To what end?

Dahlia closed her eyes and tried to shake the unsettling notion away. Perhaps he wasn't manipulating her, she reminded herself.

Within a couple of heartbeats, she found herself looking at him again, her cynicism thinning.

He understood.

That notion stung her and warmed her at the same time, embarrassed her because no one should know this about her. And the thought brought a grimace to her face, because even though Entreri had come to understand a part of her scar, it was only that, a part, a fraction of the shame that haunted Dahlia. He had a notion of Alegni's violation, that much was clear, but how far would his sympathy carry her with him if he knew the rest of the story, if he knew . . . ?

Dahlia sighed and settled back with closed eyes once more, and though she was in a stuffy and tight cave, she felt the wind on her face, felt as if she was standing atop a cliff, a baby in her arms.

Dahlia's breathing came in rasps, and she opened her eyes and glared at Entreri, silently cursing him for reminding her of that dark past.

And yet, even that anger could not gain any lasting hold over her as she watched her quiet companion. Entreri scared her, rightly so, and Dahlia continually told herself to be wary of him.

But she couldn't deny that he also intrigued her on several very deep and very personal levels.

He knew.

He knew, and he hadn't turned away from her.

He knew, and instead of disgust, he had reached out to her.

Did she want that? Did she deserve that?

Dahlia couldn't sort through the jarring contradictions in her thoughts and in her heart.

She thought of killing him.

She thought of making love to him.

Both seemed so sweet.

Drizzt's hand snapped up to grab the small cage, but he grasped only air as the image of the woman faded to nothingness in the dimly lit cavern. He leaped around, eyes darting, and found her again to the other side.

"What trick is this?"

"No trick," she answered. "In my hand, I have a magical cage, and in that cage is the companion you hold most dear."

"Give her to me!" Drizzt demanded, but as he took a single step toward the woman, she disappeared again, only to reappear farther down the corridor.

"The panther came through the shadowgate with Lord Alegni," the woman explained. "Lord Alegni does not yet know that we have the cat, but he will surely make her pay dearly for the scars she dug into his body."

So entranced was Drizzt with the possibility of getting Guen back, with the idea that she might not be lost to him after all, that it took him many heartbeats to even register the reality that Herzgo Alegni might not be dead. His expression grew curious and he stared at the woman, at this latest image of the woman.

"Alegni is dead."

The woman shrugged. "He should be, perhaps," she replied. "And surely would be had he not arrived back to loving, clerical arms."

Drizzt didn't know how to respond.

"You will learn the truth of my words soon enough, I expect," the woman added. "He will find you, if you remain with your companions. Did you think your battle out in the forest a mere coincidence?"

"Why are you here? Why are you telling me this? Are you Alegni's enemy?"

She shook her head. "I am neither enemy nor friend. I am merely employed, by another."

"Another Netherese?"

She smiled as if that should be obvious.

"Who sent you here to taunt me?"

"Taunt? I have done no such thing."

"You dangle before me that which I most desire."

"Such a companion is quite desirable, indeed, and by more than you."

"I have the figurine," the drow argued. "You cannot have her. You cannot control her! Even were you to kill me and take the statuette which summons Guenhwyvar, she would not serve you."

"The Netherese are not impotent in the way of magic, even ancient magic, nor in the ways of planar travel," she replied. "We don't need your magical item to summon Guenhwyvar, nor will you, for all of your efforts, recall her to your side from out of the cage we have built for her. Do not doubt that."

"So you taunt me."

"No."

"But you hold her before me, with me helpless to free her."

"Helpless? Nay, Drizzt Do'Urden, you can have her."

Drizzt swallowed hard at that remark. "What do you want?"

"It is quite simple," she replied. And the drow wasn't surprised when she added, "As I already told you, you have something that belongs to us."

Drizzt rubbed his hand over his face.

"Give me the sword and I will free your feline companion," the woman promised. "A fair deal, from an honorable broker."

"You would claim such."

"Why would I lie? We do know the truth of your words. The cat, beautiful as she is, is useless to us. She will never serve us. Her heart is yours. So take her back and return to us, to me, the Netherese sword you carry on your back."

"So you can use it to kill me?" Drizzt blurted, and he thought the words ridiculous as they left his mouth, for he was merely lashing out in frustration.

"The Empire of Netheril cares nothing about you, Drizzt Do'Urden."

"Herzgo Alegni might not agree."

She shrugged as if that hardly mattered. "You were a pawn in a wider game. Do not think yourself so important in this battle, to him or to us." She reached her free hand forward and beckoned to him. "Give me the sword and take your cat, and be gone from here. These events do not concern you."

Drizzt licked his lips as he stared at that cage, its glowing bars shimmering with energy. His gaze focused more clearly and he made out those familiar eyes from behind the bars, and noted the pacing of the miniaturized panther. It was Guenhwyvar. He knew it in his heart that this was no deception.

His hand went over his shoulder and hovered near the hilt of Charon's Claw. What did he care about this sword or about Artemis Entreri, after all? Wasn't the life of Guenhwyvar worth those of a thousand Entreris? He owed the man nothing! Could he say the same about Guenhwyvar?

"Give her back to me and I will be gone from the fight," he started to respond, as his hand started to close around the wrapped hilt of Charon's Claw, but the words choked him up as he tried to speak them. He thought of Dahlia. He would have to extricate her from this battle as well, of course.

But would she even go? Would she leave Artemis Entreri?

Drizzt winced as he thought of a goblin he had met so long ago, in a place so far removed from here. A runaway slave, a goblin not of typical weal, a goblin akin to himself, in truth, in its desire to be away from its dishonorable people. He had failed that goblin, and that goblin had been hanged.

A slave.

Artemis Entreri had been a slave to Alegni, a slave to Charon's Claw. Could Drizzt really offer him back to that circumstance, whatever his desires and whatever his gain?

And yet, did Guenhwyvar deserve this, deserve to pace in tight circles in a tiny cage?

"I warn you that my masters are not benevolent," the woman said, noting his hesitation. "Your precious Guenhwyvar is not immortal in her current state, chained in a pit in the Shadowfell, surrounded by shadow mastiffs eager to tear her apart. Will they get to her before Herzgo Alegni, who is fast recovering from his wounds?"

Drizzt tried to respond. A large part of him wanted to draw out Charon's Claw and throw it on the ground before him. What did he owe Artemis Entreri?

And yet, he could not do it. He could not return the man to slavery. He could not offer one life in exchange for another.

He stood there, motionless, except that he slowly shook his head.

"You play the part of the fool," the woman said quietly. "You hold to a moral standard that Barrabus the Gray does not deserve, and at the expense of your precious Guenhwyvar. What a miserable friend is Drizzt Do'Urden!"

"Just give her to me," Drizzt heard himself saying, quietly.

"Consider your decision," the woman replied. "Sleep with it, if you can. Sleep with dreams of Guenhwyvar, staked in a pit, hungry hounds tearing her flesh and pulling her limbs off. Will you hear her shrieks of agony, Drizzt Do'Urden? Will the tortured death of Guenhwyvar haunt you for the rest of your miserable life? I think it will."

Drizzt felt as if he was shrinking, as if he was diminishing, the floor rushing up all around him to swallow him—and in that awful moment, he wished that it would!

"We will speak again, perhaps," the woman said. "I will return to you, if I find the opportunity before your Guenhwyvar is destroyed. Or perhaps Lord Alegni will find you three and take back his sword. I am sure that he will not kill you until he allows you to witness the death of Guenhwyvar."

With that, she vanished, and Drizzt sensed that he was truly alone. He danced all around, agitated, his gaze darting to every shadow.

How could he have done this? How could he have chosen the sword, chosen Artemis Entreri, over his beloved Guenhwyvar?

What a miserable friend indeed was Drizzt Do'Urden!

CHAPTER 17

THE WEB OF DROW

RAVEL MOVED WITH ALL SPEED, EAGER TO SEE THE COMPLETION OF THIS GREAT achievement. They had found a dividing chamber between the main regions of the forge and lower Gauntlgrym and the still-unexplored upper levels. Several nobles had utilized their House insignias to levitate up to the ceiling and had discerned that this place was indeed the key area of division between the two sections of the vast complex, but the long circular iron staircase that had allowed access had been destroyed, and recently, it seemed, likely in the cataclysmic eruption.

The first reports had claimed that it was beyond repair, and some of the craftsmen had estimated that it would take months to build another suitable stair. Drow ingenuity and clever ideas combined with a bit of magic had solved the riddle, though.

Ravel at last came into the chamber, and it was indeed vast, a series of criss-crossing stone walkways going off beyond his vision in every direction and with a ceiling so high that it was out of sight, even though the light was ample, relatively speaking.

With Tiago Baenre and Jearth in tow, Ravel moved out from the entrance toward a group of drow settled behind an army of goblins and orcs. Not far behind him came his sisters and many others. It occurred to Ravel that almost the entirety of his expedition was now there, in that chamber, with only Gol'fanin and a few other craftsmen back in the forge room. That notion unsettled him more than a little.

As he neared the group, Ravel noted the circular stair, climbing from the floor. Beyond it, lines of orcs and bugbears, as well as Yerrininae's drider forces, pulled hard on ropes that had been hung over pulleys fastened in the ceiling, hoisting a long section of curving stairs high into the air.

"We were able to salvage more of the original stair than we believed," Brack'thal explained, and Ravel started to nod to his older brother, until he realized that the mage was addressing Berellip, who was standing behind him, and not him.

"Finally," Ravel intervened, with a tone reflecting as much disgust as relief. He knew that this, like the battles with the elementals in the forge room, would serve his brother's reputation dangerously well, and so he wanted to establish himself as the leader here, and not let Brack'thal and Berellip speak around him.

Brack'thal stared at him incredulously and started to respond—some impertinent insult, no doubt—when a brilliant flash to the side caught the attention of all, and a resounding retort shook the stones beneath their feet. Following that came a cacophony of avian shrieks of the type one might hear when trying to steal from the nest of a crow.

"The spellspinners engage the dire corbies," Ravel said, glad that his clique was proving valuable, when indeed much of the stair's repair had to be credited to the efforts and magic of Brack'thal.

"Now!" Brack'thal cried out, demanding the attention of all, as across the way, bugbears swung heavy axes at the ropes. Magical lights appeared far above, illuminating the ceiling of the great chamber, and showing the suspended section of stairs clearly as its supports broke free. With worker goblins clambering all around it, down it fell a few feet into the waiting arms of the highest reconstructed section. The momentum of the fall drove the stairwell perfectly into place, pushing the joining pins in solidly and deep.

With a great groan, it set there and toppled forward, where the hooked tip of its high end slammed in with a resounding thud and found a secure grasp on the ledge above. Dust and stones fell down from on high, spattering the wide floor, and for a moment, all held their collective breath, fearing that the whole of the top landing would collapse. But it did not and the stairwell held.

A great cheer arose from below, from drow and goblins and bugbears alike.

The poor goblins riding the stair bounced all around, some flipping over the side to grab on desperately or to pitch over and tumble down to their deaths.

Those splattering goblins, too, were cheered, just for the joy of the gruesome spectacle.

"And now we can travel in force to the higher complex," Brack'thal announced with a victorious bow.

"And enemies can come down from above," Ravel remarked.

"Not so," said Brack'thal. "The stair is hinged. We can retract it, by half, and raise it back as needed."

Another flash off to the side showed that the battle with the dire corbies was hardly at its end.

"How many?" Ravel asked, nodding that way and desperately wanting to change the subject before his clever brother gained too much of an upper hand.

"They are thick in the tunnels," one of the other nearby drow answered.

Ravel paused to consider that, and behind him, Berellip warned, "If we press on too far and too quickly, we will invite them and other monsters around this complex to slide in behind us and cut our forces in two."

The spellspinner turned an unappreciative glare on her, and her warning only prompted him to push along more boldly, out of spite if not good tactics.

"Take a sizable force—six hands," Ravel instructed Jearth, a "hand" being a patrol of five dark elves, "and half of Yerrininae's driders, Yerrininae included, and go up to map the higher chambers."

"Spellspinners?" Jearth asked.

"One for every hand," Ravel replied. He looked to Berellip and Saribel as he added, "And a priestess for every two hands—Saribel will surely enjoy the adventure."

"As will I," Brack'thal put in.

Ravel didn't turn to look at him, but kept staring at his sisters, measuring their intent and curious as to whether Berellip would try to overrule him so openly.

"Since I was instrumental in repairing the staircase," Brack'thal added.

Ravel turned on him sharply. "You will return to the forge," he instructed.

Brack'thal's eyes narrowed, full of hate.

"Any craftsman commoner could have overseen the repair of the stairwell," Ravel stated. "Your singular talent lies in your strange affinity to these fire elementals, and so the forge, and the forge alone, is where you are needed."

For a moment, all about Ravel, his sisters, Brack'thal, Tiago and even the other drow, who surely were not as attuned to the power struggles, but obviously understood that something was amiss, stood tense, most hands shifting nearer to weapons or magical implements.

"And what of the *iblith*?" Jearth said.

Ravel appreciated that reminder of the fodder they had brought along—for himself and mostly for those who would oppose him. For more than any dark elves, more than any dark elven power, in this chamber loomed the hulking specter of the slave multitude, so thick in rank. Ravel controlled them, as Jearth had just subtly, and wisely, reminded them all.

"Take as many goblins and orcs as you deem necessary," the spellspinner offered.

"Bugbears would move more stealthily through the upper tunnels," Jearth countered.

"They remain here, to secure the stairwell."

Jearth nodded and looked to Tiago.

"I believe that I will stand beside Ravel for now," the Baenre answered that look, and his words resonated on many levels.

Ravel was glad for that, for he understood the argument that awaited him back in the forge area when he returned to face Berellip and Brack'thal. The open hatred with which his brother now stared at him promised at least that.

I did not think you would come, Jearth's fingers flashed to Saribel Xorlarrin sometime later in the higher tunnels.

Saribel regarded him contemptuously and did not reply.

You could have sent lesser priestesses, Jearth's hand flashed. *Surely you know the danger here.*

No more than the danger below, Saribel hastily flashed back. Her fingers continued, but she clamped her fist shut, shutting down the communication. "Do you think I fear battle?" she asked aloud, her voice seeming absurdly loud in the dull silence of the dusty chambers, the volume drawing looks of alarm from Jearth and others nearby.

It is not wise to . . . the weapons master started to reply with fingers emphatically waggling.

"Enough, Jearth," Saribel demanded. "If there are enemies to be found, then let us find them and be done with them."

Jearth motioned for the others to move past and he motioned Saribel aside into a small and broken chamber, one that might have served as an antechamber for a chapel, for through a second, low archway, one nearly crumbled, it connected to a large room that had what appeared to be the remains of an altar at its far end. Glancing through it, Jearth watched a patrol of goblins scurrying along.

He turned to the priestess.

"If you're so afraid . . ." she started to say, but he cut her short with an upraised hand.

"Of course I'm not," he replied quietly. "I wish nothing more than to find some enemy blood to wet my blades. But I wish our conversation private."

"Plotting?" she asked slyly.

"You see the coming battle as clearly as I."

"I hope to, indeed."

"Ravel will win out."

Saribel scoffed at that.

"You don't believe it, or you do not wish it?"

"The latter," Saribel replied with a grin, "and so, doubtlessly, the former will follow."

Jearth understood her clearly enough. Berellip preferred Brack'thal.

The weapons master shook his head, slowly and deliberately.

"You doubt the priestesses of Lolth?" Saribel asked incredulously.

I do not doubt at all that Berellip could find victory for whichever side she chose. Jearth went back to the silent hand signals, for he sensed someone just beyond the archway and wanted this critical exchange to be truly private. *But why would Saribel follow?*

Saribel's superior expression turned to one of confusion, and Jearth knew that he was on very dangerous ground. His fingers moved slowly. *If Berellip chooses Brack'thal, Berellip chooses wrongly.*

Saribel's eyes widened and Jearth added, *Tiago Baenre stands with Ravel.*

Then Tiago Baenre . . . she started to reply, but Jearth emphatically interrupted her.

If Tiago does not return to Matron Mother Quenthel, House Baenre will wage war on House Xorlarrin, he explained. *There is no exception to be found. If Tiago is killed by a corbie or a cave-in, or smitten dead by Berellip, it matters not at all. Matron Mother Quenthel Baenre has assured me of this. It was her way of ensuring that Tiago's choice would, by necessity, be our choice.*

Saribel's shoulders slumped visibly, dropping under the undeniable weight of House Baenre.

Tiago has made his choice and will not be dissuaded. He stands with Ravel.

Berellip does not, Saribel's fingers replied. *I must go to her.* She started to turn, but Jearth caught her by the arm, and when she turned back, outraged that he had dared touch her, he smiled to calm her.

"Why?" he asked aloud.

Saribel looked at him without any sign of comprehension. How had this dolt ever climbed so high among the priestesses of the House? Could it be more clearly spoken? He was offering Saribel ascension. If Berellip sided with Brack'thal, but he and Saribel turned against her, the battle would be short-lived indeed. For all of Berellip's power, and all of Brack'thal's newfound prowess, Ravel commanded the spellspinners and had Tiago at his side.

Surely you can justify your decision to Matron Zeerith, knowing that Berellip's course would have set House Baenre upon us, he dared signal.

So there it was, out in the open. As his hands stopped communicating, Jearth brought them near to his weapons. He could defeat this priestess, he believed, but only if he was quick and his aim true.

For a long while, Saribel's expression remained impassive.

"If our mission here is successful, it might well create a new hierarchy in House Xorlarrin," Jearth stated.

"Certainly Ravel would be elevated above the stature of Brack'thal," Saribel replied, her words sounding as sweet music in Jearth's ears. "Formally, I mean, for already it is clear that the Secondboy has the favor of Matron Zeerith above the Elderboy."

"Lolth blesses this expedition, and will heap rewards and stature upon her priestesses who facilitated it, either by the Spider Queen's side in a place of honor in death, or within House Xorlarrin for those who return," Jearth said with a wry grin, one that was soon reflected on Saribel's face.

A cry from somewhere ahead of them told them that battle had been joined.

"For the glory of House Xorlarrin," Saribel said, and she started away.

"For the glory of the city of Xorlarrin," Jearth offered, and Saribel glanced back and nodded.

Jearth remained behind just long enough to take a deep breath, and once again he found himself quietly admiring Ravel. For this division of the sisters had been Ravel's scheme, of course, all planned beforehand with both Tiago and Jearth.

It wasn't always possible to plot steps ahead of drow females, but it was never very hard to get them to stab each other in the back.

Jearth drew his weapons and started away, now paying attention to these most interesting chambers and corridors around him. This had been the residence region of ancient Gauntlgrym, so who knew what treasures they might find?

It wasn't often that Berellip Xorlarrin was left speechless, and Tiago Baenre was quite proud of himself for accomplishing that feat.

"There is more to Saribel than you assumed," he said lightheartedly, to convey that this Xorlarrin intrigue was quite amusing to him. He had just assured her that her sister would not stand beside her against Ravel in the probable duel with Brack'thal, executing the second part of Ravel's clever plan. Jearth divided the sisters and Tiago happily relayed that truth to the one separated.

"You presume that I will let Ravel and his spellspinners kill my brother?" she said. "You believe I have no choice or say in the matter?"

"I think the consequences give you pause. I think you're quite intelligent."

Berellip swept past him, out of the room and down the corridor to the forge area, which was glowing brightly in the distance. When they entered, they found that the anticipated fight might be farther along than they had expected, for Brack'thal stood in the center of the room, a gigantic fire elemental at his side, and several other smaller ones dancing in a circle around him.

Across the way, leaning easily on the cooling pool of an unfired forge, Ravel stood with his arms crossed over his thin chest, an amused expression clear on his face.

"Don't you feel it, Secondboy?" Brack'thal called with obvious delight. "Of course you do, but you don't want to admit it. You feel it and you fear it!"

None of the craftsmen, not goblin, bugbear, nor drow, were working, all eyes focused on these two principals in a conflict long-expected.

Berellip glanced around the room, and noted that more than a few of the blacksmiths weren't craftsmen at all, but were Ravel's spellspinners, strategically placed. Her young brother had planned well. He had seen this coming—likely had incited it—in a time and place of his own choosing.

But perhaps he had erred, it occurred to her as she noted another elemental burning a line out of a forge and rushing to Brack'thal's side, for there was no denying that the older Xorlarrin son was finding impressive amounts of power and control. Just then, as if sensing her attention, Brack'thal turned to regard her and Tiago.

"He feels it!" Brack'thal explained. "And he knows what it is. Don't you, spell-spinner?" he shouted, turning sharply back on Ravel.

"I feel that you have left your better judgment behind," Ravel answered flippantly.

"My powers grow ascendant once more!" Brack'thal said. "Where will you be then, spellspinner?" He waved his arms and looked all around, focusing on Ravel's spies. "Where will all of you be in that event?"

"Alive, at least," Ravel replied, a clear threat.

Which was more than Brack'thal would be able to say, Berellip knew, for despite his fiery servants, she expected that Ravel and the others would make short work of him. She wondered how to proceed, for it didn't seem like Brack'thal would listen to any reasoning, and she hated the thought of his demise at that time, both because of the implications to Ravel's standing and because, on a practical level, Brack'thal's work with the elementals, however the fool was managing it, was proving quite valuable here at the all-important forge.

Tiago Baenre stepped past her.

"Would that not be a wondrous thing?" he said loudly, commanding attention.

"Ah, Ravel's rothé makes his appearance," Brack'thal shouted back.

Tiago laughed it off, resisting the urge to fling his sword into the mage's forehead—and it would not have been a difficult throw. He walked steadily toward Brack'thal. As he neared, so that only Brack'thal could hear, he whispered, "You cannot win."

Brack'thal puffed his chest out defiantly.

"Berellip stands with Ravel," Tiago said, and the mage deflated almost instantly. He looked past Tiago to Berellip, who, understanding what Tiago had just related, nodded solemnly to confirm it.

Brack'thal's eye twitched, and he licked his lips as he turned his gaze from Berellip to Tiago and then to Ravel, who was slowly approaching, a smile slowly widening. Ravel nodded left and nodded right, and from the shadows came the spellspinners, staves and wands in hand, fingers rolling eagerly around them.

"Not one of those you thought your ally will stand with you against Berellip," Tiago quietly informed Brack'thal.

The mage spun on Berellip. "Sister!" he implored her.

"Dismiss your pets back to the forges," she ordered. "We have much work to do."

"Sister!"

"It is ended!" Berellip roared at him, and she came forward forcefully, even throwing a spell before her, one that smote a minor elemental with a burst of water, and the creature dissipated into a blast of fog with an angry hiss.

"Eight legs?" she asked Brack'thal, and the blood drained from his face, for that particular reference loomed as the worst curse any drow might hear. Berellip had just informed the mage that his fate lay among Yerrininae's band!

243

Brack'thal, clearly caught and overwhelmed by the turn of events, held up his hands unthreateningly and began complying, dismissing his pets to the various forges.

By the time Berellip and Ravel reached him, only the largest remained. Brack'thal looked to it, then back to Berellip, and fell on his knees before her.

"Kill me, I beg," he said.

"It will not be quick," she promised wickedly, and he accepted that with an eager nod, for better to be tortured to death than to be transformed into a wretched drider!

"Sister," Ravel intervened, and Berellip, Brack'thal, and Tiago all turned to regard him curiously. "Spare him, I beg of you."

It seemed like every creature in the room held its breath.

"He is valuable. His work here has been beyond reproach," Ravel explained to Berellip's stunned expression.

"Such weakness," she whispered back, hardly believing her ears. "You would show mercy?"

"Only if Brack'thal declares allegiance to me," Ravel stated, and he struck a superior pose, towering over his kneeling brother. "Only if this is ended, by decree, by surrender, and I am named here and now the Elderboy of House Xorlarrin, with Brack'thal afforded all rights as Secondboy."

"I would rather die," Brack'thal replied.

"Would you rather sprout six extra legs?" Tiago remarked.

"Would you?" Ravel asked, referring to Brack'thal's claim and not Tiago's threat. "Then your claim of your powers returning rings hollow in your own ears."

He said it loudly, so that all around could hear, so that those spellspinners he knew had recently come to consider siding with Brack'thal would hear.

Berellip silently congratulated Ravel. He had played this perfectly, for either way, Brack'thal was caught. If he didn't agree and was thus killed, he would be admitting that his claims were false, and so Ravel would secure the spellspinners in his entourage once more. And if he did agree, he would be bound by his words. It was not often that drow males flipped their titles, as Ravel had demanded, but it was not unprecedented, and such a pact was surely binding. If Brack'thal agreed, any future action he took against Ravel would be construed as an affront to House Xorlarrin, invoking the wrath of Matron Zeerith.

"Well?" Berellip prompted.

"So be it," the defeated mage replied, lowering his gaze.

Ravel was to his side in an eye-blink, grabbing him under the shoulder and hoisting him to his feet. "You are a noble of House Xorlarrin," the young spellspinner quietly said.

Brack'thal stared at him hatefully.

"Go back to the tunnels with your pet," Ravel ordered. "Continue your important work."

The mage was more than happy to comply, and he hustled away, and as Berellip and Ravel swept the room with their stares, drow and goblins and bugbears fell all over each other to get back to their tasks.

"Follow," Berellip demanded of the two males beside her. She led them into the chambers she had taken as her own, and closed the door behind them as they entered, before grabbing Ravel by the arm and spinning him around.

"I have had enough of your subterfuge," she said.

"I am drow," he replied with a grin.

Berellip didn't blink.

"This is ended," Ravel told her. "And know that I am as weary of looking over my shoulder for you as you are for me." He turned for the door and Berellip shifted to block his egress.

Now Ravel didn't blink, and after a few heartbeats, Berellip let him leave.

"He is always full of surprises, that one," Tiago remarked.

"And you support him."

"Matron Zeerith supports him," Tiago corrected. "And Matron Mother Quenthel does so, out of respect for your mother." When Berellip didn't immediately reply, Tiago added, "This is ended, and know that I am the weariest of all."

He stepped past Berellip for the door.

"Mercy," Berellip said with a disgusted chortle. "He granted Brack'thal mercy, and mercy undeserved."

"Do not think him weak," was all that Tiago bothered to reply as he left the room. He glanced back as he stepped through the door. "All of this intrigue has excited me," he informed her. "I will return to you in short order."

"And if I refuse?"

"You're a priestess of Lolth," Tiago said with a bow. "If you refuse, I will leave."

"And if I do not refuse, you will be indebted to me," Berellip said, and Tiago could see the traps being set behind her glowing red eyes. He thought about it for just a moment, then nodded, and with a knowing smile bowed again and was gone.

For indeed, Tiago understood the task Berellip had in mind. Ravel had shown uncharacteristic mercy. Now that she knew of her younger sister's treachery, Berellip would not.

The Baenre noble caught up to Ravel just beyond the forge area, the young spellspinner sitting by a small table lifting a glass of Slow Spout, a Duergan brew so named because after it swirled around inside the imbiber for some time, it inevitably put the fool on his hands and knees, "spouting" it back up. The thick and bitter ale was more commonly shared among the goblins and kobolds of Menzoberranzan than among the drow, whose tastes and sensibilities were more usually attuned to the finer liqueurs, like Feywine or brandy.

There was no doubt that Slow Spout could accomplish the task, though, if that task was to dull the senses.

"A strange choice of celebratory drink," Tiago remarked, holding his hand out to refuse Ravel's offer of a cup. So as not to be rude, the young Baenre drew a small flask from under his coat, unscrewed the top, and took a small swig.

"Why did I let him live?" Ravel asked before Tiago could.

"That is the question most formed by drow fingers at this time, yes," Tiago replied.

Ravel looked aside, his expression very somber and very sober, despite the libations.

Tiago caught the significance of that look and suppressed the burning urge to prompt the spellspinner as his own curiosity began to bubble.

"Brack'thal's claims," Ravel said, shaking his head.

"What of them?"

Ravel looked his Baenre friend directly in the eye. "He was not wrong."

Tiago tried hard not to reveal his shock, but still he fell back a step.

"I feel it," Ravel explained.

Tiago shook his head, too emphatically, perhaps. "There is some trick at play here with Brack'thal, some secret item or one old spell returned. His work with the elementals . . ."

"Impressive work," Ravel said.

"And you're fooled by it."

Ravel took another gulp of Slow Spout. "Let us hope that is the case," the spellspinner said, and he sounded less than convinced.

CHAPTER

18

A COMPANION'S TRUST

HERZGO ALEGNI STEPPED THROUGH THE SHADOW GATE, ARRIVING IN A SMALL chamber built into a stalactite hanging above a vast underground cavern. It had been only two days since the disastrous fight in the forest, but the tiefling warlord was feeling much better. He had used Draygo Quick's failure to force the withered old warlock into redoubling the efforts to heal him, and to give him more reinforcements.

Herzgo Alegni knew they couldn't fail again. Not now. Not here. Too much was at stake, and this time, failure would mean the end of his coveted sword and the end of his reputation.

Effron was already in the portal chamber, staring out a small window beside the chamber's one exit, an open door leading to a landing and a circular stair that ran around the rock mound.

Alegni walked up beside the twisted warlock and pushed him aside. Effron stuck his face into the window opening and tried to hide his surprise.

There before Alegni, across a dark underground pool, loomed the front wall of the ancient dwarven complex of Gauntlgrym, like the façade of a surface fortress, but tucked into the back of the cavern, the castle wall coming up right near to the ceiling. There were parapets up there, Alegni could see; that wall, this whole cavern, including the stalactite in which he stood, had been prepared for defense of the complex.

"Directly below," Effron said, and Alegni leaned out and looked down, to see another landing just below his position, an ancient war engine set upon it.

"Ballista?" he asked, not quite sure of what he was viewing. It looked like a great mounted crossbow, a ballista, except that it was covered on top with a large fanlike box. A pair of Shadovar moved around down there, working on the contraption.

"An unusual design," Effron explained. "They are set all around the cavern. Balogoth the historian called them volley guns."

Alegni looked back from Effron to the ballista, and held up his hand as Effron started to explain what he had meant by that title. For there was no need—the name alone described the purpose of that fanlike box all too well.

"Will it throw?" he called down to the Shadovar on the ledge below.

The pair looked up and fell back a step at the unexpected sight of their warlord.

"Will it throw?" Alegni demanded again when neither answered.

"We do not know, my Lord Alegni," one replied. "We have replaced the bowstring, but the arms are so ancient, they likely have little tension left in them."

"Attempt it."

The two looked at each other, then scrambled to a crate lying nearby—one they had brought from the Shadowfell—and began pulling forth long arrows. One by one, they loaded the fanlike box, sliding the bolts in from behind. Then one shade grabbed the huge crank and slowly pulled back the string.

The throw arms creaked in protest.

"It won't work," Effron said, but Alegni didn't even bother to glance back to look at him.

When the crank was set, the second shade took hold of a lever. This one didn't move easily, and it took him a long while of trying before he looked to his companion helplessly, and obviously desperately afraid.

They wouldn't want to fail their warlord, Herzgo Alegni understood, and he liked that show of fear.

After much tinkering, with one shade even crawling under the edge of the box and digging at the wooden catches with a small blade, they finally managed to ease the cartridge into place.

Herzgo Alegni held back a mocking chuckle when they fired the ballista, for only one side, one throwing arm, moved with the release. Out the front came the arrows, barely thrown, more falling off to tumble straight down than actually flying free. And those that did come forth barely cleared the stalactite—the shades could have hand-thrown them farther.

Down below on the cavern floor came a couple of curses and shouts of protest.

"The wood is too old," Effron said.

"I know that," Alegni replied. "It is an interesting design."

"In their day, the many ballistae set in these towers could have filled the air with swarms of arrows," Effron explained. "It is a design worth copying, I believe, as does Balogoth, who is hard at work in diagramming the crossbows and those curious hoppers."

Herzgo Alegni swept his gaze around the cavern. "We do not have enough soldiers," he surmised. "It is too large, and too filled with cover. They will slip through our ranks."

"There is only one door, as far as we can determine," Effron replied.

Alegni looked to the vast wall and the single opening in its center. Rails came through that door and a couple of carts, ore carts likely, lay discarded in the sand before the cavern pool.

"As far as we can determine," he echoed. "Dahlia and her drow companion have been here before, have been inside the complex. If there are other entries, they will know of them."

"I sent only a single patrol inside the door for that reason," Effron replied. "Should our enemies get to the door, they will be held by our warriors that we can catch them from behind. The rest of the forces are scattering out among the cavern, trying to cover every angle of approach."

Effron paused for just a moment as Alegni stared out the window, but there was something remaining, the warlord knew, and so he turned back on the twisted warlock.

"If they are even coming here," Effron said.

"They are," Alegni said without hesitation. He knew it to be true, and feared it to be true, for he knew, too, what primordial beast lurked in that ancient complex across the dark pond. "Do you doubt your own hirelings?"

Effron could only shrug at that, for indeed it had been Glorfathel, acting on information from Ambergris, who had informed Herzgo Alegni of the trio's destination. The Shifter had confirmed to Effron that the three were in the outer tunnels of this region just a short while before, immediately after her failure to barter the panther for the sword, though that bit of information had not been disclosed to the warlord.

Herzgo Alegni scanned the vast cavern, picking out groups of his forces here or there setting positions for the ambush. He noted that all of them were on the near side of the dark pool, though, opposite Gauntlgrym's wall.

The tiefling licked his lips. It seemed a solid enough plan, for even if the trio managed to get through to the lake, how would they cross and get into the complex before pursuit, in the form of javelins and arrows and magical spells, caught up to them? Still, the thought of them doing just that nagged at Alegni. He had underestimated these three before, to a disastrous outcome.

"Send more into the complex," he said.

"We can barely keep watch over the cavern approaches with our forces out here now," Effron replied. "If we thin the ranks further. . . ."

"If they get in ahead of us, or enter through another door we have not discovered, will we ever find them?" Alegni replied.

"How many?" Effron asked.

"What is inside the door?"

"A large audience hall with several tunnels, some to the mines far below, it would appear, for they have rails as if for ore carts. And some to the upper levels. We have not explored them in any depth."

"Why not?" the aggravated tiefling demanded.

"My lord, we have been here for only a short while."

Herzgo Alegni glared at the twisted little tiefling warlock. Effron was correct, of course, and Alegni had to admit that the fact that they had even located this place and had now spread out to put some semblance of an ambush posture into place was indeed impressive. He had to admit it, indeed, but not openly, and never to Effron.

"From where will they enter?"

"There are at least four entry tunnels opposite the wall," Effron replied.

Alegni's eyes widened and his nostrils flared, his balled fists clenching at his sides.

"I have dispatched patrols along all four!" Effron quickly added, and he seemed to shrink before the specter of Alegni. "We are trying to discern which of them might lead to the surface."

"Trying?"

Effron didn't seem to know what to say, or how to react. He held his good hand up plaintively before him, then dropped it and shrugged and shook his head.

"I am not surprised," Alegni said, turning away. "And I have not forgotten your failure on the bridge in Neverwinter, I assure you."

"I battled the cat," the twisted warlock replied, but softly, his voice lost as he tried to maintain some semblance of steady breathing.

"I am used to you disappointing me," Alegni went on, ignoring his reply. He moved for the door to exit the chamber, but stopped just outside and turned back on Effron, just long enough to add, "You have disappointed me since the day I first saw you."

Effron fell back as Alegni exited the chamber and, mercifully, moved out of sight—mercifully, because wouldn't the hulking tiefling have driven his point home even more cruelly had he noted the moisture gathering around Effron's curiously unmatched eyes?

The hand of Shadovar hunters moved with practiced precision, leap-frogging their way along the lichen-lit corridor. One strong young tiefling huntress rushed up to a jag in the wall, fell flat against it, and peered around and ahead, then held up her fingers—one, two, three—signaling the others.

Zingrawf Bourdadine, a burly male of considerable reputation, glided past her silently into the next position, followed closely by a sorcerer and another fighter, a halfling shade. As they got into their respective positions, they signaled back to the huntress, who held up her fourth finger, clearing the way for the last of the hand, another female tiefling, to move past her.

The huntress eagerly leaned out a bit more, waiting for her companions to call her into the lead. They weren't ready for her yet, as the last of the band had barely caught up to the next position in line. She stood straighter once more, leaned back, and took a deep breath, preparing for her next dash.

It wasn't until she put her head back that she realized that something was unusual, that this section of wall wasn't quite what it had seemed, for it wasn't just a jut in the wall, but an alcove behind it, one she hadn't really noticed because it was . . . occupied.

A hand reached around her and slapped against her mouth. A second came around from the other side, holding a knife that went fast against, and across, her throat.

Artemis Entreri eased her down without a sound.

Alfwin the sorcerer crouched lower and peered ahead more intently, cursing the near absence of light. He had thought the next stretch of corridor clear, and had signaled as such, but now something had the hair on the back of his neck standing.

He focused his senses. Had he heard a slight sound? Had he caught a tiny flash of movement? His upraised hand became a fist, the signal to hold, but it was too late, for the last of this leapfrog cycle, the second tiefling female, was already too near to him, and without cover other than the rubble he had taken as his position.

She crawled up beside him and followed his gaze ahead, to where the corridor bent slightly to the left.

A few heartbeats passed.

The woman pointed to the left-hand wall, right where it curved, and a low overhang that might provide her with some cover. With practiced ease and perfect silence, the skilled warrior moved to that point, and the sorcerer came out behind her, easing along the right-hand wall, trying to get a view beyond his companion.

All seemed clear and quiet. He motioned for her to continue.

She crept beneath the overhang and turned the corner.

A movement farther to the left had her standing faster and turning to defend, but too late as the spinning weapon cracked her against the side of her head and sent her staggering into the middle of the corridor.

Alfwin called out for his trailing companions and stepped forward, wand extended. He tried to sort out the blur of shadowy movement before him, two forms of similar size entangled and crossing the corridor left to right.

He was about to shoot into that tangle, hoping he would hit the right target, when a third option showed, a bit farther along.

As he let fly, so too did his opponent, countering the warlock's black bolt with a lightning strike.

No, not a bolt of lightning, but a missile sizzling with lightning energy, the sorcerer realized as the streaking arrow burrowed clear through his shoulder to explode against the wall behind him.

He yelped in pain and shock and leveled the wand again.
Then he was blind.

The sorcerer's fiery bolt had stung him, bubbling the skin of his leading forearm, but Drizzt held his ground without flinching and called on his innate drow powers, a remnant of magic from the emanations of the deep Underdark, to fill the corridor before him, the region around the warlock, with a globe of absolute darkness. He kept Taulmaril level, methodically setting a second arrow and letting fly, the glowing arrow seeming to blink out of existence as it disappeared into the darkness.

He had to win, and he had to win fast, he knew, for these tight confines could surely favor a wizard. His enemy might fill the whole of the corridor with a wall of biting flames, or send forth a plague of insects.

Drizzt wouldn't give him the chance.

He drew back and fired again.

When the fighting broke out up ahead, Zingrawf and his halfling companion signaled back and called back for the tiefling huntress, then turned and advanced, seeing the form fast approaching.

They had no idea that the form was not their female companion, for she lay dead in an alcove.

Entreri rushed to catch up, and he, unlike the burly tiefling in front of him, didn't hesitate when the corridor brightened suddenly in a flash of lightning.

The halfling warrior separated then, running ahead to join the duo up front, and almost caught up to the spellcaster when they both disappeared into absolute blackness.

Again the burly trailing tiefling stopped, and again Entreri did not, for he knew well the tricks of Drizzt Do'Urden and had seen similar globes of darkness many times in his battles beside and against the drow.

He could have simply skewered the bulky fighter with his sword then, but he saw little fun in that.

"Well met," he said instead.

The burly male froze for a third heartbeat, then, finally figuring it out, it seemed, and spun around fiercely, sweeping the breadth of the corridor with his large battle-axe.

Entreri, far too clever to be caught by such a clumsy and obvious move, let the weapon harmlessly pass, then waded in behind and thrust his sword into the tiefling's shoulder. Mocking the lumbering brute with laughter, the assassin easily stepped back to avoid the backhand slash.

Entreri could have gone in again—so many openings presented themselves in the tiefling's awkward posture—but a streak of silver flashed over the tiefling's shoulder and had Entreri ducking for his life.

He started to call out for Drizzt to cease, but another arrow cracked against the stone, showering Entreri and the tiefling in sparks. Entreri dived to the far side desperately, and knew he was vulnerable to the tiefling now, to that heavy axe.

But his opponent seemed no longer interested. The brute lurched forward and half-turned, showing Entreri a smoking hole in his back where an arrow had struck.

From the darkness globe came the other warrior, backstepping, arms up defensively, and futilely, before him.

A lightning arrow blew right through him and flew on to drive into the chest of the burly tiefling.

Drizzt's right hand moved in a near-perfect circle, reaching back over his shoulder, accepting an arrow from his enchanted quiver, and coming around to nock, pull, and fire, before beginning its circuit anew.

A line of arrows streamed out, Drizzt swaying the bow, left to right and back again, shooting low and shooting high.

He glanced only once at Dahlia, who crouched atop the warrior she had felled.

An image flashed in Drizzt's head then, of Dahlia reclining with Artemis Entreri, of Dahlia entwined with Artemis Entreri, locked in passionate play.

Drizzt's face, so calm and determined until that moment, struck an angry grimace and he stepped forward.

"He is done," he heard Dahlia say, but he kept firing.

The elf reached up to grab at his arm, but Drizzt pushed past her and increased the barrage, skipping arrows off the stone, left and right, and off the ceiling as well.

"He is done!" Dahlia insisted, but she was speaking of the sorcerer, and Drizzt was aiming past the sorcerer, to the other Shadovar enemies behind his darkness globe, and at a companion he knew to be there.

The corridor flashed like a raging thunderstorm, stone smoking and cracking, the air sizzling with lightning energy.

The burly tiefling warrior somehow continued to stand, though likely more because the repeated blows were holding him aloft than out of any sense of balance or even consciousness.

Against the wall, Entreri called out for Drizzt to stop, but his words seemed thin indeed against the thundering cacophony of the barrage.

The stone right before his face fractured as an arrow skipped past, shards stinging his eyes. He rolled out from the wall and swept the feet out from under the tiefling, then flattened out, accepting the crashing weight as the brute fell atop him.

But could even this burly blanket stop a shot from that devastating bow?

"Heavily enchanted," Glorfathel warned as Ambergris edged toward the magnificent, gem-studded throne on the tiled stone dais.

"Cast protections, then," Afafrenfere said, eyeing those marvelous baubles hungrily.

Glorfathel laughed at the monk. "No mage in the Shadowfell or on Toril would be foolish enough to touch that throne. It is imbued with the power—"

"Of dwarf gods," Ambergris finished for him, and she was very near to the throne. She glanced past it, to a small graveyard of cairns. A curious sight indeed, for who would put such monuments so near to such a throne in the middle of an audience hall? Two of the cairns were larger than the others, and as she focused on the grandest of them, Ambergris realized yet another mystery: these were new. They hadn't been placed in the last tenday, perhaps, but the graves were certainly not nearly as ancient as everything else they had seen in the complex.

"What secrets might ye be keepin' here, Clangeddin?" she asked softly. "And what powers, mighty Moradin?" She reached her hand out tentatively.

"Dare not," the elf warned, and Afafrenfere swallowed hard.

Ambergris stiffened immediately as her thick fingers touched the burnished arm of the great chair, as if some bolt of power had shot down her spine. She sucked in her breath and held the pose for a long while, the other two staring on incredulously.

They could not begin to understand the rush of power traveling through the dwarf at that time. She saw flashes of the last disciple of the dwarf gods who had touched this throne, and then a clear image of him sitting there. She noted his red beard and one-horned crown, and her lips moved to form the name of "King Bruenor?"

She held on a bit longer, but the energy proved too great. She focused on the vision, as if trying desperately to convince this famous dwarf king that she, too, was of Delzoun heritage, that she truly was of the Adbar O'Mauls! But Ambergris carried no royal blood, and so the throne rejected her, but kindly, energy building until she could hold on no longer.

The dwarf staggered backward.

"It canno' be," she mumbled, but she knew that it had been, indeed. This was no deception.

"What?" Afafrenfere asked, stepping up beside her. His arm slipped out toward the throne.

"It'll eat ye," Ambergris warned.

Afafrenfere turned on her. "Then you do it," he said. "Pluck a gem or two!"

Ambergris stared incredulously, then laughed at him. "Not in ten elf generations," she said. "I'd rather be pluckin' a gem from betwixt a red dragon's back teeth."

"Well, what are we to do with it, then?" the exasperated monk asked. "It's a king's treasure and more."

"Much more," said Ambergris.

"We're to leave it alone," Glorfathel said. "As anyone who's ever been here has left it alone, or suffered deadly consequences, no doubt."

Not everyone, Ambergris thought, but did not say.

"The graves, then," the monk suggested.

"Touch a stone and I'll be making another one for yerself," Ambergris said, without leaving a hint that she was interested in any debate. Her nostrils flared and her eyes widened, almost maniacally, and Afafrenfere backed down.

"You can never take the pride from a dwarf," Glorfathel said with a laugh. "No matter how much you might darken her skin."

Ambergris nodded, glad that the elf had justified her level of rage.

As Glorfathel led the way to the tunnel they had been tasked with guarding, Ambergris let her stare linger on that wondrous throne, and once more she pictured a red-bearded dwarf sitting there, king of kings. Her last look before they left was back to the graves, to the grandest of the group, for she figured who might be buried there.

She managed a slight and inconspicuous bow as she departed.

"Drizzt!" Dahlia yelled, and grabbed at the drow's arm. "It's over!"

He shoved her away and began anew, the image of her coupling with Entreri burning in his thoughts.

He would sweep clear this corridor all the way to Gauntlgrym!

An arrow flew free, but its lightning glow was stolen even as it left Taulmaril. A second went similarly dark, and even a third before Drizzt even realized it, even noted Dahlia, crouched to the side with her magical staff extended, the energy of Kozah's Needle absorbing the magic of Taulmaril with each release.

She was protecting him!

Drizzt's eyes widened with rage. Instead of reaching for another arrow, he took up the bow as a club, thinking to bash Dahlia aside.

The darkness dissipated then, and both paused and looked to the corridor.

The sorcerer sat awkwardly against the wall, legs and arms splayed wide, chin on his chest and wafts of smoke, even a bit of flame, rising from several holes in his torso. Taulmaril, the Heartseeker, had lived up to its name. Beside, curled into a defensive ball, lay the smoking husk of a halfling shade, and a larger form lay very still farther along. The walls were pitted with holes, smoke rising from them, and shards of broken stone lay all around.

"What have you done?" Dahlia demanded, rising up.

Sobered by the scene, confused indeed, Drizzt lowered Taulmaril and stepped past her, peering into the quiet, smoky corridor.

He almost set another arrow and let fly when the third body in line shifted suddenly, but he had no time as out from under it came Artemis Entreri, a knife flying before him, and blades drawn in a desperate charge.

Drizzt deflected that thrown knife by dropping Taulmaril in its path, and out came his scimitars to meet that charge.

Entreri barreled in, sword thrusting once and again, leading him into a turn that brought his dagger around from on high, chopping down at the drow.

But Drizzt, too, rolled, and opposite the assassin, outpacing that dagger. The drow came around with a sidelong swipe of Twinkle, which Entreri expectedly parried.

Drizzt stopped in mid-turn and burst forward, thrusting Icingdeath, and had Entreri simply executed a block on Twinkle, the drow would have found a clear opening.

But the assassin was too clever for that, and had fought this particular opponent before. Instead of merely meeting the leading slash with a block and bat to drive it out wide, the parry had rolled Entreri's blade over the scimitar.

Entreri let Drizzt's momentum carry Twinkle out harmlessly wide, disengaging his blade and coming forward with a thrust of his own.

Both could have scored a killing blow, but to do so would have meant accepting a similar fate.

So both crossed to block instead, sword and scimitar meeting with a heavy crash and locking tight between them.

"Stop!" Dahlia yelled out, her voice strained and teeth chattering for some reason that neither combatant understood, or cared to even notice.

Entreri's dagger stabbed for Drizzt's throat. Drizzt's free scimitar flashed across to block, then the drow punched straight out at Entreri's face.

The assassin ducked the blow and the two went into a clench, arms tangled.

So Entreri found another weapon and head-butted.

As did Drizzt, their foreheads cracking together between them, and both fell back a couple of staggering steps.

And both meant to leap right back in and be done with this.

But a long metallic staff knifed between them like a blocking bar, its tip slamming into the far wall, and with that impact, Dahlia released the energy of three of Taulmaril's enchanted arrows, and a bit from the staff as well, lighting the corridor with a stinging, explosive blast.

Nearly blinded, the woman still caught the motion as the two leaped away, two who seemed as one warrior leaping back from a mirror. Both half-twisted in the air, executing a barrel roll, turning and diving into a headlong roll then coming back to their feet at exactly the same moment and in exactly the same turn to spin around to face each other once more, at the ready, feet wide, blades leveled.

"Are you brothers, then?" the stunned Dahlia asked.

"He would have me dead!" Entreri yelled at her.

"I will," Drizzt replied.

"I will join against he who makes the first move," Dahlia warned.

"First move was his," Entreri accused.

"Last move will be mine, as well," Drizzt promised.

"Desist!" Dahlia demanded.

"No!" they both shouted back.

Dahlia leaped between them more directly, looking from one to the other with clear confusion. "You need him!" she implored Entreri. "That you might be rid of the sword!"

The assassin backed and straightened, and so did Drizzt. "The sword?" they both said together.

A horrified Drizzt threw his scimitars to the ground and reached over his left shoulder, drawing forth Charon's Claw and taking it up before him in both hands.

"The sword," he said again, figuring it all out.

All of it.

The suspicions, the images of Entreri and Dahlia locked in passion, the urge to kill Artemis Entreri. . . .

With a growl, the drow leaped to the side. He started to yell and didn't stop as he repeatedly bashed Charon's Claw against the corridor wall.

"Drizzt," Dahlia gasped and started to go to him, but Entreri came up and held his arm before her to block her in place.

"The sword is telling him to kill me," Entreri quietly explained.

Drizzt played out his energy, his rage, scraping and chipping stone but not marring the fabulous red blade of Charon's Claw at all. Still, he was making his point to the sentient and wicked weapon: He was the master, Charon's Claw the servant.

Finally, he stopped, and with a last look of disgust at the sword, he slid it back into its scabbard across his back. He retrieved his scimitars and similarly slid them away, then looked to his companions, looked past his companions, to the carnage in the corridor, a trio of bodies that could easily have been four.

He let a few heartbeats pass, to let the tension dissipate a bit, before meeting the gaze of Artemis Entreri. He didn't apologize—what would be the point?—but he offered a nod to assure the man that he, and not Charon's Claw, was back in control.

Artemis Entreri returned his sword and dagger to their holsters.

Behind Drizzt, the woman warrior whom Dahlia had overwhelmed groaned and rolled, and even tried to prop herself up on her elbows. Dahlia was there at once, delivering a strong kick to the shade's side, and as the woman tried to curl up, Dahlia stomped down hard on the back of her neck, pinning her in place.

"If you move again, I will shatter your neck," the deadly elf warned.

Drizzt came up beside and grabbed Dahlia by the arm, trying to pull her away. She resisted at first, but the drow looked at her plaintively and tugged more insistently.

As soon as Dahlia lifted her foot from the woman's neck and stepped back, and before Drizzt could reach down to assist the captive shade, Entreri shoved past him and grabbed the warrior by the hair and arm, and roughly yanked her from the floor.

"Your sword?" he asked, noting her gaze, for indeed, her long sword lay on the floor not far away. "Yes, do retrieve it, that I might finish what should already have been done." With that, the assassin shoved the shade to the side and back to the ground, near her weapon.

She looked at the weapon, then back to Entreri, who had drawn his weapons once more and stood waiting, and beckoning.

Drizzt watched the spectacle in dismay, a telling reminder to him of who this man, Entreri, was, or he had been at least. Lost in the nostalgia of better days, had he deceived himself? Had he allowed that which he wanted so badly, a return to a time and place, to blind him to the reality of Artemis Entreri?

He glanced the other way, to his other companion, who watched eagerly, and with a grin. And Drizzt understood that expression; Dahlia wanted to see this fight, wanted to see Entreri cut the shade to pieces.

Drizzt swallowed hard and reminded himself that Dahlia had good reason to hate the shades, and that these were his sworn enemies—they had been in the tunnel looking for him and the sword, no doubt.

"Pick it up," Entreri said to the shade. "Pick it up and stand. My companions will stay to the side. You against me, and if you win, perhaps they will let you go."

"Hardly," Dahlia remarked, drawing a smirk from Entreri.

Drizzt caught the silent exchange between the two. They were of like mind, and following desires that he did not, could not, share.

Once again, an image of Entreri and Dahlia in an embrace, a passionate kiss, flashed through his mind, but he growled it away and answered Charon's Claw with a wave of anger and an image of his own: a deep pit, its sides swirling with the rush of powerful water elementals, its bottom the fiery maw of the primordial.

"I know you, Barrabus the Gray," the shade said, still on the floor and propped again on her elbows. "I will not fight you."

"Coward."

The shade shrugged. "I know you. I once fought beside you."

Entreri tilted his head, regarding the woman more closely, but Drizzt saw no flash of recognition there.

"As I know this elf, Dahlia, champion of the Thayans."

"Then you know that you will die here," Dahlia replied, and Drizzt winced once more. He almost wished that Entreri would just step over and end this torment, for the shade and for him.

He stepped over instead, between Entreri and the shade, and he reached his hand to her. When she took it, he helped her to her feet, her weapon still on the ground.

"Your patrol came looking for us," Drizzt said.

"No," the shade said, and shook her head.

"Do not lie to me or I will let my companions have you. Answer my questions and—"

"And what?" the shade and Entreri asked together.

"And Drizzt will let her go," Dahlia said with a mocking chortle.

"Will he, then?" asked Entreri.

"I will," Drizzt said to the shade directly. "Answer my questions and run away the way you were going, the way from which we came."

The shade glanced past Drizzt to Entreri, then to Dahlia. "I do not believe you," she said, looking back directly into Drizzt's lavender eyes.

"It's all you have," he calmly answered. "And it's not so difficult a question. Your friends are in the entry cavern to Gauntlgrym, it would seem. I would know their numbers."

"You ask me to betray Herzgo Alegni, as Barrabus betrayed him!" the woman snapped.

"Alegni is dead!" Dahlia declared, and the woman looked at her curiously, as if her statement was purely ridiculous.

"Speak that name again and I will bash in your skull," Dahlia promised, and spat at the shade's feet.

Strangely, that threat seemed to bolster the shade. She stood taller, as if accepting her fate, and so, no longer afraid. Drizzt had seen this before, indeed had felt such feelings of his own in times past, and so he understood that his moment to garner any useful information was fast passing.

"You cannot escape," the shade said to him.

"They're in the cavern," Drizzt replied.

The shade smiled and nodded. "They're waiting for you, and if you don't come to them, they will find you. And kill you."

Her smile was sincere, Drizzt understood, for she had gone past the point of fear and fully into acceptance. His thoughts spun—he recalled the cavern, the stalagmites and hanging pillars, so much like Menzoberranzan. He considered the layout of the place, the shallow underground pond and the beach before the great wall of Gauntlgrym.

"Go, then," Drizzt said, stepping aside and motioning back down the tunnel, not toward the surface as he had first indicated, but back the way the Shadovar patrol had come. "Go back to your dark friends and deliver my word. They will not find us. They will not retrieve this foul sword. There are many tunnels in the Underdark. They are the ways of the drow, not the Netherese."

The shade stared at him. He could feel Entreri's glare burning into his back.

"You will not do this," Dahlia said.

Drizzt turned a stern look her way, a silent warning.

"Go," he said to the shade, though he didn't look back at her. "I will not offer again."

The shade started tentatively, looking around at the three, not knowing from which would come the killing blow. She eased past Drizzt, who turned to stare at Entreri, then sidled past the assassin.

Entreri moved to the side a step, turning as the shade passed, and Drizzt pointedly moved up as well, putting himself between the assassin and the shade.

She broke into a run, nearly tripping over the corpse of one of her companions.

"I have witnessed many stupid things from you, drow," Entreri remarked, moving around behind Drizzt and bumping him as he did, "but nothing more foolish than this."

Drizzt slowly turned, first to see Dahlia, who stared at him hatefully, as if he had just betrayed her, then, as he came around to see Entreri . . . Entreri, who had retrieved Taulmaril from the floor, and who had only bumped into Drizzt to cover the fact that he had taken an arrow from the quiver on Drizzt's back!

The assassin drew back on the bowstring, leveling the shot at the shade, who was still in easy range.

And Drizzt couldn't get to him in time.

"Entreri, no!" the drow said, and he was pleading as much as commanding.

Entreri did pause at that, at the curious timbre in Drizzt's voice, likely, and he glanced over.

"Do not, I beg," said Drizzt.

"That she will go and warn her allies of our approach?" The assassin ended with a growl and set his sights on the fleeing shade woman once more.

"Kill her," Dahlia agreed.

"That she will go and tell them we discovered their ambush," Drizzt replied.

Entreri did let fly, and Drizzt winced, but the assassin had turned the bow a bit, and the lightning arrow flashed in the corridor, cracking into stone with a solid retort, and the uninjured shade yelped in surprise and scrambled along.

Artemis Entreri stood straight and stared at Drizzt, recognizing that the drow had something in mind, some plan that would use the fleeing shade to their advantage. He tossed the bow back to Drizzt, never blinking, never unlocking his stare from that of Drizzt.

More passed between the pair in that moment than the potential practicality of sending the shade on her way. Drizzt saw something else in Entreri's eye.

And Drizzt understood something quite profound: Artemis Entreri had trusted him.

CHAPTER 19

CAUGHT BETWEEN A SHADE
AND A DARK PLACE

THE TUNNEL RAN SMOOTHLY FOR A LONG WAY, THEN CAME TO A DEEP DROP, but fortunately, the fleeing shade hadn't bothered to remove the dangling rope that her hunting party had set. Down went the three companions, moving swiftly and silently, trailing the female. Soon enough, the tunnel opened onto a ledge that ran perpendicular, angling down toward the cavern below. The view below was not open to them. A wall of about chest height blocked the edge of the perpendicular walkway. Drizzt and Dahlia both knew they had come to the right place, though, surely recognizing the hanging stalactite towers.

The three crept up to the wall, exiting the tunnel.

"She delivered your message," Entreri remarked, peering over the edge.

Down below, the cavern buzzed with activity. Shades came out from many of the stalagmite mounds, gathering into ranks and battle groups. Some were already moving for the base of the walkway on which the companions stood.

Across the large cavern loomed Gauntlgrym's wall, the underground pond still and dark before it, except for a pair of small rowboats shuttling a handful of shades toward the beach.

"Be quick," Drizzt said, and he sprinted off, crouching low and close to the walkway's outer wall, Entreri and Dahlia close behind.

As they neared the bottom, now with enemy soldiers not far away, Drizzt stopped, looked to Entreri, and nodded. As Drizzt reached for his whistle, the assassin drew out his obsidian figurine.

"How deep is the lake?" Entreri mouthed, and Drizzt could only shrug. He didn't know, though it was a good question, but what choice did they have?

Again they exchanged looks and nodded. Drizzt blew his call for Andahar as Entreri dropped the statuette to the ground, summoning his nightmare steed. Surprised cries erupted almost immediately. Entreri's hellish mount came into shape right before him with a burst of flame and smoke, and Andahar materialized in the cavern beyond the walkway, galloping hard for Drizzt. The unicorn skidded to a stop and the drow grabbed the white mane, glistening even in the low lichen light of the large cavern, and pulled himself astride. He turned as he settled, reaching a hand out for Dahlia, but she was already on her way, vaulting nimbly to her seat behind him.

Entreri came by first, thundering out into the cavern, sword waving as he bore down on the nearest Netherese.

"Give me the bow!" Dahlia cried, grabbing at it.

"No!" Drizzt yelled back before he could even consider the response. The vehemence of that reply shocked him and confused him, for it had come unbidden, a sudden reaction to the notion of Dahlia taking Taulmaril—to the notion of Dahlia wielding Catti-brie's weapon.

Drizzt bent low and urged mighty Andahar on, the unicorn's hooves cracking hard against the stone. Before them, Shadovar scattered from Entreri, who veered left around a stalagmite mound.

Drizzt went right around the same one, and steered Andahar even farther to the right. Confusion was their ally, he knew, and so better to split the focus of their determined enemies. Both steeds ran on, winding paths around the many mounds, leaping the rails for ore carts whenever they crossed. Drizzt didn't even draw his blades, letting Dahlia with her long staff prod and swipe at any enemies who ventured, or were caught, too close.

Javelins and arrows reached out at them. Drizzt bent low and kept his course anything but straight. All around him, he heard shades calling out for others to take intercepting angles to cut them off.

Few ever got near to them, though. Their mounts were too swift and too agile, their surprise too complete. One poor shade rushed out in front of Andahar, apparently not even realizing that he was in the unicorn's path. He got run over, the sure-footed unicorn not slowing or tripping in the least as it trampled him. Even with their distracting zigzagging and enemies scrambling all around, all three made it to the pond in short order, coming in almost side by side.

The dark water hissed in protest as the fiery hooves of Entreri's nightmare splashed in. Drizzt leaped Andahar high and long, the unicorn splashing down hard some ten strides from the shore and running on.

"How deep is it?" Entreri asked again of his companions, who were now before him.

Dahlia glanced back and shrugged. When she had first come through here, she had utilized magic.

The water quickly rose to the top of Andahar's legs, slowing the run dramatically; Dahlia tucked her legs up under her to try to keep her high black boots dry. Suddenly their progress seemed so dangerously slow!

"We'll be swimming," Dahlia called to Drizzt, leaning in close.

"Then we swim," he replied.

"They have archers," Dahlia argued.

"Should I stop, then, so we might—" He ended abruptly, an arrow reaching out at him from the far bank.

Andahar reared and kicked at it, but it slipped through and dug hard into the unicorn's breast. Had the steed not so reared, Drizzt surely would have taken the bolt.

As they splashed back down, Drizzt tightened his legs around his mount and pulled Taulmaril free from his shoulder.

More arrows reached out at him—to the side, he heard Entreri's mount shriek, an unsettling, otherworldly howl, and knew that the nightmare had been hit. It would take more than an arrow to bring down that hell steed, of course, but what of its rider?

More arrows came forth, but Drizzt responded with his own magical bolts, launching them out at the nearing bank. He could hardly get a good shot, aiming straight ahead while mounted, but he sprayed off many arrows in succession, trying to at least keep those archers dodging around and unable to take careful aim.

"Come on," he called to Andahar and at the pond as they slogged through. It wasn't getting any deeper, at least.

"Boat!" Entreri called from Drizzt's left, and the assassin fell back a bit as Drizzt turned.

Indeed, the drow saw not one, but two boats full of Shadovar rowing in from the side, angling to intercept. A shade in the prow of the trailing craft held a bow.

But now Drizzt was shooting across his body, and Andahar's bobbing head was not obstructing him at all.

His first arrow took that archer, lifted him into the air, and dropped him off the back of the boat. Then the drow concentrated on the nearer craft and sent a stream of lightning its way. The three shades on the craft ducked and dodged. One's head exploded with the impact of a bolt and the other two, apparently having seen enough, jumped into the dark, brackish water.

Drizzt shifted for the second craft, but he paused in curiosity, for behind the boat, what seemed like a wind-whipped silvery spray danced across the top of the water.

But there was no wind in the cavern.

Unable to sort the mystery, the drow focused again on the task at hand, sending an arrow at the remaining manned boat, and some other missiles back toward the shore for good measure. His first shot skipped in low, purposely so, and exploded against the hull, splintering planks.

"Those are fish, not ripples," he heard Dahlia say behind him, and prompted by that, he turned back to aim for a second shot at the remaining threat.

The shades within the craft had ducked out of sight, though, and splashed frantically at the water threatening to swamp them.

It wasn't until Drizzt regarded the "wave" of fish again, and considered the sudden screams, that he understood their sudden desperation.

The fish had swept over the pair of shades in the water, leaping all around them and biting at them voraciously. In this light, Drizzt couldn't make out the changing hue, but he knew from the horrible and desperate sounds that Shadovar blood was fast mixing with the dark water.

Screams came from the second boat, too, as those vicious little fish made their way in through the splinter, the boat's open wound, that Taulmaril had caused.

"Faster! Oh, faster!" Dahlia begged him, for though most of the fish had stopped to feast, another leaping wave swept their way.

Drizzt held Taulmaril up, bowstring drawn, and motioned to the woman.

"What?"

"Catch it!" the drow implored her.

Dahlia stared at him in puzzlement for just a heartbeat, then held Kozah's Needle out near the tip of the arrow.

Drizzt let fly and the staff swallowed the lightning energy.

Andahar whinnied loudly, in obvious pain. Beside them, Entreri and his steed cried out.

Dahlia plunged her staff into the water and released the lightning energy, and how both horses and all three riders yelped at that painful sting.

But they pressed on, silver fish now floating all around them, dead or stunned. More were coming, though, but Drizzt ignored them. For the water had become shallower, and the drow drove Andahar on, and all of his shots were aimed before them as he swept the beach with magical lightning.

Entreri's steed charged across the wet sand first, steam flowing from its black, glistening mane. Straight for the doorway they ran, Drizzt and Dahlia riding close behind. The assassin rolled down and dismissed his mount immediately, that he might retrieve the obsidian statuette, but Drizzt did not similarly send Andahar away as he and Dahlia leaped down to the ground. Instead, the unicorn reared and turned and thundered off at the nearest enemies, lowering his ivory horn.

The three companions scrambled through the narrow entry tunnel and burst into the large audience hall beyond, to be met by a line of shade warriors. Drizzt and Entreri entered first, side by side, their blades working ferociously to drive back the stabbing pikes. One polearm thrust in between them and Drizzt sprang upon it, driving it to the ground, then jumped away, crossing before Entreri, who side-flipped the other way, back behind the drow, a perfect somersault that landed him on his feet, blades still working in harmony.

As he had gone across, Drizzt took a trio of pikes with him, tying up the line and forcing the shades to fall back. In that one instant of respite, Drizzt glanced down to his right, to the magnificent throne, and he imagined, but could not see, the grave of his dearest friend just beyond.

The enemies before him proved to be a skilled and well-practiced team, and their short retreat formed them into a defensive, blocking semi-circle around the entry tunnel.

And from the other side of that tunnel came the sounds of pursuit, and one voice in particular, a voice too familiar to the companions, particularly to Entreri, lifted above the others.

"Hold them!" a tiefling warlord screamed.

"He lives!" Dahlia cried in denial, in horror, in anger, as she skidded into the chamber behind her two companions.

"No time," Drizzt started to yell back, for he expected that Dahlia would simply turn around and go after that most hated tiefling. Drizzt understood that desire well! Alegni had indeed survived and had taken Guenhwyvar, as that strange Shadovar woman had claimed. The drow's mind spun wildly. He wondered if Alegni might have his beloved companion in tow. In the middle of his fighting, he managed to brush a hand across his belt pouch, silently calling for the panther, hoping against hope that perhaps Alegni had erred in bringing the cat, Drizzt's cat, who was more than a magical creation, who was a loyal friend.

He shook it all away when a pike nearly skewered him. He continued to silently beckon for Guenhwyvar, but again called to Dahlia to fight forward and not turn around.

But no need, for Dahlia had already rushed past behind him, moving to the side. She planted her staff and vaulted up high, clearing the Shadovar line, pikes coming up behind her as the warriors tried to turn around to meet the threat.

Entreri, understanding Dahlia's tactics, was already moving, though. He too swept behind Drizzt, coming in hard against the shades, driving them and turning them and cutting them down, tying up that corner of the defensive formation.

Drizzt rushed beside him, then behind him, moving along the wall away from the tunnel mouth—and just in time, as some burst of black magical energy soared in through the opening, an aimed cloud of burning, biting smoke. It split the shade line in two, those in the middle of the formation falling back and falling away, flailing in pain.

As he came free behind the assassin, Drizzt again called upon his dark elf powers, and reached forth at the enemy battling Dahlia. Purplish flames erupted around the shade, outlining him in dancing faerielike fire. Caught by surprise, the Shadovar nearly dropped his pike, and did drop his guard.

He recovered almost immediately, trying to realign his weapon.

Too late.

Dahlia's flail swiped across and shattered his jawbone, and as he lurched, the elf warrior turned a circuit, bringing her second spinning weapon around in a powerful backhand. This one cracked the back of the fighter's skull and launched him head over heels in a flip that left him on his back on the stone floor, twitching and shuddering uncontrollably.

Again, Drizzt called on his innate magical powers, the powers wrought of his deep Underdark homeland, bringing forth a globe of impenetrable darkness right before the entry tunnel, and right in front of those enemies coming in pursuit.

"Go, go!" he yelled at Entreri, coming up on the man's left and adding his spinning scimitars to the fray.

Entreri rolled behind him and came around clear of the tangled flank, and sprinted after Dahlia in a dead run across the vast hall, and Drizzt, with his magical anklets speeding his every step, disengaged from the pikemen and went in swift pursuit.

The three easily outran the more heavily encumbered Shadovar, making a straight line for an exit tunnel ahead and to the right.

But more shades came in from the side, and once again, arrows and javelins flew their way.

With speed and acrobatics and more than a bit of luck, they all got into the cover of that tunnel, and ran along, Drizzt and Dahlia both trying to sort out their way to the lower levels, Entreri just keeping pace.

They went around a corner and Drizzt pulled up short, motioning for the other two to continue. He went down low to one knee and slipped back around the corner with his bow in hand, and he mowed down the incoming shades with a line of deadly missiles.

"Here!" he heard Dahlia call for him, and he ran off, thinking he had bought them some time, at least.

But not much time, he realized as a powerful explosion wracked the corridor behind him. He glanced back to see sparks arcing along the walls of the corner where he had just been kneeling, and heard the renewed pursuit.

They passed through a series of chambers, guessing more than knowing which doors to burst through. They turned another corner, and another beyond that, speeding for a heavy, partially ajar metal doorway. Entreri shouldered it, crashing through, Drizzt and Dahlia close behind, and as the large room opened into view before them, all three saw and heard a similar door opposite them slam shut.

Entreri made for it with all speed, Dahlia close behind, as Drizzt slammed the door behind him. He looked for a locking bar, but none was to be found. But some furniture still remained, including a heavy stone chair frame, so he pulled it into place before the door and propped it at an angle to somewhat secure the portal.

Across the room, Entreri tugged at the other door and banged on it, but whoever had exited had already secured it.

"Now where?" Dahlia asked, leaping around and scanning for other doors.

But there were none to be seen.

"Now where?" she asked again, more insistently.

"Now we fight," Entreri replied. "That was Alegni's voice," he added, and spat on the floor.

"Kill him, at least, before we die, then," Dahlia said, and Entreri nodded grimly.

"Whatever you do, Drizzt, get me to him," Entreri said. "I will salute you with my final moments of life, for whatever that might be worth to you."

Drizzt regarded the two, standing so easily beside each other, both seeming perfectly comfortable with their fate—as long as they could get to Herzgo Alegni. He couldn't imagine the hatred that drove them, and once again he was reminded of their unspoken bond, their sharing of something deeper, something he couldn't comprehend, let alone partake.

Drizzt did recognize that either of them would die happy if that death came after the killing blow upon Herzgo Alegni. How could someone hate another so much, he wondered? What had happened, what violation, what violent betrayal or continued torture, to facilitate such venom?

A thunderous retort hit the door behind him, and Drizzt scrambled to set the chair frame back in place. He heard the report as a hail of missiles hit the door, and heard too the calls for pursuit and the multitude of footsteps.

He turned to view his friends, equally doomed, but found himself looking behind them, at the other door, which had silently opened.

Dahlia grunted, looked curiously at Drizzt, then collapsed to the ground.

A bolt of lightning hit the door behind Drizzt, crackling as it climbed around the metal and once more throwing the chair aside.

Drizzt started for Dahlia; he turned for the door.

Then he was blinded.

The drow had come.

CHAPTER 20

"BREGAN D'AERTHE!"

DRIZZT KNEW. HE FELT THE STING OF A CROSSBOW BOLT, AND ANOTHER AND a third, and the ensuing, almost immediate burn of drow poison, familiar from so long ago, coursing through his veins.

He knew. He heard the thunder of the approaching Shadovar. There was nowhere to run, nowhere to hide. He wanted to fight at least, to offer some last and fitting expression of Drizzt Do'Urden. If this was his end, as surely he believed it to be, then it should match the way he lived his life.

He wondered about the afterlife, and hoped there was one, and a just one. One where he would find again his friends lost, find his love, Catti-brie, and he even managed a grin in the magical darkness as the strength left his knees, as the scimitars fell from his grasp, in imagining the meeting between Catti-brie and Dahlia.

The grin was gone before it even began. Catti-brie and Dahlia . . . and Drizzt.

He hoped he would find Catti-brie, for the thought of spending eternity beside Dahlia . . .

He was on the ground then, though he felt nothing. He resisted the drow poison enough to remain awake and somewhat cogent, but his physical abilities were absent, and not to soon return.

"Bregan D'aerthe!" he heard Artemis Entreri cry, and Drizzt hoped that perhaps this was Jarlaxle's band, that perhaps they might survive.

Entreri clarified, "We're agents of Bregan D'aerthe!"

Clever, Drizzt thought. Ever was Artemis Entreri clever—that is what made him doubly dangerous.

He sensed forms passing by him, moving over him, but he could not lash out at them, and thought that he should not lash out at them.

The irony of a drow rescue was not lost on the groggy and fast-sinking dark elf ranger, nor was the notion that it would indeed be a very short reprieve.

The room's door burst open under the weight of ranks of Shadovar pressing forward.

A wall of poisoned crossbow bolts came at them. The room blackened before them. A second magical darkness engulfed their front ranks, and a third magical darkness hit the throng behind that one.

And in that confused frenzy, a fireball erupted, biting flames curling Shadovar skin, blistering Shadovar hands as they tried to hold to metal weapons. Turning and thrashing, disoriented in the darkness, tripping over the bodies of their front ranks lying helpless on the ground under the spell of drow poison, the charge abruptly halted.

"Press on!" Herzgo Alegni screamed from the back when he recognized the stall.

"Drow!" came the responding shouts. "The dark elves have come!"

"Effron!" Herzgo Alegni shouted. He hardly knew what to make of that, and certainly he didn't want a battle with a drow force. But neither would he let that sword, or his hated enemies, Entreri and the wretched Dahlia, escape! He spotted the twisted warlock by the entrance to the tunnel in the room ahead of him.

"Fill the room with deadly magic!" Alegni yelled at the warlock.

"There are Shadovar in that room, my lord!" a shade lieutenant near to Alegni dared to argue.

Hardly thinking of the movement, hardly even registering his own reaction to the lieutenant's words, Alegni punched the shade in the jaw, and the shade dropped to the floor in a heap.

"I will have them!" Alegni bellowed, and all around him cowered under the power of his voice and the very real threat behind his demands. "I will have that sword!" He regarded the shade he had hit. Normally, the warlord refrained from such public corporeal punishment of his charges, other than his open torment of Barrabus the Gray, of course. He put a hand out to help hoist the shade back to his feet, but when the lieutenant hesitated, staring at him suspiciously, Alegni retracted the hand and quietly warned, "The next time you so openly oppose my orders, I will answer with my sword."

He moved forward to find Effron and his magic-wielding forces filling the room at the far end of the corridor with blazing lightning, clouds of acid, balls of fire, and bubbling poisonous ooze. Prodded by a continually yelling Alegni, their barrage of deadly magic went on and on, shaking the stones of Gauntlgrym.

They could see none of it, of course, as the drow darkness lingered, and finally as both barrage and darkness began to thin, the Shadovar forces pressed on.

To find an empty room, with not a body to be seen and the back door closed and sealed once more.

"They could not all have escaped," Effron remarked when Alegni entered the scarred battlefield. "Some of our enemies were slain here, I am certain."

"You're guessing," Alegni growled back at him.

"Reasoning. None could have withstood our concentrated assault."

"You know little of the drow, I see."

Effron shrugged, that curious motion with one of his shoulders always behind him.

"So some were killed," Alegni mused. "Dahlia, do you think?"

Effron swallowed hard.

"You would not wish such a thing, would you, twisted boy?" Alegni teased. "To think her dead, but gone from you. To think her dead without you being able to witness the last light leaving her blue eyes. That would hurt most of all, wouldn't it?"

Effron stared at him hatefully, not blinking. "Do you speak for me or for yourself?"

"If she is dead, then so be it," Alegni said as convincingly as he could manage. "And Barra—Artemis Entreri?"

"If he is dead, I will take up Charon's Claw and bring him back, that I might torment him for another decade to repay him for his insolence and treachery."

"He resisted the sword before. Could you ever trust him, or in your ability to control him, even with Claw back in your grasp?"

Alegni smiled at that, but didn't really have an answer. In any case, both Dahlia and Entreri were gone, either still fleeing or dead. Or captured, Alegni mused, and under the control of these dark elves that had so suddenly appeared before his forces.

The tiefling warlord couldn't hold to his smile, for the arrival of a sizable drow force, if it was indeed that, certainly complicated his quest.

"If they're alive, and these were their allies, then they continue toward the primordial beast," Alegni said to Effron and all of those nearby. "That is the worst potential, so continue our march. Fill these tunnels with Shadovar. Find that beast!"

"If they are dead and the drow have taken the sword, they will likely bargain its return," Effron remarked quietly as the forces organized and set out once more.

Alegni nodded. "But we prepare for the more immediate potential."

"We have lines of warriors strung out far ahead in the corridors," Effron assured him. "We have found the main stair to the lower levels."

"Send word of this new enemy, then," Alegni ordered.

"We do not know them to be an enemy," Effron reasoned.

That rang as curious in Alegni's ears—hadn't they just fought a vicious and quick exchange, after all?—but as he considered the suddenness with which the two alert and powerful forces had met, perhaps there was some truth to Effron's claim. Perhaps the drow had inadvertently happened in the way of the Shadovar advance, and had reacted to force with force, as Alegni surely would have done.

Perhaps, but the desperate tiefling wasn't about to take any chances.

"Get us to the primordial," he told Effron, "with all haste and without mercy for any who stand in our way."

Drizzt still had his scimitars and still had his bow, but they wouldn't do him any good, even though his physical senses and abilities were beginning to return. Magical tentacles had grown out of the stone and grabbed him—and Entreri and Dahlia, who were seated back to back with him—fully immobilizing them all.

He heard Dahlia groan, only then beginning to awaken. Entreri was perfectly conscious, and Drizzt doubted that any of the bolts had even struck him.

"Bregan D'aerthe?" a finely dressed drow warrior standing before Drizzt remarked, his voice clearly full of doubt. "What's your name?"

He was speaking in the high tongue of Menzoberranzan, a language Drizzt had not heard in a long, long time, but one that he recognized, and one that returned to him with amazing speed and clarity.

"Masoj," Drizzt answered without hesitation, pulling out a name from his distant past.

The drow, a warrior noble if his dress and fine swords were to be believed, looked at him curiously.

"Masoj?" he asked. "Of what House?"

"Of no House he will admit," Artemis Entreri put in, also speaking perfect Drow.

A soldier beside the noble drow stiffened and moved as if to punish the man for daring to speak out, but the noble held him back.

"Do continue," he prompted Entreri.

"Masoj, of a House that offended the Spider Queen," Entreri explained. "None will admit it, save Kimmuriel, who leads Bregan D'aerthe."

"You are of House Oblodra?" the warrior noble asked Drizzt, bending low to look Drizzt in the eye.

In the lavender eye, Drizzt knew, and he feared that his reputation and strange eyes might precede him and ruin everything.

Drizzt shook his head. "I will admit no such thing," he said, the proper response.

"You are related to Kimmuriel, then?" the warrior noble pressed.

"Distantly," Drizzt answered.

"Jearth," came a female voice from the side, "the Netherese flank us. We have no time to tarry."

"Kill them and be done with it?" Jearth, the warrior noble, replied.

"It would seem prudent."

"They are of Bregan D'aerthe, they claim," Jearth replied. "If Kimmuriel's forces are around, I would have them on our side, would you agree? It should be easy enough to facilitate their aid, particularly with Tiago Baenre among our ranks."

Drizzt's thoughts whirled as he tried to place the names. Jearth sounded somewhat familiar to him, but he knew of Tiago not at all. But Baenre! Of course, the mere mention of that powerful House sent Drizzt's memories spinning back to his decades in Menzoberranzan.

"Bregan D'aerthe?" the female echoed incredulously. She started around to Drizzt's left. "A drow, an elf . . ." She paused just long enough to spit upon Dahlia, and Drizzt winced, considering what might soon happen to poor Dahlia, given her heritage and the hatred between the elf races.

"And a human," the female continued as she walked, but she bit off that last word, and Drizzt craned his neck enough to see her, to notice the surprised expression on her face as she looked over Artemis Entreri.

"Priestess," Entreri said to her with proper deference.

The female continued to stare at him with obvious curiosity.

"I know you," she said quietly, and seemed unsure and tentative.

"I have been to Menzoberranzan," Entreri replied to that look. "Before the Spellplague, beside Jarlaxle."

Drizzt held his breath, for Entreri had left Menzoberranzan beside him, and after they had wrought great damage. Reminding this priestess of that time might also remind her of the escape, and the identity of Entreri's companions during that escape!

"You would be long dead then, human."

"And yet I'm not," Entreri replied. "There's magic in the world, it would seem."

"Do you know him?" the noble warrior asked the priestess.

"Do you know me, human?" she asked. "Do you know Berellip Xorlarrin?"

There came a long pause. Drizzt craned his neck even farther, catching a glimpse of Entreri as the seated man studied the drow priestess before him. Drizzt knew the name, the surname at least, and it brought him little comfort. For House Xorlarrin had been among the greatest of Menzoberranzan, potent with magic and formidable. Drizzt swallowed hard yet again, for he recalled then this warrior noble, Jearth Xorlarrin, who had been through Melee-Magthere, the drow academy, not long before him. He considered it great luck indeed that Jearth had apparently not recognized him, for though a century and more had elapsed, few dark elves had eyes the color of Drizzt's.

This whole thing seemed so perfectly absurd to Drizzt—until, of course, he considered that Jarlaxle had been involved. Whenever Jarlaxle was involved, absurdity was soon to follow.

"I do," Entreri replied to the priestess, and Drizzt just sighed helplessly.

"Where, then?" the female demanded.

"On a ledge on the edge of the Clawrift," Entreri answered without hesitation, though there was a bit of a question in his voice, as if he wasn't completely sure and was afraid—rightly so!—to get it wrong.

Berellip began to laugh.

"How could I ever forget?" Entreri asked with more confidence. "Did you not use your powers to dangle me over the abyss in the moment of my ecstasy?"

"It was about pleasing me, human," she answered. "Your discomfort mattered not at all."

"As it must be," Entreri replied.

"Berellip?" asked the incredulous warrior noble, who was clearly more flum-moxed even than Drizzt. "You know him?"

"If he is who he claims to be, he was my first *colnbluth* lover," Berellip answered, using the drow word for anyone who was not drow. She laughed. "My only human lover. And quite skilled, if I recall correctly, which is why I didn't drop him into the Clawrift."

"I was there to please you," Entreri said.

Drizzt could hardly believe what he was hearing, but he resisted shaking his head or wearing a stupefied expression and being obvious—if he was to be taken seriously as a member of Bregan D'aerthe, after all, then such news should not be so shocking to him.

"He was brought to Menzoberranzan by Jarlaxle," Berellip explained to Jearth. "And graciously put at the disposal of those among us who were curious about the prowess of a human."

"He is who you believe him to be?" the warrior asked skeptically.

"On the edge of the Clawrift, indeed," Berellip said, and her voice revealed that it had probably been a pleasant experience—at least from her perspective.

Drizzt didn't know whether to laugh out loud or scream at the absurdity of it all. He chose—wisely—to remain silent. Once again, images of his escape from Menzoberranzan, Entreri beside him, had him holding his breath. If Berellip or Jearth put the pieces together, if they had learned that Entreri had fled Menzoberranzan beside Drizzt Do'Urden, the result would be catastrophic indeed.

"They're Bregan D'aerthe, then," Jearth declared.

"So it would seem," Berellip answered, and Drizzt breathed just a little bit easier.

"An elf?" Jearth asked incredulously. "I would not suffer her to live."

"Take her as you will," Berellip started to answer, but Entreri interrupted.

"She is Jarlaxle's consort," Entreri blurted to Drizzt's continuing surprise. "His most valuable spy, as you can imagine, for she navigates the villages of the elves and Eladrin with ease."

Simply in looking at Jearth, Drizzt realized that his assassin companion had just saved Dahlia from a certain fate of rape, torture, and ultimately, murder.

"You let *iblith* speak for you?" Berellip asked Drizzt, moving around to stand before him.

Drizzt held his breath yet again. She had recognized Entreri—what might happen if she recognized him? Certainly she was old enough to know the stories of Drizzt Do'Urden, traitor to his people.

"He is Jarlaxle's *colnbluth*," Drizzt explained at length. "I serve Kimmuriel."

"And which leads Bregan D'aerthe?" Berellip asked.

"Kimmuriel," Drizzt said without hesitation, though he was flailing blindly, for he had no idea of what he was talking about, and had even less of an idea of what Berellip and Jearth might know of the inner workings of Jarlaxle's band.

"Then why do you allow him to speak?"

"In deference to Jarlaxle," Drizzt replied. "That is our edict from Kimmuriel. All deference to Jarlaxle. I am here to serve as Kimmuriel's eyes, as Jarlaxle's *colnbluth* and his elf consort scout out this most curious place."

"Weapons master," came a voice from the back of the room, out of Drizzt's sight. "The Shadovar move to flank us. We must move at once."

Jearth looked to Berellip.

"Free them," the priestess said. "We will need their blades. Put them in a tunnel where the fighting will be especially fierce. My memory is that Jarlaxle's toy was exceptionally fine with the blade, as well as his spear."

She leaned in close to Entreri and said quietly. "If you fight well, you may survive, and if you do, I will allow you to please me once more."

To that point, the groggy Dahlia had been perfectly still and perfectly silent, but she gave a little gasp at that remark, Drizzt noted with more than a passing interest.

"She must have been an amazing lover for you to remember her after all of these decades," Dahlia said to Entreri when the three were moving together and alone a short while later.

"I don't remember her at all," Entreri replied.

"But . . . you mentioned the incident," Dahlia protested. "This Claw . . . ?" She held up her hands helplessly.

"The Clawrift," Drizzt explained. "A chasm in the drow city."

"And he remembered it, and the encounter with her beside it," Dahlia said.

Drizzt didn't look at her, figuring that it would only confirm the intrigue he clearly heard in Dahlia's voice. Again came those flashes, images of Dahlia and Entreri entwined in passion. But now Drizzt understood the source of them—partly, at least—and so he pushed them away and silently warned Charon's Claw to shut up.

If it was Charon's Claw, and that was the rub. For in his heart, Drizzt understood that the sentient sword was not planting the whole of his feelings regarding Dahlia and Artemis Entreri. The sword had sensed some jealousy within him and was fueling it, likely, but Drizzt would be lying to himself to pretend that he was not honestly bothered by the level of intimacy between Entreri and Dahlia, a level that far exceeded his own with this elf woman who was his lover.

"Not at all," Entreri said.

"I heard you!" Dahlia protested.

"That was the chosen place," said Entreri. "For all of the noble priestesses who were curious about the prowess of a human."

"You said she magically dangled you over the ledge," Dahlia protested.

"They all did."

Both Dahlia and Drizzt stopped and stared at him.

"Lovely ladies, these priestesses of Lolth," Entreri mouthed dryly. "Not very imaginative, but. . ." He just shrugged and moved along.

Drizzt thought back to those long-ago days, when Jarlaxle had taken Artemis Entreri to Menzoberranzan, and there the assassin had been like a slave—not necessarily to Jarlaxle, but to any and all of the drow who deemed to use him as they would. Drizzt had learned of some of Entreri's trials in those days, for Drizzt, too, had gone to Menzoberranzan at that time to surrender, and had been promptly imprisoned there until a dear friend had come to get him. He had left the city beside Artemis Entreri, a daring escape.

Beside Entreri and Catti-brie.

She had come for him, daring the deep Underdark, defying the power of the drow, risking everything for the sake of a foolish Drizzt, who truly hadn't appreciated the value and responsibility of friendship.

Would Dahlia have come for him, he couldn't help but wonder? He had to let it go, he scolded himself. Now was not the time to consider the past, or the reliability of his present companions. They could fight, and fight well, and now, with the tunnels full of deadly enemies, that was enough.

Indeed, in short order, the three companions found themselves alone and hard-pressed once more, for the Shadovar were all about the upper levels of the complex, like a creeping and pervasive darkness.

"We have to get down below quickly," Drizzt explained as he hustled beside Entreri, Dahlia just behind them, along a corridor lined by many rooms on either side. These had been dwarven living quarters in ancient times, obviously, the residences of Gauntlgrym.

"There is only one descent that I know of," Dahlia agreed. "Alegni will move to block it."

"If he even knows of it," said Drizzt. As he spoke, he noted that a door ahead of Entreri on the right-hand side of the corridor was slightly ajar, and it seemed to him as if the cracked opening had just shifted slightly.

Drizzt called upon his magical anklets to speed his movements. He darted across in front of Entreri, barreling into the door full speed, bursting it wide and charging into the side room. A group of four shades awaited him, or more accurately, had planned to spring out at him and his companions.

The first fell away, slammed by the door. The second instinctively reached for his tumbling companion, then spun back and threw his arms up to defend, but too late as Drizzt's scimitar cut across his throat, the drow rushing past.

"Right!" he heard Dahlia cry as he engaged the remaining two, and he understood that this ambush had been coordinated from more than one room.

No matter, though, his task lay before him.

He batted down a pointing stave with a backhand right, and the flummoxed sorcerer couldn't even finish his spell. Drizzt's left scimitar went across the other way, batting aside a thrusting sword. Without even turning his hips, the drow deftly rolled his weapon over that sword and came back in the other way, neatly parrying a thrust of the attacker's second sword.

Only then, in recognizing the two-handed fighting style, did Drizzt come to understand, too, that this shade was of elf heritage, perhaps even dark elf heritage.

Again, no matter, for he hadn't the time to ask a question. He stabbed out with that left hand, forcing the shade back, then retreated himself a few fast steps. He reversed his grip on Icingdeath in his right hand and stabbed it out behind him, perfectly timing the strike to halt the charge of the shade who had been slammed by the door. Axe up high for an overhead, two-handed chop and coming in fast, the fool had no defense. He couldn't turn, couldn't stop, couldn't dodge, and couldn't get his weapon or even an arm down for a block. He took the stab in his gut, the curving blade working upward, through his diaphragm and into his lung.

The shade staggered back, the blade sliding out, and he gasped and tried to find his balance.

But Drizzt turned even as he retracted the blade, a spinning circuit that gave him a forehand slash with Twinkle that chopped the shade to the ground.

As he came around, Drizzt darted out and leaped high, crashing down atop the mage, who was again trying to enact some spell. Drizzt yelled in his face, trying to disorient him, and unleashed a barrage of blows, left and right, tearing at the mage's robes, bashing him around the skull.

He hit the shade a dozen times or more in the heartbeats he had before the swordsman leaped at him, and then he had to hope it would be enough as he found himself engaged with the skilled warrior.

The very skilled warrior, Drizzt realized almost immediately, as those swords came in at him from a multitude of angles, seemingly all at once, so fast and perfect was the execution of the elf shade.

Entreri started into the room right behind Drizzt, but on Dahlia's call, the assassin leaped into the air and turned sidelong. He planted his feet against the door jamb and launched himself back the other way, falling to the ground in a roll and coming back up right beside the opening right-hand door.

He flipped his dagger into his right hand as he went, and stabbed out hard behind his hip, catching a shade in the gut as it crossed the threshold into the corridor. Even as the dagger plunged in, Entreri flipped his grip on the hilt and ripped it back out, then rolled his arm up and over, stabbing behind over his right shoulder, this time plunging the small blade into the lurching shade's eye.

As that one fell, more poured out.

"Drow, we need you!" Entreri yelled.

"Drizzt!" Dahlia foolishly added.

Even Entreri was too engaged, however, to understand the possible implications of shouting out that particular name in these tunnels. The second shade out the door, heavily armored and with sword and shield, came at him fiercely, driving him back.

And he heard another door, one at least, opening behind him.

The shade had gained the advantage at the start of the fight and showed no intention of letting it dissipate, working his blades ferociously and with deadly precision, keeping Drizzt on his heels, his scimitars spinning to block and deflect.

He tried to come up even, but the shade pressed harder.

Drizzt began to see the patterns in his opponent's movements. His warrior instincts took over, his vast experience led him to more careful and controlled parries, and soon enough he was managing a counter with almost every block.

Eventually he would fight himself back to even footing, and then, he knew, he could soon enough gain the upper hand on this lesser, though very good, fighter.

A cry from the hallway told him that "soon" was likely too long, and his pause nearly cost him as the shade pressed wildly. Twinkle and Icingdeath caught the thrusts and turned them out, and blocked the heavy slash, but Drizzt understood that it would take him many back-and-forth exchanges to even get back to where he was before Dahlia had cried out.

He managed a glance to the side as he turned his opponent, circling to his right to face the door, and that quick glance told him that Entreri and Dahlia—and he, stuck in this room—were surely in trouble. The hallway was filling with enemies.

A third shade rushed out of the room—or tried to until Dahlia stabbed the woman hard in the face with the end of her staff.

Entreri noted it and started to call out to her, for he knew the enemies were entering the hall behind him, and the armored shade before him pressed him hard. Dahlia didn't need his prompt, though, understanding well the dilemma. She quick-stepped forward and prodded ahead with Kozah's Needle, thrusting it into the lower back of Entreri's opponent. There, too, the shade was armored, and Dahlia hit a metal plate.

So she let loose a burst of lightning energy from her magical quarterstaff.

The arcing energy leaped across the metal plates, curling and biting at the warrior, coming together from either side in a blinding and bursting dance across the bars of his full-faced helmet.

His next swing came awkwardly, as the lightning crawled around him like an angry swarm of biting insects, and Entreri easily dodged, rolling under the blade. As the nimble assassin came around, stepping behind the lurching sword and passing on the shade's right, he managed to bash his sword across that faceplate, stunning the armored warrior.

Entreri rushed past the open doorway, where another shade loomed, and past the door to Drizzt's room, catching a quick glance as he went.

Reflexively, Entreri tossed his dagger into the air and swept his left hand across and back again past his belt buckle, extending it out as he crossed Drizzt's room.

"Drow, be quick!" he called to Drizzt, and he caught his dagger and fell into another roll to avoid a sweep of a Netherese axe. He turned as he rolled over, coming up beside Dahlia.

"Drow!" they yelled together.

Drizzt heard their summons, and he surely understood, but again, had no idea how he might extricate himself—until his opponent lurched strangely and turned stiffly to keep up with the dancing drow.

And Drizzt understood from that look of pain on his enemy's face, that Entreri had thrown his belt knife into the elf shade's side.

The shade's right arm drooped. He fought to keep his defenses in place, but the spasms of pain denied him.

Drizzt winced as the shade winced. His sense of honor screamed out at him that this was not a fair fight, and against a truly worthy opponent. Only for a moment, though, as he realized the foolishness of such a lament, particularly given that he had gone in there one against four.

He worked his scimitars more furiously, mostly down-angled for his parries, for he noted that the lower angle brought more pain to his opponent.

The ring of metal on metal and a surge of movement in the hall reminded him that he needed to be quick, and so he fell back with his left foot, inviting a thrust from the shade's injured right, and when that blade came forward, instead of picking it off with Twinkle, Drizzt swept Icingdeath across and under, coming back fast after hooking the sword and driving it with his own blade back across to his right.

He stepped left as he did, dodging his hips to avoid the stab of the shade's left-hand blade until Icingdeath and the hooked sword could fully intercept the thrust.

Which cleared the opening for Drizzt's left hand, and Twinkle struck hard and true, and the shade fell away, throwing his swords as he went, hands reaching for a torn throat.

"Drizzt!" Dahlia yelled.

"We can't hold the door!" Entreri added, and then more quietly asked Dahlia, "Will you quit calling his name?" He barely got the warning out and expected no reply, for the press was too great, with too many enemies blocking the corridor before them. Entreri's words to Drizzt rang true, for they had to retreat.

Both started to call out again, and both gasped in surprise as a bolt of lightning exited Drizzt's room and slammed into the shade facing Entreri.

Not a lightning bolt, they both realized, but a lightning enchanted arrow, and it drove right through that shade and burrowed into the one in front of Dahlia. Before that pair had even fallen away, another arrow exploded into the side of the first one's head.

Dahlia stabbed her staff into the face of the mortally wounded shade still standing before her, driving him back and to the ground.

"More!" she cried, and on cue, a third lightning arrow screamed out into the corridor.

And simply disappeared.

And then came a fourth, and Dahlia's teeth started chattering and her thick braid began to writhe with energy as if it was a living serpent.

"Hold!" Entreri cried as the third came out to be absorbed. He rushed across the body of the fallen shade, driving hard into the next rank, forcing them back with a flurry of stabs and thrusts.

Dahlia leaped past him as he cleared the immediate corridor, and thrust her staff down against the stone floor, releasing the pent up lightning energy.

The whole of the corridor seemed to leap under the power of that retort, shades twisting and falling, staggering aside in shock, mental and physical.

"Go! Go!" Entreri yelled, grabbing her and spinning her around and pushing her back the way they had come. He moved right behind her, Drizzt coming fast on his heels. The drow didn't continue, though, spinning around and falling low and letting fly a stream of lightning arrows at the confused enemies.

"Forward!" the drow ordered to his companions, turning them around.

The shades scattered and fled, the trio in close pursuit—until they crossed a side passage that rang out as familiar to Drizzt and Dahlia, one they both believed would take them to the lower chambers.

Off they ran, Drizzt sealing the end with a globe of magical darkness. Then he paused as Entreri and Dahlia spread out beyond, seeking the proper routes.

The drow held perfectly still, craning his neck in concentration. He heard the slightest of footfalls, and sent a line of arrows into and through the magical darkness.

He ducked out of sight around a corner, and not a heartbeat too soon as a Shadovar wizard responded with a stream of magic missiles, and a second mage added a line of biting fire.

On charged the shades, and Drizzt leaned out and drove them back once more, the Heartseeker's arrows cutting holes through rank after rank, three shades dropping with the first shot alone.

Drizzt ran off.

Only a heartbeat later, the area where he had been crouching exploded in a fireball, then a second and third.

"Keep running," he warned Entreri and Dahlia as he crossed by them, and he tossed something at Entreri.

The assassin caught it: his buckle knife.

On they ran.

CHAPTER

21

THE SHIFTING WEB OF ALLIES
AND ENEMIES

BRACK'THAL STOOD IN THE ORANGE-GLOWING CHAMBER, STARING DOWN past the swirling water elementals to the bubbling lava maw of the primordial beast. The mage rubbed his thumb across the ruby band on his index finger, for through that ring, he could hear the call of the primordial, and could understand it.

Parts of it, at least, for this being was truly beyond Brack'thal's comprehension, even with the assistance of the ring. This was a most ancient power, a god beast. Though it was quite above him, its primary call carried a simple enough message: the beast wanted to be freed.

Brack'thal looked down to his right, to the narrow mushroom stalk bridge that had been put in place to cross the pit.

His gaze moved out through the continual mist across the pit to the archway, barely visible through the fog, and the small antechamber beyond. He pictured the lever, and spoke the word for it—not in the drow tongue or in the common tongue of Faerûn, but in a language he knew from his ring, the language of creatures of the primal plane of fire.

The primordial roiled hopefully, far below.

Ambergris hustled to the door ahead of the rest of her hunting band. This portal opened into the main corridor, she knew, and knew, too, that her band of Shadovar hunters had arrived in time to intercept the trio. She didn't waste any time, sprinkling some powdery substance down on the floor and drawing it into specific shapes as she quietly chanted her spell.

"What is it?" Afafrenfere said, coming in through the room's other door.

"Keep yerself back," the dwarf warned, holding up one hand. "There be a powerful ward placed on this portal."

By the time she rose and turned around, several others had entered, including the sorcerer who had been designated as the patrol's leader.

"Glyphed," Ambergris explained, moving toward them.

The shade wizard looked at her curiously. "This one, you check?" he asked suspiciously, for they had come through a dozen such doors.

"I been checking most," Ambergris replied, to a doubtful look.

"Check for yerself then, fool," the dwarf said. "Meself's looking for another way about."

"Go to the door," the wizard ordered Afafrenfere.

"Don't ye move," Ambergris remarked, drawing the wizard's icy stare.

The dwarf returned that with a grin, and looked knowingly to Afafrenfere, who indeed was making no movement toward the portal. The others didn't know about Ambergris and Afafrenfere's allegiance to Cavus Dun, but Afafrenfere had not forgotten it, nor the fact that such affiliation superseded any orders he might be given here, other than those coming directly from Lord Alegni himself.

"Dwarf says it's glyphed," the monk replied, crossing his arms over his chest.

"Do not delay!" the wizard commanded, turning all around. He focused on another of the shades, a female standing beside him, and threw the woman forward. "Go! Go! Before they pass us by!"

The woman glanced at Ambergris only momentarily before easing toward the door. She neared tentatively, sliding one foot before the other.

She almost made it, and was even reaching for the door handle, when the glyph of lightning exploded, throwing the poor shade through the air, the thunderous retort shaking the floor and walls.

"Well done!" Ambergris congratulated the sorcerer, and the others fell back, except for the poor victim, of course, who went crashing aside, her hair dancing, her teeth chattering, blood running from her eyes.

The sorcerer stared at the dwarf hatefully.

"Our enemies know we're here now, I'm guessing," the dwarf taunted. "But if ye're not sure, ye might want to set off another alarm or two."

"Now we go through!" the sorcerer demanded.

Ambergris huffed at that. "Another glyph or two remaining," she warned with a shake of her hairy head, and she walked past the sorcerer, muttering, "Idiot," as she went.

That proved more than he could tolerate, and he reached out and shoved the dwarf . . . who didn't budge. Ambergris did move, though, sweeping her large mace across and swatting the sorcerer aside. The shocked mage grunted as he slammed into the side wall, then groaned and slumped to the floor.

"Gather the idiot," Ambergris instructed Afafrenfere and one other. "We got to backtrack and with all speed if we're hoping to catch them three afore they get on much more."

Ambergris, of course, was hoping for no such thing.

She turned to another pair of shades. "The two o' ye bring her along," she ordered, pointing to the lightning-wounded woman. "Might be that I can save her. Might not."

The three companions heard the thunderous report and moved with as much caution as they could muster. They soon slipped past the lightning-scarred door, then rushed away, Drizzt in the back, the Heartseeker trained on the hallway in case any enemies might come forth behind them.

Soon after, though, the drow took up the lead once more. "This way," Drizzt instructed, for he recognized the area clearly, and knew they were nearing the great stairwell to the lower levels.

Indeed, a short while later, they entered the last expanse, the door that would take them to the stairwell landing visible down the corridor before them. As they approached, the door swung open, and Drizzt almost let fly an arrow—until he recognized a fellow drow coming through.

At the same time, movement from behind had the trio looking back over their shoulders, to see more dark elves moving toward them. And not just any drow, Drizzt understood as he regarded the male leading the small cavalry patrol, for this one rode astride a powerful lizard, and it and he were armored in the finest of drow materials and craftsmanship. This was no commoner drow, but a House noble, and likely from one of the greater Houses.

A second rider followed close behind, and Drizzt recognized Jearth as Jearth called out to him.

"Where are your forces, Masoj?" Jearth demanded, riding up beside his mounted companion. "Where is Kimmuriel, or Jarlaxle, at least?"

"These are the agents of Bregan D'aerthe?" the other rider asked, and he looked doubtfully at Drizzt, and became even more skeptical as he regarded Entreri, and nearly spat on the floor when his gaze fell over Dahlia.

"They are," Jearth replied.

The other rider could barely contain a laugh. He focused on Drizzt once more, and looked at the drow curiously—so much so that Drizzt lowered his gaze. "Tell Jarlaxle that House Baenre wishes to speak with him," he said, and he walked his strong lizard through the trio, forcing them aside and nearly trampling Dahlia. And when Byok, his lizard, tried to bite at the woman, the Baenre noble only barely held it back.

Other riders rumbled past in his wake, some taking their sticky-footed mounts up on the walls.

"Ride with me," Jearth instructed Drizzt.

Drizzt looked at him curiously.

"The stairwell has been dropped to prevent the shades from getting below," Jearth explained. "I will take you down."

"What of my companions?"

Dahlia, who could not understand the drow language, slapped Entreri on the shoulder, and he leaned in, translating quietly.

"*Iblith,*" the weapons master said with a dismissive wave. "No proper mount would accept such a rider. Come along, we haven't much time."

Drizzt was shaking his head before he had even formulated a proper response. "Jarlaxle's consort," he said at last, motioning to Dahlia. "He will not be pleased if I abandon them."

"That is Jarlaxle's problem."

"And mine," said Drizzt. "I am tasked with protecting them."

"They cannot get down through this route."

"If Bregan D'aerthe arrives, it will be up here, in any case," said Drizzt. "We can avoid the shades, and we will strike at them as they advance."

Jearth looked at him incredulously, then stared at Dahlia and Entreri. "They are *iblith,*" he said with obvious disgust.

Drizzt shrugged sheepishly and reiterated, "Jarlaxle's consort."

Jearth shook his head, apparently accepting that reasoning as sound, which, of course, it would be to anyone who knew Jarlaxle. The weapons master of House Xorlarrin started off after the others, passing through the door and going over the lip of the landing without missing a stride.

"We can't stay up here," Entreri remarked as soon as the three were alone. He noticed that Drizzt was hardly listening, and prompted him, "Drizzt?"

"We saw him die," Drizzt said to Dahlia. "Down below, in the primordial's chamber."

She looked at him curiously before asking, "Jarlaxle?"

Drizzt nodded. "Twice now, we have spoken his name openly to these dark elves, as if Jarlaxle was still alive."

"Word has not reached other drow," Dahlia reasoned. "It hasn't been that long a time."

"That first rider who passed you was a noble of House Baenre," Drizzt said, and he shook his head to indicate that he couldn't quite sort this out. "If Jarlaxle had fallen, House Baenre would certainly know."

"We don't have the time to discuss this," Entreri warned. He looked back the way they had come, drawing the gazes of the other two. "We're supposed to hide up here? We have to get from this tunnel and into some side chambers, then."

"Of course not," said Drizzt. "The primordial is below, so we need to get below. Let the drow clear out from the large chamber and we will descend."

"They said that the stairwell to the lower level is broken. Do you know another way?"

"Dahlia the Crow can get us down," Drizzt replied, but he said it absently, and was hardly thinking of that at the time, despite their precarious position.

House Baenre surely would know if Jarlaxle had met his demise.

"Do as I say," Berellip said to her obstinate younger brother.

"It is my expedition," Ravel countered.

Berellip slapped him so hard across the face that his legs nearly buckled beneath him. He staggered to the side a step, and came up staring not at Berellip, but at Tiago and Jearth, who had just returned from the upper levels.

"How long do we have?" Berellip asked Tiago, and not Ravel.

"They will find another way down, if they haven't already," Tiago replied. "The Shadovar have sorcerers among their ranks and will not be deterred by the absence of a stairway. And sorcerers can surely sense the magic of the primordial. They will find the forge in short order, I would expect."

"We must defend the forge," Ravel insisted, coming back to stand before his sister.

"No open battles," Berellip declared. "I'll not lose Xorlarrin drow to the likes of the Netherese. Why are we even fighting the minions of the Shadowfell?"

"Mostly we have been running, not fighting," Tiago remarked.

"It's possible that Bregan D'aerthe is hovering about," Jearth interjected. "Kimmuriel's scouting party came into Gauntlgrym ahead of the Shadovar, it would seem."

"They would be a great asset," Berellip remarked. "But at what cost?"

"Who can know?" Tiago asked, and started away. "I am off to the forge. Do I organize a defense or a retreat?"

"We don't know how many of the Netherese have come," Jearth warned before Berellip could decide.

"Both," the priestess demanded of Tiago, at the same moment that Ravel said, "Defense."

Ravel looked past Berellip as he spoke, though, to see Jearth shaking his head at Ravel, warning him to back down.

"Shut down the forges and prepare a retreat," Berellip then added, staring hatefully at Ravel the whole while.

"The narrow and dark tunnels will favor us, should we need to continue any fighting with the Shadovar," Jearth put in. "We would err in standing against this unexpected enemy in pitched battle."

"We have ample fodder for that," said Ravel.

"Do we?" Jearth replied before Berellip could chime in. "The Shadovar ranks include many wizards—not to match the power of your spellspinners, likely," he quickly added, seeing Ravel's scowl. "But enough to wipe out our goblinkin allies, and we'll need them to secure the complex when the Netherese depart or are dispatched."

"And Menzoberranzan won't send us any more of the vermin anytime soon," Berellip added evenly, and undeniably threateningly, Ravel understood.

Ravel rubbed his eyes, trying to sort it all out. What had brought this new force to Gauntlgrym, and why now, at this precise moment? He had been so close to his ultimate triumph! The whole of Gauntlgrym was soon to be his, a city for House Xorlarrin, blessed by House Baenre. Matron Zeerith would hold him in highest standard and no more would Berellip or Saribel or any of his other sisters dare lift a snake whip his way.

Berellip had moved away by this time, no doubt confident that Tiago Baenre would heed her command and not his, Ravel realized. And he didn't disagree with that conclusion, for in truth, Berellip's order to stand down was by far the wiser course. Let the Shadovar move forward. Lead them down the long tunnels of the Underdark, the haunt of the drow.

And why were they fighting against the Netherese, anyway, he wondered? Perhaps there was no love between the denizens of the Shadowfell and those of the Underdark, but neither, to Ravel's knowledge, were there any avowed hostilities.

"We must discern why they have come, and why they are attacking us," he said, drawing the attention of Berellip and Jearth and the others in the room, including Tiago, who hadn't yet departed and was watching the play quite attentively. Ravel looked to Jearth and asked, "Who started the fighting in the upper halls?"

"When two such forces come together unexpectedly in a dark and dangerous place. . . ." Jearth remarked, as if that should explain everything. "And it appears that the Shadovar were already engaged against Kimmuriel's scouting band, in any case."

"Perhaps they're our enemies, then," Ravel said. "Perhaps not."

Berellip took a step toward him.

"In either case, we'll not share Gauntlgrym," the Xorlarrin spellspinner decreed. "This is our complex now, and the Shadovar will accept that, or they will feel the sting of drow metal."

"Should we assemble in the great stair cavern for your magnificent battle, then?" Berellip asked with dripping sarcasm.

Ravel knew better than to take that bait. "No, dear sister," he said. "You were correct in your assessment. Forgive me my anger, but understand it in the context that we are so close to that which our family has wanted for millennia. It is not so easy for me to give it away."

Berellip scowled and Ravel quickly added, "Even temporarily. But indeed, you are correct. Let us stretch their lines into corridors of our choosing. If they are foolish enough to pursue, let us fight them with proper drow tactics, on proper drow battlefields."

Berellip stared at him for a while longer, then nodded slightly—and it seemed to Ravel as if she and he had made some progress in resolving their unspoken rivalry. He wanted to lash out at her for publicly slapping him, of course, for ever had he been a prideful male. But no, he would do no such thing. He needed her, more now than ever.

"Go to Yerrininae," he instructed Jearth. "The fierce driders will be hungry for battle, but I'll not lose them, even if it meant a hundred dead Shadovar for every slain drider."

"Let the goblins engage them as we stretch back our lines?" he asked, and pointedly did not instruct, Berellip.

She slowly shook her head.

Not even the fodder.

Ravel's face brightened suddenly with an idea. "Brack'thal, then," he said. "Let our brother strike at the invaders with his fiery pets. Surely the Shadovar will not even be able to place the blame upon us should we come to negotiations, given the current lord of these halls."

Berellip stared hard for many heartbeats, but eventually she nodded her agreement, and even managed a congratulatory smile for her brother.

"I will instruct him," Tiago said, and with a nod, he jumped astride Byok and headed for the forge.

Ravel watched him go suspiciously. He alone knew of the treasure Tiago sought in the forge, the sword and shield Gol'fanin was even then creating, and he wondered if the Baenre would be patient enough to surrender the forge to the Netherese, even temporarily. He shook the thought away, though, for wasn't Ravel's own stake here at least as great? When he turned back to Berellip, he was glad of his sister's expression indeed, but whatever gains in understanding he and Berellip had made to diminish their personal squabbling seemed a minor victory next to the new threat that had interrupted their plans.

This was to be Xorlarrin's city. They were not about to let a group of Shadovar chase them off . . . for long.

"So they came here to join in with the drow's friends," Glorfathel remarked glumly, shaking his head. "Our task just got much more difficult."

"Nah," Ambergris replied, but Alegni's voice spoke over her.

"The drow risk war with Netheril, then," he said. "Do they understand that?"

"We cannot know, but perhaps a parley," Glorfathel started to answer, but Ambergris interrupted.

"Ain't no drow friend o' Drizzt Do'Urden," she said. "If they runned into a drow patrol, then that one's likely dead already."

"How do you know that?" Alegni asked suspiciously.

"Amber Gristle O'Maul, o' the Adbar O'Mauls," Ambergris answered with a bow. "The name o' Drizzt Do'Urden's well known in Citadel Adbar, don't ye doubt. And he ain't no friend of his kin. They come to catch him afore. They started a war about him. Nah, Warlord, if Drizzt runned into them drow, and them drow figured out 'twas Drizzt, then Drizzt is caught or dead, don't ye doubt."

"Then the other drow might not even know what they have," Glorfathel offered. "Perhaps there is hope for a parley."

"We don't even know if they have him, or the sword," Effron argued.

Herzgo Alegni closed his eyes and listened for that silent call once more, listened for the telepathic voice of Claw, his beloved sword.

"They may still be in the upper levels," Effron went on, speaking to him directly and drawing him from his contemplations.

The warlord shook his head confidently. "It does not matter," he said.

"If we wish to catch them . . ." Effron started.

"We wish to stop them first," Alegni declared, and all four looked at him curiously. "They seek the primordial," he explained. "They look to destroy Claw. That is why they have come," he added, looking at Ambergris, who had first posited such an opinion.

"You cannot know that," Effron replied, even as Ambergris nodded her agreement with Alegni.

Alegni's glare came as a clear warning to the twisted warlock. "The sword calls to me. Press on with all speed. We must find the beast quickly and secure the area around it. They will come to us, or they will flee and the threat to the sword will be diminished."

"There are other drow about," Glorfathel reminded him.

"If we encounter them, and they have captured or allied with our enemies, let us tell them what they have and who they have," Alegni replied. "If they cooperate, then the fighting in the tunnels above will be forgiven. If not, then let us pay them back for those we lost. In the aftermath of such a battle, so will be declared war between Netheril and the drow, and the Empire will send us an endless line of soldiers."

"I can find the primordial," Glorfathel assured him. "Its magic resonates all around us."

Alegni nodded and motioned to his nearby commanders to tighten up the ranks, that they could press on with all speed.

The giant crow swooped down from on high, one end of a fine elven rope in her beak. She alighted atop the highest remaining stair, near the hinge that had allowed the clever denizens below to fold half the stairwell down over the lower half. It was a marvelous design, but Dahlia had no time to consider it at length then. She reverted to her elf form and tied off the rope as tightly as she could, then waited as the two up on the landing pulled it even tighter and tied it securely above.

Drizzt went first, sliding down under the line, a leather belt pouch looped over the cord as a makeshift handle. Entreri came close behind, and even as he started, and before Drizzt had set down on the stairs, Dahlia became a crow again and flew back up.

She understood Entreri's impatience when she arrived at the landing, given the unmistakable sounds of an approaching force. She didn't even revert from the crow form, using her beak to pull free the knots.

And quickly she was gone, swooping again from on high, soaring past her two friends as they scrambled along the stair, and down to the bottom to ensure that the large chamber was indeed empty.

The three companions entered the tunnels quickly and made for the forge, and for the pit of the great beast. Dahlia couldn't help but notice that Drizzt grew quite agitated. He kept dropping his hand into his belt pouch—where he kept the panther figurine, she knew.

"What is it?" she quietly asked him as Entreri moved out ahead.

He looked at her curiously, but she grabbed his wrist, for his hand was again in that pouch.

Drizzt winced, his expression full of anger. "She is worth the lives of fifty Artemis Entreris," he stated.

"What?"

He muttered something undecipherable and pushed past her to catch up to the assassin.

Hustling to be done with Entreri, once and for all, Dahlia presumed, and it struck her then how greatly, how viciously, her drow lover wanted Entreri to die. Perhaps it was the call of the sword again, or maybe, she mused, Drizzt simply hated Entreri that much.

CHAPTER 22

FIRE GOD

BRACK'THAL BREATHED A SIGH OF RELIEF THAT HIS INVISIBILITY SPELL LASTED long enough for him to get through the small tunnel from the forge room and into the primordial's chamber. He had lost his elemental pet, sending it down a corridor after some Shadovar, he believed, though he had not seen them. Without it, the drow wizard felt naked indeed.

So he had quietly slipped back to the forge room, and had entered invisibly, but to his dismay, had found no ongoing breaches, no little fiery creatures rushing around. The one forge that had not yet been repaired had been fully shut down.

Even worse, during his invisible creeping around, Brack'thal overheard Tiago Baenre telling his blacksmith friend that all of the drow would be retreating from the forge and into the deeper tunnels in light of the Netherese advance.

They would surrender this hall and the primordial, and Brack'thal couldn't allow that.

This was his source of power. Through his ruby ring, the wizard felt the primal murmurs of ancient magic resonating powerfully within him. It was not a sensation he was about to let lapse.

He stood on the edge of the deep pit, cursing the water elementals swirling around its sides, trapping this godly creature of such beautiful power. He couldn't dismiss those water elementals. His magic couldn't touch them in any effective way. Because of his affinity with the Plane of Fire, those creatures from the Plane of Water were even farther from his influence, and even more dangerous foes to him.

Brack'thal could hear the beast below. Its whispers flitted around his mind, promising him all that he had lost and more. He had been formidable in the tunnels against the corbies and dwarf ghosts, formidable in his work on the stairwell, and formidable in his dealings with his wretched little brother. All because of this godlike primordial.

The old drow mage heard the call clearly. The primordial demanded release. But Ravel and his band had properly secured the mechanisms for controlled releases only, allowing a bit of the primordial to fire the furnaces. The ancient traps would keep the beast under control.

The primordial wanted release. Brack'thal could hear that lament most clearly of all.

And in that release, Brack'thal alone among his kin would find any gain, would rise in power above Ravel.

Brack'thal crossed the mushroom-stalk bridge to the anteroom and stood before the lever. This was the key, he believed, and if he pulled it, the primordial would be free. On a different and more pragmatic emotional level, the wizard surely understood the danger in such a scenario. Would he even be able to survive and escape the cataclysm sure to follow? The voice through his ring told him to trust, and he found himself reaching for the lever.

His hand didn't quite get there, though, for a multitude of images came to him then—imparted from the primordial, he knew. He saw a glittering throne set with magnificent gems, a dwarven throne for dwarf kings.

Only a dwarf could pull this lever, Brack'thal understood then, and only one who had sat on that throne. This was a typical failsafe for dwarves, as it was for the drow, for both races elevated their own above all others. Only a Delzoun dwarf could pull this lever, and only one who sat on that powerfully enchanted throne, thus, only one of royal lineage.

With a growl, Brack'thal grasped the lever anyway and began to tug. When it wouldn't budge, the wizard moved behind it and put his shoulder to it, pushing with all of his strength. When it still wouldn't move at all, Brack'thal cast a spell of strength upon himself, his thin arms bulging with magical muscle.

He might as well have been trying to move a mountain.

Sometime later, the mage stood on the edge of the pit back across the bridge once more, but he didn't look down to the primordial any longer, his eyes focused back on the narrow hallway that had led him there. His mind's eye was looking past that corridor, too, to a forge that was not really a forge.

Perhaps there was another way.

Tiago Baenre's eyes sparkled in fiery reflections and in clear intrigue as he looked at the strange items lying on the tray before Gol'fanin. He focused first on the delicate and narrow sword blade that seemed as much the stuff of magic as metal, silvery but nearly translucent, and with shining little points of light sparkling back at him from within their glow.

"Diamond dust," he whispered.

"Mingled with the glassteel," Gol'fanin confirmed. "Both creations are thick with the stuff, lending the metal its hardness and edge. You'll not break this sword, nor dull its deadly cut, and that shield will deflect the cudgel of a mountain giant."

"Magnificent," Tiago breathed. His gaze moved lower on the sword, to the unfinished hilt and the quillon and guard, and truly they were nothing like Tiago had ever seen before, a conical cage of black metal crisscrossing into the likeness of a spider web and fanning out away from the blade to cover the wielder's hand.

"If that was the extent of their powers, I'd agree," the blacksmith replied, and he was grinning slyly when Tiago glanced at him.

"How strong?" Tiago asked, indicating the sword's seemingly delicate quillon.

"Strong enough to block the blow of a giant's cudgel," Gol'fanin assured him. "And to defeat a considerable amount of magical energy thrown your way. A lightning bolt striking the blade will dissipate into a shower of harmless sparks when it runs across that quillon. If one even gets near the blade, for that shield can easily defeat such magic."

Tiago almost giggled at that point. He had known that these would be exceptional implements, but now that he saw them in person, the extent of their magnificence was just beginning to dawn on him.

He looked from the sword and shield to the side of the tray, where the sword grip and matching shield grip and straps waited for the blacksmith's expert hands. They, too, were black, gleaming like polished onyx. Each was shaped like an arachnid, with its legs pulled in tight, creating ridges to better secure grasping fingers.

Gol'fanin picked the sword grip up and handed it to Tiago, who grasped it as if the weapon was attached. Never had he felt such a secure grip on any sword! It seemed to him as if the handles were grabbing back, tightening and securing his hold. He brought the item up before his eyes, marveling at the fine detail, for indeed it seemed the perfect likeness of a beautiful spider, the pommel resembling the arachnid's head and set with a pair of dull emeralds, little spider eyes. The other two for the shield were identical, except that their eyes were blue sapphires.

"How long?" the eager young warrior asked.

"There is much yet to do," Gol'fanin replied, and he took the handle back and gently replaced it on the tray. "More enchantments and more hardening, and then I must, of course, properly attach the handles."

"How long?" Tiago asked more insistently.

"Another tenday."

The Baenre warrior slumped at that news. A tenday if they remained in the forge, but alas, it was not to be.

"Could you finish your work in Menzoberranzan?" Tiago had to ask.

Gol'fanin looked at him incredulously, his expression full of horror, and that alone provided all the answer the young Baenre needed. He looked over his shoulder to the room's main exit, trying to formulate some defensive plans to secure and hold this particular room that would convince the Xorlarrins to stand their ground.

But it was a fool's errand, he knew. The room was too open. It would favor their enemies if those enemies managed to get in. The losses would prove too great to the drow expedition, even if they ultimately held the forge.

Tiago looked back to the implements, the sword and shield that would make him the envy of every weapons master in Menzoberranzan. Items that would strike terror into the heart of Andzrel, the pretender who held that coveted rank within the hierarchy of House Baenre. Tiago would replace him. With these weapons in his hands, he would cast Andzrel aside and take his rightful place.

But not quite yet.

Gol'fanin smiled at him and took up a handle. With a grin, he moved for the sword blade.

Brack'thal couldn't begin to sort out the many valves and blocking pins and pipes lining the small chamber beneath the false forge. "Dwarven idiocy," he muttered, trying to follow this line or that, trying to figure out which piping might lead him to the one furnace that had been shut down because the goblins hadn't yet repaired the feeds.

He moved to a wall where a throng of pipes exited through the stone, the image making him think of a great organ lying sideways. Which forge in line was the broken one, he asked himself?

"Which forge?"

The mage tried to envision the room above him, counting back to the broken forge . . . or should he be counting forward?

He did not know whether the top pipe or the bottom connected to the next forge in line. He couldn't even remember which forge in the line he had just climbed through to get there!

"The script," he said, growing desperate, and he found some lettering—ancient Dwarvish lettering. He couldn't begin to decipher it, but there were spells for such things.

Brack'thal stepped back and took a deep breath, trying to recall the spell for comprehending such languages. A heartbeat later, he gave a little whimper as he realized that he had not memorized that particular dweomer this day, nor did he have any such scrolls in his possession.

"By the gods," the frustrated wizard said, and he slapped his hand against the pipe in pure exasperation.

And the fire within the pipe began to talk to him.

He held his hand in place, staring at the ruby band, his connection to the Plane of Fire, and to the primordial godlike being in the nearby pit. He didn't need to understand the ancient Dwarvish language, he realized, and he didn't need to count the pipes. For the god-beast understood the design, its living fiery tendrils weaving their way through the maze. Now it spoke to Brack'thal. Now it showed him the controls, the valves, the plugs . . . the plug sealing off the broken forge.

He saw it all, so clearly, all the channels and controls, all the valves to dampen the flow of pure fiery power. He rushed around, spinning those valves wide, freeing the beast!

So giddy with power was he that Brack'thal sang as he danced, and laughed as he twirled the valves. He could feel the energy mounting all around, the primal scream of a primal god.

The pipes clanged and banged as if tiny gnomes were within them, rapping metal hammers. Valves groaned and hissed in protest as too much energy pressed at their huge screw mechanisms.

And the building roar of the flames sounded to Brack'thal as a chant to the greatness that was magic before the Spellplague. Pure magic. Unblemished magic. Power.

The pipes glowed angrily, bluish metal turning orange, but Brack'thal did not remove his hands from them. Had he not been wearing his ring, the skin would have melted from his fingers and palms, would have dripped to the floor as melted goo.

But this god-beast would not harm him. He understood and could trust in this most ancient power.

He felt the energy growing. Deeper along the channels, past the wall, a great roar began to mount, preternatural, like the scream of a world being born in fire.

"Be easy," Gol'fanin warned. "It is not yet properly set."

As he lifted the scimitar, Tiago Baenre hardly heard the blacksmith. The handle was loose but the grip superb, and even though it was not yet solidly set, Tiago could feel the perfect balance—perfect balance because it seemed to him that no blade was attached to the handle! He could see the translucent lines of the glowing scimitar, the sparkles of the diamond dust, but if he closed his eyes, his mind would tell him that he held an empty metal hilt and nothing more. With a slight twist of his wrist, the blade changed its angle, a wake of silvery blur behind it, and it took all the discipline Tiago could manage to stop from swinging it around—which would have likely launched the blade from the handle to fly across the room.

"What magic?" he asked.

"That remains to be seen," said the blacksmith. "The djinni will imbue them."

"You must know more than that!"

"*Vidrinath,*" Gol'fanin said, nodding to the weapon Tiago held, the one with the emerald eyes. He looked to the shield. "*Orbbcress.*"

Tiago rolled *Vidrinath* over in his hand and spoke the name, the drow word for the songs priestesses would sing to the young students at the Academy when they went into their Reverie repose. He understood then the power of this blade, so akin to that of the hand crossbow bolts, and spoke the name again, "Lullaby."

And for the shield, "Spiderweb."

He considered the potential. He let his mind wander down the paths hinted at by those particular names—names hardly chosen at random, he knew. "Tell me more," he bade Gol'fanin, or started to, for his words were lost in a rumbling deep within the cavern stone, and a cacophony of sharp metallic rapping sounds.

Tiago looked curiously at the blacksmith, who could only shrug. Together, they turned back to the main forge. Inside the oven, the fires danced wildly, forming angry faces and spitting sparks at them.

For a moment, the young Baenre wondered if this was expected, but Gol'fanin's expression dispelled that notion. "What is it?" he asked.

A half-dozen structures down to their left sat the darkened forge, the forge of the last breach which had not yet been repaired or refired, and from that oven came a tremendous bang. Suddenly, it teemed with fire, so fully that an angry orange glow emanated from its stones. Other dark elves cried out in warning, goblins scrambled, falling all over each other. Tiago and Gol'fanin ducked behind the main forge for protection.

The broken forge exploded, a giant fireball reaching across the cavern. Spurts of lava and lines of fire blasted from the wreckage of the forge. Amid the rubble, where the oven used to be, stood a mighty fire elemental, roaring and crackling and swinging its torchlike arms all around.

Other forges, too thick with primordial fuel, began to vomit, spewing forth jets of white-hot flames, and from those flames leaped more elementals, smaller ones, darting in frenzy, chasing down goblins and biting at them, dragging them down and swarming over them, lighting their clothes and hair aflame, shriveling their pallid green skin.

Screams mixed with the roaring flames and the continued throaty rumbling within the stones, and above that symphony of insanity, Tiago could not be heard. He shouted anyway, "Flee! Flee!" for the room was lost, the fight over before it had even begun. They could do nothing before the bared might of the primordial.

Nothing but burn.

A barrage of fire and lava came forth from the main forge, tossing aside the trays and the unfinished shield, and the implements: the tools, the scroll tube, the djinni bottle.

Tiago's eyes widened with horror and he started forward. "Orbbcress," he whispered as if he was speaking of his child. Gol'fanin tried to hold him back, but he broke free and rushed amid the flames, ignoring the heat and the stings. He would not lose these items, even at the cost of his own life.

He came out of the sub-chamber unafraid of the firestorm engulfing the forge room. Torrents of flames whipped around, elementals leaping to and fro, consuming the flesh of those creatures, goblinkin and drow alike, who had not escaped the conflagration.

Brack'thal did not care. The smell of burning flesh hung thick around him, but that only meant that his god-beast was feasting well this day. The wizard stepped right through the deep fires, his ring protecting him fully. Even more, he heard the song of the elementals, reveling in their freedom and calling to him, who had freed them.

He imagined himself as the Chosen of this primordial—did these ancient god-beasts even have such minions? He could be the first, a being of great power, with deadly fire at his easy disposal, ever ready to smite his enemies.

Or to melt his brother.

He continued across the room, moving for the small tunnel to the primordial pit. It was calling him, then, he believed, likely to congratulate him.

Brack'thal slowed his steps as the primordial voice rang out loudly, and once again, the room began to resonate with elemental power.

The forge of Gauntlgrym was not merely a dwarven contraption, was not simply a clever clockwork of levers and pins and valves and piping. It was a magical construct, full of energy as old as the fabled Hosttower of the Arcane of Luskan. And as such and given its role in containing such a beast as a primordial of fire, it had been carefully imbued with magical contingencies.

Brack'thal started again for the tunnel at a swift pace, then a trot, then a sprint. Just before he reached the entrance, though, his nostrils filled with a new odor, salty and pungent.

"Brine?" he asked, puzzled.

He looked up at the corner where the wall met the ceiling, to those curious green rootlike tendrils running like veins through the lower complex. Small knots, like tiny corks, popped from a thousand places at once, and water sprayed like rain across the room. Salt water. Brack'thal couldn't begin to sort it out, for he did not understand that those tendrils ran to the harbor in distant Luskan, out into the dark and cold waters of the Sword Coast.

The fire elementals roared and fought back, reaching up to throw flames at the tendrils, and so great and pure was their fury that it seemed to Brack'thal as if they would surely win out against the clever irrigation.

But a greater rumbling came forth again, from the primordial's room. Knowing that it wasn't his god-beast speaking, knowing the sound to be ominous, the wizard ran again for the small archway.

But he fell back with a cry as the river rushed forth from that corridor, pouring into the forge room. And no normal river this, for as it spread into the room, giant humanoid forms broke free of it and charged to challenge the fire elementals. The water elementals fearlessly attacked their foes, extinguishing the small fiery mites with a single splashing stomp.

Brack'thal watched as one great water elemental faced a gigantic fire beast. Without fear or hesitation, the watery beast threw itself against the creature of fire, which roared in protest—Brack'thal felt its agony clearly.

A tremendous burst of steam replaced them both, the two bodies mingling to disastrous results. More so for the fire elemental, the wizard realized. The joining wrought steam, and from the steam would come anew the magic of the Plane of Water.

Brack'thal cried out and threw himself against the wall just beside the archway. More and more watery beasts came forth, sloshing and splashing and rushing into the fire.

Finally it let up, the battle raging throughout the forge room, and Brack'thal heard again the voice of his god-beast, and this time it was a cry of pain.

The wizard ran into the corridor and stumbled out into the chamber beyond, right to the edge of the primordial's pit.

He noted immediately that the swirl of water around the sides of that deep well had diminished greatly, and he glanced back to the forge room, understanding then that many of the elementals previously holding back the primordial had come forth to meet the great challenge.

Water poured down from the ceiling above, raining into the pit, and steam obscured his view.

"Now," he bade the primordial. "You must come forth now."

He reached his thoughts through his ruby band, sending them to the primordial, bidding it to leap from its captivity.

He heard the bubbling below, and he fell back with a cry, and just in time, for the primordial leaped, or tried to, as the remaining elementals reached their watery limbs out to block it.

A small burst of rock and lava got through, lifting up over the edge of the pit to splash down on the floor right where Brack'thal had been standing.

For a few heartbeats, the wizard believed he had been betrayed. His ring might have protected him from the heat of that stony vomit, but the weight of it would surely have crushed him. Had this god-beast spat at him to pound the life out of him?

His confusion became curiosity a moment later, though, when that splattered lava reformed and regrouped, and stood up on thick rock legs, thrice his height. The drow wizard's eyes sparkled in reflections of the monstrosity, the lava elemental, a creature of tremendous strength and magical power.

It stalked over to stand towering above the wizard, and how small and vulnerable Brack'thal felt at that terrifying moment. He sucked in his breath, fearing it to be the last he would ever draw.

Tiago and Gol'fanin sat against the corridor wall many twists and turns away from the forge room. Other drow milled around, most gasping for breath, or grimacing against the sting of multiple burns.

Tiago pulled back the hood of his *piwafwi*, a very powerful cloak indeed, as it had been enchanted in the magical chambers of House Baenre. The young Baenre had not a mark on him, and thanks to his quick actions and the blacksmith's own enchanted garments, Gol'fanin had come through unscathed, as well.

More important to both of them, Orbbcress and Vidrinath, the scroll, and the djinni bottle had survived and now lay at Gol'fanin's side, covered in a thick blanket

"We were to abandon the forge anyway," he said to his companion. "Let the Shadovar deal with this new intrusion."

"If the primordial has broken free, the entire power of Netheril will not put it back," the old crafter replied. "The forge of Gauntlgrym is lost to us."

Calls of "Steam!" filled the area, echoing from the corridors leading back to the forge room.

"Perhaps Gauntlgrym has awakened to the threat," Gol'fanin offered, and he and Tiago stood up and started away.

"What has happened?" came a cry from the other way, from Berellip Xorlarrin as she and the other House nobles rushed down the hallway, many other drow beside them, and a few of Yerrininae's driders marching in rear guard behind them.

"A major breach," Tiago replied. "The forge room was overwhelmed by flames and lava and creatures of the Plane of Fire."

Jearth rode his lizard right past the young Baenre and down the corridor leading back to the forge room, rushing out of sight.

"Where is Brack'thal?" Ravel asked, and the look he tossed at Tiago made it clear that he hoped his brother was still in the room, preferably dead.

"You tell me," Tiago replied, his voice thick with intrigue, for all of them were surely thinking that Brack'thal, broken and angry, might have had a hand in this disaster. "I've not seen him."

"Find him!" Berellip snapped at the nearby commoner drow, and they nearly fell over each other as they started scrambling away.

"We lost a small group of bugbears, all of the goblins in the room, and a few drow as well, I fear," said the young Baenre, but his casual tone belied his claim that he feared any such thing. In fact, he didn't care. Gol'fanin had survived, the recipe had survived, and all the pieces and ingredients needed to finish Lullaby and Spiderweb had survived. Did anything else really matter?

All eyes turned back behind the Xorlarrin nobles, where Yerrininae moved past his drider rear guard and up to join the conversation. "The Shadovar approach in great numbers," he warned.

Berellip nodded and started to speak, but Ravel beat her to it.

"Let us fade back to the deeper tunnels," he said. "Let them deal with the danger in the forge room, and then deal with our magic and our blades as we see fit."

"And our negotiations," Berellip said.

"It would not do well for House Xorlarrin to begin a war between Menzoberranzan and the Netherese Empire," Tiago warned in support of the priestess.

Berellip gave him a quick glance and a nod—a nod of appreciation for his support, Tiago realized.

Nothing could eliminate drow infighting quicker than an external enemy.

Ravel took the lead then, ordering and arranging his forces so they could begin their quick retreat from the area. As that ensued, Berellip moved near to Tiago, and she had just reached him when Jearth returned with news that a great battle was underway in the forge room, water against fire.

"This is a most marvelous design," Ravel declared loudly. "Do not underestimate the skill of dwarves and the ancient magic their allies employed."

He reminds us that it was he who led us to this place we will soon call our home, Berellip's fingers flashed to Tiago.

Tiago's hand subtly replied with a single question: *Saribel?*

Berellip looked at her sister—at her sister who had schemed against her. Saribel was hard at work issuing commands to those around her, seemingly oblivious to Berellip's hateful glare.

Tiago saw the sting on Berellip's face, and understood where the necessity of the desperate situation was forcing her even before she answered, *Stand down.*

She couldn't let Tiago kill Saribel at that time, not until they knew the extent of Brack'thal's role in this great breach. Saribel had double-crossed Berellip with her intent to side with Ravel over Brack'thal, but if their suspicions about the Xorlarrin Elderboy proved true and Matron Zeerith learned of Brack'thal's ultimate treachery, how strong would Berellip's claim against Saribel sound?

Indeed, given the victory by Ravel, Tiago had held no intention of killing Saribel in any case, not that he would have told Berellip that little truth.

Besides, Berellip might be the more important priestess, but Saribel was by far the better lover. A minor detail in the greater scheme of things, perhaps, but those minor details often allowed Tiago greater enjoyment in life, and to him, that, after all, was the whole point of . . . everything.

Brack'thal instinctively tried to make himself smaller, curling down and defensively bringing his arms in tightly. He almost laughed at that reflexive movement, for it would do him little good when this mighty elemental decided to crush him into a smoldering pile of gore.

The blow did not fall.

Gradually, Brack'thal summoned the courage to peek out at the beast, which stood towering above him, very near. But it made no move against him, and so the mage slowly unwound himself to stand up straight before it.

Only then did he hear the voice of the lava beast, calling him through the power of his ring.

"Master."

The primordial had given this gift to him, the mage thought, and he nearly squealed with glee.

His giddiness proved short-lived, though, as a rumble from without, from the forge room, told him that the creatures of water had won out and were now fast returning. At that same time, a huge spray of water began from above the primordial pit, the magical tendrils bringing even more water into the complex in response to the primordial's attempt to break free.

And among that falling water came more than one new water elemental, diving into the pit and once more strengthening the swirl of containing waters around its walls.

Brack'thal looked through the mounting steam toward the room across the way, where the lever remained fully engaged. He could never free his god-beast as long as that lever kept open the connection between Gauntlgrym's devices and the power of the sea.

He had to find a way to throw that lever! He would need a dwarf . . .

A rush of water in the corridor to the forge room broke him from his contemplation, and he realized that he had to get out of that chamber at once.

And as he realized it, so too did his lava elemental. The mighty creature moved with incredible grace, the joints of its rocky appendages molten and fluid. It rushed to the wall beside the corridor, and there it seemed to flatten and widen as it pressed into the stone. Whether it was some powerful magic, like the dweomer known as passwall, or simply the intense heat, or perhaps a bit of both, Brack'thal could not tell, but the stone hissed and melted. Even as the returning water elementals began to pour in from the other corridor, the lava elemental departed, burrowing through the stone as easily as Brack'thal might move through water. Lava streamed behind the beast and dripped all around, and the stone seemed to simply part, leaving a sizable glowing corridor in its wake.

Given the protective magic of his ring, the dripping molten stone would not bother him, and so the mage ran off after his pet, winding its way from the room in a tunnel of its own making.

CHAPTER 23

INTERSECTION

DRIZZT STARTED AROUND THE CORNER, BUT FELL BACK ABRUPTLY AND TURNED to his companions, his expression one of concern and surprise.

"What?" asked Entreri, who was growing more impatient and agitated with every step. Even as he finished the question, though, he and Dahlia both understood the drow's hesitance, for a wall of steamy fog rolled along the perpendicular corridor. The temperature in the area climbed dramatically, the air growing so humid that the greenish tendrils of the Hosttower above began to sweat and drip almost immediately.

"It is passable," Drizzt informed them.

"Then go," Entreri snapped back.

Drizzt continued to hold his position. He glanced around the corner again, and when he turned back, beads of sweat showed on his face.

"This tunnel continues to bend around the forge room," Drizzt replied. "Perhaps there would be an easier way in."

"Or a less obvious advance than the main corridor," Dahlia agreed.

Entreri started to argue, clearly wanting to be done with all of this, wanting to be done with everything, but when Drizzt held up his hand, the assassin went quiet, for he, too, had heard a distant rumble. On Drizzt's motion, they backtracked quickly the way they had come, taking up a mostly concealed position some twenty strides back.

The unmistakable sound of an approaching force grew around them, then rumbled down the corridor against the rolling steam. The first forms, ghostly in the fog, crossed the corridor. Even before a couple happened out into their side tunnel, in clear view, the three companions understood the composition of the force. These were Shadovar, making directly for the forge room.

"We could have gone in before them," Entreri whispered, his jaw clenched, the veins standing out on his forehead.

But both Drizzt and Dahlia, who knew the layout of the forge room, knew of the small archway and single tunnel leading to the primordial pit, understood the futility of that argument. Had they gone in, they would have had to flee immediately out another exit of the forge room, or would have surely found themselves trapped in the primordial chamber.

"We go in behind them, then," Entreri said.

"We would never make it to the archway," Dahlia replied, and though he didn't know the specifics of what she might be talking about, her point was clearly made.

"What, then?" he asked.

"We go past the steam corridor," Drizzt suggested. "Let us learn the layout of this entire region, and learn it well. We'll find our way in, but we can't rush in there behind the shade forces and hold any hope of getting to our goal, to say nothing of getting back out."

Even though that last part of the statement seemed to hold little persuasion to Entreri, Drizzt noted, the assassin didn't argue. If they went in there and were stopped by the multitude of shades, Entreri would find himself right back in the position of Barrabus the Gray, or worse.

They had to wait a long while for the Shadovar forces to pass by, then they moved quickly, crossing the steamy corridor and moving with all prudent speed.

Drizzt again took the lead, opening a wide distance between himself and his two companions. He dropped his hand into his belt pouch and quietly called out for Guenhwyvar again and again, hoping against hope that the Netherese forces had been foolish enough to bring her along, and that she would hear his call and appear to him.

He thought of the strange woman he had met, with her enticing offer.

Nay, not enticing, for in truth, Drizzt could not put a man, any man, even Artemis Entreri, back into slavery again, whatever his gain. He simply couldn't do it.

And in his heart, Drizzt knew that he wouldn't get Guenhwyvar back that way, anyway. The trickster would never have willingly given the magnificent panther to him. He could not bargain in good faith with the Netherese.

He thought of the shadow gate he had seen in the forest. His answer lay there, he believed. He would have to go to the Shadowfell when he was done with this ugly business, when Charon's Claw—and Artemis Entreri—was destroyed.

Flanked by Effron and Glorfathel, Herzgo Alegni glimpsed the forge room through a thick cloud of steam. Fires burned all around the place as the battle of the opposing elemental monsters raged.

"Destroy them," he instructed his spellcasters.

"Not easily done," said Effron.

"A slow process," Glorfathel agreed.

"Bah, but I'll be turnin' the tide for ye," said Ambergris from behind, and she pushed her way through the trio, even daring to shove past Alegni himself.

He looked at her curiously, too surprised to lash out, and more curiously still when he saw what the cleric held: a small jug of curious design. It seemed to be polished from one piece of wood, its thick neck offset from center, and stoppered with a large cork fastened to the decanter with a gold link chain. Circles and triangles of red and green ran around the circumference of the jug in a repeating, but hardly perfect, pattern, as if this item had been crafted by some village woman in a remote jungle.

Ambergris whispered something under her breath, talking to her magic item, it seemed, and she pulled out the cork with a loud popping sound. A few more words and a stream of water poured forth, splashing the floors before her.

"What is that?" Effron asked before Alegni could.

Glorfathel just laughed, having no definitive answer. "Always full of surprises is that one," he explained. "It is why Cavus Dun so quickly accepted her."

Ambergris continued to walk out from the doorway, her magical decanter spraying in wide sweeps before her. The others watching from just outside the room all gasped in unison as a large fire elemental rushed through the steam to meet her, reaching at her with flaming limbs.

The dwarf laughed at it. She had already fortified herself with resistance spells, and when the stream of water became a geyser, the weapon she carried proved effective. Ambergris staggered back a step just trying to control the powerful flow.

The elemental, too, staggered back, diminishing before their eyes as the geyser assailed its fiery core, cooling it, shrinking it.

The dwarf laughed all the louder.

"Where is the primordial?" Herzgo Alegni asked.

"Nearby, surely," said Glorfathel.

"Get me to it," Alegni ordered.

"Let's hope we're not too late," Effron said.

Herzgo Alegni closed his eyes and opened his mind, and heard again the whisper of Claw, of the sword that was still very much intact. "We're not," he stated with confidence.

Thanks to the magical sprinklers of the curious tendrils above, the remaining water elementals, and the dwarf with her perpetual decanter of water, the Shadovar secured the forge room in short order. They couldn't stop the occasional outbursts from the forges, or the appearance of fire beasts now and again, for they knew nothing of the sub-chamber that controlled the flow of primordial power.

They found the small corridor and the primordial pit, and soon enough, there stood Herzgo Alegni, Effron, and the trio from Cavus Dun. Like all who had entered this place, they lingered at the side of the pit, staring in awe at the swirling water and the rumbling of the godlike primordial from far below.

Other concerns did not allow them to linger, however, for they noted the second exit from the room, a small tunnel still glowing with streaks and puddles of red lava.

"Newly cut," Glorfathel remarked. "The work of the primordial, I would guess."

"What happened here?" Alegni asked. "Did the dark elves do this as they retreated?"

"Perhaps this is why they fled," said Effron. "They could not control this power."

"But did they take the sword with them?" Glorfathel asked, and no one had an answer.

"Set a perimeter around the room," Alegni ordered as he stared down this curious tunnel. It looked as if a ball of fire had just rolled through the stone, melting and disintegrating it as it went. "Secure the halls and corridors, and determine proper emissaries to send to find these unexpected dark elves. Let us determine their intent."

"Ye'd bargain with drows?" Ambergris asked skeptically.

"If they have Claw, they will return it for a price, likely," the warlord replied. "The drow don't want war with us."

"A hefty price," said the dwarf.

Alegni stared hard at her and for a moment almost gave in to the urge to strike the annoying dwarf. But he calmed and let it go. She was speaking the truth, likely.

"Cross that small bridge," Alegni told Afafrenfere. "Ensure that these are the only two exits from the chamber. I'll take this room as my own for now, and you four shall remain with me." He turned to Glorfathel and Effron. "Find other warlocks or sorcerers or some type of wizard who can help to secure the pit."

"Secure it how?" Glorfathel asked. "There is a beast below beyond all of our power, Lord Alegni."

"Secure its edge," the warlord explained. "I'll not have our enemies throw the sword over the side."

"We mustn't let them get near to the pit in the first place," the elf insisted. "I know of a few potentially helpful dweomers against such an attempt, but we cannot secure it as you would demand, certainly."

"Send scouts along this tunnel, then," Alegni replied. "And we'll make our camp right here, before the pit and the primordial. Let them come to us and let us be done with them."

He would take all precautions, but Herzgo Alegni truly doubted that his enemies would come to him in that place. They had joined with, or been taken by, these other drow. Likely the latter, for these dark elves had been in this place for some time, judging by the work Alegni and his minions had seen in their charge through the lower levels. The expertly crafted and repaired, and purposely dropped stairwell alone showed that Alegni and his force had stumbled upon a determined dark elf settlement.

Had this curious ranger, Drizzt, known about that, he wondered, and not for the first time? Had Drizzt led the other two here to find reinforcements?

He turned to the dwarf as he considered the pressing question, for she had insisted that could not be the case. She claimed to know of Drizzt, quite a bit of his history, actually, since he had settled in a dwarven citadel near to her own place of birth. Drizzt would not willingly fall in with others of his race, she had assured Alegni. He was a rogue, an outcast, and his head would be a greater trophy than Claw even, in the eyes of the Spider Queen's followers.

In that case, the dark elves, not Drizzt and his two companions, likely now had the blade, and likely had the three Alegni pursued, as well, either dead or wishing they were.

He hoped that was not the case, even if he could bargain to get back the sword and the three living prisoners. He wanted more than that. He wanted a fight.

He wanted to pay back the traitor Barrabus, and most of all, he wanted to defeat Dahlia yet again, to pull her into his grasp, battered and terrified.

Oh, that one he would pay back most dearly, he fantasized, and he looked at Effron as he did, crystallizing his hatred.

Drizzt, Dahlia, and Entreri moved quietly and cautiously, but with all considerable speed, for time was against them, they knew. The Shadovar force had entered the forge room, and so the shades controlled the small tunnel to the primordial chamber, and it was a force the three of them couldn't hope to fight their way through.

Perhaps the Menzoberranyr would return to battle the Shadovar, perhaps not.

To Drizzt, that point was almost moot in any case. They had fooled the dark elves for the time being, but it would not hold, he feared. And what might happen to him and his companions if those dark elves learned of his true identity?

To Drizzt's thinking, then, they would follow this corridor around the forge room and see if they might have a way to slip in and quickly be done with the sword. He didn't think it likely, for though he hadn't fully explored the region the last time he was there, he was fairly confident that there were no secret tunnels that he and the dwarves of Icewind Dale had missed.

What, then?

They would leave, and with all speed. Entreri would have to wait for his freedom from Charon's Claw. Perhaps they would travel to Waterdeep to find better guardians for the weapon. Perhaps they would learn of another way to be rid of it—maybe they would ride a merchant ship far off the Sword Coast and drop it deep into the cold ocean. Perhaps they would leave this place and return at a later date for a second try at the primordial—though, given the arrival of the drow in force, and now the advent of the Shadovar in Gauntlgrym, Drizzt didn't see how that might happen without an army marching beside them.

The ranger put it all out of his mind. He had to focus on the immediate situation if they hoped to survive.

That situation changed abruptly as Drizzt rounded a steamy corner to find an unexpected intersecting tunnel, one crossing both left and right. He stopped and looked both ways, trying to make sense of it, for this was no ordinary corridor, nor was it of any conventional construction, nor was it very old.

Dahlia and Entreri caught up to him, and both seemed equally at a loss as they stared into the red-veined tunnel, which seemed as if it had just been melted through the stone.

"Could it be the beast?" Dahlia asked.

"It's some mighty magic, and some fire," Entreri replied.

"A small side eruption?" Drizzt asked, for surely he noted lava among the darker stone. One orange pool of it glowed brightly not far away, and even as the three looked on, it cooled to black.

"We caught a bit of luck," Entreri said, and he started in to the right, which seemed the logical direction heading back toward the primordial.

Drizzt grabbed him by the shoulder almost immediately, though, and held him back. "The floor won't be consistent or safe. Let me lead. My sword will protect me if my foot breaks through a cooling crust and into the molten lava." He rolled Icingdeath in his hand and put its blade into the nearby lava, which cooled all the faster as the frost brand stole its heat energy.

"The other way," Dahlia whispered behind them, and both turned, and both figured that the elf had lost her direction sense in the dark tunnels.

But Dahlia wasn't talking about their course to the primordial chamber, she was warning them of movement in the other direction. Far down the tunnel there came a flash of light. It seemed as if the fiery creature digging the tunnel had swerved back to the other side to flicker into view.

Drizzt sheathed Twinkle, but held Icingdeath as he started off, quick-stepping all around to find the most solid footing for his following friends. More than once, his foot broke through thin crust and tapped into still-hot lava, but Icingdeath protected him and he quickly readjusted to mark out a path for his less-protected companions.

He feared that they were wasting too much time, and almost told his companions to go back to the intersection and wait for him to scout out the movement up ahead.

Almost.

He picked up his pace as the corridor swung a bit to the right, then slowed greatly when he came back to the left, and saw the tunneler, a fiery monstrosity that appeared as if some wizard had conjured a fire and earth elemental to the same spot, joining them as one melded monster. And there was the wizard, a drow, moving along right behind the beast.

Drizzt put an arrow to Taulmaril, unsure of how to proceed.

Dahlia and Entreri came up beside him.

"Go back the other way," Entreri whispered.

"Bregan D'aerthe?" Drizzt whispered back. Perhaps they had found a powerful ally, or at least someone who could better inform them of the path ahead of them.

Drizzt stepped out from the wall and gave a short whistle.

The drow ahead stopped and spun around, and Drizzt held up his hand and flashed the signal of alliance. But to his surprise, the wizard cried out and fell away, and waved frantically for his companion elemental to turn back and attack.

"Bregan D'aerthe!" Drizzt called out, but it hardly seemed to matter.

"Wonderful," Entreri remarked.

Drizzt growled against the cynicism and stepped out, drew back, and let a lightning arrow fly into the chest of the approaching monstrosity. The creature staggered just a bit, but then came on. Drizzt fired again and again, but he had no idea of whether his enchanted arrows were having much of an effect on this fiery stone beast.

"Run," Entreri said.

But Drizzt didn't. He kept up his line of arrows, and when he heard the wizard behind the beast beginning the chanting of a spell, he angled his bow and began skipping arrows off the side walls.

A line of fire appeared from behind the elemental, rushed right through the beast, and swept down at Drizzt and his companions.

"Run!" Entreri called more frantically from behind, and this time, Drizzt heeded the assassin—but not in the direction Entreri had intended. Icingdeath in hand even as he held his bow, trusting in the frost magic to protect him from the bulk of the fire and minimize the flames as they passed him by, for the sake of his companions, Drizzt charged. He got off one more arrow, aiming for the elemental's face, trying to blind it or distract it, then flung the bow and his quiver back toward Entreri and Dahlia. In the same motion, he drew out his second scimitar, and sped on even faster, closing the ground quickly and, at the last instant, cutting right to the wall and flattening out to shinny past the beast.

It swung out at him with a heavy and glowing limb, and Icingdeath slashed at it and bit at it hard—and not just with its fine diamond edge, but with its magic, its enchanted hatred of creatures of fire. The elemental roared, like boulders against boulders, and thrashed around as the powerful scimitar grabbed at its very life essence, and Drizzt had to resist the urge to charge in closer and strike again and again to bring the elemental down.

He went past it instead, still using the wall of fire to cover his movements, and burst free at the mage. He came through the end of the fire just strides from the drow, who shrieked in surprise and lifted his hands, thumbs touching, and sprayed forth a fan of fire.

This, too, Icingdeath minimized. Those fires stung Drizzt, but they did not truly hurt him, nor did they slow him, and he raced past and the mage ducked aside. He was too close to effectively stab or cut, but he punched out with his left, the pommel of Twinkle crunching into the drow wizard's face and staggering him backward. He fought hard to hold his balance as Drizzt fell back over him—and surely Drizzt could have finished him then, for the wizard clearly wasn't prepared for an enemy to so quickly circumvent his powerful pet.

Drizzt rushed in close, preventing any somatic spellcasting movements. Again the wizard flung a fan of fires at him—and Drizzt noted that the drow focused on a curious ring as he did—and again Drizzt's scimitar minimized the effect. He closed further and loosed a barrage of punches at the drow, driving his pommels all around the wizard's head and chest.

He had to be done with this quickly, he knew, and he attacked all the more furiously, expecting that monstrous elemental to come charging in from behind.

"Run!" Entreri said to Dahlia, and he grabbed her hard as she started off after Drizzt. "Run!"

"No!" she shouted, then both jumped as the bow and quiver bounced down in the diminishing line of fire before them.

"Grab it!" Dahlia ordered.

"I'm no archer!"

The elemental issued an earthquake roar and thrashed around, then charged at them.

"Grab it!" Dahlia yelled again, setting her long staff out before her. "Just shoot!"

Spitting curses, Entreri took up the bow, grabbed an arrow from the quiver, and let fly at the approaching monster. The arrow barely got away before Dahlia's magical staff swallowed it.

"What are you doing?" Entreri yelled at her.

"Just shoot!" she yelled back through chattering teeth.

He did, and again, and Kozah's Needle ate the bolt, and arcs of lightning magic danced all around the metallic staff, stinging Dahlia's hands as she stubbornly held on. She rushed forward and thrust the end of the staff against the charging fiery behemoth, and in a great flash of lightning, the monster was thrown back a step.

Another arrow almost hit the beast, but Dahlia's staff got it at the last instant. She struck again, a lesser blow, but one that stole the monster's momentum.

They worked in rhythm, Entreri putting arrows into the air and Dahlia's weapon absorbing them and redirecting the magic against the elemental with brutal, enhanced strikes. Shards of stone and bursts of flame accompanied each hit as the elf warrior chipped away at the elemental's magical form. Never did

Dahlia more need that extended reach, for she had to stay out of the sweeping radius of those explosive, rock and fire arms.

She had to be perfect in her dance and in her strikes.

But still the lethal behemoth came on, and Dahlia and Entreri had to give ground.

Drizzt had gained a great advantage with his desperate charge, catching the wizard by surprise, and he was experienced enough against spellcasters to understand that he needed to press that advantage through to a swift victory.

The mage flailed, trying to block, but the blows came too swiftly and from too many angles. One got through cleanly to crunch the mage's skull, and he staggered back against the wall, waving his hands out defensively before him.

And calling again on the ring, Drizzt recognized, and across came Icingdeath, cutting that hand in half, fingers flying. The mage howled and crumbled, and Drizzt spun and circle-kicked him hard in the side of the head, laying him low.

The ranger spun back the other way, just in time to see the flash and hear the report of thunder again as Dahlia struck the behemoth and Kozah's Needle released its lightning charge. He took a quick step but pulled up short, for there before him lay the severed piece of hand, four fingers intact, and a ruby band on one. Reflexively, the drow dropped and pulled off the ring, hardly thinking as he slipped it onto his own finger.

He felt strange. The ring sang to him as if in accord with his scimitar . . . but there was something more.

Drizzt staggered under the weight of that magical burden. He eyes blurred as if he was looking at the world suddenly through a haze of fire.

And in his mind, he heard the elemental's confusion, its anger, its desire to destroy and consume, and a sense of particular hatred . . . for him.

"Keep shooting!" Dahlia prompted, and Entreri did, one after another, each missile being eaten by the magical staff. She kept thrusting it forth; she had to, or the magical energy would throw her aside.

The staff ate an arrow, then a second as she jabbed at the beast.

But the beast turned and ran away.

The staff ate a third. Dahlia tried to call out for Entreri to stop, but the lightning energy had her jaw clenched so tightly, she couldn't speak.

The staff ate a fourth.

A fifth.

She had to slam it down and release the blast, but the beast was getting away. The beast was charging Drizzt!

Dahlia threw Kozah's Needle like a spear. It hit the elemental with a tremendous explosion, jolting the whole of the corridor with such power that it lifted Dahlia right into the air, to fall back down and stumble.

And the elemental swung back and charged, and hardly seemed hurt.

"Oh, by the gods," Entreri mumbled, thinking that he and Dahlia were surely doomed. He put up Taulmaril and pulled back for one last shot, one last desperate and angry act of defiance.

And he saw a form in the air behind the elemental: a leaping ranger, cape flying behind him, one scimitar grasped in both hands, up high over his head.

Drizzt slammed into the beast, plunging Icingdeath through its back, the magical, fire-hating blade diving deep into the creature's core being, the very magical energy that gave it form.

How it thrashed and swung around, Drizzt holding on desperately, legs flying wildly.

But he held on, and Icingdeath feasted.

The elemental spun and thrashed in frenzy.

And then it died and melted in on itself, a pile of smoking rock and lava in the middle of the corridor.

"Well, that was fun," Dahlia remarked as Drizzt pulled himself off the pile and staggered back a couple of steps.

CHAPTER

24

FAMILY REUNION

THE DROW WIZARD GROANED AND GROWLED, CLUTCHING THE STUMP OF HIS halved left hand.

"Where does it lead?" Drizzt asked him. The ranger crouched before the wizard, looking him in the eye. "Where does it lead?"

The wizard spat at him.

"Your life depends on this," Drizzt said. "Where does your tunnel lead? Where did you come from?"

Artemis Entreri pushed Drizzt aside and roughly grabbed the wizard by the hair, yanking his head back and putting a dagger to his throat.

"It goes to the primordial?" Entreri demanded in perfect Drow inflection.

"Leave it alone!" the drow wizard yelled at him.

Entreri smiled and looked back at his companions. "Take that as a yes," he said.

"What are we to do with . . . ?" Drizzt started to ask, but he stopped with a gasp as Artemis Entreri drove his dagger through the front of the drow's throat, angling up and into the mage's brain. The drow stiffened, legs popping straight out, and began to tremble.

Entreri yanked the blade out, wiped it on the wizard's robe, and stood up, turning to face the incredulous stare of Drizzt and the amused expression of Dahlia.

"You didn't think I would leave a drow wizard alive behind us, did you?" Entreri said to Drizzt with a snort, and he started past.

Drizzt stood there staring at the slain drow. Blood flowed heavily from the wound under his chin. His hands had fallen to his sides, giving Drizzt a clear view of the one he had cut in half. From a tactical level, Drizzt could understand Entreri's brutality, of course, but still, the callousness with which he had executed the mage had jarred Drizzt.

Would his old friends have treated a helpless prisoner in such a manner?

He wasn't sure, given the desperation of their current situation, but still, the casual brutality of Artemis Entreri had once again shocked him.

"Come on," Dahlia said, moving to Drizzt's side and taking his arm affectionately. "We haven't much time."

Drizzt looked at her, angrily at first. But that couldn't hold against Dahlia's responding look, one that reflected great understanding toward him—surprisingly so, Drizzt realized, since Dahlia hadn't been nearly as shocked as he when Entreri had struck.

"The world's an ugly place," she said quietly. "If we're not ugly enough to defeat it, we will be dead."

The cynical truth stung Drizzt profoundly, but Dahlia's insistent tug reminded him that they didn't really have the luxury of standing around and debating the issue. Drizzt retrieved his bow and quiver, and they caught up to Entreri just before the intersection. He crouched on one knee, staring across to the other tunnel, motioning them to hold still and get down.

As they crept up, Entreri slipped off to the left into the perpendicular tunnel, and Drizzt and Dahlia moved right. By the time they put their backs to the wall across that main corridor and right beside the one the wizard's elemental had burrowed, they understood the assassin's sudden caution, for they heard the approach of several Shadovar.

Drizzt looked across to Entreri, who motioned for him to hold his ground. With a nod, the assassin turned around and disappeared into the lava tunnel.

Drizzt eased an arrow onto his bowstring and listened intently. He heard a grunt followed by the sound of someone falling to the ground, followed by a short yelp of surprise and a quick scraping of metal on metal.

He spun around in front of the tunnel, leveling his bow. One shade lay on the ground, and a second joined him there as Entreri rolled his sword over the shade's and plunged it through the creature's throat.

The assassin fell back, giving Drizzt a clear view of the third of the group, who started sprinting back down the tunnel.

Heartseeker's missile caught him in the back and lifted him into a short flight before he crashed face-down on the still-smoking black stone.

Beside the drow ranger, Dahlia swallowed hard, and when Drizzt turned to regard her, he noted with surprise that she was staring at Artemis Entreri, and with obvious appreciation of the man's deadly skills. Drizzt, too, looked toward his old nemesis. A thought flashed in his mind to take out the man with a line of deadly arrows, but he dismissed it immediately, knowing it to be a desperate cry from the incessant sword.

But still . . .

"He's good," Dahlia muttered.

"I might not use that particular word," Drizzt whispered back.

"I'm glad he's on our side."

Drizzt wanted to argue, but he didn't.

"Quickly now," Entreri said to them, motioning them along.

"Why, Lord Alegni, here they come," Glorfathel remarked.

Alegni's smile widened, his eyes sparkled, and he clenched his fists eagerly. They hadn't begun to properly prepare for this, having just secured the forge room, but that didn't matter to the tiefling. He just wanted his revenge.

"Go," Effron called to the few others in the room. "To the forge and gather a great force! Send others through the tunnels to prevent any escape. Go!"

"On me way!" Ambergris replied, yanking back a pair of shades who had started for the tunnel to the forge room and rambling past them. Afafrenfere sprinted to catch up, but the dwarf slugged him in the gut as he started past her.

"Go protect the lord, ye dolt!" she scolded, and she disappeared into the small corridor.

"Which of them carries the sword?" Glorfathel asked.

"The drow had it in the forest," Effron answered. "Strapped across his back."

"I will stop that person, then," Glorfathel declared. "We cannot allow him to get anywhere near the primordial's pit."

"You have magic to counter such an attempt?" Alegni asked, his voice betraying his anxiety, for to lose that sword to the primordial would be disastrous indeed. He felt a sting of regret that he hadn't properly prepared his defenses, but the simple fact that they had managed to get between those who would destroy Claw and this fiery beast was no small thing.

The tiefling warlord surveyed his forces, and looked to the forge room tunnel. He had only a pair of magic-users, Glorfathel and Effron, and a handful of warriors. It should be enough, he figured, even without Claw to dominate Barrabus.

"Five ranks!" he ordered. He motioned to a pair of rogues and sent them away. "Find them and strike them down." He signaled for a pair of warriors to go off right behind them, then pointed to a second group of Shadovar warriors. "You four in next—meet them twenty strides inside the tunnel if they get past the first line." As that second line hustled into place, Alegni turned his gaze on the remaining two warriors. "Each of you with me, third rank!"

"Effron and you, monk"—he waved absently at Afafrenfere—"behind me, but within the chamber. Destroy any who manage to slip past and get near the chamber."

"And I in the back, near the rim," Glorfathel agreed, moving into position opposite the tunnel, before the primordial pit. "Though expect that I will not await their entrance and will strike at them from here."

"Do not kill the female elf," Effron said.

Alegni glanced at the twisted warlock, then nodded to Glorfathel to signal his agreement with that command. Indeed, he wanted Dahlia alive. Alegni reviewed the positioning, then moved toward the tunnel entrance flanked by the two shades.

He looked again at the corridor to the forge room, hoping the reinforcements to this room and those circling the approaching trio would be quick. He couldn't take any chances, nor would he tolerate another escape.

Out of the tunnel came Ambergris, huffing and puffing, and nodding Alegni's way as if to signal that reinforcements were close behind.

Artemis Entreri led the way. The corridor was mostly cooled, the floor solid, but enough glowing lava along the walls and floors remained to provide ample light.

So the assassin moved stealthily, in perfect silence, shifting from shadow to shadow. Still, even with all of his considerable skill, the shade rogues were no novices and it was good fortune alone that allowed Entreri to see them before they noticed him. He went flat against the wall in an advantageous spot, and held his breath.

As they neared, he noticed other forms coming along as well.

Entreri clenched his jaw tightly. He was so close! But the way was blocked. He could smell his freedom in the brine and smoke of the distant chamber, yet he could not get there.

"No!" he growled as he leaped from the wall, sword leading, dagger slashing as he turned past the first shade.

The first fell. The second managed to shrug enough so that the dagger cut at her shoulder and not her throat, as Entreri had intended. She fell away with a cry and broke off into a run back the way she had come.

"Come on!" Entreri called to his companions, and he started after her, then fell back with a cry of surprise of his own as a lightning missile streaked past him, taking the shade rogue in the back and laying her low.

On came the shade warriors, but on came Dahlia and Drizzt in support.

Another arrow flew off . . . and disappeared.

"Will you stop doing that!" Drizzt scolded, but Dahlia laughed at him and sprinted on, right past Entreri and into the pair of enemies. She led with a stab of her staff, into the ceiling just before the enemies, and the shocking burst of lightning halted them and blinded them momentarily—just long enough so that when they came out of the blindness, they were met by a pair of whipping and spinning flails, a fierce barrage that had them back on their heels before they could begin to formulate any coordinated movements.

And so they were still on their heels when Dahlia's companions rushed past her to engage them. These two could not have matched Drizzt Do'Urden and Artemis Entreri on even turns, but now, caught so abruptly, they were quickly doomed.

A scimitar stabbed straight out, driving the one before Drizzt back. The drow's second blade went across at the other, distracting him as Drizzt cut across to confront him.

Entreri rolled behind the drow and sprang forward, and the first shade, busy trying to gather some understanding of the darting ranger, never saw the sword coming.

Drizzt turned his blades over and over before him, driving back the remaining shade, keeping the poor fool completely focused in a desperate attempt to block the rolling barrage.

So when Entreri rushed past on his flank, that shade was helpless against the dagger thrust. That alone would have proven a mortal wound, but Dahlia, close behind Entreri, only sped the process with a tremendous pair of heavy flail swings, cracking his skull.

He fell into the wall and slumped, and Drizzt, too, rushed past.

"Many more!" Dahlia cried, spotting the next four in line.

"Turn back!" Drizzt said, but Entreri lowered his head and ran on, determined to be done with this wicked business.

Dahlia hesitated, thinking to turn, but only until she looked past the next line of shades, to see the familiar hulking tiefling coming behind them.

By the time Entreri had engaged, she was right there beside him.

Determined to be done with this wicked business.

And so was Drizzt, for he would not abandon his companions. As he joined them in their line of attack, he saw the others behind, and still more in the steamy chamber beyond that.

"So be it," he said aloud.

Ambergris ran across the floor toward Glorfathel. The elf wizard shifted all around, head moving as if he was a hunting bird waiting for a mouse to appear among the many cracks in a woodpile.

"Whatd'ye know?" the dwarf asked, sliding into place beside the wizard. Ambergris looked to the tunnel as she did this, and could understand easily enough why Glorfathel was having so much trouble picking out a clear shot. Just before them, but still in the room, Effron similarly bobbed, every now and again launching some black bolt into the tumult of the darker corridor. Beside him, Afafrenfere danced around nervously, air-boxing and glancing back at Ambergris, nodding eagerly and rather stupidly.

Ambergris sighed.

"The narrower corridor aids our enemy," Glorfathel said. "We cannot flank them or overwhelm them."

"And yerself can't find a clear lightning line," the dwarf said.

Glorfathel didn't seem to be listening to her at that moment, though, his face brightening.

"The drow has the sword," he said, and he stopped bobbing, and stopped blinking.

"Aye, we were knowin' that," the dwarf replied.

Again Glorfathel didn't seem to hear her. He seemed locked in his focus, pinpointing Drizzt, holding perfectly still as he waited for the drow to show himself more fully. So much like a hunting animal did Glorfathel seem that Ambergris almost expected him to start tamping his feet as if readying to spring.

He brought one hand out before him, lining up his angle, and rolled his fingers to reveal a small metal bar. Smiling, eyes glittering in the glow of the room, Glorfathel started casting.

He chanted slowly, softly, and his voice began to rise in volume, his words coming faster and more forcefully as he rose to a towering crescendo.

Ambergris grabbed him by the arm. "Hey, wizard . . ."

Glorfathel nearly choked on his words. He pulled away roughly, staring incredulously at the stupidly grinning dwarf. He went right back to focus on the hallway, arm and magical component out before him. He seemed quite flustered and quite intent all at once, obviously trying to find his target and his composure before he lost the moment.

"Hey, wizard," Ambergris said again, just as Glorfathel settled once more.

Glorfathel gasped angrily and snapped his gaze over her.

"Ye got a spell o' levitation for yerself or meself?" the dwarf asked.

Glorfathel stared at her as if she had lost her mind, then turned back to the situation before him and as he began moving his arms into spellcasting position again, he answered emphatically, "No!"

He started chanting for his lightning bolts once more, and hardly caught the significance when Ambergris quietly replied, "Good."

Glorfathel did feel the dwarf's strong hand slap hard against his back, though, and felt it more keenly as the dwarf's other hand slapped up between his legs to grab him by the crotch.

He managed to say, "What?" but that was all, as Ambergris lifted him over her head and pitched him back over her shoulder and over the ledge, into the primordial pit.

Not even bothering to turn around and admire her handiwork, the dwarf fell right into her own spellcasting, waggling her fingers.

Before her, Afafrenfere stared blankly, for he had seen the throw, and apparently he had not yet figured out that he was the target of the dwarf's coming dweomer.

The four shades standing before them were not novices to battle, and had fought and trained together for a long, long time. Drizzt knew that almost immediately. The shades' coordination of movements was too precise to indicate anything less.

They stood four across in the tight tunnel, and that alone showed a level of trust and familiarity, for their movements and efforts had to be straightforward, or properly angled outward on a diagonal—and not a block or thrust of theirs could come as a surprise to the others in line, else risking a catastrophic entanglement.

With Dahlia next to him on his left and Entreri beyond her, the three companions fought ferociously, going for the fast kill. Time was not their ally.

Drizzt set his scimitars to rolling again and rushed forward, trying to break the line. But the shade to his opponent's right thrust out to intercept.

Dahlia moved perfectly to intercept that thrust, her spinning flail cracking at the blade.

But the shade retracted and came ahead again, and Dahlia had to fend a similar attack as Drizzt, but from the third shade in line.

Entreri slapped that thrust away, freeing up Dahlia, but then he faced an attack from the far end, and Dahlia from the next, and Drizzt, again, from the second.

The shade line held.

"You have failed, Barrabus," Herzgo Alegni said from behind the fight. "And you will be punished."

Dahlia, not Entreri, reacted fiercely, driving forward to get at the most-hated tiefling.

She was driven back before she ever started, and only fast reactions by Drizzt and Entreri at her sides prevented her from taking multiple hits from those shades flanking her intended victim.

In the effort, Entreri got cut across his right forearm by the fourth shade, the one holding the end of the line on his side.

Behind the four, Herzgo Alegni laughed.

"Faster, faster," Drizzt prompted his friends, and all three pressed ahead, blades stabbing wildly, scimitars rolling, flails spinning.

The four shades responded with a barricade of parrying swords.

One flicked a dagger out suddenly, throwing for Dahlia.

Entreri picked it off with a slight turn of his sword.

A dagger came at him, as well, but Dahlia's flail batted it aside.

One came for Drizzt, then a second, but his scimitars took them from the air cleanly, and he hardly slowed his rolling barrage of blows.

Artemis Entreri flicked his own dagger, feigning a throw at the shade to his right, but actually spinning it at a backward arc.

In came swords, left, right, and center, to block, and the assassin's suddenly free hand went to his belt buckle, brought forth the knife, and launched it at a lower angle in one fluid movement.

It disappeared into a tangle of swords and flails, but the grunt of the targeted shade signaled a hit.

Entreri spun a complete circuit—Dahlia reflexively sent a flail snapping across to protect him as he turned—and when Entreri came around, he held sword and dagger once more, for he caught the fake throw behind him perfectly.

The shade before Dahlia, Entreri's buckle knife deep in his gut, could not maintain the pace, and the elf pounced, sending a straightforward barrage of spinning poles at him.

His companions left and right defeated that attack, but Dahlia side-stepped to the right as she worked the weapons.

And Drizzt rolled behind her to take her place as she took his, and Icingdeath flashed ahead past those defenders still trailing Dahlia.

The shade carrying Entreri's dagger took the stab in the chest and fell away.

But another was there immediately, thrust forward by Herzgo Alegni, who continued to grin.

"Well done!" He mocked them with a wicked laugh.

Drizzt knew that Alegni's confidence was justified. They had scored a minor gain and no more. The shades fought defensively, and in the tight tunnel, they three could not begin to break through in time.

In time . . . Alegni's confident grin told them that more Shadovar would soon arrive, before them and probably behind.

"Fight hard, Dahlia!" Entreri cried, and his curious reference to her only clued Drizzt in to his meaning.

The drow went forward with a double thrust, but reversed almost immediately and threw himself backward into a roll, and the instant he vacated his spot, Entreri and Dahlia both shifted in half a step to fill the gap.

Drizzt came up from his roll with Taulmaril in hand.

"Center!" he called, and the two fell apart, and the arrow streaked through.

A shade warrior slapped his sword across desperately and managed to deflect the lightning arrow, but only changed its angle so that instead of catching him in the chest, it hit him in the face, and he, too, flew away.

The other shade flanking Alegni started to fill the void, but in came the tiefling warlord instead, now roaring in anger and with a huge broadsword flashing left and right.

"Kill them!" he ordered, and he led the assault, striking mightily and often.

Entreri and Dahlia couldn't begin to counter the sheer power of those strikes with three other shades pressing in around the mighty Alegni.

Drizzt let fly again, the arrow streaking at Alegni, but Dahlia's flail ate it before it got near. He let fly again immediately, but she took that one, too!

The drow couldn't tell whether she meant to steal the arrows with her magical staff or whether her interceptions were merely the result of the furious flurry she needed to throw forth to try to slow the warlord and his minions.

To try futilely, Drizzt realized, for the four shades pressed ahead and over-whelmed Entreri and Dahlia, driving them back.

Drizzt managed one last shot, which Dahlia again stole, before he had to take up his scimitars again and leap into the fray, and he did so just in time as Dahlia stumbled backward and cried out in pain, nearly caught by Herzgo Alegni's sword slash, and struck instead by a line of searing black magic.

She turned as Drizzt stepped by to take her place, and he stayed near the center of the corridor, expecting her to flank him again on his right.

But she didn't.

Grunting in pain, she turned and ran away.

Like Glorfathel behind him, Effron tried to find an angle of attack with his devastating magic. So focused was he that he didn't realize that the sorcerer behind him had been thrown into the pit, the plummeting elf's screams drowned by the swirling thunder of the water elementals.

Nor did Effron notice Afafrenfere beside him, turning around and gaping incredulously at the traitorous dwarf.

The twisted warlock did see a shade fall away in the tunnel before him.

He did see a flash of lightning and a second fall, and saw Herzgo Alegni take up the fight.

No help had yet appeared, however, and strangely so! Effron released a spell, aiming just to the left of the warlord. He lost sight of the bolt, but his eyes sparkled when he heard a cry of pain, the voice of an elf female.

But then his eyes became heavy suddenly, and his limbs slowed and he felt as if he was underwater, then under something heavier, thicker than water . . .

He could barely move. His mind dulled as his limbs seemed to lock and freeze in place.

He fought back with all of his willpower. He managed to turn his head enough to see Afafrenfere, standing perfectly still, not moving, not even blinking.

Effron fought through the dweomer and spun around to see Ambergris the dwarf standing there, hands on hips, with Glorfathel nowhere to be seen.

"Ah, ye fool," the dwarf said. "Ye should o' stood still."

Effron's mind spun as he tried to sort it out, but one thing seemed crystal clear to him: The dwarf had cast a spell of holding over him and Afafrenfere.

Ambergris laughed, hoisted her great mace in both hands, and charged at him.

"Alegni!" Effron cried desperately, and he became a wraith and dived into the stone just an eye-blink before the sweeping mace of Ambergris.

Alegni heard the shout and it stole his momentum. He faded back from the fight just a bit and managed to look back into the primordial chamber, hoping that Effron's cry signaled the arrival of the reinforcements.

Where were they?

And worse, what was he looking at? He saw the dwarf rush off out of view to his right, mace in hand—had enemies come in behind them? Had the dark elves arrived?

The warlord swallowed hard at that awful thought and shoved the remaining shade up before him to join the other three in their defensive line. Alegni turned back as he did, to see Dahlia in full retreat.

Had his forces swung around to block that end of the tunnel, he wondered and hoped?

Were his forces detained in the forge room, battling the drow?

"Kill them!" he ordered the four shades before him, and he fell back, cautiously but quickly, trying to make sense of a situation that suddenly seemed to be fast deteriorating.

With Herzgo Alegni dropping back from the fight, Drizzt and Entreri soon came up to even footing against the four before them, and while they couldn't make much headway in the narrow tunnel, neither could the shades gain any advantages against the two supremely skilled warriors.

"Go!" Drizzt bade Entreri. "Run with Dahlia!"

"To what end, you noble fool?" Entreri asked, his question coming forth in choppy inflection as he parried a sword thrust with his own sword, then caught a second attack with his dagger and deftly turned it aside. "You've got the sword!"

Drizzt growled and batted aside a well-coordinated attack from the two before him.

"You go," Entreri yelled at him. "Better for me to die than to be caught again by that wretched blade!"

But Drizzt was thinking that if Entreri did run off, he could hold back these four for a few moments, then sprint in pursuit, his anklets giving him the ground he needed to be away. "Go!" he shouted back at Entreri, even as the assassin shouted the same to him.

And both of their cries got cut short by the screech of a giant bird, coming in fast behind them!

Both dropped low and drove forward, even going to their knees as they forced down the attention and the blades of their opponents.

Dahlia the Crow soared over them and bashed into and through the shade line, scattering the four, knocking two to the ground in the process.

"Oh, good girl," Drizzt said, leaping back to his feet beside Entreri, for now they had the advantage, all integrity of the defensive line before them broken.

Perhaps momentarily, but momentarily was all that Drizzt Do'Urden and Artemis Entreri fighting in concert would ever need.

Herzgo Alegni widened his eyes in shock as he saw Effron come up out of the floor far to the side, and saw the Cavus Dun dwarf charging at the warlock, mace in hand.

"Treachery," the warlord breathed as he began to sort it out. The monk still had not moved, obviously held by some magical spell. And Glorfathel was nowhere to be seen.

And this dwarf attacked Effron.

Alegni dived aside and to the ground, catching a sudden and overwhelming movement out of the corner of his eye. He got clipped by a clawing talon, and used it to enhance his roll and bring him back to his feet. He could only watch in shock as that giant bird—Dahlia, he knew—dived out of sight, over the ledge and down into the mist.

Where were the reinforcements?

Alegni thought of the dwarf running for the corridor to fetch them.

And then he understood. This one's treachery had been complete.

Alegni winced as Effron launched a spell at the dwarf, but one that met with magical defenses and hardly slowed her charge. Again at the last moment, Effron slipped into a crack in the floor.

But the dwarf skidded to a stop, laughing, so confident. "Ye canno' get away like that for long, ye little sneaker!" she proclaimed, and truly she seemed to be enjoying herself.

The warlord spun back to the tunnel, where four defending shades had become two, and where the superb skill and coordination of Barrabus the Gray and this drow ranger would soon win out.

And no reinforcements would be coming.

"Damn you," he whispered at Ambergris, at Barrabus, at Dahlia, at them all, for he had lost again. He yelled out to Effron, who was coming back to his three-dimensional form far to the other side of the chamber, back near the corridor to the forge room, "Effron, be gone! To the Shadowfell! Get away!"

He turned back to the tunnel and saw the last of his shade warriors go down before a cut of Barrabus's deadly sword, saw the drow ranger already coming for him.

Bitterly, Herzgo Alegni had to accept the truth: His side had failed.

"Be gone, Effron!" he called again, and he began to shadowstep, thinking of all the curses he would scream against Draygo Quick and the treacherous Cavus Dun before the Netherese Council.

The world began to fade into shadow.

But an image came to him, then, and it jarred him indeed. Herzgo Alegni saw his beloved red-bladed sword spinning down into the maw of the primordial, to be eaten by the fiery beast.

The sword cried out in his mind, begging him to fight on, promising him that it would help him, that it could control Barrabus.

Promising Herzgo Alegni that he and Claw would win.

The tiefling warlord ended his dimensional step and came back to Toril fully, the shadows around him dissipated.

Drizzt the ranger stood barely ten strides away, holding Claw out before him. This dangerous enemy reached out at Herzgo Alegni through the telepathic power of that sword, promising him, coaxing him, coercing him.

The crow swooped in.

The huge bird rolled over in mid-air and became an elf female, flying down at the distracted Alegni's back from on high, tingling with arcing bolts of pent-up lightning magic, her face locked in a murderous expression.

"Father!" Effron screamed, seeing it all before him, seeing her drop upon the unsuspecting tiefling from behind, her muscles snapping in perfect coordination and timing to lead with a tremendous chop of her magical staff.

Herzgo Alegni glanced at Effron, his twisted son, his expression revealing a deep lament.

The explosion of Dahlia's staff, the release of lightning, the momentum of her wild charge as she crashed down upon him, sent horn and bone and smoking hair and flesh flying aside and drove the mighty tiefling to his knees.

"Father!" Effron cried again, tears streaming from his strange eyes, red and blue.

"Get over here, ye little rat!" Ambergris yelled at him, and the ferocious dwarf closed furiously, mace ready to split his skull.

CHAPTER 25

IDIOCY OR HOPE?

"WHY DRIZZT, HOW VERY CLEVER AND IMMORAL OF YOU," ARTEMIS ENTRERI said, walking up beside the drow, who stood very still with Claw held vertically before him, locked in telepathic combat with the dangerous sentient sword.

"I do believe there's hope for you," Entreri added.

Those words, from that man, reached right through the drow's telepathic connection to stab Drizzt in his soul. In an instinctive moment of anger and denial, Drizzt gave in to the demands of the sword then, sending a shot of pain at Entreri.

The instant the man began to lurch, however, the drow fought back against the vile and torturous impulses of the evil sword.

Entreri turned on him hatefully, eyes threatening retribution, and Claw warned Drizzt to press the attack, to lay this dangerous enemy low.

But Drizzt growled and slid the sword away, and he continued to growl in protest as he stared at Entreri.

Entreri wanted to leap at him—he recognized that clearly enough on the angry assassin's face. But Drizzt didn't draw his weapons.

A cry from the other direction, beyond the assassin, broke the moment of tension.

It was Dahlia's cry. After crashing into Alegni and driving him to his knees, she had bounced violently and rolled away, but any injuries or pain from the punishing descent obviously mattered not at all to her, for she went right back at the warlord, who seemed already dead, breaking her staff into flails and launching a tirade, a barrage, upon Alegni. Her spinning poles crashed against his head and face repeatedly, viciously, the woman spitting curses at him with every blow, issuing words and feral sounds that seemed to come from a place far removed from her consciousness.

Artemis Entreri's sudden expression revealed to Drizzt that he understood that place and those sounds, and the drow had to admit that such recognition from Entreri stung him.

329

The assassin spun away from Drizzt and charged into the room, falling over Dahlia, hugging her arms in close to her sides as he dragged her away—and even then, in her thrashing, she managed to lift her foot and kick the tiefling warlord in what was left of his face.

Drizzt moved to the edge of the chamber and tried to sort out the curious sights before him. Alegni was dead, of that there could be no doubt. He knelt upright, but only because in the barrage of blows left and right, he simply hadn't fallen over. His head had been mashed to pulp, there was no life showing in his remaining eye, just the dull haze of death.

Entreri continued to drag Dahlia aside, to Drizzt's left. Beyond them, a familiar female dwarf rushed about, laughing crazily and beating at the stone floor with a large mace. She rushed past another shade, one Drizzt recognized from an earlier fight in the forest. This one just stood perfectly still, magically immobilized.

And another shade, the twisted warlock, appeared not far from Drizzt. The drow grabbed for his scimitars, but the broken tiefling paid him no heed and staggered to fall over Alegni in a desperate hug as he screamed, "Father!"

At the sound of that, Dahlia gave a sudden cry, and Drizzt watched her melt into Entreri's arms, as if all the strength had just been yanked out from within her. She just went limp, shaking and crying and gasping for breath.

The suddenness of that moment took Drizzt's breath away, as if a gigantic thunderclap had just stunned them all. Even the crazed dwarf skidded to a stop and simply stared.

"Curse you!" the twisted warlock shouted at Dahlia. "Murderess! Damn you and curse you! Once you tried to kill me and now you killed him!"

If his every word had instead been a punch into Dahlia's face, she would not have been more staggered or wounded. Drizzt wanted to leap over and silence this broken tiefling forever, but something held him back, some understanding that there was so much more to this story that he did not know.

"I will find you, Mother," the twisted warlock said, and Drizzt, too, felt as if he had just been slugged. "Oh, I will," the shade promised, and he began to fade, stepping back to the Shadowfell.

Entreri hugged Dahlia closer.

"Ye've got no' much time," the dwarf said then, addressing Drizzt. She lowered her mace and paced toward the drow. "I put a spell o' silence in that hall," she explained, pointing to the corridor to the forge room, "but they'll be comin' along anyway, don't ye doubt."

"Who are you?" Drizzt demanded as he tried to sort it out, and indeed, there flickered some recognition. "You were in Neverwinter . . ." He recalled this grinning dwarf indeed, though her skin hadn't been this particular shade of gray, from the inn where he, Entreri, and Dahlia recovered from their wounds with help from the clerics, including this very dwarf. Drizzt looked past her to the immobilized shade, her companion now, and her companion before, in the forest fight.

"You were there," he accused.

"Aye, Amber," the dwarf happily replied. "Castin' me spells to fix yer wounds."

"In the forest," Drizzt clarified. "In a fight."

The dwarf sobered immediately.

"Ah, so ye seen me then, did ye."

Drizzt's hands went to his blades.

"Aye, and I saved yer life, drow, when ye was hangin' upside down on the side o' the hill. Was meself that pushed that one"—she nodded toward the immobilized human shade—"aside when he wanted to leap upon ye for killin' his dearest."

"As I asked, who are you?"

"Amber Gristle O'Maul, o' the Adbar O'Mauls, as I told ye in the town," the dwarf said with a bow. "Ambergris to me friends. When I heared in the Shadowfell that ye was the target o' this hunt, I figured any good dwarf'd owe King Bruenor to see what good I might be doing."

"You're a shade," Entreri said from the side, where he still held the sobbing Dahlia. He had finally managed to get her back to her feet, at least.

"Aye, a bit, and right back to yerself, gray one." She looked to Drizzt. "I'll be tellin' ye all about it if we're gettin' out o' here, and I be thinking that we should be gettin' out o' here."

The other shade stirred a bit, the magical hold lessening its grip.

"What of him?" Drizzt asked as the dwarf walked up to stand right before the dark man.

"Brother Afafrenfere," Ambergris said to Drizzt, and she focused on the shade fully. "I know ye're hearin' me now, me monk friend," she said, nudging Drizzt aside. "We're setting out through that burned tunnel. Yerself's going through one hole or th'other." As she said that, she pointed back over her shoulder at the primordial pit. "No other choices for ye."

Ambergris looked around him to Drizzt and offered an exaggerated wink. "He's a good enough sort," she explained. "And not so dumb that he'd be goin' against us. Come on, then."

She grabbed the monk and began sliding him along toward the room's exit.

Drizzt turned back to his companions, just in time to see Artemis Entreri press close to Dahlia and kiss her intensely, passionately. He spun away to face Drizzt, smiling widely.

"You always wanted to kill me, Drizzt Do'Urden," Entreri said, and he nodded toward the pit. "This is your chance."

Drizzt eyed Entreri every step as he walked near to the primordial pit. He quickly pulled the sword off his back and tossed it to the stone nearer the pit, for he didn't want to hold it long enough to have to battle its intrusions again. He was on edge after witnessing that kiss, after all, and he feared that Charon's Claw might convince him to take a more conventional route to be rid of Artemis Entreri.

"No!" Dahlia cried frantically.

"Yes," Entreri answered.

Drizzt stared at his lover, but no stabs of jealousy assailed him. He was glad of that realization, glad of the confirmation that his insecurity had been an exploitation of the sword—at least, for the most part. Many other things assailed him at that moment. Dahlia had a child? This twisted tiefling was her offspring? He considered her visceral hatred of Herzgo Alegni then, and so much came clear to him.

He had to run to her, to hug her and comfort her, but he found that he could not. They hadn't the time! Too much was yet to do, and quickly, if they ever hoped to be away from this place alive.

He and Dahlia, at least, he thought, as he looked at Entreri.

"It's all right," Entreri said to the elf woman gently, and he grasped her by the shoulders and looked into her eyes. "It's time." He turned to Drizzt and started walking for the pit. "Long past time."

"You do it," Drizzt said to him, and the drow stepped back from the sword.

Entreri looked at it, then back at Drizzt. "That was cruel."

Drizzt swallowed hard, unable to deny the charge. He knew that Entreri could not approach the sword and throw it in, or even kick it in. If he neared the red-bladed sword, Charon's Claw would likely enthrall him again.

"You owe me nothing," Entreri admitted. "I cannot ask this as a friend. Mutual respect, then? Or might I simply appeal to your sense of honor, and remind you that the world would be a far better place without the likes of me in it?" He gave a helpless little laugh, but sobered quickly, raised his empty hands, and begged, "Please."

"Often have I entertained the thoughts of a redeemed Artemis Entreri," Drizzt admitted. "A man of your skills could contribute—"

"Spare me your idiocy," Entreri said, jolting Drizzt.

So be it.

Drizzt moved to kick the sword, but bent low and picked it up again. Immediately, Claw's powers assaulted him. He could feel the swirl of desperation, of rage, of threats and tantalizing promises mingled together in a confused and confusing jumble.

"Idiocy?" Drizzt echoed with a shrug. "Hardly. You never understood it, Artemis Entreri. Alas! Idiocy, you say, but hope is never that."

With a resigned shrug, Drizzt tossed the sword over the rim.

"I have forever envied you, Drizzt Do'Urden," Entreri cried out quickly, knowing that he had but a heartbeat left. "Envied you, and not for your skill with your blades!"

Artemis Entreri closed his eyes and leaned his head back, accepting the cool blackness, the sweet release, of death.

CHAPTER
26

EXPECTATIONS

E FFRON STAGGERED AROUND THE SHADOWFELL, TEARS CLOUDING HIS VISION. He had been caught quite off guard by his reaction to the fall of Herzgo Alegni, his father, for he had profoundly hated the tiefling. Never in his life had he measured up to Alegni's expectations, not from the moment of his rescue at the base of a wind-blown cliff to the moment of Herzgo Alegni's crushing death.

Herzgo Alegni prized strength of arm, and his broken son hardly fit that description. And indeed, the warlord had made his feelings quite clear to Effron. How many times had Effron entertained the fantasy of killing the brutish tiefling?

Yet, now that Alegni had been killed, right before him, the twisted warlock could experience nothing but grief and the most profound pain.

And the most profound hatred.

Dahlia had done this. The elf who had borne him, the witch who had cast him from the cliff, had done this.

Gradually the shaken warlock made his way to Draygo Quick, who seemed unsurprised to see him.

"The sword?" the Netherese lord asked immediately.

"Herzgo Alegni is dead," Effron said, and the pain of speaking the words had him blubbering again, his legs going weak beneath him so he had to put his hand to the wall to stop himself from toppling over.

"The sword?" Draygo Quick demanded again.

"Doomed," Effron whispered. "Destroyed, certainly, for they gained the primordial chamber."

"They? Dahlia and her companions?"

The twisted warlock nodded.

"And they killed Lord Alegni?"

Effron just stared at him.

"Impressive," the withered old lord whispered. "Twice now he faced them, and twice he lost. Few who knew Herzgo Alegni would have wagered on such an outcome."

Effron winced with every callous word.

Draygo Quick grinned at him with yellow teeth. "Callous, yes," he admitted, reading Effron's expression. "Forgive me, broken one."

"I will kill her for this," Effron vowed.

"Dahlia?"

"Dahlia, and any who stand beside her. You must afford me an army, that I . . ."

"No."

Effron stared at him as if he had been slapped. "Herzgo Alegni must be avenged!"

The old warlock shook his head.

"The sword!" Effron protested.

"We'll have our diviners seek its magical call. If it is destroyed, as you believe, then so be it. Better that than to have it fall into the hands of an enemy once more."

"I must avenge him!"

"What you plan to do is of no concern to me," Draygo Quick retorted sharply. "I will grant you that much, and nothing more. If you wish to hunt down Dahlia and her companions, then hunt."

"I will need support."

"More than you will ever understand."

"Grant me . . ." Effron started to say, but Draygo Quick cut him short.

"Then hire some. You have friends with Cavus Dun, do you not? If you believe that I will grant you more forces after these abject and expensive failures, then you are a fool."

"Cavus Dun!" Effron cried as if he had hit on something. "They betrayed us!"

Draygo Quick looked at him curiously. "Do tell."

"The wizard Glorfathel fled the fight," Effron explained. "And that filthy dwarf turned on me. She cast a spell of holding, but I avoided it. Alas, the monk did not—and the dwarf chased me around, preventing me from helping Lord Alegni in his desperate fight. Swinging her mace and laughing all the while! Were I less skilled and clever . . ."

Draygo Quick waved a wrinkled hand in the air to silence the young warlock. "Interesting," he muttered.

"I shall demand recompense!" Effron proclaimed. "Cavus Dun will repay me."

"Your attitude will surely get you cut into little pieces," said the old warlock. "If you consider that to be repayment, then truly you are an easy buy."

"We must go to them!" Effron demanded.

"We?"

"You cannot allow this to stand! The Shifter failed me, and now the treachery of the hirelings . . ."

"Easy, young one," Draygo Quick said. "I will speak with the Grandfather of Cavus Dun to learn what I may. You avoid them. Trust my judgment on this."

The way he finished the response told Effron to hold silent, and so he did, staring obediently at the great warlock, awaiting instructions.

"You should rethink your course."

"I will kill her," Effron said.

"Family matters," Draygo said with a sigh. "Ah, by the gods. Well enough, then, young fool, I grant you my leave. Go as you will."

"I will have the panther."

"You will not!"

There was no bargain to be found in that tone, Effron knew.

"Will you not help me?" the twisted warlock begged.

"On this fool's errand? Surely not. Your father failed by underestimating this band you hunt, and failed again in his attempt to right his wrong. He lost Charon's Claw, and that is no small thing. Better that he died trying to recover the blade than return without it. That is the way of the world."

His casual attitude surprised Effron, until the young tiefling realized that Alegni's failure was just that: Alegni's failure. It could not reflect on Draygo Quick any longer, and surely the old wretch was somewhat relieved to be rid of the troublesome Herzgo Alegni.

"Go and find her, then," Draygo Quick said. "You may use my crystal ball if it will guide you to Toril properly. I understand the formidability of your enemies and will not expect your return."

"I must."

Draygo Quick waved him away. "I will hear no more of this," the old wretch said, his tone becoming very sharp suddenly. He chortled and laughed at Effron. "Idiot boy, I only kept you alive out of respect for your father. Now that he is no more, I am done with you. Be gone, then. Go and hunt her, young fool, that you might see your father again so soon, in the darker lands."

He waved Effron away.

Effron staggered out of the room, heading for his own chamber, tears welling in his strange eyes once more as he tried to deny the stinging words of merciless Draygo Quick. He replaced that wound with anger, stopped, and turned around, making for the warlock's room of scrying instead.

"That was harsh, Master Quick, even by your standards," said Parise Ulfbinder, a warlock and peer of Draygo Quick. Parise, too, was a Netherese lord of great repute, and an old friend of Draygo's, though Draygo Quick had not seen him in person in a long while, the two preferring to correspond through their respective scrying devices. The mere fact that Parise had come to Draygo's tower in person had tipped the old warlock off to the importance of the visit. He entered from a concealed door even as Effron departed.

"Are they recalled?"

"Indeed," said Parise. "We have opened the gates and most of our forces are safely back within the Shadowfell."

"You heard what Effron said of the Cavus Dun trio?"

"Glorfathel, Ambergris, and Afafrenfere are not to be found among the returned," the other warlock confirmed, though his tone revealed that he really didn't care about that particular curiosity. "It is possible that Effron speaks the truth."

Draygo Quick looked to the door where Effron had departed and nodded, his expression one of great lament. Despite his parting words, Draygo had come to care for this pathetic and twisted creature, he had to admit, privately at least.

"These enemies are formidable, yet you would allow your young understudy to go in pursuit?" the handsome Netherese warrior asked.

Draygo Quick didn't lash out at the blunt remark, but merely nodded again. "He must do this. He is tied to that one, Dahlia. He must find his revenge."

"Or his death?"

"We all die," Draygo Quick replied.

"True, but it is best to choose when we allow, or cause, others to do so," Parise Ulfbinder remarked slyly, drawing Draygo Quick's full attention. "I wish to talk to you about this curious drow who has associated himself with our enemies."

"Drizzt Do'Urden."

"Yes," Parise said with a nod. "There may be more to him than you know, and likely more to him than he knows."

Draygo Quick's eyes widened as he considered that curious statement in the context of the speaker, a Netherese theorist who had been whispering dire warnings to any lord who might listen.

Down the hallway several doors, Effron lit a single candle and moved to a small table. Atop it rested an item covered by a red cloth.

Effron pulled the cloth back, and a skull-sized ball of pure crystal glistened in the candlelight before him.

"Ah, Dahlia Sin'Dalay, murderess," he said, and his eyes sparkled in reflection. "You think you have won, Mother. You are wrong."

Many heartbeats passed, not a one in the room daring to even draw breath. Entreri just stood there, head and shoulders thrown back, awaiting death. But death did not visit him.

Gradually, the assassin opened his eyes and glanced over at the others.

"You threw it in?" he asked.

Drizzt glanced over the rim, into the pit, and shrugged.

"You threw it in?" Entreri asked again.

"The primordial has it, surely."

"Ye think?" Ambergris put in with a snort.

"Do you feel anything?" Drizzt asked. "Pain? A sense of impending doom?"

"Are you asking, or hoping?" Entreri replied, and Ambergris laughed all the louder. At that moment, the monk broke away from her and leaped at Drizzt—or started to, for the dwarf kicked Afafrenfere's trailing ankle, tripping him up, and he skidded down to all fours. Before he could regain his footing, Ambergris grabbed him roughly by the shirt and his hair and hoisted him to his feet.

"Now ye hear me, boy, and ye hear me good!" the dwarf roared in his face. Still holding him by the hair, she dropped her other hand into her pouch and brought it forth, her fat thumb covered in some blue substance. As the others looked on, perplexed, she used it to draw a symbol on the monk's face, and she chanted out what seemed to be a spell in the ancient Dwarvish tongue.

"Now ye're geased," she announced, letting go and shoving Afafrenfere backward.

"What?"

"Ye got me god's wrath lurkin' on yer forehead, ye dolt," Ambergris explained. "Ye make a move at me drow friend here, or either o' his friends, and Dumathoin's sure to melt yer brains that they'll flow from yer nose like so much snot."

"B-but . . ." Afafrenfere stuttered, hopping all around and stabbing his finger in Drizzt's direction. "He killed Parbid!"

"Bah, yerselfs started the fight and ye lost, and so be it."

"But . . . Parbid!" Afafrenfere said with a great wail and keen.

Ambergris rushed up and grabbed him by the hair again and pulled him very close, so that her long and fat nose touched his. "If ye're wantin' to see yer dearest boy again, then go and strike at the drow," she said. "Been hoping to watch a good brain melt—been years and years since the last I seen."

Afafrenfere stuttered and gasped, but when Ambergris let him go, he moved back and said no more.

"Well, what of ye?" the dwarf asked of Entreri. "Ye dyin' yet?"

Entreri stared at her incredulously.

"Then let's be gone afore we're all dying," the dwarf said. "That silence spell I throwed in the hallway ain't for lastin'!"

She started off, slapping Afafrenfere to fall in line beside her as she made for the elemental's tunnel. She pulled out her magical decanter as she entered and summoned its spraying water once more, wetting the hot stones before her, and laughing indeed as the swirls of steam arose around her.

"Nothing?" Drizzt asked Entreri again. He walked over and crouched beside the sobbing Dahlia, hugging her close.

"Well?" he asked of Entreri yet again.

The assassin just shrugged. If he was dying, he didn't feel it.

Drizzt gently pulled Dahlia up beside him and started off. Entreri fell in line, following the dwarf.

Entreri looked at Drizzt coldly.

"Not even a bit of pain?" Drizzt asked, and he tried hard to sound disappointed.

Artemis Entreri snorted and looked away. He was alive. How could it be? For the sword had been keeping him alive for all of these decades, surely, and now the sword was gone. Or perhaps the primordial hadn't destroyed it—perhaps its magic was strong enough to survive the bite of that most ancient and powerful beast.

Or maybe it was destroyed, and the mortal coil of Entreri would begin to age again, that he might live out the remainder of his life as if he had been in stasis all these years.

Either way, he figured, he was still alive, and more than that, and he knew it profoundly: he was free.

He put his arm around Dahlia and pulled her close, signaling for Drizzt, who seemed less than thrilled at that movement, to take up the lead.

They moved through the complex with all speed, and encountered no shades, who, unbeknownst to them, were fast departing through magical gateways, and encountered no Menzoberranyr drow, who had moved to the deeper tunnels of the Underdark to weather the Shadovar advance.

Expecting pursuit, of course, Drizzt didn't slow the pace at all. With the help of Dahlia's raven cape, they got through to the upper levels and pressed on to the throne room and the complex exit.

Many hours later, Tiago Baenre and Gol'fanin moved quietly to the entrance of the forge room and peered in. The battle of elementals continued, water against fire, but were much diminished, for the floor was ankle-deep in water, a situation surely not conducive to the spawning of creatures of fire.

Still, the forges glowed orange, overheated by the flow of primordial power, and every so often, one erupted, spewing forth a line of blazing flames that hissed angrily across the giant puddle and sent swirls of steam into the air.

We can get to the underchamber, Tiago's hands flashed.

Where we'll be cornered and slaughtered? the old blacksmith signaled back.

By whom?

Gol'fanin looked at him doubtfully.

"They've left," Tiago announced aloud, for if he believed those words, after all, then why was he bothering to use the silent hand language?

"All of them?"

"We've seen no sign of the Shadovar."

"We've gone no farther than this place," Gol'fanin reminded. "Perhaps they came in and engaged in battle with the elemental forces in the forge, then fell back to a more defensible position. Would that not be your own choice, as it was Ravel's?"

Tiago had to admit that.

"Wait for the scouts," Gol'fanin advised. "Before we go in there, let us make sure that our efforts are worthwhile."

Tiago put a hand on Byok's saddlebag and the unfinished sword and translucent shield strapped beneath it. Truly he was torn, for in those few moments before the primordial had broken free and chased them from the room, Tiago had felt the promise of Lullaby and Spiderweb.

"If we restore control of the room and the Shadovar come back to this magnificent place, will they so willingly depart a second time?" Gol'fanin asked.

Despite his desires, Tiago knew that he was waging a losing argument.

"It will take tendays to ensure that they are truly gone from this vast complex," Tiago lamented. "I'll not wait that long."

Gol'fanin stared into the room for a few moments before offering a compromise. "We can discern in but a few hours if our enemies are far enough removed from the forge room for us to venture in. So let us not restore it until we are certain of the security of the complex. Not fully, at least. For I need only the one forge fired, and only for short amounts of time. I understand the design of the subchamber well enough to facilitate that which is needed."

Tiago's eyes flashed with hunger. "Then go."

"When the scouts—"

"Go now," Tiago ordered. "I will stay here and watch over you. The scouts will catch up to us soon enough, and I will put them all around the area."

The old blacksmith looked him over for a bit, then shook his head at the impatient young warrior and splashed into the room. He discerned the pattern of the fire-spewing forges easily enough and made his way to the trap door disguised as another forge. Fortunately, the chamber within the fake oven was not full of water, and when Gol'fanin managed to open the door, he saw that the room below was neither flooded nor full of fire. Still, the pipes below glowed angrily and threateningly, so the blacksmith adjusted and tightened his magical garments and put on his magical gloves before venturing below.

Sometime later, Gol'fanin was back at the room's great forge, implements and unfinished items at hand, preparing to continue his solemn work. The rest of the room continued to roar with unbridled fire, hiss with angry steam, and rain briny water, but Gol'fanin expected that would prove to be no more than a minor nuisance. Coincidentally, the blacksmith had just tapped his small finishing hammer against the flat of the shield, had just begun his actual work on the items, when he noted the return of Tiago, and surprisingly, the young Baenre approached from out of the corridor to the primordial pit, though Gol'fanin had not seen him go down that way, and as far as the blacksmith knew, there were no other entrances to that critical chamber.

"We found the wayward Xorlarrin brother," he said.

"And Brack'thal has information?"

"He is quite dead."

"My sympathies to the Xorlarrins," Gol'fanin replied, and of course he meant no such thing.

"He was killed by the blade," Tiago explained. "And found in a new tunnel, recently dug, or melted, it seems."

Gol'fanin didn't hide his intrigue, but Tiago had no answers for him.

"Perhaps the work of his own pet elemental," the young Baenre offered. "We cannot know."

"Your Xorlarrin lovers can find out. The dead are not so silent to the calls of a priestess."

Tiago shrugged as if it did not really matter. Berellip's main concern and motivation in talking to the dead Xorlarrin mage would be to learn if Ravel or his agents had killed Brack'thal, which wasn't likely the case.

"And the Shadovar?" Gol'fanin asked.

"We have found signs of their march to this place, but none of their retreat. Yet they are not to be found."

"Back to the Shadowfell, then."

"And so Gauntlgrym is ours."

"Counsel Ravel to proceed cautiously," the blacksmith advised.

"But you will continue your work?"

"Of course."

"Then I hold no sense of urgency."

The five companions rested in Gauntlgrym's great entry hall, far to the side of the great throne and the graves.

"Touched it," Ambergris said to Drizzt when he walked up beside her, to find her staring across at the throne.

"Come," Drizzt bade her, and he started that way. He led her right past the throne, though, to the small group of graves.

"King Bruenor," he explained, pointing to the largest. "Here in Gauntlgrym, he fell."

"Word was that he died in Mithral Hall," Ambergris replied. "We held a great drunk in his honor." She paused and laughed. "But we knowed, elf, we knowed," she said.

The way she addressed him, "elf," had Drizzt back on his heels, for it was a nickname he had heard before, and spoken with similar inflection and affection.

"Glad that he found his road," Ambergris said solemnly. "His reputation always called him as one for the road and not the throne."

"His shield dwarf," Drizzt explained as they paced to the other larger cairn.

"The Pwent," Ambergris mumbled, and that came as a bit of confirmation to Drizzt that this one could indeed be trusted.

"And the others who fell in the fight for this place," Drizzt explained of the other graves. "Battlehammer dwarves from Icewind Dale."

Ambergris nodded and quietly whispered a prayer for them all.

Drizzt patted her on the shoulder and led her back to the others. He paused before he got there, though, and looked the dwarf straight in the eye. "Geas?" he asked, his voice full of suspicion.

Ambergris looked at him stupidly.

"Your shade friend," Drizzt clarified, and the dwarf snickered.

"Chalk," she explained. "Blue chalk and nothing more . . . well, a bit o' magic suggestion to convince the dolt."

"So if this Afafa . . . Afrenfafa . . ."

"Afafrenfere," Ambergris explained.

"So if this Afafrenfere tries to kill me, I'll not find Dumathoin coming to my rescue?"

The dwarf showed a gap-toothed smile. "He won't try," she assured Drizzt. "That one's a flower, but he ain't hopin' to be a daisy. Not the smartest, not the bravest, but a gooder heart than them Netherese butchers e'er deserved. Ye got me personal guarantee on that."

For some inexplicable reason, that seemed more than good enough to Drizzt.

EPILOGUE

I N THE DARK OF GAUNTLGRYM'S THRONE ROOM, A SHIFTING STONE STOLE THE quiet.

Then came a grunt, and more sounds of rocks sliding against each other.

A black-bearded dwarf crawled from under the pile, then reached back and grabbed at something he had left behind, grunting with exertion as he tried to extricate it.

"Durned thing's stuck," he muttered, and with a great tug, he pulled free a most curious helmet, one set with a long and oft-bloodied spike.

His effort sent him flying over backward to crash against the stones of the nearest cairn, where he lay on his back as the dust settled.

"Durn it," he cursed, seeing the trouble he had caused, and he rolled to his feet and began replacing the dislodged stones. "Don't mean to be desecratin' yer tomb . . ."

The words caught in his throat, and the rocks fell from his hands.

There in the disturbed tomb before him was a curious helm, with a single curving horn, the other having long before been broken away.

The dwarf fell to his knees and dug the helm free, and saw too the face of the dead dwarf interred within.

"Me king," Thibbledorf Pwent breathed.

Nay, not breathed, for creatures in the state of Thibbledorf Pwent did not draw breath.

He fell back to his bum, staring in shock, his mouth wide in a silent scream.

If he'd had a mirror, or a reflection that would actually show up in a mirror, Thibbledorf Pwent might have noticed his newest weapon: canine fangs.

Arunika's imp, released from its duties by the succubus, loped around the swirling mists of the lower planes, seeking its true master.

It found the hulking balor seated atop a mushroom throne, clearly expecting the visitor.

"The devil is done with you?" the great demon asked.

"The threat to her domain is ended," the imp replied. "The enemies have moved along."

"The enemies?" came the leading question.

"The Shadovar."

"Only the Shadovar? I grow weary—"

"Drizzt Do'Urden!" the imp spat, a name it, Druzil, hated as much as anything in all the world. "He has left Neverwinter."

"And you know where?" the demonic monster roared.

Druzil shifted uncomfortably from foot to foot.

"You can find him?" the beast demanded.

"Yes! Yes! Yes!" Druzil squealed, for a hint of anything but that response would have surely gotten the wretched little imp squished flat by the merciless balor.

The demon began to utter a sound that seemed a cross between a purring giant cat and an avalanche.

Druzil understood that, for it had been near to a hundred years, at least, and Errtu, twice-banished by this dark elf, Drizzt, was, or soon would be, free to carry out his revenge.

More than a tenday passed before Berellip and the other priestesses joined Ravel and the others in the forge room. The lower reaches of the complex had been fully scouted, and some drow had even gone up to the top levels, though the stair remained folded, with no signs of Shadovar to be found.

Now the work had begun in earnest to secure and repair the forge room, while a team of goblin masons worked to seal the strange second tunnel leading from the primordial chamber to the outer corridor.

And Gol'fanin's work on Lullaby and Spiderweb proceeded with all speed.

Tiago was at his side, as usual, when the Xorlarrin nobles caught up to him.

"It was Masoj and his companions who killed Brack'thal," Ravel said, before they had even exchanged proper greetings.

"Truly?" Tiago asked.

"Truly," Berellip said, her tone showing that she didn't appreciate even being questioned on this matter, for it was she who had spoken to the spirit of her dead brother. Such conversations were usually vague and often unreliable, they all knew, but Berellip seemed quite confident.

"Masoj?" Gol'fanin dared to ask, for it was not his place to interrupt the conversation of nobles.

"Masoj Oblodra," Tiago explained. "Of Bregan D'aerthe."

"Oblodra?" Gol'fanin said with surprise, before he could bite back the further indiscretion. "That is a name not often spoken among the folk of Menzoberranzan. Not since the Time of Troubles."

"An Oblodran captains Bregan D'aerthe," Jearth reminded, referring to Kimmuriel.

Gol'fanin seemed satisfied with that, and he went back to his work, but he muttered "Masoj?" repeatedly under his breath, as if trying to recall something.

"There are implications here," Berellip warned, staring at Tiago.

"If the agents of Bregan D'aerthe killed your brother, then they did so in a battle of Brack'thal's choosing," the young Baenre answered evenly. "Bregan D'aerthe does not go against nobles of a major drow House."

"Without the permission of House Baenre," Berellip added, making her suspicions clear.

Tiago laughed at her. "If I had wanted your crazy brother dead, dear priestess, I would have killed him myself."

"Enough," Ravel put in. "Let us continue our work and our exploration. We will discover soon enough why this happened. And we already know," he added, looking hard at Berellip, "that Brack'thal almost surely initiated it."

"It was Brack'thal who sabotaged the forge room and drove us out," Tiago said. "If it was Bregan D'aerthe, I should pay them well for saving us the trouble."

Berellip and Saribel both glared at him for that remark, but Tiago wasn't about to back down.

"Need I remind you of your brother's . . . shall we say, instability?"

Berellip huffed and swung around and swept out of the forge room, Saribel in her wake. With a helpless shake of his head to the impertinent Tiago, who was not making his job of keeping his sisters under control any easier, Ravel followed.

"They are brilliant," Jearth remarked a moment later, and Tiago turned to see the Xorlarrin weapons master admiring the half-finished sword and shield.

"You met this Masoj . . . Oblodra?" Gol'fanin asked, never looking up from his work or indicating which of the warriors he was addressing.

"Yes," they both answered.

"An agent of Bregan D'aerthe?"

"So he claimed," said Jearth. "So claimed his companions as well, a human and an elf."

The blacksmith gave a little laugh and did look up at that remarkable information.

"A human who once came to Menzoberranzan, beside Jarlaxle," Tiago added.

"I knew of a Masoj once, though not an Oblodran," said Gol'fanin, who didn't hide the fact that he suspected much more than he was letting on, something that was not lost on the two warriors. "He was a wizard?"

"A warrior," said Tiago.

"Carrying three blades," Jearth added. "A great broadsword strapped across his back and a pair of scimitars."

The blacksmith nodded and went back to his work. With the conversation apparently at its end, Jearth excused himself and went back to his duties.

"Do you think that Bregan D'aerthe will cause us trouble here?" Tiago quietly asked. "Surely Kimmuriel and Jarlaxle understand that the Xorlarrin move to Gauntlgrym was sanctioned by Matron Mother Quenthel . . ."

"Bregan D'aerthe is no worry of yours," Gol'fanin assured him. "But Masoj . . . ah, Masoj."

"What are you speaking of?" Tiago demanded.

"Do they not teach history at Melee-Magthere any longer?" Gol'fanin asked.

"You try my patience," Tiago warned.

"I make your weapons," Gol'fanin retorted.

"What, then?" Tiago demanded, or begged. "What do you know?"

"I know only what you have told me. But I suspect more."

"What?" the exasperated Tiago shouted.

Gol'fanin chuckled a bit more. "Scimitars? A drow carrying scimitars and traveling near the surface with *iblith*."

Tiago held up his hands, completely lost by the leading statement.

"What more can you tell me about this curious rogue?" the blacksmith asked. Tiago snorted.

"What color were his eyes?" Gol'fanin asked.

Tiago started to answer "lavender," but choked on the word. His eyes widened in shock and he gaped at Gol'fanin and breathed, "No."

"Is it possible that a noble drow of House Baenre, surely soon to ascend to the rank of weapons master of the First House of Menzoberranzan, came face to face with Drizzt Do'Urden and didn't even realize it?" Gol'fanin asked.

Tiago glanced all around, as if to ensure that no others had heard that statement. His thoughts were whirling as he tried to recall all that he knew of the history of that traitorous rogue named Drizzt, among the most coveted outlaws ever known in Menzoberranzan. Drizzt Do'Urden, guardian of another dwarven complex, Mithral Hall, where Matron Baenre herself had been killed! Drizzt Do'Urden, who had slain Dantrag Baenre, Tiago's grandfather.

Gol'fanin held up the unfinished sword and tapped it on the shield. "These prizes will make you a weapons master," he said. "But the head of Drizzt Do'Urden? That prize will make you a legend."